THICK AS THIEVES

Center Point
Large Print

Also by M. J. Kuhn and available from Center Point Large Print:

Among Thieves

THICK AS THIEVES

TALES OF THAMORR

M. J. KUHN

CENTER POINT LARGE PRINT
THORNDIKE, MAINE

This Center Point Large Print edition
is published in the year 2024 by arrangement with
Saga Press, an Imprint of Simon & Schuster, Inc.

This book is a work of fiction. Any references to historical events, real people, or real places are used fictitiously. Other names, characters, places, and events are products of the author's imagination, and any resemblance to actual events or places or persons, living or dead, is entirely coincidental.

The text of this Large Print edition is unabridged.
In other aspects, this book may vary
from the original edition.
Printed in the United States of America
on permanent paper sourced using
environmentally responsible foresting methods.
Set in 16-point Times New Roman type.

ISBN: 979-8-89164-022-1

The Library of Congress has cataloged this record
under Library of Congress Control Number: 2023947837

For my wonderfully supportive parents,
Diane and Rich.
. . . Sorry for all the swearing in here.

CHAPTER ONE
Ryia

"Are you sure this is a good idea?" Evelyn Linley, ex-captain of Dresdell's Needle Guard, waded through the puddles in Ryia's wake, swiping a rain-soaked red curl out of her face.

"Of course I'm sure. When have I ever had a bad idea?" Ryia answered, holding a hand to stop Evelyn from looping around the next corner. She gave a sniff, checking for the telltale stench of danger. Her Adept senses detected nothing beyond the normal unpleasant smells that always clung to places like this, where too many humans lived crammed together in too little space.

Ryia smirked at Evelyn's silence as she waved them both forward. "See? You can't think of a single time."

"No," Evelyn said, pushing her hair back once more. It was in her face again within seconds. "The problem is that there are too many bloody examples to choose from. . . ."

"Ha-ha," Ryia said, voice dripping with sarcasm.

The fact was it didn't really matter if their current plan was a good idea, and they both knew it. It was the only idea they had.

A fork of lightning split the night, throwing the wood-shingled roofs of houses, shops, and inns into sharp relief against the rain-blurred sky. Ryia's lip curled. Edale. Land of mud, soot, and shitty memories. For ten long years she had avoided the kingdom at all costs. Now she was back—though not for long, if she had her way about it.

She and Evelyn had arrived in the stinking city of Duskhaven three days ago. Like her most recent home of Carrowwick, the Edalish capital was a tangled mess of close-knit houses crowding the edge of a river, but there were some key differences. For one, Duskhaven was about ten times the size of Carrowwick, with the filth and stench to match. And the people here were colder and harder than the Dresdellans—the lifeblood of Edale ran with coal and steel instead of Dresdell's delicate lace, and it showed. All in all, Duskhaven was a bleak, disgusting pit of a city, filled with dour bastards and sallow-faced wenches.

After weeks of hard travel on the roads of Dresdell and Edale, sleeping on the wet ground and eating gathered mushrooms and stolen bread, they had been rewarded with a pair of cots in the foulest city of all Thamorr. All in all, it was an awful lot of trouble to go through to rescue the son of a bitch who had betrayed and abandoned Ryia in the lair of her lifelong enemy.

Tristan Beckett had only been in Carrowwick about six months by the time they had traveled to the Guildmaster's island together, but in those six months, he had become the closest thing to a friend she'd had in the city. Which made the betrayal sting even more.

Bafflingly, he had turned out to be Prince Dennison Shadowwood, heir to the throne of Edale. In the end, he had only betrayed her to stay out of his father's clutches, a motivation she was uniquely positioned to understand, given her own bastard of a father. Tristan—Dennison—had also saved her life in the Catacombs, stopping the Kinetic pit fighter who had been hell-bent on tearing her throat open. Saving her skin had put him back in his father's grasp again. So she had come to Edale to return the favor. An eye for an eye, as it was. Or in this case, a harebrained rescue mission for a harebrained rescue mission.

Shit, she was getting soft these days.

On their first night in the city, she and Evelyn had learned where the prince was being kept. A drunken guard who had stared at Evelyn a bit too long for Ryia's liking had been more than happy to let the information slip, especially since it didn't seem too secretive or scandalous.

Prince Dennison was in his old quarters—a sprawling set of rooms located in the western tower of the keep. The stories all said the Shadow Keep was impregnable, but that seemed like one hell of an exaggeration to Ryia. Sure, it was situated on an island, surrounded by deep, murky water on all sides, and its walls were made of tall, solid blocks of shining obsidian. But Ryia was never one to shy away from a challenge.

The trouble would be getting Tristan—Dennison—back *out.*

Unless he had grown a pair of wings or gained some serious coordination since she had last seen him, there was no way he was going to be able to leap from his tower to the ramparts or climb down the outer wall from there or swim the width of the entire moat without attracting the attention of the guards patrolling either side. They had to find a way to get him out through the castle. Somehow Ryia doubted they were going to be able to saunter out the front gate.

Which brought them to their current predicament.

"You really think we can trust this . . . this *skiver?*" Evelyn asked.

"I think if you keep using words like 'skiver,' no one is ever going to buy that you're from Edale," Ryia said, chuckling at the Dresdellan slang. "But no. I don't trust anyone; you know that."

"Not even me?" Evelyn asked.

"Especially not you, you skiver," Ryia shot back, avoiding the question. The truth was she trusted the ex-captain from Dresdell a hell of a lot more than she was willing to admit. After all, she *had* helped Ryia escape the Guildmaster. And Carrowwick. And helped her destroy the fabled Quill—the secret relic that gave the Guildmaster of Thamorr the ability to control all the branded Adept of the world. She was starting to rely on Evelyn quite a bit, actually. Not that she'd ever say so out loud.

"Well, if you're not planning on trusting Mr. Berman, why exactly are we out in this ruddy downpour?"

"Because we can't get Tristan out without a boat. Berman has a boat. So we're going to go . . . have a chat with him."

After two days of scouring every inch of the stinking hellhole that was Duskhaven, Ryia had found a way to get Tristan—Dennison—out of the castle. And actually, "stinking hellhole" was a pretty good description of the exit she'd found.

The royals of Thamorr didn't shit in pails like the common folks of the kingdoms. They preferred to send their waste down an elaborate system of chutes and tubes that wound through the walls and cellars of their castles before leading outside. Through eavesdropping on some servants in a tavern called the Jackal's Mug, Ryia had learned the sewer in the Shadow Keep ran underneath the wine cellar. Observation proved that the mouth of the sewer was positioned along the southeastern wall of the castle. With a little luck, a boat, and the right cover, it should be possible to get in and out without anyone being any the wiser. Another bolt of lightning crackled through the sky. They certainly had the "cover" bit down. The guards would have trouble seeing the ends of their own noses in this mess. Now they just needed the other two pieces of the puzzle.

Ryia threw a hand out, halting Evelyn in the shadow of a tavern just beside the moat surrounding the castle. A pair of City Watch stomped by, rain pinging off their armor as they went. Strains of string music floated out from the tavern, a dark and powerful ballad of some sort.

Felice, even the *music* in Edale was dull.

"And once we get Mr. Berman's boat," Evelyn said, eyeing the City Watch as they disappeared around the next corner, "what do you suggest we do with Mr. Berman himself?"

Just a few months ago, Ryia would have said, *Easy, we slit his throat and throw him in the water.* But, for better or for worse, Evelyn's noble bullshit was rubbing off on her. "I already paid him," she said.

Evelyn raised one eyebrow. "And you're naive enough to think a few silvers is going to stop him from reporting a break-in to the castle guard?"

"You really think the man cares about his job *that* much?"

"No," Evelyn answered, "but if he cares about lining his pockets as much as I assume he does, he'll be very interested in collecting the coppers he'd get as a reward for turning in a pair of criminals breaking into the keep."

Ryia shrugged. "Then we'll ask him nicely to stay where he is and keep his mouth shut." She pulled a length of frayed rope from her cloak pocket, holding it up in the light of the storm. "By tying him up with this."

Before Evelyn could argue, Ryia darted out from the cover of the overhang. The sounds of rattling dice and murmured voices faded away as they splashed through the puddles, running for the lopsided hut that stood just beside the heavily guarded crest gate separating the Rowan River from the moat. The hut looked like a candle that had half melted on a hot day, the crumbled mortar barely holding the stones together as they tried desperately to collapse onto the mucky ground below. A tiny rowboat sat tethered to the side of the hut with a thick chain and a thicker lock, tossing and rocking in the wind as the storm raged on.

By the time they reached the door, Evelyn's cloak was more brown than it was black, splattered with thick, dark mud all the way from the hem flapping at her boots to the seams underneath her arms. She thrust both hands down, sending a wave of mud and rainwater splashing onto Berman's front stoop with a "yuck." She looked at Ryia through narrowed eyes. "Can't you do something about this?" she asked, waving a hand vaguely toward the sky.

"What, stop the rain?" Ryia asked, incredulous. "I'm sorry—I didn't realize I was one of the twin goddesses."

"Not stop it," Evelyn griped, wringing out the hood of her cloak. "Just keep it off our bloody heads." She wiggled her fingers in the air. "You know, with your special . . . skills?"

She was referring to Ryia's Kinetic magic. Ryia snorted. "Yeah, sorry, you didn't partner with a true-blood Adept. You've only got a cheap imitation on your team." She tapped the hatchets slung over her shoulders, then ran her fingers over the throwing axes on her belt. "These are the only things my particular *skills* have ever had any control over."

Her father's axes. The very same weapons that had cut the throats of a hundred Adept or more. Bled them dry so the sick bastard could funnel the sickly red liquid down Ryia's throat. The weapons that had made her were the only thing her telekinetic magic would ever lock onto. The objects she would have liked to have never seen again after escaping from her father's mansion were the only constant in her life since leaving that burning hellhole behind. If that wasn't one of the goddesses' sick jokes, Ryia didn't know what was.

When it seemed that Evelyn was finally satisfied with the dryness of her hood, Ryia lifted a gloved hand to the door, giving it a resounding knock. The thunder rumbled. The rain poured. The music in the tavern across the way fell into a new, equally depressing-sounding tune. No one answered. Ryia knocked again. Still there was no response.

"Are you sure this is the right hut?"

Ryia rolled her eyes. "No, you're right, this is the house of the *other* poor sod whose job is to unclog the pipeways and scrub the shit off the windows."

She knocked again. She had come across Berman earlier that day, balancing haphazardly on his rowboat as he scrubbed at the lower windows of the keep with a rag tied to a stick. When he'd come back to his house, he had found Ryia lounging on his front stoop, waiting for him. For five silver halves, he had agreed to let her borrow his boat that night, and for another five, he had agreed to keep his filthy, crooked-toothed mouth shut about it. The money didn't matter to Ryia—she had pickpocketed it all anyway.

After another knock returned only silence from inside, she lost her patience and shouldered the door open. Even without her stolen Kinetic strength, it would have been easy enough to break in. That door frame had been held together by mold and prayers to Felice, goddess of luck.

"Whuzzat!" came a disoriented reply from inside.

Berman was on his feet, but it was clear from

his red-rimmed eyes—not to mention the smell of the room—that until a few seconds ago, he had been in a drunken stupor on the moldering couch beside the cold, empty fireplace. Ryia felt the weight of the rope in her pocket. This would be even easier than she had anticipated.

"Ah, Berman, good to see you're ready for me," she said, pulling her gloves from her hands one finger at a time.

"Close the twice-damned door, would you?" he said, lunging forward and shutting it himself. With the latch broken, it just swung right back open. "Lettin' in more water than the bloody Rowan, you are."

"Sorry," Evelyn said, reaching forward to help him jam the door shut with the lone chair beside the tiny dining table. Polite as ever, she was, even when breaking into a man's home in the middle of the night.

"What'd you break down my fuckin' door for?" he asked, wiping his eyes like he was trying to rub the drunkenness away. It didn't work.

"We made a deal, Berman." Ryia leaned against the wall, pulling her cloak aside to reveal the belt of throwing axes at her hip. She then held out one hand, palm up. "I wouldn't go back on it if I were you."

"Yeah, yeah," Berman muttered, patting his trouser pockets, then the pocket of his sweat-stained shirt, before finally unearthing a small silver key. "You better bring 'er back in one piece, or you'll owe me a hell of a lot more than ten silvers."

"And I'd request that you keep to yourself and your ale tonight," Evelyn said, stalking toward him. "If you get my drift."

"If I . . . who in the hells are you, anyways?" Berman asked, bleary eyes focusing on her for the first time.

"The key, Berman," Ryia prompted. "We haven't got all night."

"All right, all right." He went to put the key in her hand, then drew back at the last second. "Don't get yourselves caught out there, neither. There's more than City Watch up on those walls at night."

He meant Adept, of course: Kinetics and Sensers, brainwashed and trapped in service to the king of Edale. The castle was bound to be crawling with them.

"Yeah, yeah, yeah. Now, the key."

Ryia scowled as she snatched the key from Berman's grip. For the first few days after she and Evelyn had destroyed the Quill and fled Carrowwick, she had been waiting to hear the news that the whole damned world was burning. That the Adept servants had all rebelled against their masters, risen up, run away, *something*. But there had been nothing. When she and Evelyn had stopped in the city of Taravan to pick up a pair of horses, she had finally seen why.

The Adept were no different from the way they'd been before Ryia and Evelyn had stolen Declan Day's ancient device from the Guildmaster. They still plodded behind their masters, dead-eyed as corpses, obedient as hunting hounds.

Ryia didn't know exactly what she had been expecting, of course. She'd known from the start that the cursed Quill could sense all the Adept in the world, could hunt them down in any corner of Thamorr. After watching Tristan—Dennison—use the Quill to take control of the Adept fighter back in the pits of the Catacombs, Ryia had thought the relic was the key to their obedience, too . . . but evidently not. No, it seemed that the Adept were bound to service by their masters' brands. And if that were true, then the only way to free the poor saps who were already branded would be to go back in time.

At least the Adept serving now were the last ones who ever would, now that the Quill was gone. She had smashed it to bits herself up on top of the wall in Carrowwick. Had watched the pieces float away down the Arden River and out to the Yawning Sea. But still. The branded Adept would continue to serve their masters until the day they died, apparently. Thousands, alive, but trapped forever in their invisible shackles. It made everything they had done seem far too small.

Evelyn was watching her carefully. They'd had enough conversations about this since Taravan that she knew the ex-captain could tell exactly what she was thinking about right now. Evelyn's hand brushed hers, and Ryia flinched away instinctively.

All right. Enough screwing around. She reached for her pocket, pulling out the length of rope.

"What's this all about?" Berman asked, drawing back.

Ryia charged forward, pushing the man down into the chair, wedging the door shut. In three deft motions, she wound the rope around him and the back of the chair and knotted it tightly. He would be able to break free eventually, but definitely no time soon, and definitely not in his current state.

Leaving Berman shouting obscenities in their wake, she and Evelyn slipped out the back door to the tiny inlet where the boat was tethered.

The rain continued sloshing down from the sky in buckets, plastering Ryia's hair to her scalp. It was still short, barely reaching the tips of her ears. Ivan had shaved her head so she could pose as a Kinetic pit fighter back in Carrowwick just under a month ago. It had been so damned convenient that for a moment, Ryia had considered keeping her hair that way. Then she had learned the branded Adept still weren't free. The shaved head had felt like a pair of shackles from that point on.

Still, watching Evelyn wrestle her own long curls back behind her shoulders as she leaned over to unchain the rowboat, Ryia had to admit she was glad to have it shorn as close as it was.

Lightning crackled across the sky, and in the white flash Ryia saw it. The Shadow Keep. The Edalish castle was situated on a hard, rocky island about the size of most of the towns they had ridden past on their road north. The water surrounding it, now sloshing around their boots, was a stagnant and murky brown.

The keep was framed by thick stone walls, each corner marked with a tall tower studded with arrow slits. A single gate stood on the northern wall, but at the moment it opened to a stretch of disgusting water. The bridge rested alongside the wall for now, but Ryia had seen it in motion. Its mechanics were powered by magic, taking a team of Kinetics to raise and lower it over the moat. Another reason it was a shame destroying the Quill hadn't instantly freed every branded Adept in the world. She would have liked to see Tolliver Shadowwood swimming through that thick, shit-filled water to get back to his castle. . . .

In the center of the walls stood the keep itself, a tall structure built of stone so dark it almost looked black. It towered over the walls, jutting so high into the sky it almost blocked the twice-damned moon. Four turrets stood from its hard, angled roof. Evelyn eyed the western tower nervously through the sheets of rain pouring from the clouds.

"Are you sure about this?" she asked. "There's bound to be a ton of guards up there. Or worse."

After all, only Evelyn would be taking the boat tonight. Ryia would enter the castle by a different path—one where she was less likely to leave a trail of disgusting stains as she led Tristan—Dennison—back out.

Ryia snorted. "Have you really forgotten how impressive I am?" She had gotten through tighter spots than this before. She would break in and get the king's brat down into those sewers to meet Evelyn before Tolliver Shadowwood and his men ever knew she was there.

For a long second, Evelyn didn't respond. Ryia stared determinedly at the Shadow Keep as she felt the ex-captain's eyes on her. "See you on the other side," Evelyn finally said.

"Enjoy the shit tunnel."

"Fuck off."

Ryia grinned, turning to watch Evelyn hop into the boat and row toward the castle walls. If this went sideways, the sight of the former captain disappearing behind the curtains of heavy rain might be the last she ever saw of her. The grin slid off Ryia's face. She kept one eye on the Shadow Keep as she looped around to the western edge of the moat.

"This had better be worth it, Tristan," she muttered, staring up at the western tower, ringed in the shadows of a fresh lightning flash.

With that, she took a deep breath and dove into the filthy water of the Duskhaven moat.

CHAPTER TWO
Tristan

Tristan Beckett awoke with a start in his tower room as a flash of lightning split the sky outside. *Just the storm,* he told himself . . . but as his eyes slitted open, his heart leapt into his throat.

There was something outside his window. Not something. *Someone.*

That was impossible. No one could scale the height of the Shadow Keep—especially not in a storm like this. But his stomach twisted as he recalled one person who could absolutely accomplish such a feat. Someone he cared for more than any other living soul in Thamorr.

Someone he had betrayed and left for dead.

Thunder rattled through the night, this time accompanied by the tinkling sound of shattering glass. Tristan gritted his teeth, peering through the darkness of his bedchamber. Another bolt of lightning rent the blackness, revealing a hooded shadow stalking across his fine woven rugs, soaked in rainwater and dripping with mud. Silver throwing axes glinted at her belt.

The Butcher of Carrowwick. She had come to kill him at last.

To be fair, he was surprised to have survived

this long anyway. He had fully expected his father to kill him the instant their ship pulled away from the Carrowwick docks. Instead, he had been locked in the captain's cabin, where the worst thing that happened was that the man who brought him his meals called him Dennison. Technically appropriate, since that was his birth-given name.

But Tristan didn't feel like Dennison. After all, Dennison Shadowwood had been a prince, sheltered and coddled. Naive in the ways of the world. Tristan Beckett was a card man. A con artist. A pickpocket. As lowly as those things might be, he would rather be any of them than prince of Edale. He would rather live in the gutters of Carrowwick forever than play son to his monstrous father again.

But Tristan Beckett wasn't just a thief. He was also a coward. He hadn't fought when his father had led him back into the Shadow Keep. He was confined to the western tower, his every step mirrored by Adept and Shadow Wardens . . . but still his father kept him alive. For what purpose? The summer sun gave way to the driving rains of early autumn, and still Tristan was alive. There was no way his father had suddenly had a change of heart. . . . No, there had to be a reason Tristan was still breathing. He just couldn't figure out what it was.

But none of that mattered anymore. Ryia Cautella had come to finish him off. He swallowed, clenching his eyes shut again as the Butcher tiptoed across the room toward him, like feigning sleep would protect him from facing punishment for his crimes back on the Guildmaster's island. He flinched despite himself as a wet glove clamped over his mouth. To muffle his screams, of course. Any second now he would feel the cool bite of her hatchets cutting into his flesh. . . .

Instead, he felt a second gloved hand grab his forearm. The rainwater soaked through his nightshirt as the hand shook him roughly.

"Get your ass up."

Up? Tristan let his eyes flutter open. "What?"

"For Felice's sake, did old Tolliver slice your ears off? I'm trying to rescue your traitorous ass. Let's go."

"Rescue," Tristan said, blinking. "Then . . . you're not here to kill me?"

Ryia's gruff chuckle echoed through the darkness. "Not this time. But fuck me over again and we'll have to talk. Fair?" She reached out to him.

Tristan grinned in disbelief, grabbing her hand and letting her pull him to his feet. "Fair."

"All right, now that you're finally up, we can get out of here," Ryia said, crossing toward the window.

Tristan hurriedly grabbed his dressing gown, belting it on over his nightclothes as he stuffed his feet into the first pair of shoes he found.

"You, er, you know I can't climb down the side of a tower in this rain, right?"

Ryia tossed a grin over her shoulder, her teeth glinting in a fresh flash of lightning. "Because in better weather you'd skitter down it like a spider, would you?"

"I'd have a better chance of it, at least." Tristan blushed, knotting the laces on his second shoe.

"Right . . . well, don't worry, Dennison, we're not going out that way."

"Don't call me that."

Ryia turned, apparently indifferent to the torrents of rain pouring in through the shattered window. "What am I supposed to call you, then? If you say *Your Highness,* I might decide I *am* here to kill you."

"No, that's not—" Tristan started to protest. He shook his head and swallowed. "Tristan's fine."

He thought Ryia would argue, but she just studied him a second, then nodded. "Tristan it is. Now, Tristan, you think you can get through this window without cutting yourself to pieces?"

"About that." Tristan crossed to the window, wincing as the rain splattered over him. The water was bone cold—how was Ryia standing there, soaked, without shivering? He grabbed the knob at the window's base and swung it inward. "You could have just opened the window, you know," he said.

Ryia blinked. "It's not locked?"

Tristan raised an eyebrow. “It’s hundreds of feet in the air, Ryia. Why would it be locked?”

“I always forget how incredible I am,” Ryia said. Her eyes flicked to the chamber door. “How many are guarding the hall out there?”

Tristan shrugged. “At least two. Usually Shadow Wardens. Sometimes it’s Kinetics, though.”

Ryia’s face slipped into a grimace that Tristan understood all too well. The Shadow Wardens were somber and dangerous . . . but the Adept were something else entirely. Tristan had seen the damage they could do—and with his father controlling *all* of them . . . The thought prickled the back of his mind uncomfortably. Control over all the Adept of the world should make his father unstoppable. So why had he not yet made his move? Why hadn’t he conquered Gildemar? He had the Quill . . . didn’t he?

“How well do you know the inside of this castle?” Ryia asked, still eyeing the chamber door.

“Well enough,” he answered hesitantly.

“Good,” Ryia said. “Can you get us to the wine cellar?”

“The—what?”

The wine cellar was one of the last places he wanted to go right now. It was tucked away in the basement, below the keep’s kitchens. The farthest point in the keep from this high, rain-soaked tower. He would almost rather try to climb down the walls with cold-numbed fingers than try to navigate their way there. Almost. "How exactly will getting to the cellar help us escape?" he finally asked.

Ryia looked him up and down. "Let's just say I hope you're not too attached to those shoes."

Before he could ask her to elaborate, the Butcher of Carrowwick disappeared out the window and into the rainy night. Her gloved hand slid back into view, beckoning for him to follow. He peered out the window after her, his dark curls sticking to his forehead as the rain drummed down on him.

"For Adalina's sake," he muttered. His rescuer was perched on the windowsill, some three inches wide . . . nothing but open air between her and the ground, so far below he couldn't even see it in the darkness.

"Come on, let's put that dancer's frame to good use," Ryia said with a wink.

"I don't think I can—" he started. Then he swallowed, looking back toward the door. His father hadn't done anything besides lock him in a luxurious tower . . . yet. But he would be more foolish than Weagar the Witless to sit around and wait for that to change. After all, the king had planned to kill him once before, in order to justify going to war with Gildemar—it was the reason Tristan had run off to Carrowwick in the first place. If his father had the Quill of Declan Day, he wouldn't need to use his heir's death as a pretense to start a war. Still, Tristan knew he knew too much. His father would find a way to silence him eventually.

The castle was quiet. The guards outside the door to his chamber hadn't even stirred, as far as he could tell. The rain and the thunder could cover for them, and Ryia had a plan.

If he was going to get out, now was his only chance.

He took a deep breath and edged out onto the windowsill.

His head spun and his heart raced as he sidled along the sill, eyes locked on the back of Ryia's hood to suppress the insistent—and insane—urge to look down. How in Adalina's name did she do this all the time?

Ryia held up a hand, motioning for him to stop, and he stood, wavering on the sill for a few long seconds as she peered into the dark window of the chamber next to his. After a moment she waved him forward. It continued on like this for what felt like a lifetime: shuffle forward a few feet, wait at the window for Ryia's all clear, then shuffle forward some more.

His legs shook, and he nearly toppled over every time a new crack of thunder boomed through the night. Ryia paused yet again as they reached another window, but this time she didn't wave him forward. Instead she knelt, balancing on the three-inch windowsill as though it were as wide as a walking path, and pushed at the base of the window. Just like the one in Tristan's chambers, it was unlatched. It creaked a bit as it swung open, but the sound was swallowed by the wrath of the storm.

Ryia crept inside, hand still raised to hold him back, peering through the darkness. After a few seconds she finally waved him forward. He almost collapsed into the room, his legs shaking as he dripped frigid rainwater all over the expensive rugs carpeting the west tower study. He eased the window shut as Ryia, apparently unconcerned with the value of the rugs, wrung out her cloak over them. When she noticed him staring, she shrugged.

"What? Would you rather I leave a clear trail so they know exactly where you went?" She strode to the door, pausing with one cheek pressed against it. She turned back questioningly. "Are there really no other guards in this tower?"

Tristan shrugged. "I mean, I'm the only person in the tower who needs guarding. And they think they know where I am." He nodded back toward his now empty chamber.

"Stupid royals," Ryia chuckled. "This is going to be even easier than I thought." She paused again, staring intently at the door, almost like she expected to be able to see through it. Her nostrils flared . . . then she nodded, twisting the knob and looking both ways before waving him on. "'Impregnable fortress' my ass," she muttered under her breath as they went.

The Shadow Keep was always quiet at night. The king and queen's chambers were all the way up in the northern tower; Tristan's brother and sister shared the southern tower. There would be chambermaids and servants in some of the corridors, and no doubt the kitchens were already bustling with preparations for breakfast, but the majority of the keep was as quiet and empty as a Borean graveyard, save for the muted rumblings of the storm outside.

It had been a long time since he had roamed these halls freely, but Tristan still knew them well. Not only the halls themselves, but the tricks, like the location of the servants' stairwell in the western tower, and the fact that the third stair behind the throne room creaked something horrible. With a mix of his expertise and what must have been dumb luck, they made it through the top seven floors of the keep without incident. Tristan sighed with relief as they passed the kitchens without being seen. The ovens were already hot, the cooks already throwing vulgar insults at one another in thick, low-Edalish accents, but they managed to sneak into the larder without being spotted.

Still, Tristan couldn't shake the strange curling

of his stomach. He paused, frowning at the larder door. The overwhelming smell of spices and strong cheeses swirled around them in the darkness.

"What are you just standing around for?" Ryia hissed. "Let's go."

"I feel like we're being watched," Tristan whispered back. It was either intuition or paranoia. He sincerely hoped it was the second.

"Watched?" Ryia snorted. She sniffed the fragrant air of the larder, frowned, then shook her head. "If someone was watching us, they would have tried to kill me by now."

"I guess . . . ," Tristan said.

Ryia walked forward across the larder, tapping one foot along the floorboards until she found a spot that sounded hollow. Her knees cracked as she crouched down and pried up the trapdoor to his father's wine cellar with her nimble fingers.

He thought he saw a flicker of fear in her eyes as she peered down into the musty darkness. It was gone as quickly as it had come, but still, he noticed her rubbing her wrists nervously as she took to the stairs, descending into the cool dark of the wine cellar.

Tristan crept down into the blackness behind her. He felt ridiculous in his fine dressing gown and court shoes, trying to mimic the motions of the black-cloaked mercenary in her silent leather boots. But thankfully, it seemed the time for stealth had passed—for now, at least. His father would never partake in wine before supper, so the earliest a servant could possibly stumble upon them here would be some twelve hours from now.

"All right, let's get going," Ryia said.

"Going? Going where?" he asked dumbly.

"That's a good question," Ryia said. Then she whispered, "Where in Felice's bitterest hell are you?"

Tristan frowned. "I'm right—" he started, but he broke off, stomach leaping into his chest as another voice sounded beneath his feet.

"I'm right under your bloody noses."

Evelyn Linley? Tristan struggled to hide his surprise. The ex-captain of Dresdell was one of the last people he would have expected to come rescue him. Of course, Ryia was also one of the last people he would have expected to do so. It seemed that tonight, Felice was just full of surprises.

"How was your crawl through royal shit?" Ryia asked, crouching down and prying at something on the floor.

A grate.

Tristan grimaced, realizing with a start where Evelyn was. Aside from using one of the waste chambers, Tristan never gave the pipes within the walls of the castle much thought, except in the summers when a few of the lower halls smelled vaguely of boiled urine. And now . . . he wrinkled his nose. This explained why Ryia had told him not to get too attached to his shoes.

There was a low scraping sound as Ryia pulled the grate aside. The unmistakable scent of human waste washed over him. As Evelyn reached a hand up to help him down, he realized the smell was coming from the ex-captain herself. He held his breath as he grabbed her hand. It was moist—he tried not to think about why. The smell only grew stronger, almost overpowering him, as he lowered himself into the pipe.

"Careful," Evelyn said, "this ruddy pipe is slipperier than a merchant on tax day."

She wasn't wrong. He almost lost his footing immediately, saved from sliding down the length of the waste-slick pipe only by Evelyn's hand. He managed to find a few grooves in the shaped stone to latch on to. Already the smell threatened to overwhelm him. Between the waste in the pipe and the spices in the larder above, his nostrils felt ready to explode.

Then, suddenly, a flint struck somewhere in the darkness, and he was temporarily blinded by the light of a bright-burning lantern. A few slow, sarcastic claps followed, accompanied by the clicking of shoes on the floor of the wine cellar above his head.

"Well done, well done."

The voice was one that sent Tristan's teeth

chattering and his heart racing. King Tolliver Shadowwood. He stalked out from behind a stack of wine barrels, flanked by four Shadow Wardens. Two gray-cloaked Adept servants slunk out of the corners as well. Kinetics.

Above him, Ryia's hands jumped to the hatchets strapped across her back.

"Not so fast, thief," his father said, taking another step forward.

"Thief?" Ryia said. She held up her hands, showing empty palms. "I've stolen nothing."

Tristan gulped. In the cellar above, his father's jaw tightened, thrown into sharp relief by the light of the lantern. "Let us not play games, gutter rat. I know what you've taken from me. The most valuable item in this world."

Tristan frowned. He wasn't sure how he felt about being referred to as an "item," but this would be the first time his father had attached any sort of value to him whatsoever. His frown deepened as his father reached out a hand, palm up.

"I would have it returned to me."

"You must have me confused with some other vagrant skulking around your castle, Your Highness," Ryia said.

"I am certain I do not." King Tolliver snapped his fingers once. "The Quill of Declan Day. If you relinquish it quickly, I may let you leave this cellar alive."

Tristan shared a look with Evelyn. They wore radically different expressions—his one of blank confusion contrasting sharply with the way her narrow face was stretched tight in dread. His father didn't have the Quill?

Ryia's rasping laugh split the tense silence. "I don't have the Quill. And if I did, I'd shove it up my own asshole before giving it to someone like you."

"You don't have it. . . ." Through the grate, Tristan saw his father rub his fingers together thoughtfully. The king then gave a curt nod.

Tristan suppressed a yelp as the Kinetics at his father's side sprang into action. They grabbed Ryia's arms, pulling them behind her back.

"Search her," said the king. His Shadow Wardens surged forward next, patting down Ryia's pockets, sleeves, waist.

"Watch it," the Butcher said in a warning tone. But the Wardens came up empty.

"Nothing but the hatchets, sir."

"Hmm," the king said. He leaned back, inspecting his fingernails. "You have already sold it, then? To whom?"

"I didn't sell it," Ryia said. She looked calm—defiant. "I destroyed it."

Destroyed? Tristan's stomach clenched. Had she really destroyed the Quill? Without it, no one would know where to find the new Adept. They would be born and just . . . exist out in the world. Wielding their powers. They could prop up their own leaders, form their own armies—armies the existing forces of the world would be powerless to stop. The kingdoms of Thamorr would crumble, and the lives of every non-magic person in this land would be in mortal danger. How could she do something like that?

Evelyn's face was white as a sheet beside him. But up above, his father just laughed.

"If you are going to lie to me, you will have to do better than that." He paced back and forth in front of her, throwing his long shadow up and down the shelves of dusty wine bottles from every corner of the five kingdoms. "Do not suppose I am not aware of *all* the Quill's powers." He nodded at the Kinetics holding her arms. "If the Quill was truly gone, these two beasts would be out for my blood at the moment, I would imagine."

For the first time, Ryia's cool mask slipped. She blinked it back into place in the span of a breath. "You're lying."

"I am not," the king said calmly. He stopped his pacing, studying her for a moment, then sighed. "Well, if you truly do not have the Quill anymore, then I suppose there was no reason for me to set this elaborate trap for you. No reason for me to allow you to break in to steal away with my worthless son . . . and no reason for me to let either of you walk free."

Elaborate trap. His father had set a trap for Ryia? He must have known Ryia had ended up with the Quill in the Catacombs, and somehow known she would come to save him. That was why he had been allowed to live, then. He—the *worthless son*—had been bait all this time.

"Elias, Oliver, lift that grate and return the prince to his chambers. The rest of you, deal with this . . . intruder."

In the pipe beside him, Evelyn's hand darted to the filth-stained sword at her belt.

"What are you doing?" he hissed. His father didn't seem to know Evelyn was there. She could still get herself out of here.

"I'm not just going to let them kill her, you git," she whispered back.

Of course, he had forgotten: this was death-before-dishonor Captain Evelyn Linley. She would never back down from a fight—not even when it was one that was clearly already lost.

Ryia moved forward a pace, stepping onto the grate before the Shadow Wardens could pry it back up. "If the Quill was not destroyed, there's only one place it could have gone missing," she said. Her eyes were locked on Evelyn's. "Tracking down whoever took it is our number one priority now."

"Unluckily for you, I know where that is," the king said, addressing Ryia as though she had been speaking to him. "So, I still have no reason to keep you alive." He tutted. "You'll have to try harder than that, thief."

A scuffle broke out above them. The shadows were too long and dark to see what was happening clearly, but Tristan heard swords leaving their sheaths and saw flashes of whirling hatchet blades cutting through the air. Beside him, Evelyn tensed. Her sword rang out shrilly as she pulled it free, and with a grunt, she pushed off from the slick base of the pipe, thrusting upward to slip the blade of her sword beneath the nearest Shadow Warden's breastplate. He slumped onto the floor of the wine cellar with a gurgle.

"Hold on, Ryia—I'm coming!" Evelyn said. Her hand slipped, and she swore under her breath as she repositioned herself, struggling to pull herself from the steep, slippery tunnel of excrement.

"No, you're not," Ryia growled above. "There are only a few people in the world who know where the Quill could be, apart from this asshole," she said, gesturing to Tristan's father. She thrust both hatchets over her head, blocking one Shadow Warden's blade before rearing back and kicking the nearest Adept squarely in the chest to knock it back a pace. "If all of us die here, you know what that means."

Tristan's breath caught in his throat. It was a fair point. The idea of his father having dominion over all the Adept was bad enough . . . but the idea of not knowing who held the beasts' leash? He shuddered as he remembered the power that had flowed through him for the instant he had pressed his bloodied finger to the Quill. The chill of control he had felt. The idea of a mysterious stranger wielding that force was truly terrifying.

"Do we have a third truant in this cellar?" the king said, his tone almost playful as he peered down through the grate, sighting Evelyn for the first time. "Good, you can keep one another company in the pits of hell."

"I don't think so," Ryia said. There was an edge of real fear in her voice as she lunged forward to stop the Shadow Wardens from prying up the grate again. "Evelyn, Tristan, get out of here. *Now!*"

Evelyn struggled forward again. She slipped and fell. Tristan caught her as she almost slid backward down the pipe. "I'm not going to leave you here," she grunted.

Ryia blocked a Shadow Warden sword with each hatchet. He forced her back three paces, pinning her to the wall of the cellar. She looked around wildly, arms restrained. Her eyes lit up as they landed on a wine barrel lying on its side just beside the grate. "Yes, you are."

She gritted her teeth, narrowing her eyes. Tristan's mouth dropped open as he saw a pair of the throwing axes at her belt quiver to life, seemingly of their own accord. It was impossible. Time seemed to freeze for a moment, and he could hear nothing but his own breathing rattling around inside his skull.

Was she . . . was Ryia . . . *Adept?* No. She couldn't be.

But as he watched, the axes sprang from her belt, careening through thin air toward the barrel, their bits embedding themselves firmly in the lid.

"Ryia, no!" Evelyn shouted. She adjusted her footing, clearly preparing to clamber out of the grate once again. Ryia's face screwed up in concentration. Tristan felt his stomach clench again as the axes pried themselves free of the barrel, speeding back toward her outstretched hands. A steady drip-drip-drip of deep red wine dropped onto the floor just beside the grate.

Evelyn reached up, latching her fingers firmly on the stone floor just outside the grate, preparing to pull herself out into the cellar. Tristan saw one of his father's Shadow Wardens slink from the shadows, sword raised, ready to strike downward and skewer Evelyn through the throat. Tristan tried to shout a warning, but his brain was still too preoccupied with the display of Adept magic he had just seen to cooperate with his mouth.

Ryia's voice seemed to be working just fine. She let out a wordless cry of anguish, reaching out to stop the blade, though she wasn't near enough to block the strike. At that very moment, the lid of the wine barrel suddenly burst into splinters.

A torrent of the finest Brillish wine rushed from the barrel, pouring straight down the grate. Evelyn lost her grip, slipping out of range of the sword just as the Shadow Warden struck.

"Stop! Stop. I said stop! Do you not see what she is doing?" Tristan's father shouted above them. "She is Adept, you fools. But how . . . ? We need to take her alive!"

"Shit!" Evelyn yelled, scrabbling at the side of the wall, struggling to keep her grip. She kept swearing, but the words were garbled by the flood of wine.

Tristan's grasp on the pipe had been tenuous at best. With the force of the bitter wine rushing toward him, it was impossible to hold on. He flailed around, trying to get a grip . . . and then he was falling, shooting down the slick pipe, his back and hips protesting with every bump in the stone. Judging from the clang of steel and constant stream of creative Dresdellan curses, Evelyn was falling right behind him. They landed in a heap of tangled limbs and filthy clothes in a rowboat tied up in the moat at the mouth of the pipe.

For a moment, they just lay there, breathing hard, letting the driving rain wash the worst of the muck from them. Tristan wasn't certain, but he thought Evelyn's chest was heaving with what felt like sobs. After a few seconds, she extracted her limbs from his, readying her sword and facing the pipe again. The last remnants of the deep red wine were still spilling from it. His stomach turned. At least he hoped that was just wine.

He leapt up as Evelyn went to take a step forward, snaring her arm. "Where are you going?"

"Where do you think I'm going, Dennison?" she snapped.

"Don't call me that," Tristan spat back. He didn't want to be connected to that name, especially not after what he had just seen. What his father had just done to Ryia.

But if she's Adept, she belongs in chains, said a voice inside his mind. The voice sounded suspiciously like his father's. He pushed the thought away. Adept powers or no, she was still Ryia . . . wasn't she? His stomach clenched with indecision.

"Fine," Evelyn said. "Where the ruddy hell do you think I'm going, *kid?* I'm going back to save her."

"Are you a damned fool?" Tristan asked. "If you go back in there, he's going to kill you."

"And if I don't, then he's going to kill Ryia! Or torture her or—"

"You don't think I know that?" Tristan shouted, grabbing her by both shoulders and shaking her. She froze, eyes wide, surprised at his outburst. He sagged forward, resting his forehead on her collarbone. "I know, okay? But you heard what she said. That Quill is still out there—"

"The Quill. Who *cares* about the bloody Quill?" Evelyn spat, pushing him away.

"Ryia does." Tristan straightened, meeting her fierce gaze without flinching. "In case you missed it, she just let herself get dragged to the Shadow Cells so we could escape. So we could tell others and go find it. You want to throw that away just to get locked up right alongside her? You think that's what Ryia wants?"

The fire blazing in Evelyn's eyes flickered and faded, leaving her face drawn and ashen. "No. No, I don't." She scrubbed her hands down her cheeks. "But if we're leaving her, we'd better have a ruddy good plan. I'm not abandoning her to rot in a prison just to fail."

"We're not going to fail," Tristan said, his mind already whirring and churning.

"Then we'd better find that damned Quill."

"Oh, we'll find it. And we'd better do it quickly." Tristan chewed his lip. "Because if it didn't leave the Catacombs with you, and it didn't leave the Catacombs with my father . . . there's only one man I can think of who had hands on it. And he's one of the last people in Thamorr you'd want to have it."

He looked up in time to see Evelyn's rain-soaked face drain of its color. "Wyatt Asher."

"Wyatt Asher," he confirmed.

The ex-captain wrestled with herself for almost a full minute, eyes darting between the pipe and

Tristan's face. Finally, she slumped back into the rowboat. "To Carrowwick?"

He nodded, grabbing an oar. He didn't want to leave Ryia here any more than Evelyn did, even if she *was* Adept. He knew what his father was capable of, after all. But if Wyatt Asher had the means to control every Adept servant in Thamorr, someone needed to do something about it. And quickly.

CHAPTER THREE
Nash

Under normal circumstances, Nash would have been thrilled to be at the helm, the wind at her back, the spray of the sea in her face . . . but these circumstances were nowhere within fifty leagues of "normal." For starters, she was sailing without her regular crew. Without a crew at all, really.

"Would it kill you to give me a hand here, Rezkoye?" she asked, wiping sweat from her brow as she called across the deck to Ivan.

Where she was running back and forth across the deck like a madwoman trying to keep *The Hardship* from sinking to the bottom of the twice-damned ocean, Ivan was sitting with his back against a crate and his nose in one of the books they had lifted from the Library of the Duality in Fairvine a few days ago.

Lifted. The word was too gentle. It made it sound like the job had been smooth and easy. In reality, they had almost died, missing the arrival of the Guildmaster's Disciples in the Gildesh capital by a whip of a seasnake's tail. It hadn't been their first near miss either. And it was unlikely to be their last, if they didn't get their act together soon.

"I'm busy," Ivan said, leafing another page forward as he chewed on the rind of a sausage. The *last* of the sausage, if Nash's calculations of their food stores were correct—they would need to make port again soon. *But where?* It was a question with no easy answer.

The Borean disguise-master was leaning so close to the paper as he read that Nash was surprised the tip of his nose wasn't smudged with ink. After almost a month on the open ocean, his hair had grown out past his shoulders, and his face was slightly hollowed from hunger and marked by a light brown beard, but he looked far from unkempt. If anything, the bastard looked more flawless than ever.

"You don't look that busy to me," Nash grumbled back. But she knew that was far from fair. After all, there was a reason they were still sailing around the western coast of Thamorr, dreading the sight of blue sails on the horizon and avoiding the Disciples as they popped up in port after port, checking all the docking ships. A reason Callum Clem was not yet master of the world.

Clem may have been wily enough to sneak the true Quill of Declan Day out from under the noses of Ryia Cautella, King Tolliver Shadowwood, and Wyatt Asher all at once . . . but no amount of cunning could get the damned thing to actually work, it seemed. At least not for long.

After leaving Carrowwick, they had sailed straight for Safrona, on the southern tip of Briel. Clem's plans of conquering the southern kingdoms before winding north toward Boreas were dashed when he realized that, no matter how many times he sliced his thumb and pressed its bloody print to the side of the Quill, he couldn't take hold of all the world's Adept for more than a half minute or so. And that half minute looked like a painful one, based on the Snake's screwed-up eyes and sweat-drenched forehead.

When the blue sails started to crowd the horizon north of the Safronish docks, Clem finally agreed to stop cutting his thumb for a twice-damned second and think of a new plan. Gildemar had the largest library in all of Thamorr . . . so to Fairvine they went. Nash had lurked in the streets gathering news as Ivan went to the library and pilfered every book he could find that had been written in the era of Declan Day. The news Nash had overheard in those days still made her stomach clench and sent her eyes darting over her shoulder. The Guildmaster was mobilizing his army in force. For the first time in history.

In the few days they were docked in Fairvine, Nash had heard rumors of Disciples cropping up not only in Safrona, but also Tychias and Cilna—every major port in Briel. The Guildmaster's men weren't hunting the streets for infants; in fact, the Disciples hadn't taken a single infant in over a month, according to the stories coming in from the traders. The rumormongers didn't know why, and Nash was obviously not fool enough to share the answer.

With his Quill stolen and his ability to track down and steal crying babies from their mothers' arms currently waylaid, the Guildmaster had found a new hobby: searching ships. Any ship docking or pulling out from the ports where the Disciples appeared was searched, deck to keel. In essence, if Nash happened to dock somewhere the Disciples were now stationed, they would be trapped. The Quill would be discovered. And after that, they would no doubt be executed.

They had just barely escaped that fate while leaving Fairvine and hadn't dared pull in at any port since. In the past week or so, Clem had mostly shifted his focus to reading ferociously alone in his cabin, pelting anyone who dared try to come inside with either something sharp or something heavy. There were still times when the Snake's two Adept froze in place up on deck, muscles all straining at once, and Nash knew Clem had decided to slice his damned thumb open again, trying to master the Quill. Then, invariably, they would resume their dead-eyed stares, proving that the Snake had failed yet again.

The namestone around Nash's neck felt heavier and heavier each and every day. In her ma's home kingdom of Briel, it was customary to hang the namestones of the dead. Nash had always assumed she would find the right place to hang her ma's someday . . . but with capture and certain death lurking just over the horizon, Nash was becoming more and more certain that instead of a beautiful forest or a windswept cliffside, Ma's namestone was likely to end up in a watery grave. The thought made Nash sick.

"If you would prefer, I can steer the ship and you can attempt to decipher the old Dresdellan texts," Ivan said coolly, pulling Nash from her thoughts. He reached for the canteen beside him. He tipped it toward his mouth, then frowned as nothing but a few droplets came out. The water was nearly out too? They wouldn't be able to avoid docking for much longer. . . .

"Tempting," Nash said. One of the sails started flapping, catching an errant wind. She turned her attention to one of the two Kinetics, standing still and silent a few paces away. "Hey, be a pal and grab that line, would you?" she called.

Both of the Adept looked nearly identical, their pale heads shaven, their cheeks marked with Clem's brand—two snakes circling a man's head like a halo. It wasn't the first brand for either of the poor bastards. Not that she was surprised at that—Callum Clem was many things, but a reputable merchant was not one of them. Nor was he a nobleman. And those were the only two types of men invited to the Guildmaster's auction to buy Adept of their own.

The Adept on the left strode forward, taking the line in hand as she had asked.

"You know you don't have to ask them, Nash," Ivan said quietly. He was watching her over the edge of his book with his startling, sea-green eyes.

"I—" Nash started, but cut off at the sound of a bloodcurdling scream. "Clem," she said.

At the same time Ivan jumped to his feet and said, "Callum."

Nash quickly waved the second Adept over to the helm; then she and Ivan both sprinted toward the hatch, nearly tripping over each other as they rushed belowdecks.

In their first few days of travel, Clem had ordered his Kinetics to divide the lower deck into three cabins connected by a single passageway using wood from the crates on board. Nash's cabin was the smallest, closest to the ladder. Ivan's was just beside hers, and the entire opposite side of the hold served as Clem's quarters. Nash skidded into the doorway, Ivan close behind, to find Clem kneeling on the deck, his hands clenched tightly into fists, his face redder than a Borean with a sunburn. A lonely leather binding lay a few inches from him, surrounded by sheafs of loose parchment that looked like they had been shredded by a cave bear.

"Callum!" Ivan said, dropping to his knees at the Snake's side. "What happened?"

"Like you don't already know!" Clem said. He rounded on Ivan, wrapping his hands around the disguise-master's throat. His unhealed thumbs left smears of dark crimson blood on Ivan's pale skin. "You set me up to look like a fool, didn't you? Didn't you?!"

"Clem, what the fuck!" Nash said, leaping forward and grabbing the Snake by the shoulders. Thankfully he was still weaker than a newly hatched gull, and she easily pulled him away from Ivan. Clem rounded on her next, but she stood her ground, placing herself between the two men. "What is going on?"

The redness in Clem's face subsided, his breathing slowing down to a normal rate as he sank back into his usual calm persona as quickly and easily as another person might slip on a pair of boots. He straightened his shirt, running one bloodstained hand over his hair, then handed Ivan one of the leaves of parchment littering the deck.

"I've been misled," he said. His eyes glittered dangerously again, the madness sparking back up as suddenly as it had left a second ago. "And if I discover it was by either of you . . . you will wish I had the mercy to throw you overboard."

Ivan seemed unfazed by the threat, despite the fact that his throat was still ringed with bloody marks from Clem's fingers. Instead, he just took the paper and began to read, his brow dipping lower with every word on the page. "No," he whispered, more to himself than anyone else. "It cannot be."

"What?" Nash asked, impatient. "Does anyone want to tell me what the hell is going on?"

Ivan opened his mouth to speak, but apparently that was too twice-damned difficult. Instead, he just passed the sheet of paper to Nash in silence. It was a study of the early Guildmasters of Thamorr, written in what looked like Middle Thamorri, the language that had morphed into Thamorri Common over the past few hundred years. There were a lot of words Nash couldn't quite decipher from that old dialect, but there was one line that sucked all the air from her lungs. It didn't mention the Quill by name, but still, it was clear what the passage meant.

Nash looked up. "So, the Quill . . ."

Clem's lip curled as he glared at her with eyes rimmed in the deepest red. "The Quill of Declan Day cannot be wielded by a man without Adept magic."

"That cannot be the entire story," Ivan said. He began to shuffle the papers on the deck, searching through them. "Perhaps there is some way to work around this safeguard of Declan Day's device. Perhaps . . ."

Ivan continued to talk, but Nash's ears were

suddenly filled with the rush of blood past her eardrums and nothing more. She hadn't wanted to give Callum Clem this twice-damned Quill in the first place. Now they were almost out of supplies, sailing up and down the coast of Thamorr, afraid to dock anywhere, on the run from . . . well, everyone.

Clem would never give up on his hopeless quest for power; the way he was drinking in the scattered pages like they were water when he was dying of thirst made that painfully clear. And somehow, amazingly, Ivan was drinking them in right alongside him. Clem's hands had been at Ivan's throat not one minute ago, and already Ivan was acting as though it had never happened. Why on earth was the disguise-master so loyal to this man? Especially now that Clem was clearly losing his marbles?

Even if the Snake *didn't* lose his mind completely, if he insisted on staying out here, parsing through old texts in hopes of making the impossible possible, they were sitting ducks. They would just float here, bobbing like a cork, until the Guildmaster managed to track them down. Nash reached up toward the leather strap encircling her throat, instinctively grabbing her ma's namestone and running her fingers over it as she thought. Callum Clem would never give up the Quill by choice, so there was only one option left. She eyed the

Quill, swaying from its chain around Clem's neck.

She was going to have to steal it.

Nash waited until well after dark, after the sun had been swallowed by the Yawning Sea and the sounds of shuffling papers had faded into silence belowdecks. She eyed the horizon to the west. The shadow of Gildemar rose like thick black smoke over the tossing waves. They had kept out of sight of the Thamorri coastline for days now, but she had slowly steered them west over the past few hours. Once she had stolen the Quill, she would take *The Hardship*'s dinghy and row herself to the mainland. The night should hide her from prying eyes on the shore, and with a little luck, she would be able to disappear into the wilderness before Clem was any the wiser.

Nash swallowed. Everyone in Carrowwick knew betraying Callum Clem was not a wise move—not if you wanted to keep your head attached to your shoulders. But they weren't in Carrowwick anymore. Without his Saints, and without the Quill, he would be just another man. A ruthless man who would surely be hell-bent on destroying her, but still, just a man.

"You there!" she called. The nearest Kinetic turned sharply toward her. She pointed to the wheel. "Man the helm awhile, would you?"

The Adept didn't nod or show any other sign it

had heard, but it walked across the deck toward her, stiff and mechanical. Its flat, dead eyes didn't even meet hers as it—*he?*—took the wheel in hand, staring blankly off into the distance.

"Keep us on course," Nash said. "I'll be right back."

She wasn't sure why she was bothering to lie to the Kinetic—she wasn't even sure if the creature could understand her . . . but still, it felt wrong to communicate with them with just snaps and points the way Clem did. She had always had what many would call a "problematic" sympathy for Adepts, but ever since she had seen the children on the Guildmaster's island, she was even more certain of their humanity. Now that she lived with two Kinetics in close quarters, she knew that they ate and slept, just like any other men (though only when ordered). Of course, Clem fed them like dogs and made them curl up on the deck to sleep. But still, there had to be something human left in them . . . didn't there?

The night wind riffled through her short, dark curls as Nash turned away from the helm, stalking across the deck toward the hatch. As she picked her way over the salt-stained slats, Nash thought about her sister, Jolie. The infant who had been stolen from her mother's arms by Disciples when Nash was barely more than a baby herself. She shot a look over her shoulder at the Kinetic now at the helm, bathed in starlight. Maybe she only *wanted* to believe there was still something human in them. That somewhere out there, Jolie was alive, just trapped in an expressionless shell like this poor sap—whether it was true or not.

Nash shook her head, turning away again. She could dwell on depressing things like that another day. Once the Quill was sold, and she was flush enough with crescents to buy a proper ship and crew and sail off into the sunset far away from Callum Clem. She tapped her ma's namestone again. She had wasted enough years of her life smuggling for the crime lords of this world. Once she escaped Clem and sold the Quill, she would finally go searching for a place she could set her ma's memory to rest. She would just have to ignore the pang in her chest that came every time she remembered that sailing far away from Clem would also mean sailing far away from Ivan. But if he wouldn't leave the Snake's side . . . there was nothing she could do about that.

Trying to stay as quiet as possible, she knelt to the deck and eased the hatch open, climbing rung after rung down into the gloom. She paused when she reached the lower deck, listening. Nothing but silence, the deep breath of sleep, and the flapping of sails up above. Finally, Clem's madness had given in to exhaustion. It had certainly taken long enough.

She crept through the hold as silently as she could manage. She had never really been one for sneaking—she was, after all, over six feet tall and built like a fort wall. Avoiding the worst of the creaky planks beneath her feet, she paused at the entrance to Ivan's quarters. *Would he leave the Snake?* He had seemed too certain all this time . . . but with the news they had gotten today, maybe there was a chance she could sway him.

"Looking for someone?"

Nash whirled around to see Ivan standing in the passageway behind her, his golden hair bathed in the moonlight streaming in through the open hatch.

"Clem still up, then?" Nash asked.

Ivan shook his head. "No, he fell asleep some time ago. I wanted to go through one last text."

One last text. Nash's heart skipped. *Last.* Was he finally ready to give up on this madness? "Did you find anything?"

Ivan's face twisted sourly. "You already know that I did not." He paused, looking at her for a few heartbeats. Then: "I know why you are here. What you're planning to do."

Nash smiled hesitantly, flashing her sharpened canines. "And? Have you come to stop me, or help me?"

Ivan's stonelike face used to be so unreadable to her, but she knew him better than that now. The corners of his lips tightened under his frustratingly perfect beard. The thin lines on his forehead grew just a hair deeper. He was either torn or pissed. If he was pissed, she could only drive him further away from her. Deeper into the chasm of Clem worship he had been sinking into these past few weeks. But if he was torn . . .

"Look, Ivan, we helped Clem get the Quill to keep it out of more dangerous hands. If he can't master its power . . . he's not going to have it much longer."

"You do not know that he cannot master it," Ivan said stiffly.

"If anyone could puzzle it out, it's probably you two," Nash admitted. "But if we don't do something quickly, the Guildmaster is going to track us down and take it. By force."

"You're just planning to beat him to it, then?"

"It's a damn sight better than sailing around in circles, waiting to get ambushed and murdered."

Ivan's lips grew tighter. "We cannot betray Callum. Not now."

"He doesn't deserve this much loyalty from you, Ivan," Nash whispered. "You know he would sell you out for a new pair of loafers, don't you?"

"I think you are forgetting something, Nash," Ivan said, putting as much sourness on her name as she had just put on his. His eyes were hardly visible in the darkness as he took another step toward her, but she could still see them flick up toward the deck above them.

"The Kinetics?" Nash guessed.

"Yes, the Kinetics," Ivan whispered. "I have seen the way Callum allows you to order them around up on deck, but do not think for a moment that they are yours."

Nash recoiled, disgusted. "I wouldn't want them to be mine." And she meant it. She had been commanding them on board *The Hardship* for the past few weeks, it was true, but she had treated them like crewmen, not servants.

Pity flickered in Ivan's eyes, and Nash felt her hackles rise. She had never liked pity from anyone, but she especially didn't want it from him. "I'm taking that Quill," she started, voice a low hiss, "and I'm going to sell it to some unlucky bastard who won't understand that he can't use it. Then I'm going to use the gold to buy myself a nice ship and enough Gildesh-made wine to last a trip all the way around the three seas."

The never-ending ocean swirling in Ivan's eyes froze solid, cracking and hardening as he stepped toward her again. Her breath caught as he stood inches from her. "If you manage to steal that Quill, the Guildmaster will not be the only one hunting you."

Nash snorted softly. "Callum Clem is unraveling. He's not the Snake of the Southern Dock anymore. Now he's just a madman with an obsession."

"I did not mean Clem."

Nash drew back a step. After all the time they

had spent together? The dangers they had shared, the betrayals they had weathered . . . He was so willing to become her enemy—her hunter—just like that, in the blink of an eye?

She stood, staring Ivan down for one heartbeat, then another. But the fight was already over. If she tried to take the Quill now, he would raise the alarm. And if he did that . . . well, the Kinetics would do what they did best. Tear her to bits and toss the pieces overboard for the sharks to fight over.

Finally, she sighed and took a step backward, raising her hands in surrender. "Fine." She shouldered past him, grabbing hold of the ladder and climbing up to the deck. For the first time in her life, she felt claustrophobic on her own damned ship.

"Where are you going?"

"To set a new course," Nash said. She didn't bother to keep her voice down anymore. Clem would find out what she was doing as soon as he woke anyway.

"A new course?" Ivan hissed. "I was not aware we had a course to begin with. Where could you possibly mean to go? The Guildmaster has Disciples in every major port along this coastline."

"We need supplies," Nash said flatly. "And I can think of one port that may have escaped the Guildmaster's attention. So far, at least."

Ivan was quiet for a moment. Then his eyes sharpened. "Golden Port?"

"Golden Port," Nash repeated, half to herself. No matter how far she ran from that cursed town, it always managed to drag her back. As she took the helm again, she found herself almost wishing she'd see blue sails on that horizon.

CHAPTER FOUR

Ryia

Ryia was already so bruised and bleeding she barely felt the Kinetic's next punch as it crashed into her cheek. Her eyes were swollen halfway shut, and she was pretty sure her nose was broken. She didn't even raise a hand to block as the Kinetic brought a knee up, burying it in her gut. Her stomach heaved, and she collapsed to the floor, spitting up the meager Edalish supper she'd eaten that night, mixed with a good helping of dark blood.

There was a snap of delicate fingers, and the Kinetic retreated. A shadow fell over her, and Tolliver Shadowwood crouched beside her, his hair spilling over his face as he met her eye.

"I know what you are," he said, grabbing her bruised chin and tilting it upward.

His words were worse than the punches.

For years, she had run from kingdom to kingdom, slum to slum, holding her secret tight. But now it was out—and to one of the most batshit crazy men in all of Thamorr. She thought of the Guildmaster's last words to her. That death would be a mercy compared to what a more curious man might do with her. With the knowledge of what she was.

It looked like she was about to find out if he was right.

"I saw what you did back there, and yet . . ." Tolliver Shadowwood tapped her cheek with one long-nailed finger. "Not a brand in sight." He moved his hand up to her freshly shaven skull. "Nor do I see a tattoo. So, not an Adept, not a Disciple," he continued, naming the unenslaved Adept working in the Guildmaster's service. "Still, you have a power only seen in the most expensive of Kinetics. Those axes . . . the wine cask . . . How is this possible?"

For roughly the millionth time, Ryia kicked herself mentally. She should have just tried to fight her way out with her hands, or not at all. The second she reached for her power, used her magic to fling her throwing axes across that wine cellar, she should have known she was asking for trouble. The exploding wine keg, she couldn't take credit for. Only her hatchets were controlled by her magic, that much had always been true. She must have just weakened the lid enough that it eventually collapsed under the pressure of the wine inside. And it was fortunate that it had.

She still remembered the feeling of panic clawing up her throat as she imagined that Shadow Warden's sword piercing Evelyn's pale, thin throat. But the wine cask had chosen that moment to burst, and Evelyn had made it out safely. That was the only bit of good news to be found in these horrible stone walls.

Ryia was defenseless now—her hatchets snatched away and hidden by this disgusting old man. And she was getting the life kicked out of her by two Adept. Two of the poor saps she had risked her ass to try to free from their invisible bonds just a few weeks ago. This was what she got for letting Evelyn Linley fill her head with all that noble horseshit.

"I don't know what you think you saw," Ryia said, pausing to spit a mouthful of blood out onto the filthy floor, "but—"

"What I saw was something that has been thought impossible for centuries now." Shadowwood's voice was almost tender as he studied her swollen face. "You have discovered how to give yourself Adept magic. And now you are going to teach that secret to me."

"And if I don't know what you're talking about?" Ryia asked. "If I don't have any secrets to teach you? What then?"

Shadowwood studied her a moment longer, then shrugged. "Well, then I would just have to hang you as a foreign invader and leave your body in the gutter where it belongs."

Two great options, then.

The rank scent of danger suddenly filled her nostrils, filtering past the blood and broken cartilage. It came from the direction of the second Kinetic, lurking in the shadowy corner to her left. Instinct took over before she could stop it, and she whipped back, ducking away from his massive fist as he brought it crashing toward her skull. The scent came from the right-hand corner of the room next, and again Ryia's body moved without asking her mind for permission. She pushed herself back to her feet, leaping out of the way as the right-hand Kinetic kicked at the empty air where her face had been just a second before.

Even before she found Tolliver Shadowwood's face again, she knew he had seen. Seen how she had jumped higher than any normal person could . . . and seen how she had dodged before her tormenter had even reared back to strike. She had given away her Kinetic powers to get Evelyn and Tristan out of this cursed cellar. Now her stupid ass had given him a front-row show of her stolen Senser magic as well.

The king snapped his fingers, and his Kinetics marched back to their corners. Ryia's heart thudded with dread as the mad king of Edale stalked toward her. He was only a few inches taller than her, but still he seemed to look down at her from a great height as he studied her.

"It seems I have stumbled upon something more powerful than I even thought," he said softly. "I think that is enough damage to my valuable *subject* today." The Kinetics seized her arms from behind, pulling them so tight her shoulder blades brushed together. "Let's see if a few nights in the Shadow Cells don't loosen that tongue of yours."

The Shadow Cells. Ryia had never seen the cells beneath the castle of Edale before, but she had heard enough stories about them from the various criminals she had run with in her day to know the basics. Even if she'd never heard anything, knowing she was about to be carted underground made her palms sweat and her skin prick. She could hear her father's voice growing louder and louder inside her head with every single step down the long, winding staircase leading into the bowels of the earth.

As the name implied, the Shadow Cells were dark as the deepest pits of the hells. They were even lower than the wine cellar—lower than the disgusting pipe Evelyn had crawled through to sneak Tristan out. The walls were slimy and wet, and the constant sound of drip-drip-dripping filled the air all around her as they entered the dungeon.

The hairs on Ryia's arms stood up, chills convulsing down her spine as she felt the weight of the earthy darkness crushing in on her. The only light came from sputtering torches on the walls, and as the Kinetics led her down the corridor, she could see the shadows of wasted figures lying on the floors of the cells surrounding them. Some lunged for the bars as they passed, reaching out with shriveled arms and baring brown-rimmed teeth. Others barely even lifted a head at the passing torchlight, choosing instead to stay curled on the rock, their ribs sticking out and the soles of their bare feet caked with filth.

Tolliver Shadowwood didn't seem to give half a shit about any of it; he just stalked through the darkness, surrounded by his halo of torchlight, head high, fancy, buckled boots clicking on the moist stone underfoot. When he reached a cell with puddles coating half the floor space, he nodded to the gaoler.

"This one will do."

The gaoler, a tall, stone-faced man with more scars than wrinkles and a wicked hand-and-a-half sword at his belt, pulled out a set of keys. He fitted one into the lock and twisted. The door creaked open with a screech that set Ryia's teeth on edge.

"Perhaps a few days of quiet reflection will help you see what needs to be done," Shadowwood said as the Kinetics bullied her into the cell. She knew it was useless to struggle in her present state, but still, she didn't go easily. She kicked and scratched, tossing her head and trying to wriggle her wrists free.

After just a few moments, though, she was on the far side of the bars listening to the lock click into place behind her.

Shadowwood eyed the moldy puddles covering

her cell floor with a curled lip, then said, "Sleep well."

The king knew exactly how much of a bastard he was being, and he clearly reveled in it.

Ryia lunged forward, thrusting her hands through the bars toward him. She missed the king, instead striking the gaoler right in his prominent gut. The man doubled over, gasping. An instant later, the Kinetics were back, pushing her away from the bars and back into the damp darkness of her cell. Shadowwood tutted his tongue in mock disappointment.

And with that, the king was gone. He took his ring of light with him, leaving Ryia alone in the gloom, listening to the constant drip of water on stone and staring at the reflection of the distant corridor torches on the puddles soaking her floor. *Sleep well.* She would be lucky to find a square foot of this cell that wasn't going to soak her to the bone with freezing, fetid water. Not that she would even be able to sleep soundly on a feather bed in a place like this. Not with the walls closing in around her, the smell of earth and decay filling her lungs.

She rubbed her wrists absently, feeling the thick, ropy scars from her father's shackles. They seemed to throb in the cool darkness, like the cold march underground had transported her back in time, bringing the scars—and the memories—back to life.

"So. What are you in for?"

Ryia managed to transform her jump of alarm into a sneer as she turned toward the voice. But the sneer melted into a look of complete shock as she saw the figure standing in the next cell.

She was tall and broad, her hands wrapped around the bars separating them. Her head was shaved bare, not even a hint of hair growing from that scalp. She must not have been here all that long. She wore the boots of a sailor, sensible trousers, and a filthy shirt that had the unmistakable patterns of salt spray hiding underneath a layer of dungeon grime.

"Nash?" Ryia asked. "Nash, how did you—" She took a step closer. The woman in the next cell was grinning at her confusion. Grinning with normal, un-sharpened canines.

"Who the hell is Nash?"

"No one." Ryia shook her head. "Nothing." Her eyes must be playing tricks. . . .

But it was no trick. Sure, it was darker than Callum Clem's nightmares in this hellhole, but she knew she wasn't mistaken. This woman—whoever she was—was a dead ringer for the smuggler Ryia had traveled with to the Guildmaster's island.

"Right." For Felice's sake, even the woman's smile was just like Nash's—minus the canines, of course. But all the cockiness was there, and the mischievous glint to her dark eyes. "Not gonna tell me what you're in for, eh?" She sucked on her cheek, then shook her head. "Well, I just hope you last longer than the poor sap who had that cell before you."

"Oh yeah?" Ryia asked, trying to sound casual despite the fact that the basement air was still squeezing her like a damned vise grip. *Shackles clanked in the darkness, tethering her to the cold stone wall. All around her was the scent of blood. She could still taste it on her tongue. . . .*

"What happened to him?"

"You clearly already know Tolliver likes to play with his food. But eventually he shoves it down his gullet," Not-Nash said.

"Thank you for that," Ryia said. "So, what are *you* in for?" She took a step closer to the bars between them, then drew back as the torchlight illuminated the other prisoner's entire face.

The woman looked haunted. The skin on her face was somehow both saggy and stretched way too tightly over her bones. She had huge, bruised circles ringing both eyes, and her cheeks looked hollow.

Ryia's revulsion was not missed. The woman cackled mirthlessly. "A regular beauty queen, I know. If one of these prissy sods would just get me a few hits of *vitalité* . . ." She picked up a small pebble from the floor of her own cell, cocked back her arm, and flung it toward the shadow of the nearest guard. He was right next to the door to the dungeons, not even in earshot let alone in range of her pitiful throw. The pebble landed on the floor with a clatter some fifteen paces shy of the man, and Not-Nash waved a hand dismissively. "And you already know what I'm in for. Everyone in Thamorr knows my crimes."

"What do you mean everyone knows your crimes? You some kind of highwayman or something?"

Not-Nash grinned again. "Something like that." She shifted in the darkness, leaning against the bars so Ryia could see the patch on the lapel of her filthy coat. The patch was old and weathered, crusted with salt spray just like the rest of her, but Ryia could still make out the stitching clearly. The symbol of a bearded skull with crystals for eyes.

"You're one of Salt Beard's?" she asked, naming the infamous pirate who had terrorized the Gildesh coast for a decade.

"I *am* Salt Beard."

Ryia raised an eyebrow, looking her up and down, then snorted. "*You're* Salt Beard?"

The woman in the next cell straightened her spine, fixing her hollow eyes on Ryia in a pointed stare. "What makes you think I couldn't be?"

"Well, you don't have a beard, for one."

The woman rolled her eyes. "That's the whole fucking joke. My beard is made of salt—can't grow one myself. Next question."

"Salt Beard's been on the seas for longer than you've worn grown-up britches."

"What can I say? I was precocious when it came to relieving merchants of their purses."

Ryia snorted. She couldn't really argue with that one—not when she herself had been cutting purses and slitting throats since the tender age of thirteen. "Fine, then there's the fact that you're in this cell at all." She gestured around them, suppressing a shiver as the dungeon walls seemed to close in on her again. "I thought Salt Beard never got captured."

"Correction: Salt Beard only gets captured when she *wants* to be captured," the pirate said, scratching one arm bitterly.

"Well, I can definitely see why you would want this," Ryia said. "Quality lodging right here."

"It was better than the alternative."

Salt Beard muttered that last bit to herself, but Ryia still heard it in the quiet of the dungeon. "I'd think a fearsome pirate like yourself would rather die on her ship than waste away in a pisshole like this."

"What makes you so sure that death was the other option?"

Ryia had no idea what that meant, but she didn't really care. She gave the woman a pitying smile. "Well, I wish I could keep you company for longer, but . . ." She pulled her hand from inside her sleeve. A glint of iron caught the distant lantern light as the dungeon keys jangled slightly on their ring. Taking them from the gaoler had been even easier than picking the silvers she had stolen to pay Berman for his boat. She cocked her head to one side. "Care to come along?"

Breaking out alone would be better for stealth, but having another prisoner loose in these halls could be a valuable distraction. Salt Beard chuckled, shaking her head.

"You're dumber than the court fool if you think these bars are the only thing stopping me from escaping this place."

Ryia shrugged, eyeing the guards at the end of the corridor. "Suit yourself."

If the pirate wanted to stay and rot in this dungeon, that was her own business, but Ryia had places to go. Syndicate lords to murder, Quills to destroy. From the looks of the Adept in Shadowwood's service, Wyatt Asher hadn't made his move yet, but it wouldn't be long before he did. The winter snows were coming, and if he intended to conquer any kingdom north of Gildemar, he'd almost certainly begin his conquest before those first flakes started to fall. She reached through the bars, fitted the key into the lock, and twisted. Making sure to push the door slowly enough to watch for any squeaking hinges, she eased herself out of the cell and into the corridor.

There was only one exit from this place, which

wasn't ideal, but at least it didn't seem all that well-guarded. Just two guards, from what Ryia could see. They weren't even Shadow Wardens, just run-of-the-mill soldiers of Edale. Ryia could take them unarmed—probably even with her hands cuffed together if she had to. She kept to the shadows lining the cells, slipping closer and closer.

Suddenly the scent of danger crashed over her like a wave, bursting through the already foul scent of the dungeon. The hairs on her arms prickled as no fewer than six Kinetics emerged from the dark spaces in the walls all around her. With her hatchets she may have stood a chance . . . but as it was, they had her pinned in seconds.

The scent of earth, mildew, and blood overcame her as they ground her face into the dungeon floor. She sank deep inside herself, running from the memories of her father's cellar. She was so distracted that she didn't even kick or struggle as they hauled her back to her cell and threw her inside, this time without her keys. The gaoler hurried over, swearing, and clicked the lock on her cell shut again. Ryia forced her mind back into her body as the man pointed at her through the bars.

"Consider this a warning, scum. Next time, you won't find these beasts so friendly," he said, gesturing toward the Kinetics, who were already slinking back into the shadows. Now that she was looking for them, Ryia could see them, lurking in the spaces between the cells closest to the doors.

The gaoler ambled away, clutching his keys like they were his firstborn child. As he disappeared back down the dimly lit corridor leading from the cells, Ryia heard a wheezing laugh from the cell beside her. She looked to see Salt Beard, curled on the floor, her hood up over her head. She lowered it as she pushed herself back to her feet, still chuckling.

Ryia wiped the blood from the corner of her lips. "A heads-up would have been great."

"Yeah, maybe. Would have been a lot less fun for me, though," Salt Beard said, running a hand over her bare head. She looked at Ryia, eyes glittering in amusement, then stuck her hand pompously through the bars separating them. "Most might know me as Salt Beard, but you can call me Joslyn."

Ryia grabbed the hand tentatively. Joslyn shook it firmly in a mocking sort of way.

"How long have you been here, *Joslyn?*"

"Few weeks," Joslyn said. She eased herself down to her cell floor. Ryia noted bitterly that at least *her* floor was dry. Then she looked from the floor to the woman's head and frowned. It was bald to the point of being shiny.

"A few *weeks?* You're kidding me."

There was no way in either hell they would've given someone in these cells a blade to shave with—it didn't even look like most of the prisoners were getting fed down here.

"Wish I was," Joslyn said wistfully. "I just hope—oh shit." She suddenly sprang back, digging in the pocket of her coat.

"What's wr—" Ryia started, then broke off as the smell overcame her. The scent of moist earth and decaying things. The scent of danger. Someone was coming. The sound of footsteps didn't reach her cell for another few seconds.

So how had Joslyn known?

Ryia looked back up just in time to see the pirate fitting a bedraggled-looking wig onto her suspiciously bald head.

"Itches like a bitch" was all she said when she noticed Ryia looking. But as the guards started their rounds, parting the darkness like curtains with their too-bright torches, Ryia pieced it all together.

Joslyn was Salt Beard. The infamous, invincible pirate. Constantly on the move, never calling one place home. Her head was still as hairless as Tristan's balls, despite being locked in this hellhole for weeks. And she had known the guards were coming before she could hear them. There was only one answer . . . but it was absolutely mad.

The guards stopped three cells away, yanked a screaming man in a bloodstained tunic from his cell in chains, then led him away up the stairs.

Ryia stared at Joslyn as the guards' torchlight disappeared, leaving them in near darkness again. She watched the pirate's nostrils flare, only calming when the dungeon door slammed shut, the guards taking the last whiff of danger out with them. This woman—this *Joslyn*—was a Senser.

CHAPTER FIVE
Evelyn

Evelyn Linley had trained with a sword nearly every bloody day of her life. She was quick with a blade and steady on her feet. As it turned out, she was neither quick nor steady on horseback.

"Need a hand there, Captain?"

Evelyn scowled up at the lily-green boy who still insisted on being called Tristan. He was lounging on the back of his chestnut-colored bay, one hand lazily on the reins while she wrestled with the thousand-pound beast beneath her own rough-hewn saddle. Where Tristan's mount was calm and obedient, her own horse, a caramel-colored creature Tristan had called a Haflinger, was all wide eyes and bared teeth. It whipped its shaggy mane back and forth again as Evelyn leaned on the reins, tugging it to the left to join Tristan.

Finally, the horse listened, stomping up the path. "Nope. I've got it under control."

"The trick is to relax," Tristan said, tossing his hair back from his face. That was a new habit he had picked up since being captured by his father. Evelyn was not a fan. "She's going to panic if you keep squeezing the life out of her."

"And tell me, Highness, how am I supposed to relax right now?"

Tristan shifted uncomfortably in his saddle, shooting an anxious glance over each shoulder. "Don't call me that."

Evelyn looked over her own shoulder. "Sorry."

Tristan had sold his fine shoes and dressing coat back in Duskhaven and had managed to trade his silken nightclothes for a rough-spun shirt and riding trousers. His boots were worn, and their horses were old and unkempt—the cheapest mounts gold could buy. In short, he looked even less like a prince now than he had back in Carrowwick. But still, it was bloody foolish to risk being identified by openly using his title. Especially just for the sake of spite.

They rode side by side down the Iron Road in silence after that, Tristan's steed trotting along obediently, Evelyn's tossing its head and huffing in irritation every time her hand so much as twitched on the reins. It had been two days since the weeping willows of Duskhaven had been swallowed by the rolling hills of the Edalish countryside. Two days since they had been swept through the pipes beneath the Shadow Keep, leaving Ryia to be captured and collared by Tolliver Shadowwood.

Evelyn's horse snorted, baring its teeth as her legs clenched. She sighed, reaching out to pat the horse's neck. It whipped its head around and tried to bite her for her trouble. Maybe Tristan had a point. It wasn't easy to relax . . . but this was what Ryia had wanted them to do. If she hadn't forced them to leave that cellar, they would just have been captured alongside her. This way, they were free—and with the knowledge that Wyatt Asher had somehow outsmarted everyone back in the Catacombs. The leader of the Kestrel Crowns must have made a fake Quill and swapped the original out before the meeting.

A dodgy move, but then again, Asher was missing half his fingers. Risks were clearly not a new concept for the man. Ryia was counting on them—counting on *her*—to get that artifact back from Asher and destroy it. For real this time. And she would not fail, though time was likely running out. Asher hadn't made his move just yet, but Evelyn had no doubt he would soon. She shot a wary glance at the slate-gray skies above. Only a fool would try to start a war in the winter. Half the roads north of Carrowwick were unpassable by mid-Verbot, which was only some eight weeks away. If Asher planned to make a play for Thamorr, Evelyn had no doubt he would do it before then.

They followed the Rowan River for another four days, then cut south when the rushing waters forked in two, the deep blue of the Rowan rushing due east through the moors of Edale, the sludgy brown of the Arden winding down toward Dresdell. For those first few days, they traveled alongside the road rather than walking on it. After all, only a complete git would parade the kidnapped crown prince of Edale around the well-worn roads of his own father's kingdom. But as the days wore on, it became clearer and clearer that the king was not sending men after them.

Good news, Evelyn tried to reason with herself. If Shadowwood didn't know where they were, it meant he didn't know where they were headed. And if he didn't know their plans to return to Carrowwick, it meant Ryia hadn't cracked and told him. She swallowed. Hopefully that meant the Butcher was still fighting . . . and not that she was dead.

A stupid thought. A mad old fool like Tolliver Shadowwood would never get the best of Ryia. But still, her stomach squirmed. It wasn't just Shadowwood Ryia would have to outlast or overpower. The Shadow Keep had hundreds of guards, scores of Shadow Wardens, and dozens of Adept. Even Ryia wasn't strong enough to fight them all. Not forever, at least.

But it was no use obsessing over it. Ryia had sent them to Carrowwick to get the Quill, and she was right. Stopping a man like Wyatt Asher from becoming lord of Thamorr was obviously worth the sacrifice of one measly life. Even if that life belonged to someone who had become more important to Evelyn than she could have predicted over the past few months. Something she and the prince had in common, she knew.

Tristan had his share of faults, like the fact that he started complaining about the itch after only three days without washing, or the fact that he suggested they stop at every bloody town they passed, despite their dwindling pouch of coin. But he was nearly as worried about Ryia's fate as she was. Evelyn knew if she suggested they ride back to the Shadow Keep to spring her the second they managed to get the Quill back, he would be on board. Most nights, that knowledge was the only thing that stopped her from slapping the shite out of him.

On their third day following the Lilac Road southeast along the Arden, they reached the first flax farms. When she and Ryia had left the city, the farms had been teeming with knee-high green shoots topped with pale blue flowers. Now the fields held only long rows of dry, golden stalks, bare and bent in the haste of harvesting. It made it feel like a whole bloody season had passed since she had last been here when it had really only been a few weeks. The dread in Evelyn's belly pulsed at the thought. Winter would be here in less than two months' time. How long did they have before Asher stopped dithering around and finally made his move with the Quill? Thankfully, they were almost to Carrowwick. The tall, familiar city walls came into view before the picked-over fields were behind their horses' flicking tails.

A sick feeling swept through Evelyn as she took in the slanted rooftops, the circling gulls, the broad, jarlike tower of the Bobbin Fort in the distance. It was lucky they weren't approaching from the south, where she would have had to ride past the gleaming white stones of the Linley Manor, perched on a hilltop just outside the city limits. Still, the sight of the silver-tipped helmets guarding the gates was more than enough to send her stomach churning again. In another bloody life, that would have been her, taking her monthly shift at the city gate.

But it wasn't another life. Not really. She had marched the streets of Carrowwick wearing the purple-and-silver armor of the Baelbrandt throne just a few months ago. There was a good chance the guards up there knew her face. She may have lived with them in the barracks, trained with them, ordered them around when she was a captain. Meaning she and Tristan weren't just going to march into the city on horseback—not unless she wanted every gutter rat and nobleman to know the disgraced Captain Evelyn Linley was back in town.

What she wouldn't have given for one of Ivan Rezkoye's brilliant disguises right now.

But they didn't have Ivan. They had one set

of clothes each, a few scraps of food, and two horses older than the legends of the Ophidian.

She and Tristan pulled their horses to a stop at the nearest farm flying the flag of the merchant's guild. Beets and leeks, from the looks of the cart being loaded. Evelyn stayed back with the horses while Tristan did the talking. When all was said and done, he had traded both their mounts for a few coppers and safe passage into the city, sitting on the back of the beet-trader's cart. Evelyn wasn't sure what explanation Tristan could have given other than *Hello, we're wanted criminals. Care to help us sneak into the city?* But clearly, he had thought of something.

The trader was nice, if a bit friendly for Evelyn's taste. But she had to admit, the last place anyone who knew her would expect to find Evelyn Linley was on the back of a bloody beet cart.

"Where are you two comin' from?" the trader asked as they clambered into the bed of his cart. Evelyn tiptoed forward until she found a bare spot on the cart's ledge, careful not to bruise any of the beets.

Tristan was ready with an answer. "West coast of Edale, over by Willow Water Grove. Been on the road for near a month now." He shot the trader a smile that was all too gleaming white for someone on the road for a month. "I'm looking forward to steady meals and soft beds, that's for sure."

The trader nodded toward Tristan. "Hopefully

those coins'll get you at least a few nights of those."

"I'm sure they will." Tristan smiled again, wistfully this time. "Just make sure to take care of those horses. The bay was my uncle's. Shame to see her go."

For the first time since meeting the prince of Edale in that smoky room in the Miscreants' Temple, Evelyn understood how Tristan had lasted so long with the scum of the southern docks. The boy had a silver tongue—he lied more smoothly than Gildesh silk.

"I'll treat 'er right," the trader said. Evelyn grabbed hold of the sides of the cart as it rumbled into motion, bumping down the Lilac Road toward the western gate of Carrowwick. "Don't you worry about that."

Evelyn held on tight, wincing at every bump that rattled the cart as Tristan chatted pleasantly with the beet trader. The pair of them sounded like old drinking pals by the time they crested the last hill before the walls. As the gate came into view, Evelyn sucked in a sharp breath, then prodded Tristan with an elbow.

"Tristan," she hissed.

"—and then my ma said, 'If that wine was Brillish, I'm the queen of Boreas,' " Tristan was saying, telling the end of a riotous story involving a series of escapades that Evelyn was certain held not a single grain of truth.

The merchant laughed so hard he had to wipe his eyes. Tristan joined in, smiling broadly and clapping the man on the shoulder.

"Tristan," Evelyn hissed again, a little louder this time. She smacked him on the knee.

"Ow," he said. "What?"

Evelyn didn't answer, just pointed toward the gates with her chin. Tristan followed her point, then paled to roughly the same shade as a winter melon. The gates were not flanked by the Needle Guard. No, it was twin swirls of vivid blue that billowed in the early autumn wind. Disciples. The Guildmaster's private soldiers—the only Adept in Thamorr besides Ryia who retained control over their own minds and bodies.

The merchant caught them looking, and the mirth faded from his face quickly.

"Ah yeah, them . . . ," he said, lowering his voice, even though they were still well out of earshot. "Showed up about a week past."

"What do they want?" Tristan asked.

But Evelyn already knew—they were here looking for the Quill. What else could it be?

"Not right sure," the merchant said. "Sensers, though, the both of them. So, nothing to fear."

His lips pursed like he didn't quite believe himself. Then he looked them both over suspiciously, as though starting to regret his decision to cart two complete strangers past a pair of ruddy Disciples. Evelyn didn't blame him. She swallowed nervously as they clattered forward. Disciples had seen her on the Guildmaster's island. She had been in disguise then, but still, these were Sensers. Would they recognize her somehow?

The cart rattled to a stop. Evelyn held her breath as the tattooed, blue-robed figures began to poke and prod, first at Tristan's pockets, then the compartment under the merchant's bench. Evelyn's pulse was the only thing she could hear as the Disciples moved to the back of the cart where she was sitting. Thankfully, the Guildmaster's soldiers seemed more interested in the beets than the dirt-encrusted woman sitting among them. They passed into the city without incident, and as soon as they were out of sight of the gates, Evelyn gave Tristan a nod and jumped off the cart, tucking to roll to a stop beside a clothier called the Noble Fit.

Tristan followed suit, rolling clumsily as he hit the cobblestones. Evelyn sprang to her feet, reaching a hand down to help the boy up. "Before we saw those Disciples, I thought you were going to ask Father Beets to adopt you," she said, nodding down the road.

Tristan dusted off his filthy shirt and gave her a dazzling smile that didn't quite reach his eyes. His mind, like hers, was still on the Disciples, no doubt. Evelyn didn't blame him. "The more questions you ask a man, the less time he has to ask questions of you." He tapped his temple with one finger. "Being nice can pay off, Captain. Think about it."

"I'll keep that in mind," Evelyn said, pursing her lips sourly. "Though I wouldn't bet on Wyatt Asher handing over the Quill just because some prissy git shoots him a grin."

"Shh," Tristan said, eyes wide as he glanced back toward the gate. But there was no need for him to worry. The Disciples were far behind them now, surely patting down some other poor, nerve-stricken travelers, and the merchants and guards and ladies surrounding them all hurried past, far too busy to spare half a glance for two poor sods in dirty trousers.

As they wound their way south through the city streets, the neat doublets and long gowns were replaced by torn coats and mud-stained trousers. Seedy taverns and run-down disorderly houses took the place of tailors and sweets shops. Tristan grew steadily stiffer beside her as they slipped from the merchant's quarter to the manufacturing district and finally to the slums.

When they passed Flaxen Row, Tristan slowed almost to a stop beside her. "What in Adalina's name . . ."

"Callum Clem is dead—what were you expecting?" Evelyn asked. But her lip curled as well. The Lottery was . . . different these days. Without the Harpies and Saints to keep him in check, Wyatt Asher had clearly wasted no time spreading his reign over the entirety of the Southern Dock. Sure, there were the usual sailors, seedy merchants, and other poor bastards who didn't have enough silver to afford an apartment north of the Lottery, but Kestrel Crown tattoos peeked out at them every few steps. On forearms and throats. Evelyn even saw one idiot with the mark inked onto his face.

The late afternoon sun glinted off the chop in the harbor as they cut along the east dock. Tristan let out a low whistle as they strolled past the Carrowwick Fair. The Harpies' old black market was a shadow of what it had been. As a former guard in the city, Evelyn was happy to see the seedy trade spot dying. But still, she couldn't help but wonder what Ivan would say if he could see it now. Barely three stalls open where there had once stood more than a dozen, all of them selling *vitalité* and dormire's blood and other cheap gutter-rat goods.

In their Edalish farm scrub, they might look like strangers to the city, but even strangers to the Lottery would be able to sense that wandering around after dark was a good way to get your purse cut. The syndicates seemed to have crumbled to dust, and Evelyn didn't want to risk accidentally showing allegiance to one of the fallen gangs, but there was still one place that would be safe.

She paused at the corner of Spindle Lane and Keel Alley. No part of the Lottery was nice, but these narrow alleys along the southeastern wall made the Catacombs look like a bloody paradise. The locals called it the Shanty. It was the only part of the Lottery so piss-poor that none of the syndicates had ever bothered to claim it, as far as Evelyn knew. Probably home to more rats than humans. All that was left were a few run-down apartments and a tavern or two even Ryia wouldn't trust the ale from.

When she stopped again, she was in front of a building with a peeling door and a sign swaying lopsided from a single corner. It read THE CELLAR MOUSE. Evelyn wrinkled her nose. Just what people wanted on their minds before entering a seedy inn—rodents.

Tristan seemed to be of the same mind. He wiped his hands on his trousers like he thought he had been infected already. "You aren't really thinking of staying here, are you?"

Evelyn snorted. "You used to sleep above the bloody Miscreants' Temple, didn't you? How much worse can this place be?"

Not waiting for his reply, she shouldered the door open. The common room of the inn was exactly the sort of tavern that Ryia liked: a single, poorly lit room filled with freebooters and cockroaches and ripe with the smells of fish and body odor. Not that Ryia liked any of those things specifically, but it was the kind of place where half the gits in there were piss-drunk and the other half had their hoods up and their eyes hidden. In other words, the kind of place where it was easy to slip by unnoticed.

"Keep your hands on your purse, Beckett," Evelyn muttered as they stepped inside.

"What about your purse?" he protested. "They're just as likely to cut yours as they are mine."

Evelyn tapped the hilt of her sword. "I'd like to see the bastards try." A pair of hooded men in the corner sized them up. Evelyn stared them down, hand still on her sword. Eventually they looked away. Either they were bloody cowards, or they knew how to spot someone well-trained with a blade. Evelyn didn't really care which, as long as they stayed the hell away from her.

Tristan sank back into his old con-man persona as they strode through the smoky room. They passed a table where a bleary-eyed man shoved a small pile of dingy silver halves into the hands of a rat-faced woman in return for a tiny purple bottle of dormire's blood. Another table held a group of drunken freebooters who looked like they were about a breath away from spilling blood over a raucous game of Bobbin Draw. Beside them was a man with his head on the table, a puddle of drool forming at his lips, his hand still clutching a cup of wine the color of piss.

At the back of the room stood a filthy bar

tended by an equally filthy woman. A cockroach skittered across the bar as Evelyn and Tristan approached. The woman picked up a wooden cup, smashed it onto the roach with a crunch, then wiped the bottom of the cup on her apron before setting it back down beside the barrels. "What're you lot after?" she asked. Her voice was rough, like a cart rattling over thick gravel.

"We'll take a room," Evelyn said, sliding a small pile of coppers across the bar. They stuck to the surface immediately, and Evelyn withdrew her hand.

"And we wouldn't say no to a meal and a few ales," Tristan added with a wink, throwing down the last silver half they had.

Evelyn shot him a look as the woman scooped the coins up, tipped them into her pocket, and turned to find them a room key. "We don't have time for a few ales, you dolt."

An exaggeration, she knew. But still, they were short on time already. The weather was beginning to turn. What if Asher made his move while they were in the city? Or, worse, what if the Disciples came down to the Lottery and pried the Quill from Asher's remaining fingers before Evelyn had the chance to do the same? Felice had smiled on them enough to let them steal the Quill from the Guildmaster once . . . but Evelyn doubted the goddess of luck would be so kind if they tried to take it a second time.

"If you go straight to your room in a place like this, they'll assume you have something to hide," Tristan said.

Evelyn glanced around the room, brow raised. "Tristan, every bloody person in this room looks like they have something to hide."

"Not like that," Tristan said. "I mean they'll assume we have gold. Which means . . ." He drew a finger across his throat, dropping his hand to his side hurriedly as the innkeeper turned around again, holding out a rusted, pitted key and two mugs of ale. Evelyn tried not to wonder whether one of those mugs was the one that had been used to bludgeon the cockroach to death.

They took their seats at the table beside the sleeping man—although "sleeping" was a kind word for it. "Passed out drunk" was more like it. His gentle snores were drowned out by the sounds of increasingly rowdy card games in one corner of the room and a man playing the flute for coins in the other. After a few minutes, a dirty-nosed, reedy boy came from the back room of the inn. He shared some shouted words with the innkeeper, then slipped over to their table.

"Two suppers for—well fuck me sideways, is that Tristan Beckett?"

Tristan's eyes widened as he whipped his head around. He had been watching the nearest card game with interest, but now his gaze fell on the serving boy. "Cam? Is that you?"

"Yeah, it's me. Shit, I thought you were dead!" He was a twitchy sort of boy, built like a jackrabbit, with arms and legs too long for his body. He rubbed one thumb nervously. A barely healed blister marked the skin all the way from his first knuckle to his second, like it had been shaved away neatly by a blade. He nodded at Tristan's hands, which were folded on the tabletop. "Surprised you're not, still sporting that old mark and all."

Evelyn glanced down at Tristan's hands. He folded them hurriedly, but she still caught sight of the mark on the prince's wrist. The brand of two snakes encircling a Saint's head like a halo. Suddenly the scar on this boy's hand made more sense. "You were with the Saints?" she asked.

Cam's eyes bulged, and he glanced over his shoulder one way, then the other, like he was expecting a crossbow bolt to take him in the throat any second, but no one in the common room even glanced in their direction. "Are you two mad?" he whispered when he finally turned back around. "If you're smart, you'll hide that mark. Fuck—burn it off if you can. And you won't say that twice-damned name again. At least not till you're good and well shot of me."

"All right, Cam, calm down," Tristan said, hurriedly shaking his sleeve over his right hand, hiding the mark. "Is it really that bad?"

"Worse," Cam said. He shot another glance

over his shoulder at the innkeeper. Satisfied that she was immersed in conversation with the rat-faced dormire's blood dealer, he set the plates down in front of them, then eased himself into the chair beside Evelyn and rested his elbows on the table. "Roland's dead."

"What?" Tristan asked, dropping his spoon almost as soon as he picked it up. Grayish, fish-scented slop splattered over the table.

Cam nodded grimly, wiping the stew from his face with his blistered hand. "Not just him. Rolf, too. And Birgit. Just about every fucking one of us."

"What in Adalina's name . . .," Tristan cursed, running a hand through his greasy hair. He froze as he realized which hand he was using and tucked it gingerly back into his sleeve to hide the mark again. He swallowed. "What about Ivan? Or Nash? Heard anything of them?"

Evelyn shifted in her seat uncomfortably. This was all her bloody fault, after all. Hers and Ryia's. If they hadn't made their own plans, betrayed Clem, and gone after the Quill on their own, there was a chance Clem might have ended up with it. Then none of the Saints would have died. Not that Evelyn regretted it—the idea of Callum Clem wielding the Quill of Declan Day was even worse than Tolliver Shadowwood having it. Or Wyatt Asher. Still, she dreaded Cam's answer.

The reedy boy shook his head. "Don't know,

but I haven't seen or heard from either one of 'em. If they're not at the bottom of the Arden, then they're probably nestled up in the Upper Roost. Either way, they're dead, as far as I'm concerned."

"The Upper Roost?" Evelyn asked, frowning.

"Where'd you find this one?" Cam asked Tristan, disbelieving. He turned back to Evelyn. "Big Crown hideout. Where the Lottery king himself takes his shits and fucks his whores."

Evelyn blinked. After spending two months joined at the bloody hip with Ryia Cautella, she thought she'd heard just about all the foul language there was to hear. Cam put the Butcher's tongue to shame.

"So, he's still there, then?" Tristan asked. "Asher, I mean?"

Cam shrugged. "Far as I know. But do I look like a motherfucking Crown to you? Shit." He jumped to his feet as the innkeeper turned toward him and bellowed his name across the common room. "Get rid of that mark or keep your ass clear of the docks, all right, Tristan?"

With that, the gangly youth backed away from their table, disappearing behind the swinging door that led to whatever shite kitchen had turned out the bowls of slop still sitting, untouched, on the table in front of them. There was silence for a few seconds while they both sat there staring after him. Then Tristan cleared his throat.

“Well, that saves us some time,” he said, picking up his spoon again and delicately nudging the pinkish-brown chunks in his bowl.

“That it does,” Evelyn said. She grabbed her cup, raising it to him. “About bloody time we had some good luck.” She went to lift the cup to her lips, then remembered the cockroach and thought better of it, setting it back on the table and tapping on the rim with one finger. “Assuming . . . you think it’s there?”

“I’m assuming he keeps it on him.” Tristan glanced around under the pretense of scratching the back of his neck, making sure the surrounding tables were still too busy drinking and gambling and feeling each other up to notice them. “Or that cursed bird of his.”

Evelyn picked up her dented spoon, stirring the stew absently. It would be just like Wyatt Asher to take the most powerful relic in Thamorr and put it in his kestrel’s filthy talons. “So. Tomorrow?”

Tristan took a bite of his stew and grimaced. “Tomorrow.”

They were going to break into the hideout of the Kestrel Crowns, and they were going to rob the new king of Carrowwick’s underworld. Evelyn took a sip of lukewarm ale. For her entire life, she had bowed down to Adalina, goddess of toil, but hard work wouldn’t be enough to save them this time. Tonight, her prayers would be to the goddess of luck.

CHAPTER SIX

Ryia

Ryia lost count of the days in the darkness and despair of the Shadow Keep. Whoever had designed this damned pen had done their best to make it impossible to track time. There were no windows, no pattern to the guard shifts, and even meals were irregular, if they came at all. A lump of gruel and a heel of yesterday's bread—was that meant to be breakfast or supper? Who the hell knew. The fact that her brain kept flashing her back to a different dark, damp cellar only made it harder for her to keep track of the present. Her father's voice haunted her, hiding in every scuff of foot on stone, every drip plinking down from the ceiling.

It's in the blood . . . it's in the blood.

"I know it's in the twice-damned blood," Ryia muttered, answering a man who had been dead for over a decade.

"What?" asked a voice—a real one this time. Joslyn.

Whatever torture Ryia was going through, trapped in memories of her past, Joslyn seemed to be going through something roughly one hundred times worse. She peered through the darkness at Ryia through haunted, skeletal eyes. The pirate had bags the size of knapsacks under each eye but still barely slept, preferring to pace until Ryia chucked a pebble at her head through the bars and told her to knock it off. Pools of thin, stringy vomit dotted the floor of her cell, sending the smell of stomach acid and spent food mixing with the fishy wetness of the dungeon.

"Nothing," Ryia said. "Go back to your own muttering."

"Fuck off," Joslyn said darkly.

Things continued on like this. Ryia spent half her time crouched in the miserable dark of the Shadow Keep, and the other half crouched in the miserable dark of her father's cellar, trapped deep inside her own head. How long had she been down here? Had Evelyn and Tristan made it to Carrowwick yet? How close was winter? All questions she had no way of answering. Not from this horrible cell.

After Felice only knew how many days, Tolliver Shadowwood and his Adept returned to Ryia's cell for another "friendly" chat. The Adept still obeyed him. That meant Evelyn and Tristan hadn't made it to Carrowwick yet. Which meant she had only been down here a week or so. *Or they just failed,* said another voice—one that sounded suspiciously like the Guildmaster. She could see him, silhouetted against the flaming manor in her mind's eye.

"Shut up," she muttered to the hallucination, retreating into her mind as Shadowwood's Adept began to beat the shit out of her again. Stupid, brainwashed assholes. She was saving these Adepts' lives by not coughing up the truth. They were the Adept closest to Shadowwood, and if she told the king that drinking their blood could give him the ancient Adept magic, they would absolutely be the first to die.

After what felt like hours, the king finally called off his attack dogs. It seemed like the man wasn't willing to kill her yet, but he was willing to get pretty damned close. She winced, feeling her ribs as the Adept filed out of the cell, the door clicking shut behind them. Definitely bruised, maybe even cracked. That would make breathing fun for a while.

She nearly sank to the floor of her cell in exhaustion as his footsteps started to disappear down the corridor, but she hesitated as she heard his voice again.

"This again? I swear to Adalina . . . ," he muttered under his breath.

Moving slowly so as not to jar her throbbing head, Ryia peered curiously through the bars of her cell. The king's little recessional had stopped halfway to the door. Shadowwood stood, straight-backed and arrogant, the gaoler beside him, toying with his keys. Nothing abnormal there.

The Kinetics, however, were a completely

different story. They were . . . frozen. All four of them—almost like they were having a fit. They stood with their arms out at their sides, their legs solid, mid-step, all their muscles bulging and tensing at once. Ryia wrapped her fingers around the bars, peering into the shadows where the prison guard Adept lurked. They too were stiff—not in the normal, blank, Adept way, but almost in agony. Their eyes were wide and rolling, their jaws clenched, fists tight. Realization struck Ryia over the head like a club. They froze the way the Kinetic had back in the Catacombs when Tristan had saved her life. He had tried to master the Quill, and he had managed to stop the Kinetic pit fighter from killing her.

Wyatt Asher must be trying to master the Quill now.

"Come on, then, gaoler!" Shadowwood shouted. "Don't just stand there—slap them out of it!"

"No fear, Your Highness, I will manage this," the sniveling gaoler said, swallowing.

He started prodding one Kinetic gingerly. Then shook the man's shoulder, like he was trying to wake him from a deep sleep. When that didn't work, he resorted to the king's suggested slapping, cracking the Kinetic across the face with his open palm. None of it seemed to faze the brainwashed Adept.

The seconds ticked by as Shadowwood grew more and more frustrated. Then, without warning, the Adept servants all seemed to take a breath at once, sinking back into their steps like no time had passed.

"Finally," the king muttered. And a few moments later they were gone.

Ryia allowed herself to slump down to the floor of her cell. She nursed her various cuts and bruises as she stared after the king and his guard. The king had said, *This again?* How often was this happening, exactly? How many times had Wyatt Asher tried to get the Quill to work for him?

And how long would it be before he finally succeeded?

Hurry, Evelyn and Tristan . . . if you're even still alive. The dark thought consumed her as she watched the lantern flames flicker in the corridor. She barely even registered when Joslyn began to speak to her from the adjoining cell.

"What in Felice's deepest hell do you know?"

Ryia spit a mouthful of blood onto the floor, wiping her lips as she turned to face her. The pirate captain looked like a ghost at this point, dark and haunted, her cheekbones too pointed, her eyes set too deep in her face. "What?"

Joslyn wrapped one hand around the bars separating them. She nodded toward the door with her chin. "He's an ass, but he's not just beating the hell out of you for fun. What's your secret?"

Ryia paused, studying her. Then she shot the pirate a blood-soaked smile, nodding at the wig still sitting lopsided on her head where she had thrust it the second the dungeon doors had creaked open. "You tell me yours first."

Joslyn patted the wig, straightening it irritably. "What, you've never seen a woman go bald before?"

"I've seen plenty of bald women before," Ryia said, rocking backward to sit on the damp floor, her back resting against the bars on the opposite wall of her cell. "They're just usually not quite as . . . talkative as you." Joslyn eyed her suspiciously, and Ryia just shrugged. "If you didn't want me to figure it out, you should have kept that ratty-ass thing on your head this whole time."

The pirate hesitated for a heartbeat, then sniffed. "Figure what out?"

She was going to make her say it, then? Fine. Ryia leaned forward, elbows on her knees, and whispered, "That you're an Adept."

"Huh, is that so?" Joslyn said slowly, running her tongue over her teeth. She turned her gaunt face side to side, pointing to both cheeks. "Where's my brand, then?" She pulled her wig from her head, bowing until the light from the torch down the corridor shone off the bald dome. "And where's my tattoo? There are some holes in your theory, girl."

"Are there?" Ryia said. "Or are there just some holes in your story?" She looked the pirate up and down scathingly. "You're awfully young to be running your own crew. Especially one as big as the crew on Salt Beard's infamous *Ophidian Fang*. And you said you've had that crew since you were barely off your mother's tit."

"Did I say that?"

Ryia waved a hand. "I might be rephrasing a bit."

Joslyn sucked one cheek. "I don't know how things work wherever you're from, but out on the seas, people tend to follow talent over experience."

"Exactly my point," Ryia said, grinning her sharpest grin. "So, exactly what talent were they following, I wonder?"

"You think I bullied them into following me with my amazing Kinetic powers, do you?"

"Maybe," Ryia said, pretending to mull it over. "But I think that if Salt Beard was a Kinetic, the whole damned coastline would be talking about it." She cocked her head to one side. "No, I think it's far more likely that your crew has no idea what you are. I think you just happen to have a suspicious knack for knowing which way to sail to avoid trouble. A knack for choosing the least dangerous ships to target—the ones that look fully armed but are short men, that kind of thing. That sound about right?"

Joslyn didn't answer. Ryia pushed herself to her feet, sloshing over the wet floor to stand in front of the pirate, arms folded.

"I've seen your nose twitching like a hound on the trail, Salt Beard. You're a Senser. A strong one too—that's how you've managed to avoid the twice-damned flood of Disciples that I bet the dear old Guildmaster has sent after you since you managed to escape that hellish island of his." She gestured toward the door to the dungeon, shut tight behind them. "I'm guessing he doesn't know?" she asked, meaning Shadowwood. "Good. Keep it that way, or I have a feeling you'll have more than a dark cell and *vitalité* withdrawal to look forward to," she finished, indicating the patchwork of bruises covering her own face.

"You seem to know an awful lot about the Adept," Joslyn said, eyes narrowing in suspicion.

Ryia shrugged, lazily grabbing hold of one of the bars. "Maybe I'm one of the rich assholes who goes to that island to buy myself some brainwashed muscle."

"If you're rich, then I'm a priest in the Church of Adalina."

"Oh, fuck off." But Ryia couldn't really argue. With her threadbare black cloak and boots worn almost through to the socks at the heels, she looked about as much like a wealthy merchant as Tristan looked like a brawler.

The conversation trailed off after that, but Ryia thought she felt the pirate's eye boring into the back of her head as she curled up on the cold, wet floor to fall asleep. As she lay crumpled against her cell bars in silence, the scent of danger suddenly wafted toward Ryia from the far side of the bars. The smell of rich peat soil and earthworms and decaying things cut through the fishy moist scent of the dungeon. Without even thinking, Ryia lunged away from the bars. Her good hand darted up, snagging Joslyn's wrist just as she struck out with a sharpened bit of rock, aiming right for where Ryia's neck had been an instant before.

"Are you out of your twice-damned mind?" Ryia yelped. She twisted sharply, and Joslyn's hand spasmed in her grip. She dropped the stone. Ryia let go of her hand, and she wrenched it back. "What the hell was that?"

But the pirate didn't answer. She pointed at Ryia through the bars, her face caught between disbelief and amusement. Amusement won out, and she started laughing. It sounded just like Nash's laugh, a low rumble like thunder that erupted into a booming chuckle.

"What is wrong with you?" Ryia asked. The smell of danger had vanished, but she kept her hands up just the same. The bitch had just tried to stab her, after all.

"You're Adept too." Joslyn's laugh dissolved into a coughing fit. When she recovered, she cocked her head to one side. "Kinetic for sure, no one moves that fast. But I saw your nose flare right before you moved. You're both, somehow." She looked toward the dungeon door. "That's why he wants you. That's what he's after."

"You were really going to stab me." She wouldn't have been able to smell the danger if Joslyn had only been bluffing.

The pirate shrugged. "Look, if you were Adept, I knew you'd dodge or block it. If you weren't . . . then maybe I was looking to shut you up before you could spill my secret to that old sad sack of a king."

Ryia paused, then chuckled darkly. It was exactly the kind of thing she would have done herself. Maybe not now—these days, a voice that sounded an awful lot like Evelyn's pestered her when she tried to do anything too underhanded—but in all those years she'd been on the run from the Guildmaster? She had done much worse to far nicer people just to stay alive and free.

"That's one hell of a trick you're doing there, with that stubble," Joslyn said, pulling her ratty wig from her head and fiddling with the tangled hairs. Ryia wondered absently what poor creature had given its fur to make it. "What is it? Short little rat hairs or something?"

"The hair is real," Ryia said, running a hand over the crown of her head.

"You were never taken to the island, then?"

Joslyn gave a low whistle. "How did your parents pull that one off?"

Ryia took a deep breath, turning around and leaning her back on the bars separating her cell from Joslyn's. Was she really about to say this out loud on purpose? But if there was anyone who would understand . . . She had given up hope years ago that someone like Joslyn even existed on this twice-damned continent. Another free Adept, on the run.

"I wasn't born Adept," she finally said, whispering so quietly she wasn't sure Joslyn heard at first.

"Huh." Joslyn was silent for a long time, then cleared her throat. "And here I thought the concept of making Adept died out with the Eis Yavols a thousand years ago."

Ryia whipped around so quickly, she almost slipped on the puddle under her boots. "What?"

All this time, she thought her father had been the only son of a bitch crazy enough to try to create his own Adept.

Joslyn raised one eyebrow. "You *do* know where Adept come from, don't you?"

"Their mothers, just like anyone else," Ryia guessed.

"I don't mean *now*." Joslyn shook her head. The distant light of the torches by the door threw the shadows of her hollow cheeks into sharp relief. "I mean the *first* Adept."

A cheer went up from the doorway. Ryia looked over her shoulder to see one guard celebrating as the other fished a pair of silver halves out of his pocket. She turned back to Joslyn. "Believe it or not, the deepest secrets of the Adept and their history aren't exactly common knowledge to those of us who didn't grow up at the Guildmaster's knee."

"Watch it."

"Or what?" Ryia snorted. "You going to come flailing at me with another pointy rock?"

Joslyn scowled, but it was the same kind of scowl Nash had always given her—the kind that was basically a begrudging chuckle. The dungeon door creaked open. Ryia's stomach clenched, but only two long shadows broke the beam of light streaming in from the stairwell. Guard change.

Ryia retreated to the corner of her cell while Joslyn shoved her wig back onto her head. The pirate curled up on the floor of her cell and Ryia leaned against the stone wall facing the door. She tossed a small pebble from hand to hand, winking at the guards as they strode past. She and Joslyn waited as the new guards finished their rounds, not daring to return to their shared wall until both those silver-helmeted heads were beside the door to the dungeon, bending low as they stole sips from a smuggled wineskin.

After a pause, Ryia made her way back toward

Joslyn's cell. "So. Where did they come from? The first Adept."

Joslyn lay still a moment longer, then rolled over to stare at her through the bars and shadows. "It's a story every young Adept is taught before Division." She noted Ryia's blank stare and pushed herself up to sit cross-legged. "Before we're separated into Kinetics and Sensers. The kids too young to be showing their magic yet."

The pirate leaned back on her palms, her voice settling into a formal-sounding tone, reciting something she had obviously heard a hundred times or more. "Thousands of years ago, before the borders of the five kingdoms were drawn, the land of Thamorr was wild and full of magic. Ophidians ruled the seas, cougars the size of carriages roamed the wastes in the south, and massive, shaggy white bears hunted in the mountains along the northern coast."

"If you're going to tell me Adept are descended from twice-damned cougars, I swear to Felice . . . ," Ryia started.

Joslyn cocked her head to one side but plowed on without acknowledging the interruption. "For centuries, the people living in the north avoided the mountains at all costs. They named the bears Eis Yavols, or Ice Devils, and for a long time, any man stupid enough to enter the mountains never came out again."

"Why don't we speed ahead to the part where

the first bastard survives?" Ryia said, shooting a glance over her shoulder toward the door. As much as she hated to admit it, she desperately wanted to hear this story, and if Joslyn took an age and a half to tell it, there was a chance mad old King Tolliver would come back, and she would never get the opportunity.

"All right, fine," Joslyn sighed. "You're ruining the drama, though. Yes, eventually, a man named Leonid Piekov made it out. He had puncture wounds on his arms and legs, an inch around, and at least three times as deep. Bite marks, from an Eis Yavol, he said. He made it home, got bandaged up, and for a few days he went back to normal. But soon Leonid's fellows started noticing some strange things. He seemed stronger than he had been before he went into the mountains. Faster, too."

"He was a Kinetic," Ryia guessed. She frowned. "But how?"

"Eis Yavol venom," Joslyn said. "The people of the north figured that out after a while. And you know what they did then."

Ryia could guess. Humans in any era were selfish assholes; that much was always pretty predictable. "They started hunting those shaggy beasts?"

Joslyn nodded. Her eyes glittered in the torchlight. "Emperors and kings from all over Thamorr sent their men into the mountains to capture the things. Then they baited them to bite. The venom killed some, but the ones who survived gained the powers of speed and strength. Some could even move things without touching them."

"The Kinetics, I know, I've got it," Ryia said. "What about the Sensers?"

"Well, once the queens in the south heard about the bears up north, what do you think they did?"

Ryia nodded. "Cougar hunting?"

"Cougar hunting," Joslyn agreed. "Properly, Ignifeles hunting, in the old Brillish tongue. But yes, survivors of a bite from the Ignifeles ended up with heightened reaction time, an uncanny ability to sense danger before it smacked them square in the face."

"And a bite from an Ophidian?" Ryia asked, snorting. "What powers did that grant?"

Joslyn shrugged. "No one ever survived that one, from what the Adept histories say."

"But they tried."

"Wouldn't you?"

Ryia shrugged. But the pirate had a point. If a bite from two different legendary creatures had resulted in magical powers, maybe the bite of *any* mythical beast would grant some kind of magic. Assuming you could survive the bite, at least. Still, she wasn't believing this story in the slightest.

"Okay, so that's where the first Adept came

from. What about all the ones since then?" Ryia raised an eyebrow. "Eis Yavols died out centuries ago, and I've never even heard of a twice-damned Inga-fellus."

"Ignifeles," Joslyn corrected.

"Whatever. Since those animals are deader than a snitch in the Miscreants' Temple, shouldn't there be no more Adept?"

Joslyn shook her head, then leaned forward, resting her elbows on her crossed knees. Her eyes looked sharper than they had since Ryia had met her—more alive. She was enjoying having someone to share this tale with. "Don't you see? The venom gave the people magic. It mixed into them, became part of them."

"It's in the blood . . . ," Ryia muttered under her breath. The words her father had said, over and over again in the darkness. They had obviously turned out to be true. Was this further proof of it?

"Exactly."

Ryia frowned. "And the Guildmaster knows this? Then why isn't he breeding you poor sods like cattle on that twisted-ass island of his?"

Joslyn's snort echoed off the dripping walls all around them. "Don't think he wouldn't try it if he thought it would work." She shook her head. "No, people learned pretty fast that any child born of two Adept was stillborn. So then, people who survived the bite paired up with ordinary non-magic people. The kids lived, but they didn't have the gifts. But sometimes *their* kids did. Or their kids' kids."

Ryia nodded slowly. "So, you could figure out if a child might be Adept if you could track their bloodline? All the way back to the beginning, I mean."

"At this point, I'm not sure there's a soul on this continent who doesn't have a bit of the old magic in their blood," Joslyn said thoughtfully. "But whether there's enough of the venom to actually make a child Adept depends."

"Depends on what?"

"How shit that kid's luck is," Joslyn said bitterly. She shook her head to clear it. "So, how did King Sad Sack figure out what you are?"

Ryia shot a glance over her shoulder, peering around the rest of the dungeon. The guards at the door were now immersed in a game of dice. The cells across from them were open and empty, as was the cell nearest Ryia. The prisoner on the far side of Joslyn's cell was asleep, kicking and muttering fitfully to himself. He'd been turning madder and madder since Ryia had arrived in this pit—no doubt withdrawing from something a hell of a lot stronger than *vitalité*. There was no one else who would hear.

She leaned back on her elbows. "Well, it was either my reflexes or the fact that I swung a hatchet around midair like I had it attached to an imaginary string." She gave the pirate a bloodstained grin. "We may never know for sure."

Joslyn stared at her blankly for a second, then grabbed the bars between them, trying to shake them. "What the *hell,* Cautella!"

Ryia raised one eyebrow, lying back down on the cold, wet stone. "Keep your wig on."

Joslyn charged on as if Ryia hadn't spoken. "I didn't know you were a twice-damned telekinetic."

"Well, if I'd realized you were going to go absolutely batshit, I definitely would have mentioned it sooner," Ryia said drily.

"That whole stunt with the key . . ." Joslyn peered at her through the bars, looking her up and down like she thought she was secretly a lizard in a human suit. "What are you *really* doing down here?"

"What am I—" Ryia started. She shook her head, snorting with disbelieving laughter. "I'm a prisoner, Joslyn. Just like you."

"Look, Cautella, even the weakest telekinetic Adept could bend these bars into a Dresdellan twist roll like *that*." The pirate snapped her fingers. "You could get out of this cell any time you wanted."

"Settle down there, Senser." Ryia scoffed. "You're dead wrong. I am just as stuck in this cell as you are. The only things I can control with these powers are my weapons. My hatchets and my throwing axes." Ryia flexed her fingers, studying them in the darkness. "And I had those ripped from my hands about three seconds before I had the shit kicked out of me for the first time."

"Just your axes?" Joslyn asked. "Why would—"

"Because they made me." Ryia gritted her teeth, suppressing the memories as they threatened to flood over her for the thousandth time since she'd been dragged down into this horrific place.

"You were, what, cut by these hatchets, and they gave you Adept magic?" Joslyn narrowed her eyes, cocking her head to one side. The distant torchlight reflected off the shiny dome of her hairless head. "What are they made of?"

"What—no," Ryia said, shaking her head. "They're regular steel hatchets. And . . ." She took a deep breath. "It wasn't me they were cutting. It was . . ."

"Other Adept," Joslyn guessed as Ryia fell silent.

Ryia nodded. For years she hadn't been able to look at the hatchets without seeing her father slashing them through Adept throats. Without remembering how he had gathered the blood as it pooled, then forced it down her throat. But eventually she had come to love the weapons as her own so much that even now, a week or more after she had been stripped of them, she felt naked without them.

"So the only thing you can control with your powers is the same tool that was used to . . . what, murder a bunch of Adept and steal enough of their blood to turn you Adept?"

Ryia looked up, pissed, as Joslyn started to laugh.

"That's fucked up," the pirate wheezed. "First off, that's not how Kinetic powers work, but even if it *was,* wouldn't you only be able to control the same items as the Kinetics whose blood you stole? Why would the steel that spilled that blood matter? It doesn't make any sense."

Ryia opened her mouth to argue, then shut it again. She didn't really understand much about Adept magic, other than how to use her own stolen, bastardized version. Could Joslyn be right?

But she'd never been able to control anything else—if she could, she would have figured it out by now, wouldn't she? She thought about the time on the Guildmaster's island when the blue-robed bastard himself had her bound and unarmed. If she had been able to strangle him with his own robes, or bring the bell tower crashing down on his sneering face, she would have . . . wouldn't she? She had always been able to *sense* her hatchets. To hear them whispering to her, feel them tugging at the corners of her awareness, ready to spring to her fingertips at any moment. She'd never heard anything else whisper to her.

Unless she just hadn't been listening.

Feeling very foolish, Ryia narrowed her eyes, reaching out with her left hand and breathing deeply. She focused on a pebble about three paces away, just beside the biggest puddle on the floor of her cell. Could she lift it? She gritted her teeth, grinding them together as she willed the pebble to rise . . . to roll . . . to shake . . . *anything*. But the little fragment of rock remained stubbornly still and lifeless. No, just as she had thought. Joslyn was wrong. Her powers started and ended with those hatchets.

"Well, the good news is we might not have to deal with old Tolliver's bullshit much longer. With the both of us trapped down here, the Guildmaster won't be far behind."

"I don't think you need to worry about the Guildmaster anymore," Ryia said, picking her fingernails more violently than was necessary.

"That won't be true until he's looking up at us from beneath the waves," Joslyn said.

Ryia paused in her fingernail picking, running a hand through her hair. It was greasy and caked with muck from her attempts to sleep on the slime-covered floor of her cell. "He doesn't have the Quill anymore."

Joslyn froze. "How do you know about the Quill?"

Ryia leaned back on her elbows, tossing a pebble into the air and catching it deftly with the same hand. "Because about a month ago, I stole it." Joslyn raised an eyebrow, and Ryia shook her head. "Don't get too excited. Someone else stole it from me. Someone who might be even worse than the Guildmaster."

"As long as it wasn't one of his Disciples, then we have nothing to worry about."

"I wouldn't be so sure about that," Ryia said, laughing mirthlessly. "Some of the most terrible men in this world are the ones without a stitch of power in their blood."

"You don't think I know that?" Joslyn asked, her too-deep eyes glinting in the near darkness. "But no regular person can take control of the Purified. Not for long, at least."

"Are you sure about that?" Ryia asked, eyebrow raised at the word "Purified." Was that how the Guildmaster saw the Adept he brainwashed? "Didn't you just see what happened to those Kinetics of Shadowwood's?"

"Was *that* what that was, then?" Joslyn said. "Well, I'm guessing whoever has it is *trying* to use it. But without Adept powers, they're not going to be strong enough to succeed."

Ryia chewed her lip, looking back to the blank corridor where the Adept had frozen.

Wyatt Asher didn't have full control of the Quill . . . not yet. But could Tristan and Evelyn pry it away from his clawed fingers before he figured out what Ryia's father had all those years ago?

CHAPTER SEVEN
Evelyn

A chill breeze tugged at Evelyn's braid as she stood in the shadows of a defunct apothecary. Autumn had begun in earnest; winter would be upon them in six weeks' time. They were running short on days to stop Wyatt Asher. But if all went to plan, this would end tonight.

Moonlight glinted off the small brass key in her fingers as she held it up, examining it. She didn't know exactly how Tristan had managed to get his hands on it, but she could guess. The boy was surprisingly skilled at picking pockets, for a prince. The key fit the lock of the doors at the Kestrel Crowns' run-down apartment building, the Upper Roost.

But getting the key was only the first hurdle—and probably the least dangerous one. She peered through the clear night toward the tall, skinny building sticking up into the sky like an axe handle. Half the shutters were missing, and the wooden siding was cracked and chipped, dry as a bone in some places and sprouting mold in others. Ryia would have found a way to scale the bloody thing, steal the Quill, and probably slit Wyatt Asher's throat for good measure.

A pang shot through Evelyn at the thought, and she pushed it away quickly. Ryia wasn't here. Evelyn was the only one here, and she could definitely not scale a building that tall and unsteady unless she was interested in breaking her own neck. No, for her there was only one way in—the door.

Unlike when they had gone to the Guildmaster's island, there were no building plans or sketches of the Crowns' hideout. All they had to go on was the fact that Tristan thought he had once heard that the building was originally an inn, back before the Crowns took it over.

Evelyn glanced up at the sky again. The blackness of night was starting to lift. The bells at the Church of Adalina had chimed out four in the morning when she first stowed herself in this corner, crouching in the shadows like a ruddy cockroach in the kitchens. Since then, she had seen a few figures stumble drunkenly down Flaxen Row, watched a pair of street mutts fight over a scrap of chicken, and tracked the shadows of three different men returning to the Upper Roost. None of them were Wyatt Asher, but if she had timed this as well as she hoped she had, he would already be in his chambers, fast asleep.

If not . . . well, there was no bloody use standing here worrying about it, was there?

Wishing for the hundredth time that she was wearing one of Ivan's disguises instead of her own face, Evelyn broke free of the shadows, trying to walk like she belonged in the depths of the Crowns' territory. Fitting in in this hellhole wasn't as difficult as it would have been just a few months ago, she realized. With her tattered cloak and sunken, travel-weary cheeks, she was suited to the part.

Her heart jumped twice in her walk to the door, once when a rat skittered across her path, and again when the cry of a bird sounded out overhead. *Not a kestrel,* she told herself, forcing her steps to stay unhurried, *just a gull, you git. Relax.*

The alley behind the Upper Roost was darker than most of the alleys in the Lottery, and that was saying something. It was the kind of place people from the streets north of the trade docks would give at least three blocks' berth. The angle of the Roost prevented even a glimmer of moonlight from reaching the uneven mud covering the ground. A fool might say there could be anyone lurking in the darkness there, but Evelyn wasn't a fool. This close to the Roost, the only people lurking in the darkness would be Kestrel Crowns. She kept one hand on the hilt of her slender sword as she turned into the darkness, creeping up to the door.

There were no Crowns stationed outside. Likely, Asher believed no one in this city would be brave—or fool—enough to waltz right into the place that housed the deadliest members of the most powerful syndicate in the city.

Eyes straining, Evelyn could just make out the peeling paint, all black with a faded white kestrel skull set right at eye level. Subtle. Resting one hand on the frame, she leaned against the door, pressing her ear to the rotting wood, listening intently. For a second, she wished she had Ryia's Senser abilities—imagine how much easier it would be to creep around unseen if she could smell every ruddy threat before it even showed itself. But she knew she didn't really wish for that power—not with all the strings that came attached.

She could hear timbers creaking and groaning behind the door, but they sounded far away—some to her left, some the right, some above her head. There was also the sound of scraping and banging—sounds Evelyn knew well from her time spent meandering around her father's manor, looking for Saoirse, the pretty head cook. They were the sounds of a kitchen preparing a meal. A good sign for Tristan's hunch about the Roost's layout—Dresdellan inns almost always placed the kitchens right inside the back door.

In short, the Upper Roost was quietly humming with life, but none of it seemed to be in the corridor behind this door. If the kitchens were just preparing breakfast, then hopefully, Wyatt Asher was still tucked up in his bed, dreaming whatever twisted dreams men like that thought up. There was really only one way to find out. Taking a deep breath, Evelyn slid the key into the lock and twisted. She had to wrench it hard enough that she was half-worried she'd break the bloody thing in two, but eventually the lock gave way.

The door creaked as she swung it open. *Shite*. Evelyn paused, one foot over the darkened threshold, waiting for someone to appear in the eerie hall before her, but no one did. The kitchen stood to her left. Lantern light flooded into the dark hallway from the crack beneath the door, as did the smells of honey bread and something vaguely fishy. She sniffed again. Crab cakes? She raised an eyebrow. The Crowns were eating like lords these days, then. Though she supposed she shouldn't find that surprising—Carrowwick had always had a healthy criminal underworld. Now it was headed by a single man who could probably afford to eat whatever he damn well pleased.

Evelyn crept past the kitchens, peering left and right as the entry corridor came to an end. To her right was a hall where the floor was so well-worn that the floorboards were stripped nearly down to nothing. She could hear voices there, muffled through the thin walls, and what sounded like boots being yanked off and thrown onto the floor. The area that would have been the common room, back when this was an inn, made into some kind of sleeping chamber now, from the sounds of it. But Wyatt Asher was not the type to bed down with his underlings.

She opened the door to her left instead, smiling when she saw a dark, decrepit stairwell. In any inn, the priciest rooms were on the top, up where the windows could tempt a real breeze—one that didn't smell like piss, if you were lucky. Surely that was where Wyatt Asher's chambers would be. She mounted the staircase, walking slowly with her feet pressed up against the edge of each stair beside the wall—in a building this old, the nails would surely be creakier than her nan's knees had been. The closer she stayed to the wall, the softer those squeaks would be.

The door on the second floor hung wide on its hinges, revealing a large, open space lined with bedrolls and heavy-breathing bodies. The third floor opened to a long corridor lined with scuffed doors. The door on the fourth floor looked like it had been ripped off its hinges by some kind of beast—a piss-drunk Crown bruiser, more likely. Roaches scuttled past her feet on the landing of the fifth floor, and she sprinted past the sixth-floor landing altogether, running on tiptoes, rounding the corner up the stairwell just as someone started trudging down the stairs with heavy steps behind her.

The higher she climbed, the less worn the stairs

were. Where the ancient varnish on the lower stairs was almost completely worn away, now there were steps that still shone with the reddish gleam of wood stain. Fewer feet had trod these. A good sign. The walls around her creaked and moaned as the autumn wind gusted outside. She could feel the Roost swaying beneath her feet as she crept up the last flight of stairs.

The door here, all the way up on the ninth floor of the Roost, was the first one she had seen that was closed. The handsome door fit with the dilapidated decor of the Roost about as well as a peacock fit in a chicken coop. It was made of what looked like Edalish walnut, stained coffee black. The kestrel-skull symbol of the Crowns was worked into the wood with an unmistakably expert hand, and the handle was made of heavy brass instead of rusted iron. If she'd had any doubts that these were Wyatt Asher's quarters, the presence of a massive Kestrel Crown standing guard on the landing outside the door quelled them instantly. She ducked back behind the corner as soon as she caught sight of the man, then peered around slowly, heart pounding a steady path up her throat.

But there was nothing to fear. As it turned out, "standing guard" wasn't quite accurate. The Crown was fast asleep, his head slumped against the wall, his hands gripping a cheesecloth sack. *Dormire's blood*. Evelyn tutted softly. "Oh, Asher would not be pleased if he could see you, my friend," she whispered.

Patting her sword, as though assuring herself it was still in her belt, Evelyn mounted the last few steps, then reached gingerly over the passed-out man. She twisted the handle and pushed the door inward. It swung silently on well-greased hinges, revealing a massive open space.

A desk littered with papers, silver halves, and sealing wax stood against one wall, and six tall-backed chairs encircled a table in the adjacent corner. A wardrobe and a bed large enough for a warhorse stood on the opposite wall, and a tall perch surrounded by white bird droppings and bits of bone was placed beside the only open window. The long red curtains billowed in the breeze, but that was the only movement in the room. No torches were lit, and the bed was empty and cold. Wyatt Asher wasn't here.

She supposed that explained the less-than-stellar guard detail at the kingpin's door.

"What kind of git isn't in his own bed at four in the bloody morning?" Evelyn muttered, easing the door shut behind her. Never mind that she also was not in her own bed at four in the bloody morning, making her, by her own statement, a git as well.

Her stomach sank. Asher wasn't here. Would she even be able to attempt this again? She winced as a cool breeze rushed in through the open window, whispering of an early winter. They had used up all their luck getting here, it seemed. Now . . .

Evelyn shook herself to the present. Asher wasn't here, but there was still a chance the Quill might be. Tristan had been certain the Crowns' leader wasn't stupid enough to leave the thing unattended in his chambers, but it seemed foolish not to at least look when she was already here. This wasn't over yet.

But nearly an hour of quiet searching—interrupted periodically by moments of panic when she thought the dormire's blood–huffing guard outside might be stirring—proved Tristan right. She checked the desk drawers, the closet, tore apart and remade the bed. On the side of the table she found a secret panel, but all that lay behind it was a small tube and a packet of darts tipped with scorpion venom or poison from the pale-leaf flowers in Briel no doubt. Illegal? Absolutely. Something the Needle Guard could have his head for—probably the reason he kept them so well-hidden. But she wasn't Needle Guard anymore, and she wasn't looking for any old contraband. Only the Quill of Declan Day.

Her eyes flicked to the open window as the bells in the Church of Adalina rang out north of the trade docks. Five tinny gongs marking five o'clock in the morning. She patted her trouser pocket, assuring herself that she still had the key.

Not that it mattered. No doubt the Crown Tristan had stolen it from had already noticed it was missing. There was little to no chance they would be able to infiltrate the Roost again. But what else could they do? Confront Wyatt Asher on the streets of the Lottery? She snorted. That had to be about as suicidal as waltzing up to Duncan Baelbrandt with a knife in hand these days.

But if they wanted to stop Asher before he made his move with the Quill . . . maybe that was a risk they had to take.

Taking one last look at the room to make sure she had replaced every pillow, copper, and scrap of parchment exactly as she'd found it, Evelyn turned to the door. Just as she reached for the heavy, bronze handle, she froze, stomach leaping into her throat at the sound of heavy footsteps banging up the staircase.

She hoped they would get off at the floor below . . . but of course that wasn't her luck. The footsteps rounded the next landing, marching straight up toward her. They were accompanied by voices, garbled by the thick black wood of the door. One male, one female, as far as she could tell. Then she heard the screech of a kestrel. *Shite*. Heart slamming around in her chest like a caged bat, Evelyn turned from the door, looking around wildly as the male voice started shouting at the sleeping guard.

Evelyn caught the words "useless" and "fucker"

as she frantically searched for somewhere, anywhere, to run. Her eyes finally fell on the wardrobe, and she sprinted toward it on tiptoes, sliding inside and burying herself behind a dozen of Asher's nearly identical plain black cloaks just as the door to the chamber swung open.

Through a gap between the doors of the wardrobe, Evelyn watched two shapes enter the room. One was tall and angular, his arm held out in front of him to support the weight of a bird. It shrieked, flapping into the air and winging its way over to the perch beside the open window. The second shape was smaller than the first—an outline Evelyn recognized. She ground her teeth so loudly she was almost surprised Asher didn't hear her.

Tana Rafferty. The bitch who had convinced Tristan to betray Ryia on the Guildmaster's island . . . and then betrayed Tristan herself the second she got him back to Carrowwick. Evelyn's hand tightened on her sword hilt, but she took a calming breath. Leaping out of the shadows in the heart of the Crowns' hideout was a terrible idea. She might be able to slice Rafferty's throat before she was bludgeoned to death by two dozen of Asher's cronies, but still, she would be killed before she made it five steps down the stairwell. Which would certainly prevent her from getting the Quill back.

She held her breath, pressing herself farther

back into the softness of Asher's cloaks as the Crowns' leader shut the door to his chambers behind him, then turned to his second-in-command.

"Well, what is it, Tana? What news is so secretive you had to drag me from the Satin House, through the streets, and up nine flights of stairs to hear it?" Asher sounded agitated—understandable, seeing as it seemed like Rafferty had interrupted a visit to one of the most expensive brothels in Carrowwick. Evelyn watched, eye pressed to the crack in the wardrobe, as Asher took off his cloak, watching for a flash of silver and listening for the heavy thunk of metal in the pocket—any sign of the Quill. There was none.

"Trust me—when you hear this news, you'll be glad I didn't list it out in front of that girl," Rafferty said, her voice just as inappropriately sweet and girlish as Evelyn remembered. She crossed to the open window, giving the restless kestrel a stroke on its beak before closing the pane. "Whores have their mouths open almost as often as their legs. One word of this in there, and it would have been all over the city faster than a jackrabbit on *vitalité*."

"At this hour, Tana, is all this really necessary?"

Tana grimaced. "I'll let you be the judge of that."

Evelyn leaned forward, eyes narrowing. She

was here for the Quill, true . . . but still, her curiosity got the better of her. Whatever news Rafferty had, she was going to some ruddy great pains to keep it quiet. Maybe she could use it as leverage against Asher to get him to give up the Quill? Unlikely, but worth a shot . . .

"Callum Clem is alive."

Evelyn felt like she had been clubbed across both temples. She was not the only one who was stunned by Rafferty's pronouncement. Asher went silent for two full breaths, then took a step forward, one bony hand stretched out in front of him as though he could fend the words off like a cloud of gnats.

"What did you say?" His voice was low with either anger or fear; Evelyn couldn't tell which.

"Clem," Rafferty repeated grimly. "Somehow, the Snake weaseled his way out of the Catacombs that night. Made his way down the coast. The word is he's been spotted in Golden Port with his smuggler and that gorgeous Borean piece of ass."

Evelyn's breath caught again. Nash and Ivan—it had to be them. All three of them had been in the Catacombs that night . . . and had managed to slip away unseen. They'd let the whole bloody Lottery think they were dead while they ran off to . . . Golden Port? But why? There had to be more to it than that.

Then it hit her, the realization smacking into her skull like a crossbow bolt. She and Tristan were chasing the wrong man. Silently she sank to the floor of Asher's wardrobe, eyes wide in the darkness. Callum Clem had the bloody Quill. He'd double-crossed them in the Catacombs before she and Ryia ever had the chance to double-cross him in kind.

They needed to get to Golden Port . . . and fast.

CHAPTER EIGHT
Ryia

In the depths of the Shadow Cells, Ryia's life fell into a pattern of familiar misery. The only breaks from the silent darkness came in the form of nightmares, phantom images of her father lurking in the dungeon, and Joslyn's wildly exaggerated stories of adventure on the high seas. In between these, Ryia attempted again and again to lift the pebbles on her cell's floor using Kinetic magic. No matter what she tried, the stones wouldn't whisper their damned secrets to her.

Stupid, she thought as she gave up yet again. The hatchets were the only thing she could control. She had known that since the day she'd fled her father's manor. A few words from a Senser-turned-pirate wouldn't change that. Nothing could.

The guards had just delivered another dose of hard bread and thick, grayish slop when Tolliver Shadowwood returned. Ryia barely looked up as the lock clicked, the light of Shadowwood's lantern filling her cell as he stepped toward her.

"You're not too bright, are you?" she said lightly, dipping the heel of her bread into the slop and scooping up a mouthful. "You'd think you would have figured it out by now—it doesn't matter how hard you have your servants beat me." She took a bite, finally looking up as she chewed. "My tongue isn't budging."

"Oh, I'm well aware of that by now, gutter rat," Shadowwood said. Ryia shrugged, turning back to her meal. "Fortunately, if your mouth will not talk, there is another part of you that might. . . ."

A cold tingle of fear worked its way down Ryia's spine. She pushed it away, eyes filling with defiant fire as she met the king's gaze again. But that fire vanished when she saw what he held in his hands.

A flat, sharp blade. And a bucket.

"What are you—" she started, but before she could get the rest of the question out, the Kinetics Shadowwood had brought with him surged forward. They grabbed her arms and legs, pushing her back until she was stuck between their dead-eyed gazes and the stone wall of the back of her cell. There was no chance of escape, but that didn't stop her from fighting like a cornered street dog.

"Go ahead, keep flailing. I don't mind. It just means I might get more than I came here for," Shadowwood said. He sounded amused. The bastard.

He was right, though. He just wanted a sample, but if she kept struggling, he might well end up cutting somewhere that could bleed her dry. She should just let him take what he wanted.

But no. If he took this blood from her, he could figure out her father's secret. The fact that he was even *taking* her blood meant he was close. Much too close. Shadowwood would learn the secrets of Adept magic. How many throats would he slit once he knew the power Adept blood could give him? Too many.

The Kinetic holding her right arm slammed her backward again. For a second, her shoulder went numb, and her arm fell limp. *No, no, no.* Shadowwood's razor cut down, striking toward the inside of her elbow. She was pinned. There was no way to stop it. Panic surged up in her, and a scream filled her ears. Not a scream, a ringing sound. A high-pitched note, spiraling through her skull. It resonated with the deepest part of her, familiar and foreign all at once. The king lost his grip on the razor, and it slipped sideways, clattering to the stone at his feet.

The ringing sound stopped all at once. Ryia blinked. What had just happened?

Had she done that?

She was still dazed when she felt the bite of a blade sinking into the crook of her opposite elbow. *Shit.* She thrashed as she felt the blood coursing down her arm, but that only made the liquid flow more thickly, pooling like a disgusting cocktail in the bottom of the bucket the king had placed beneath her hand.

"That should do. For now, at any rate," he finally said delicately. He nodded at someone behind him, and a servant rushed forward with a roll of gauze. The girl didn't meet Ryia's eyes, just wrapped the fabric quickly around her still-bleeding arm, then hurried away.

"Don't fret, I'll be back soon. . . ." Shadowwood shook the bucket gently. Ryia almost vomited as she heard the blood—*her* blood—sloshing around inside.

For her entire life, Ryia had thought there could be nothing worse than the years she had spent chained in the basement of her father's manor in southeastern Edale, but she'd been wrong. Her father had been a twisted son of a bitch, sure, but Tolliver Shadowwood was something far worse. Somehow both more rigid and more erratic at once. For the first time, she felt genuine empathy for Tristan's betrayal back on that island. If she'd had a soul, she might have sold it just to be rid of this fucking man.

King Tolliver nodded at the gaoler, wiping his fingers gingerly on the hem of his doublet as the man unlocked the cell, ushering him out. The king's careful, delicate motions reminded her of Clem. Truthfully, the king reminded her of Clem in a lot of ways. The two could have formed a Society of Soulless Bastards if Clem hadn't gotten himself killed back at the Catacombs. Maybe they could join up in the ninth circle of

Felice's hell whenever Shadowwood finally kicked it.

Of course, he was a lot less likely to kick it anytime soon if he learned the secrets her blood held. Maybe someone would assassinate him before he got the chance. A dark hope for a dark place.

Ryia looked down at her hands, the light bathing them fading as the king and his entourage exited the dungeon, taking their torches with them. Something had happened with that razor blade. She didn't think the king had dropped it by chance.

She thought of the clear, ringing note she had heard. Had that just been panic? Or had it been something more?

Frowning, Ryia stepped forward, placing her hand on a rusted iron bar of her cell. It was cold and rough on her palm . . . but beyond that, she felt nothing. *Or did she?* Not caring how stupid she looked, she closed her eyes, reaching out with both hands now. There was something there . . . unless she was imagining it. A grating song, almost, just out of range of her hearing, like words whispered behind a closed door. It was different from the feel of the hatchets, but still solidly there.

She reached for the unfamiliar chorus of the rusted bars with the invisible string she usually pulled to control the hatchets. The same invisible string she had unwittingly pulled on that razor a few moments ago. Once she was sure she had a grasp on it—or as sure as she could be in something she only half believed—she yanked.

Her eyes snapped open as a sound like a gong rang out over the dungeon, echoing off the dripping walls.

No way.

The bars were still intact, but the one in her right hand now had a small kink right at the base. Just about an inch, but it was unmistakable, even in the darkness. She and Joslyn shared a look, then both turned toward the torchlight, nostrils flaring as the scent of danger wafted toward them. The guards. Of course they would have heard that.

"What are you bastards doing back there?" shouted a voice from the end of the corridor. "Which one of you made that damned racket?"

Joslyn's eyes sparkled at her as she shoved her wig back onto her head, turning to sit in the opposite corner of her cell. *I told you so,* she mouthed.

For once, Ryia didn't have a retort. Her heart felt like it was rolling over inside her rib cage, spinning and pounding like a tiny carriage wheel on uneven ground. She felt almost dizzy as she stared at the small bend in the bar. Now that she knew what to look for, she could feel the iron in the bars calling out to her the way her hatchets always did. And it wasn't just the bars. She could feel the stone beneath her, the water in the puddles; all of it had a different feel, a different song . . . but she could sense all of them now, tugging at that space tucked away in the back of her mind.

The pebble she had tried and failed to lift for days was resting at her feet. Its whisper was gravelly and subtle. She seized that energy . . . then clenched the fingers of her right hand into a fist. The pebble shook and shuddered, then cracked neatly in two, breaking open as though she'd struck it with a chisel.

She kept her eyes down at her boots, her knees hugged up to her chest as the guards stalked past, rattling the bars as they went, shouting obscenities at each prisoner, and waving their torches to make their shadows dance long on the floor. In the torchlight she could see Shadowwood's Kinetics, lurking in the darkness. If her magic could bend bars and shatter stone, then Joslyn was right, no cell could hold her. The Kinetic guards would be another challenge, though. If she could figure out how to get past them . . .

She narrowed her eyes in thought, remembering what had happened the second day Shadowwood had come to watch his Kinetics tenderize her like a fine cut of steak. The day Wyatt Asher had last tried to seize control of the Adept. Shadowwood's

Kinetics had been frozen—helpless—for nearly a full minute. The dungeon guards clanked away down the corridor, returning to their post by the dungeon door. Ryia studied the Kinetics as they fell back into shadow, barely visible in the darkness of the dungeon. Her mind whirred, forming a skeleton of a plan. No one would go through the trouble of stealing the Quill of Declan Day only to give up figuring out how to master it. It was only a matter of time before Asher would try to seize control of the Adept again, she was sure of it. And this time, when he did, she would be ready.

"What is it?" Joslyn asked, clearly reading something in Ryia's expression.

Ryia held her hands out in front of her in the near darkness, flexing her fingers before looking up to meet Joslyn's gaze. "We're getting the hell out of here."

CHAPTER NINE
Nash

After four days holed up in the Gull's Gullet Inn, Nash knew two things. First, that Callum Clem was about three steps from the madhouse, and second, that coming to Golden Port had been a huge mistake.

As soon as they'd docked, Nash had taken a sack of coins to the neighborhood north of Skuller's Lane, rented a room at the Gullet, and bought enough bread, cheese, and dried meats to last a month or more. After all that, she had still had enough coin left over to buy Clem some of the tea he was so twice-damned obsessed with from the little port's only apothecary.

Golden Port was used to grimy sailors flashing too much gold to have been earned in any honest way, so that had not been an issue. What Golden Port *wasn't* used to was real wealth. Clem had always been a proud son of a bitch, so instead of listening to Nash and dressing in simple clothes to blend in with the crowd, Clem had stridden off the gangway in his finest velvet-lined coat and clicking boots, flanked by his two stone-faced Kinetics.

No one had attacked him directly—not even

Golden Port thugs were stupid enough to jump a man flanked by a pair of Adept servants. But they'd taken one look at his fancy servants and his ridiculous coat and assumed he was a rich bastard . . . and in a place like this, flaunting wealth was an invitation to get robbed. They had decided to start with *The Hardship*. When Nash had returned to the cog after what was supposed to be a single night of good rest and hot food before heading back out into the waves of the Yawning, she'd found it completely ransacked . . . and it wasn't just their meager supplies that were missing.

The thieves had stripped *The Hardship* down to the boards. Furniture, sails, and lines had all been lifted under the cover of night. Dock security in Golden Port was worse than a joke, but Nash had never seen anything like this. They didn't have the gold to buy all their supplies over again *and* rig the ship with new sails. Their options were then to either camp out in the city until they could con their way into enough coin to outfit themselves again, or just buy the sails and hope they didn't starve.

In the end, Nash only convinced Clem to go with the first option by reminding him that no supplies would mean no tea. The man was inches from losing it, but he was still as pretentious as ever. It was strangely comforting, no matter how annoying—a wink through this hollow shell of a man to the sly mastermind who had kept the

Saints alive and prospering for the better part of three decades back in the Lottery.

But as it turned out, Clem wasn't up to much conning. He would barely leave their twice-damned room. Most of the time, he just sat hunched over the Quill as it danced over whatever scrap of parchment he could place under it, watching intently as it placed dot after dot on map after map of Thamorr. Watching as it marked out the location of every soul in Thamorr with Adept magic . . . though what he expected to do with that information, Nash didn't know. He refused to listen to reason. Even when Nash brought back the news that Disciples had been spotted in Luxim, just a few miles south along the coast, Clem simply waved her away like she was a pesky gnat and resumed his stewing.

Ivan, on the other hand, barely sat still long enough to blink before hurrying back out into the city, doing Felice only knew what. The disguise-master was as unreadable as ever, but Nash had spent enough time with him to know something was wrong. There was no point in asking what that something was—it had to be the same thing that was wrong for her. The fact that they were stuck in the darkest corner of the darkest slum in all of Thamorr, watching the Guildmaster slink toward them across the map while Callum Clem slowly but steadily lost his twice-damned mind.

With her two companions flying off opposite

sides of the deep end, Nash was left with no one to talk to but the two Kinetics Clem had brought along with them. Of course, they were Adept, so they couldn't talk back, but that didn't stop Nash from trying. Maybe she was starting to fly off the deep end herself.

Their room was crowded, with a desk, a fireplace, a chair, two beds, and a cot crammed into a space no larger than the back room of the Miscreants' Temple back home. Clem slept fitfully on the largest bed by the window, hugging the Quill to his chest like a rich brat might hug their favorite doll. The two Kinetics stood, framing the door like they were expecting an attack at any second, hands at their sides, eyes blank yet sharp, just like always. Nash sat in the battered chair beside the desk, tossing a set of dice onto the pitted wooden surface. The desk was covered in stains, burn marks, and dark smudges that were probably old blood. The dice rolled to a stop, showing two fives, a four, a two, and a one.

"Bah," Nash said. "A real stew cup, that roll." She looked up at the Adept on the right. He was pale as a snowstorm. Probably born in Boreas. She wondered if his mother had screamed as loudly as hers had screamed for Jolie when he was taken.

"Mind if I roll for you? All right, great." She tossed the dice again. Four fives and a one. She wagged a finger at the Adept. "Another merchant's roll? I'd say you were cheating if I didn't know better." She tossed the dice back in the cup, squinting suspiciously at him. "But maybe you *are* cheating. Using that telekinetic shit." Nash wiggled her fingers at him. He didn't even react, and she sighed, turning to the left-hand Adept. "All right, your roll."

She upended the cup, then jumped about a foot into the air as the inn door banged open. Clem sat bolt upright, brandishing the Quill like it was a conductor's baton. His Kinetics sprang to life at his wordless command, seizing the dark shape as it entered the room and slamming it against the wall beside the fireplace.

The figure didn't so much as twitch a finger in protest, and Nash knew instantly who it was.

"It's Ivan—let him down," she shouted.

At the same time, Ivan, pinned to the wall, said, "Callum, it is me. I apologize for startling you." His voice almost sounded bored, despite the fact that his throat was locked in one Kinetic's fist as the second stood with his grime-encrusted nails about an inch from his perfect face. Still, there was a glint of something in his sea-green eyes. Fear? Had the Disciples slunk their way into these dark slums at last?

But no. At second glance, Nash saw the glint was something else entirely. An expression Nash hadn't seen in those eyes in weeks.

Hope.

Clem wiped his eyes gingerly, then stuffed

the Quill into his shirt pocket with one hand and waved the Kinetics off with the other. They released Ivan immediately, slinking back to their posts beside the door.

"What is so important that you felt the need to burst into the room like an overzealous Needle Guard?" Clem asked sourly.

A tone like that from Callum Clem would have made half the Saints back in Carrowwick soil their britches, but Ivan was completely unbothered. He bent down, picking Clem's boots up from the floor and holding them out to him.

"Put these on."

Clem stared at the boots, looking more like his old, commanding self than he had since leaving Carrowwick as he raised one eyebrow just a hair above the other, fixing Ivan with his most dangerous stare. "Did you just give me an order, Rezkoye?"

Ivan didn't waver. "You are still interested in learning to wield the Quill, are you not?" He shook the boots slightly. "I believe I have found a way. But I do not think you will want to walk through this *pizhlache* in your bare feet."

Clem paused a moment longer, then snatched the boots from Ivan's hands, swinging his legs off the edge of the bed to lace them onto his feet.

Nash turned to Ivan, incredulous. "You found information about the Quill of Declan Day *here?*"

She'd spent the first half of her life in these

piss-soaked alleys, and in all that time, she had seen about as much magic as she had kings and princes. Golden Port was the last place in all of Thamorr Nash would have expected to hold some dark secret about the magic that bound the Adept.

"The Quill? No," Ivan said. "We do not need information about the Quill; we already have the *verdammte* Quill. What we need to know is how to use it."

Clem stopped lacing halfway through his second boot. "Tell me exactly what you have found, Ivan. I do not intend to trudge through the streets of this deeply inferior city without purpose."

Ivan hesitated a moment, his lips thinning. The expression was barely there, but Nash thought she could read it, clear as a cloudless sky over the Luminous Sea. He had been hoping to save this detail for when they were already out of the room—maybe even for when they were already to whatever mystery location he was leading them to.

Could it be a trap?

The thought bloomed, unwelcome and uninvited, into Nash's skull. But it was a stupid thought—one born of the string of betrayals she had been forced to deal with since leaving Carrowwick to start this stupid mission in the first place. If Ivan intended to betray Clem, he would just have let her steal the Quill that night on *The Hardship*. No, whatever plan this was would benefit Clem . . . Ivan just didn't trust the Snake to see that.

"I have found a man with knowledge of the history of the Adept," Ivan said evasively.

"A scholar? In Golden Port?" Clem asked.

"Not exactly a scholar. More of a . . ." Ivan waved a hand, vamping as he searched for the right word. "*Kroniclar*."

Nash snorted, any inkling of hope she might have felt a moment ago evaporating in her chest. She wasn't fluent in Borean by any means, but she had spent enough time in Borean port cities to know quite a bit of the harsh northern language. Even if she hadn't, she would have known that word. She had known it since childhood—the childhood she'd spent running around, helping her father lug nets and lines and fish around these very docks.

"Let me guess: You met Gavril Bornchev?" Nash asked. Ivan's lips grew even thinner, and Nash turned to Clem. "Kick those boots back off, Clem. This will be a waste of time."

But Clem's eyes sharpened. He leaned forward, resting an elbow on his knee and fingering his chin thoughtfully. "I will be the judge of what wastes time."

Privately, Nash thought that lately Clem was something of an expert on wasting time, but all she did was shrug and lean back in her chair, motioning for Ivan to continue.

"*Herrn* Bornchev fled from Boreas just after the fall of the Avendroth Crown," Ivan started.

"Before that, he was an adviser for King Leonid Avendroth. Very close to the throne."

"And since then, he has been a crackpot living just outside the gutter telling his batshit stories to sailors for crumbs and coppers," Nash finished.

When she was younger, she had liked Bornchev's stories. They were all old Borean legends of magic and giant bears the size of fishing ships—fables and myths, nothing more substantial than pipe smoke on the wind.

Ivan gave her a level stare. "And what of this Quill of Declan Day? A few months ago, would you not have said that was *mullshiss* as well?"

Nash pursed her lips. He had a point. She had seen a lot of things since leaving Carrowwick that one fateful evening in the dead of summer that she would have called horseshit if someone else was telling her the story. Adept children, talking and fidgeting like normal children? A writing stick that could find and enslave all the magical people of the world? All of it sounded crazy, but it was true.

Of course, that didn't mean *everything* anyone said was true. But it meant there was at least a chance.

Clem looked between them, then fixed Ivan with his stare again. "And this Bornchev. What song has he sung that sent you running to find me?"

"The story of the fall of the Avendroth Crown, Callum. He said it was the sixth Guildmaster who hunted the king down and Disciples who slaughtered his line. And he said that for a price, he will tell me why."

Clem's cobalt eyes narrowed. "And you think this will somehow solve all our problems?"

"I do."

"Why?"

Ivan took a deep breath. "Because the stories say the Avendroth Crown fell because King Leonid was using *Yavol's* own magic."

Nash suppressed an eye roll at that. Stereotypically, the Borean people were a superstitious lot, but she would never have assumed Ivan Stone-Face would buy a single word of it. Surely Clem was going to tear him apart for even suggesting something so foolish. But when Clem spoke again, his voice was breathless.

"You think he figured out how to turn someone Adept?" he asked.

Ivan nodded grimly. "And I think *Herrn* Bornchev can tell us how he did it."

Clem paused for a long moment, but Nash had worked with the man long enough to know what he was going to say. Finally, he grabbed Nash's coat from where it lay, slung over the side of the cot, and threw it to her.

"Then let's go speak with this *Herrn* Bornchev."

With the constant threat of Disciples wafting on the winds, Nash tried to convince Clem to leave his Kinetics back at the inn. Clem wouldn't hear a word of it. The man had made himself a legend in Carrowwick by daring to walk the streets alone, and unarmed, in velvet loafers, at just over five feet tall. Now he wanted his Adept bodyguards within arm's reach no matter where he went. At least he had agreed to disguise them. Only Nash's clothes were large enough to fit the bulky Kinetics. One wore a spare shirt and pair of trousers, the other had Nash's salt-stained coat buttoned up over his robes, leaving Nash shivering and coatless in the chill autumn wind.

Ivan took the lead, but Nash didn't need help finding Bornchev's apartment. It was above the weaver's shop on the edge of Skuller's Lane. Just a few doors away, past a tavern called the Searat's Shanty and a stoop that somehow always held men playing dice, stood the apartment where she had grown up. The place her mother had died. The place from which Jolie had been taken.

Why the *fuck* had she decided to put in at Golden Port again?

Ivan led them around the back of the shop and up a rickety wooden staircase Nash had climbed dozens of times before. He knocked twice on the battered door at the top. After just a few seconds, it whipped open to reveal the face of Gavril Bornchev.

It had been over a decade since Nash had last seen the man, but somehow he looked exactly the same. He had to be at least ninety years old by now—though how anyone survived to be ninety in a place like Golden Port, Nash couldn't figure. His hair was the color of the foam on top of a wave, and his eyes matched Ivan's for color almost exactly—that distinctly Borean mix halfway between green and blue. Wrinkles scored his face like the grains in a slat of old wood, and his long, thin neck cracked as he cocked his head to one side.

"You have the gold?" he asked Ivan, barely sparing a glance for Clem, Nash, and the Kinetics.

Ivan looked to Clem. The Snake of the Southern Dock examined the old storyteller shrewdly for a few seconds, but Nash knew it was just an act. If Clem wasn't planning to entertain this bullshit, he wouldn't have bothered to drag his ass out of the Gullet in the first place. Finally, he reached into his fine coat pocket and produced a small, jingling bag. The last of their coin. Disciples could be pulling into port at any moment. Their ship had no sails, and they had barely enough food to get through breakfast, and they were spending their last coin on *this*.

Felice help them.

The inside of Bornchev's apartment was just as Nash remembered it. She felt like she was ten years old again, following Andrée and Louis into the gloom to listen to whatever stories the old Borean man would tell them. She couldn't remember him ever charging them as much as a copper back then—and she would have remembered something like that, since she had been nearly twenty before she'd regularly had two coppers to rub together. Either the man had a soft spot for children, or he thought Ivan and Clem looked like suckers he could scam into paying him a crescent's worth of silver for a few stories. If the latter was the case, the man was right.

Bornchev creaked the door shut behind them. He motioned for them to sit with one hand, feeling through the bag to count the silver halves inside with the other. There were only three chairs in the room. Clem took one without question, and Bornchev took one of the others. The Kinetics, of course, made no move to sit, standing on either side of Clem as still and stoic as the carved beasts on the gates of the castle in Fairvine. There was an awkward moment where both Ivan and Nash stared at each other, then the chair.

"You should—" Ivan started.

Nash raised an eyebrow. "If you're about to offer me that chair because I'm a twice-damned lady, I'll introduce you to my handmaids," she said, indicating her balled fists one after the other.

Ivan held up both hands in silent surrender, then took the chair directly across the table from

Bornchev while Nash leaned against the support holding the peak of the roof up in the center of the room. For a few long moments, no one spoke. The clatter of looms filtered up from below, where weavers made fishing nets of every size, strength, and weave imaginable.

Bornchev reached into a cabinet beside the table and pulled out a dusty brown bottle Nash recognized. *Stervod.* Specifically, *stervod* smuggled in illegally by the Gold Lords, the biggest syndicate in Golden Port. The Gold Lords always cut their stock liberally with river water, but Bornchev clearly didn't mind. He poured himself a healthy glass, then waved it around, offering. They all shook their heads, and Bornchev shrugged, lifting his cup and taking a deep draft of the foul-smelling stuff as he looked around at their faces.

"So, we have a Borean pretty boy, a lord and his guards . . ." Clem straightened pompously at that. Nash rolled her eyes. "And . . ." Bornchev cocked his head the other way as his eyes fell on Nash's face. "Well, that face is about three feet higher off the ground than the last time I saw it, but I still know it." He wagged a finger at her around his cup, smiling with his crinkled eyes. "You have listened to my stories before."

Nash was surprised to feel a swell of emotion rising in her throat at being remembered. She swallowed it, running her tongue over her teeth to hide the lapse in her uninterested expression. "I have. But I've heard you have a new one for me today."

"I do." Bornchev smiled at her with just as toothless a grin as she remembered. It was infectious. Despite the fact that they were quite possibly wasting their last hours on this nonsense, she couldn't stop herself from grinning back.

When Bornchev sank into the rhythm of his story, the experience was just like she remembered it. His rich voice filled the apartment, his descriptions almost solid, tangible things as they hung in the stagnant air all around them. It was a story everyone in Thamorr knew pieces of, but the details were things Nash had never heard before.

"The lands of Boreas have always been the wildest in all of Thamorr, its people the hardiest, with backbones of iron and hearts of fire," Bornchev began. "We are a difficult people to rule over, and so from the beginning of this land, our rulers have been cold as the winds through the mountain passes, and as hard as the frozen earth beneath snow."

"And as vicious as *verdammte* cave bears," Ivan muttered under his breath, his hands balled into fists.

Bornchev turned his stare on him, looking vaguely amused. "Yes, that too. But if you believe the Tovolkovs are brutal, it is good the

Avendroth Crown fell before you were born. Because you would never have survived it."

Ivan pursed his lips tightly, which was as good as a derisive snort from just about anyone else. Bornchev didn't seem to notice.

"I was still a young man when I served King Leonid," Bornchev continued. "Back then, Volkfier was hardly large enough to be called a city, and Kroniv was nothing more than a few shacks at the base of the mountains for the fur traders to sleep off their *stervod*. But there was one thing in Boreas that was far stronger then than it has been in all the decades since."

"The *medev*," Clem guessed. He was leaning forward now, his elbows resting on his knees, his eyes shining with greed. No, more than that. Hunger.

"Exactly." Bornchev nodded, giving him that infectious toothless smile. "The *medev* of today are strong warriors, but they are merely an early-winter frost, where the *medev* of the Avendroth Crown were a snowstorm. The soldiers of Boreas were so strong in those days that Leonid grew greedy. I advised him against his war with Edale, but . . . you know how men of power can be.

"Edale had iron mines, and the armies of Boreas had need of iron. It does not take an expert strategist to see why he wanted to claim the land for the north. Some of the greedier advisers agreed. But those of us with sense left in our skulls remembered the only law consistent in all of Thamorr."

"The Guildmaster's will," Clem said.

Bornchev nodded again. Each Guildmaster of Thamorr had ruled the land with his respective iron fist since the era of Declan Day, centuries ago. When Declan Day had ended the Seven Decades' War, he had forbidden war among the kingdoms of Thamorr. Any differences between kingdoms or squabbles between kings could be settled by Kinetic single combat, but outright war? One army crashing into another like two waves meeting in the wake of a ship? That hadn't been tolerated since the leashing of the Adept. Of course, there were a few kings scattered throughout history who had been thick enough to try it. And their stories all ended the same way. The same way their own story was likely to end if they were still in Golden Port when the Disciples arrived.

"The Guildmaster's will," Bornchev repeated. "But it was far worse than that alone. For decades, the king had been hiding a secret from the rest of Thamorr—most importantly, from the Guildmaster. And his first attack on Edale revealed his secret to anyone who was looking, lighting it up like a lantern in the darkness. Normal men did not fight the way the *medev* fought. Regular soldiers did not leap higher than the gazelles of Briel, nor did they wield a bastard sword in each hand, swinging them as though they weighed no more than summer reeds."

"They were Adept," Nash said.

She had always heard legends about the old soldiers of Boreas. The way a single soldier could take on a full battalion without sustaining more than a scratch. The way their swords moved faster than the eye could see, slicing off their opponents' heads before they could even reach for their own blades. Nash had always assumed that, like all old stories, they were full of it.

"I do not know if they were Adept," Bornchev said, taking a thoughtful sip of his watered-down *stervod*. "I knew these men. They did not look like those two." He waved at Clem's Kinetics, who were staring blankly at the opposite wall, backs straight and arms at their sides. "These men were just . . . *men*. They drank with us in taverns. Some had wives and children. But yes, they were as strong as any Kinetic I have ever seen fighting in the pits."

"And how did they become so strong?" Clem asked. There was no question about the hunger in his eyes anymore. He looked like a street dog eyeing a pile of bones. Nash swore he was almost salivating.

Bornchev shook his head. "That was one of King Leonid's greatest kept secrets. Whenever a guard was raised to the *medev*, he would complete their transformation himself, and each *medev* was sworn to secrecy on pain of death."

Clem's fists tightened, his face beginning to slide into its most dangerous smirk. Ivan stilled him with a hand.

"You do not know for certain, but you said you had an idea of how it was done," Ivan said, urging. He looked nearly as desperate as Clem did, his eyes narrowed, almost pleading with Bornchev as he, too, leaned forward, just a few inches, hanging on the storyteller's every word.

Bornchev hesitated a moment, filling the silence by taking another sip from his cup. "I do have an idea," he finally said. "It is the reason I fled Boreas in the first place."

"You didn't flee when the Guildmaster came to clear out Avendroth's halls?" Nash asked. Growing up, she had always heard the rumors about Bornchev. That he had worked in Avendroth's court and was living in Golden Port in hiding from the Guildmaster after fleeing during the crown's fall.

Bornchev smiled at her sadly. "No one fled then. There were no survivors of the Guildmaster's raid on the Reclaimed Castle that night. Not a single *medev*. Not a single servant. Not a single one of the king's children. I do not think they even allowed the horses to live."

Disgust pooled in Nash's belly at that. The king had clearly mucked things up, but the Guildmaster had punished even the *servants?*

There was no need to kill someone just because of the mistakes of the man whose chamber pots they scrubbed.

"No," Bornchev continued. "I fled just before that day. A few weeks prior, the king was raising his newest *medev*, and I grew curious. I dared to peek into the throne room during the ceremony, and I cannot be certain, but I believe I saw him marking the forearms of his soldiers with something. A long white blade."

"A sword?" Nash asked, puzzled. If a slash on the arm with a sword could make someone a Kinetic, half of the continent would be brimming with magic.

"Not a sword. A dagger," Bornchev said, looking at Ivan.

Nash had no idea what that meant. She shared a look with Clem, who seemed similarly perplexed, but Ivan perked up immediately, straightening in his chair.

"A dagger . . . with a white blade . . . you cannot mean the Eisfang Dagger?"

"The very same. It would make sense why the ceremonies took place in the throne room, where the dagger was kept," Bornchev said, looking only at Ivan now.

"Would anyone care to explain what this dagger is?" Clem asked, picking a piece of lint from his trousers and flicking it away.

"It is an ancient Borean artifact," Ivan said. "It

is said to have been made for the very first king of Boreas some thousand years ago. And every Borean king has carried it since."

" 'Carried' is a strong word," Bornchev said with a chuckle. "Every Borean king has kept it locked up tight in a case since then, though. For centuries, possession of the dagger was what gave a man the claim to the throne. If the dagger was lost, so was the crown."

The irritation had melted from Clem's face now. He was leaning forward again. With his head cocked to one side and his eyes narrowed to slits, his resemblance to a snake was more pronounced than ever. "And drawing blood with this dagger . . . you believe that is what gave the old *medev* their powers?"

Bornchev leaned back in his chair, arms spread wide. "I cannot say for certain. But yes. I looked at the arms of every *medev* I saw from that night until the night the king discovered what I had seen. Until the night I had to flee the north with nothing but the coat on my back. All of them had identical scars." He mimed the action, pushing up his left sleeve. "Three inches long, just below the elbow."

Clem looked down at his own arm, and Nash knew he was imagining the cut there. Imagining the feeling of Adept magic rushing into his veins. Imagining taking hold of the Quill's power, once and for all.

"And this Eisfang Dagger," Clem began, tripping slightly over the Borean word. "What do you think happened to it?"

"The Guildmaster would have taken it in the raid," Ivan said wearily.

Perfect. Another dead end. Unless Clem was batshit enough by now to try to steal from the seventh Guildmaster of Thamorr *again*. Which he just might be . . .

But at the end of the pitted old table, Bornchev was shaking his head as he poured himself another glass of *stervod*.

"No, he did not. It is said that his rage was something terrible when he could not find the dagger. That is why he killed every last member of the Avendroth line, because not one of them would tell him where it was kept."

Nash narrowed her eyes. "So it's still in Boreas somewhere?"

Bornchev turned his greenish eyes on her, cocking his head once again. "Not just *somewhere* in Boreas. It is inside the Reclaimed Castle. In the possession of Andrei Tovolkov. Without it, the other lords of Boreas would not have allowed him to claim the throne." He took another swig of *stervod*, then swirled his cup thoughtfully. "Though I do not believe he knows the dagger's true power."

Clem leaned back in his chair, folding his hands in his lap. He tapped his right pointer finger against the back of his opposite hand. It was a pose Nash had seen many times before. One that made her stomach turn, though she couldn't quite put her finger on why. It was the posture Clem adopted when he was on the precipice of making up his mind about something. When his plans were nearly complete inside that twisted head of his.

Finally, he said, "Who *does* know of the dagger's true power?"

"Aside from the Guildmaster and his Disciples?" Bornchev asked. He leaned back in his chair too, spreading his arms with a wide smile. "Just me. And now you." He winked at Nash. "Not bad for a handful of silvers, now, is it?"

"Not bad at all," Clem said. His right hand twitched.

Nash saw what was about to happen an instant too late to stop it. Both Kinetics leapt forward, one circling around the table, the other bounding right over it. Nash blinked, unable to look away as they tore into the kind old storyteller with their bare hands, filthy nails digging into the man's throat. Bornchev's eyes barely had time to widen in shock before the light left them. Blood pooled around his body as it fell, spilling from him in rivers Nash swore rushed faster than the Arden as they spread across the dust-coated floor toward her. She took a step back, swallowing a wave of nausea as the first trickles reached her boots.

"What the hell did you do that for?" she shouted at Clem. He wouldn't take kindly to her talking to him like that, but the words came out before she could stop them.

The Snake was already on his feet, delicately brushing off his coat. The gleam was back in his eye. Seeing that glint of victory reflected in Clem's gaze as he looked down at the broken body of an innocent old storyteller sent chills racing one another down Nash's spine.

"Prudence, Claudia," he said lightly. Nash gritted her teeth. He knew calling her by that name pissed her off. "Now we are the only ones who know what we are after. Surely you see how that benefits us? If I'd left him alive, he could have sent any number of our enemies chasing after us."

He held his trousers out of the way as he stepped gingerly over the old man's body. He then grabbed his pouch of coins back from the dead man's grasp and raided the cabinet for good measure. Inside were another two small leather pouches. Clem drew them out, jingling them merrily.

"This should be enough to get us out of this pisshole, don't you think?"

Nash swore she heard him humming a cheerful Gildesh jig under his breath as he stalked out the door, his Kinetics close behind.

She set her jaw, lifting her eyes to Ivan, still

sitting in the chair beside the toppled *stervod* cup. "Still think you're betting on the right horse, Rezkoye?" she asked bitterly.

Ivan opened his mouth to respond, then shut it again without speaking. He pushed himself stiffly to his feet, following Clem out the door without a word, leaving Nash alone with the pooling blood and the dead man.

"I'm so sorry," she whispered, bending over Bornchev's corpse to close his eyelids.

She wanted nothing more than to lose herself in the streets of Golden Port. To abandon her hopes of using the Quill to gain enough riches to buy herself a new ship and crew. Right now, she didn't care if she never set sail again, she just wanted to flee from Callum Clem's sinister face and even more sinister plots. Nash gripped the namestone tucked beneath her shirt. But she was in too deep now. She knew too much. If she didn't follow Clem, she had no doubt she would end up just like Bornchev. No matter what she wanted, she was either stuck with Clem, or she was dead.

Stuck with Clem it was.

Some would say that was cowardice, but to Nash, it just felt like good sense. She cleared her throat, blinking the remnants of her welling tears from her eyes, and followed Ivan and Clem back out into the city.

CHAPTER TEN

Ryia

For the next few days, Ryia and Joslyn traded shifts. One slept while the other sat awake, watching the Kinetics in the shadows like a dog watched a clumsy child with a snack, waiting for them to seize up, frozen as Asher tried to take control of the Quill. In that time, Ryia tested the limits of her newfound power.

She floated bits of stone from the floor, made ripples in the puddles without touching them, and snatched Joslyn's wig from her head so fast the pirate barely had time to clamp her hands over it before it flew across the dungeon into Ryia's fingers. Nothing responded as quickly or obediently as her hatchets, but the power was clearly there.

There were still limits to the magic. Mainly, focus. It was difficult enough to focus on doing something with her body—walking, talking, fighting—while controlling an object through telekinesis, but controlling two items at the same time with the power seemed impossible. It was like the intangible strings of magic got tangled up with each other, knotting together and making her lose control over everything.

It was difficult to gauge what time it was without access to sunlight, but based on the way the on-duty guards were bitching and moaning about how they wished they were out at the tavern, Ryia guessed it was sometime after nightfall when she took her next shift.

The guards at the end of the hall were two of the most incompetent souls the Edalish army had to offer. Alton and Gareth were their names, and both of them were dumber than the hero's idiot sidekick in a children's story. Alton was taller than Nash and skinnier than Tristan, and Gareth was just the opposite. Half the time they were drunk, swigging from hidden flasks and belching loudly. The other half they were playing dice, betting coppers, and trading obvious lies about the fights they'd won and the women they'd fucked. Charmers.

Tonight, it was the latter. Ryia could barely keep herself from rolling her eyes as Alton launched into a lengthy tale about how he had seduced the crown princess of Briel on their last trip to the Guildmaster's auction. Oh, what she wouldn't give for the chance to shut that man up with a punch to the face.

A few seconds later, Felice heard that prayer.

Ryia's skin prickled in the darkness as a flash of movement caught her eye. Several flashes, in fact. Squinting through the dim light, she could see the Kinetics stiffening and straining. Not at a flat, alert attention as they usually were, but a tense, taut stillness, muscles pulled tight in what looked like agony as their jaws clenched, tendons throwing harsh shadows against their necks.

It was time.

Ryia picked up a small stone and chucked it at the back of Joslyn's head.

"What the—" the pirate said, sitting up. But she stopped when she saw Ryia's face.

"Ready?" Ryia asked.

"Like I haven't been ready since the second I got here."

Ryia grinned, then glanced at the distracted guards as she extended one hand toward the bars separating her from the corridor.

"If you leave me behind, just remember I'll get out of here eventually," Joslyn whispered, clearly misreading Ryia's expression. She tapped the side of her nose. "And there's not a single corner of this twice-damned world where you could hide from me."

"I'm not a total asshole," Ryia said. "Get ready to run like hell."

That was the only warning she gave. She stretched her stolen Adept magic out toward the bars of her cell . . . then she yanked. The rusted iron quivered for a moment before yielding to her power. One bar slowly bent outward, bowing like a stalk of wheat in a strong wind.

"Careful now," Joslyn whispered, breathless.

Sweat beaded on Ryia's forehead as she pulled back from the power. The iron bar wavered to a stop, leaving a gap just wide enough for Ryia to squeeze her slight frame through.

"I'll need more space than that," Joslyn said.

"You don't say," Ryia whispered back, sarcasm dripping from her tongue.

Joslyn stretched out her neck, then flexed one bicep. "You'll be grateful for these muscles later on."

"That a proposition?" Ryia asked, looking back toward the still-oblivious guards again as she positioned her hands over the bars to Joslyn's cell.

"You wish," Joslyn snorted.

Joslyn's cell bars weren't as cooperative as Ryia's. She grunted softly, struggling to focus her power. Finally, the bar relented. Instead of bending gently under her Kinetic power, however, it screeched like a dozen angry alley cats fighting over the same scrap of meat, then split from the floor, clanging deafeningly as it toppled. The pirate slipped through the space, joining Ryia in the corridor.

"Subtle," she said, glancing toward the entryway as the guards began to stir.

Ryia shrugged. "You said you needed a bigger gap."

The guards yanked their swords from their sheaths as Ryia and Joslyn turned toward the door.

The poor bastards didn't stand a chance.

Shouts of alarm and confusion rang out from the cells on either side of the corridor as Ryia sprinted toward the guards at full speed. The Kinetics, still trapped in their silent fits, did nothing. But that wouldn't last long. She and Joslyn needed to get out of this dungeon—now.

Ryia leapt off the stone floor, easily clearing Alton's sword as he swung it toward her. Midair, Ryia laid herself out in a front flip so high her boots almost touched the ceiling. She snatched the guard's sword from his grasp as she sailed overhead, whirling to level it at his throat as she landed.

"Hello there, gentlemen," she said, treating the men to her most carnivorous smile. She nodded toward the door behind her. "You wouldn't happen to know where I might find the key to this here door, would you?"

Gareth curled one lip, but the impression of toughness was undercut by the shake in his voice. "You don't really think King Tolliver would be thick enough to leave the keys locked in here with us, do you?"

"I do," Joslyn said. She had sidled up behind Alton and lifted the heavy iron key ring from his coat pocket without him even noticing. He swore loudly as she held them up, jingling them merrily.

He moved to slash the pirate across the throat with his sword, but she was ducking before he even twitched in her direction. Still holding the sword to Gareth's throat with one hand, Ryia extended her other toward Alton, feeling the vibrations of his weapon slithering toward her through the air. *Come on.* She sent up a silent prayer to Felice for her newfound Kinetic power to cooperate.

Alton yelped with surprise as the blade twisted in his hand, bending his wrist back, back, back, until he was forced to let go. The sword zoomed through the air into Ryia's outstretched palm.

"Oh, I could get used to that," she said, twisting the second blade so it caught the torchlight. "Now, what do we do with these two?"

Joslyn cocked her head to one side as she examined the two unarmed guards. "I'm sure you've heard that the *Ophidian Fang* never takes prisoners?" she asked, naming Salt Beard's infamous ship. "There's a reason for that."

Ryia pursed her lips. She knew Joslyn had a point. If they left these two buffoons alive, they'd follow them or sound the alarm or do something else monumentally stupid that could end in her death or recapture. The smart thing to do would be to kill them. *Dead men ring no bells*. Her old mentor's voice rang in her ears—the one she had served under in the assassin's guild back in Briel when she was little more than a girl.

For almost a decade, she'd followed that man's advice. She had followed it to the point that she had slit his throat to keep him quiet the day he learned what she really was.

But now she had a new voice ringing inside her head. A sharp voice with a violently Dresdellan accent and obnoxiously uptight morals. She hesitated for a long moment, then sighed, lowering both swords.

"Cautella, what are you—" Joslyn started, but Ryia ignored her.

She focused all her energy on Gareth. Or, more specifically, on the dark-green guard cloak slung around his shoulders. On its quiet, rasping whisper. Tugging the strings of her Adept power, she knotted the cloak firmly around the bars of the nearest cell, then turned to Alton. He was already trying to run, but luckily he weighed about as much as an overfed street mutt. Her hand darted out, snagging his cloak. He choked as it stopped him in his tracks. She reeled him in like the world's ugliest fish before tethering him firmly to the bars beside his partner.

"They'll get out of that in about four seconds, Cautella. For Felice's sake, how have you survived this long?"

"No they won't," Ryia said, taking a step toward the men. She lifted her swords, clapping them firmly on the temples with the hilts in quick succession. Both slumped forward, held up only by their firmly knotted cloaks.

Joslyn pursed her lips to one side, looking Ryia

up and down with a pinched expression. The pirate thought she was a twice-damned softheart.

Ryia was surprised to find that she wasn't upset by that in the least.

"You going to stand here staring at me until those Kinetics wake back up? Because if you don't mind, I've got somewhere to be," Ryia said wryly.

"A bathing chamber, maybe?" Joslyn said, striding forward and trying one key in the lock. She gave Ryia an exaggerated wink. The key didn't turn. Joslyn removed it and examined the others on the ring in the torchlight.

"Right, because you smell like a twice-damned Gildesh rose," Ryia chortled.

Joslyn tried another key. It didn't fit either. "Call me a Gildesh anything again and I'll rip your arms off."

The comment reminded Ryia so much of Nash that she couldn't help but crack a smile. Joslyn tried a third key. This one clicked when she turned it, and the door swung inward. She looked back to Ryia. "Not sure what you're laughing at—it's a real threat."

"I'm sure it is."

Ignoring the pirate's glare, Ryia stalked through the open doorway and mounted the stone staircase beyond.

It was definitely nighttime. The lower corridors were deserted, silent except for the scrabble of rodent feet on hard stone and the distant clump-clump-clump of boots on the floors above. Joslyn took the lead, winding through the hallways, sniffing deeply at every corner before choosing which way to go. Ryia's Senser abilities had never failed her before, but Joslyn's magic was stronger. She wrinkled her nose at corners where Ryia scented nothing but mildew and maybe a hint of hearth smoke. Neither of them knew the way out of this mazelike keep . . . but as long as they managed to steer clear of the guards, Ryia didn't much care how long it took them to find their escape.

Joslyn led them around another bend, and Ryia held up a hand. She recognized this place. It was the hall leading to the wine cellar. Could the escape route Evelyn used still be an option for them? She curled her lip. She didn't relish the idea of crawling through lukewarm, royal shit, but it would be a damn sight easier than trying to find the servants' entrance, which was their current plan.

"Where are you going?" Joslyn hissed, but Ryia ignored her, tiptoeing through the cool darkness toward the door to the larder.

It was early enough in the morning that she didn't even hear cooks and servants bustling around. It couldn't be much past midnight.

"Cautella," Joslyn whispered, warning.

Ryia moved to take another step forward, then

stopped abruptly as she finally scented the danger Joslyn had probably been smelling all along. Her nostrils tingled with it . . . the faint scent of decay and congealing blood. Holding her breath, she pressed herself against the wall, peering around the corner toward the larder. She swore silently.

Two guards stood positioned outside the doorway. Unlike Alton and Gareth in the dungeon downstairs, this pair actually looked competent.

"Will you listen to me now?" Joslyn breathed, raising an eyebrow. She nodded the other way, gesturing for Ryia to follow.

Ryia started to turn but froze when she caught sight of a familiar glint at one of the guards' waists. Or rather, several familiar glints. Anger surged up her throat like bile, unexpected and violent, and her grip tightened on both the stolen guard swords in her hands. Her hatchets. One of these green-cloaked sons of bitches had seen her hatchets among the prisoners' confiscated weapons and decided to claim them for himself.

Whatever complicated history she had with those hatchets, they were *hers*. She could feel them tugging at her already, like they were beckoning to her.

"Don't worry, darlings," she muttered. "I won't leave you here."

"Cautella, don't—" Joslyn whispered again, but it was too late.

"Hey, asshole," Ryia said, stepping around the

corner and into the light. She nodded at the belt. “You have some things of mine. I’d like them back.”

“That so?” he grunted, sounding amused. He looped his thumbs behind the worn leather of the belt, examining it fondly. “Not sure why you’d think that. They’re mine.” Ryia’s teeth ground together as the man reached back, running a thumb over the cold, shining steel of the left-hand axe blade. “I’ve seen what weapons like these can do. I’ve been waiting for the chance to try them out on something that bleeds. . . .”

The guard was no Kinetic, but he was still quick. Quick enough that, if it wasn’t for Ryia’s Senser powers, he might have managed to draw some of that blood he was so damned excited to see. As it was, she was able to roll out of the way, lifting one of her stolen swords to block the hatchet—*her* hatchet—as it swung down toward her. The hatchet’s steel bit rang out shrilly as it collided with the sword blade. The sound was deafening. It almost seemed to grow louder as it echoed off the stone walls around them, but Ryia didn’t care.

All she could see were her throwing axes glinting at his waist. This bloodthirsty, cocky son of a bitch. He reminded her of someone, but she couldn’t quite put her finger on it. Before she had the chance to consider it much further, a twinge of danger pulled at her nostrils from her left. She lifted her second sword just in time to block the blade of the other guard as he swung toward her.

"Oliver, check out the filth on her," the second guard said, addressing the bastard trying to kill her with her own weapons. "She's up from the dungeons."

"Or she's just never heard of soap before," the guard named Oliver said with a snort.

Ryia smirked, spinning rapidly on her heels to bring both swords screaming toward Oliver the hatchet thief. He managed to block one, but barely. The other scored a long, thin mark on his cheek. He hissed like an aggravated snake, and Ryia's smirk widened. "Oh, I'm from the dungeons, all right. Tortured and underfed, and I'm still kicking your ass."

"What—" the second guard started. "How did she . . . ? I'll go sound the alarm."

Ryia turned to stop him, but Joslyn was way ahead of her. The pirate slid around the corner, sticking out an arm the size of a tree branch as he ran by. She caught him right in the neck, and he stumbled, crashing to the floor.

"No you won't," Joslyn said grimly. She grabbed the sword from the man's hand as his arms windmilled through the air. Before he could catch himself, she ran the blade through his throat. His eyes bulged, and he gurgled wetly.

Ryia tore her eyes away with difficulty as the rank scent of blood and dust and death sliced into her from the direction of the remaining guard. Oliver's face showed only amusement and determination as he leapt toward her again, both hatchets raised over his head, ready to split her like timber. Again, his resemblance to . . . someone . . . was striking. She still couldn't place who it was, but the resemblance filled her with a sense of loathing and disgust. She raised the swords over her head, blocking both hatchets, then twisted to free herself.

"Are you planning on using your skills anytime soon, or were you just going to dick around like this all night?" Joslyn asked. "Because I'll leave your ass behind."

Right. Something clicked into place in Ryia's brain, and the next time Oliver came at her, she didn't try to block him. She dropped her stolen swords to the floor with a clatter and raised her empty palms instead. She could feel the hatchets singing to her with their familiar, sinister song. Reaching out with her Kinetic power, she tugged the hatchet in his left hand slightly to the right . . . then down. The bit sliced into the man's throat, and he sank to his knees, blood bubbling out from between his lips. Breathing hard, Ryia lowered her hands, then stalked toward him.

He was laughing. Or as close to laughing as a man bleeding out from his throat could get. "I did want to see them spill blood," he wheezed. And as his choked laughter faded away to silence and stillness, Ryia realized what loathsome, horrible ass this guard reminded her of.

Herself.

More specifically, the version of herself she had been until a few short months ago. A version of herself she could still feel inside her bones: cocky and heartless and filled to the brim with self-hatred. The version of herself that still made her stomach lurch in fear at the thought of trusting another soul with a handful of coppers, let alone her life.

She shook her head. No time to unpack that right now. The fight had taken only a few minutes, but Felice herself couldn't get away with a sword fight in a silent castle without being overheard. There would be more guards here in minutes if she was lucky—Adept if she wasn't.

"Joslyn, open that door," she said, nodding toward the wooden door the dead men had been guarding as she tugged her hatchets free of Oliver's still-grinning corpse and belted them back around her.

The pirate opened the door, then looked at the larder inside with a raised eyebrow. "Is now really the time for a snack?"

"Just trust me, would you?" Ryia grumbled, elbowing past her into the darkened larder.

"Sure, you've given me no reason not to trust you so far. Other than leaving those guards alive in the dungeon, then picking a fight with others just to get back a couple of piss-poor axes," Joslyn said, easing the larder door shut behind them and locking it.

"Insult my hatchets again and you'll find one in your throat," Ryia said, but there was no bite to the words. She was too distracted, patting at the floor looking for the hollow board that led into the wine cellar.

When she found it, she was unsurprised to find the trapdoor nailed firmly shut. She slowly started tugging at the nails one by one with her Kinetic power, but apparently whatever son of a bitch had nailed this up had used half the iron in Edale to do it. Already the hall outside the larder smelled faintly of danger. They would have only a few minutes. Throwing stealth and subtlety aside, Ryia aimed her newfound magic straight for the wooden floorboards.

The anxiety buzzing in her ears seemed to help channel her power. The boards split with a bang like Borean blasting powder. One firm kick sent them tumbling down into the wine cellar below. There would be no hiding their tracks now—speed was their only remaining weapon. She leapt through the hole in the floor, not bothering with the rickety ladder, landing in a puff of dust on the floor of the wine cellar.

The floor shook a bit as Joslyn landed beside her, rattling the dusty wine bottles all around them. The pirate inspected the bottles with a whistle. "A few of my old crewmen would give their left hand for a stash like this." She ran a finger along one of the bottles, drawing a line in the dust. "Course, a few of them are missing their left hand anyways, so I guess that's not saying much."

"Help me with this, would you?" Ryia grunted, grabbing hold of the grate beneath her feet.

Joslyn stooped down beside her and hefted the grate all by herself, pushing it to one side. The pirate then leaned back, waving a hand over her face. "Do I want to know what's down there?" she asked, wrinkling her nose.

"I think you already know," Ryia said. She wasn't looking forward to sliding down a quarter mile of human waste any more than Joslyn was, but she wasn't nearly as uneasy as she should have been. She was underground, about to crawl through a cramped tunnel that was also underground. A week ago, just the thought had been enough to make her want to vomit. Now?

Now she could feel the stone in the floor and the ceiling calling out to her. She could sense the vibrations in the pipe beneath her. She doubted she would ever *enjoy* being beneath the surface of the earth, but the walls around her didn't feel like the enemy anymore. Now they felt . . . maybe not like friends, exactly, but allies. Shields and weapons, just waiting for her to call them into action.

They were already twenty yards or more down the pipe by the time Ryia heard the door to the larder splinter back open behind them.

"Where does this lead?" Joslyn asked. Her voice was nasal, like she was trying very hard not to breathe through her nose.

Ryia didn't blame her. She looked over her shoulder at the pirate as she crawled. "How strong of a swimmer are you?"

"You know I've quite literally spent my entire adult life on a ship, right?"

"Fair enough."

Evelyn and Tristan had escaped by rowboat, but there would be no boat for her and Joslyn. Just the thick, sludgy water of the moat and the light of the stars. She would have her Kinetic strength to help her make the swim, but Joslyn would have only her arms. Arms that were, admittedly, about as broad as a pair of mainmasts.

The first breath of air outside the pipe was still tinged with refuse and mold and rotting things, but it tasted sweeter than the finest Gildesh pastry. She took a deep breath in, then dove headlong into the greenish water. It washed away the three-inch layer of unspeakable things that had built up on her hands and knees during the steep downhill climb through the Tunnel of Hell, then started in on the coating of grime and sweat that had settled over her down in that foul prison cell.

Joslyn hadn't been lying about her swimming skills. Even without the help of Kinetic magic, she reached the rocks on the far side of the river moat before Ryia did, pulling herself out of the water and shaking out her dripping sleeves as Ryia rolled onto the bank beside her. Apparently, the guards didn't care enough about their posts to crawl through shit, because no shining, helmeted heads appeared in the mouth of the pipe that was now a few yards upriver. But that luck couldn't hold for long. Within minutes, Adept and guards and hounds and Felice only knew what else would come streaming out of the gates, and the first place they would look would be the banks surrounding the moat. It was time to move. But to where?

"You coming?"

Ryia looked up at Joslyn, who was wringing out the hem of her coat a few steps away. "Coming where?"

Joslyn nodded toward a set of docks, silhouetted in moonlight, just past the nearest bridge. "It's been a long-ass while since I've been on a ship. I think it's time."

"I suppose you've got some gold for passage tucked up your ass, then?" Ryia asked, squeezing half the river out of her shirt.

Joslyn smiled mischievously back at her. "You let me worry about that."

Ryia wasn't sure exactly how Joslyn managed

it, but just a quarter of an hour later, the pair of them stood on the deck of a river barge heading west. Ryia was not at all sorry to leave the stinking hovel of Duskhaven behind. The city shrank into the distance as the barge followed the flow of the Rowan River toward the Yawning Sea.

CHAPTER ELEVEN

Tristan

"Oh, come off it—you call that a wager? There's going to be more coin in our cups than our pockets by the end of this game if you keep betting like that!"

Tristan had fallen back in step with his old Lottery persona almost the second Evelyn had stepped out the door to stake out the Upper Roost. It felt like slipping into a pair of boots he had recently outgrown—well-worn and familiar . . . though something about it just didn't fit quite right anymore.

Tristan's opponent scowled at him over the table in the common room of the Cellar Mouse as the men gathered around hooted and hollered. If there was one thing Tristan had learned from Ivan Rezkoye, it was that being watched by a crowd made men do stupid things. Things like bet too much gold on a game with a stranger. The man scratched his beard with one filthy hand, then threw down another few silver halves.

"That enough to shut you up?" he grunted.

"I guess," Tristan sighed. He turned to the gathered crowd with his most dazzling smile. "Who wants to count us off? How about you?"

He winked at a pale-faced woman beside his opponent.

She nodded, blushing just a bit at his grin. He and the other man each grabbed a single copper as she laid her hands across the table between them.

"Three . . . two . . . one . . . Fly!" the woman said.

Tristan and the other man each threw their coppers down onto the tabletop. The bearded man's caught a bad bounce off a knife gouge in the table and skidded sideways. He frowned and grabbed another coin. Tristan's first throw was dead on, but too low. Instead of bouncing into his cup, it tinked gently off the side. He hadn't missed a copper bounce since his third day in the Lottery all those months ago. In his defense, he was a bit rusty. And he was using his left hand—keeping his right under the table to hide Callum Clem's deadly brand.

Even left-handed, his second bounce landed true. It sprang straight up in the air, glinting in the lantern light for a second before landing in his lukewarm ale with a plop. Another plop on the other side of the table told him the bearded man's throw had been true as well.

"Save Thamorr!" the crowd started to chant. "Save Thamorr!"

That was the name of the game, after all. Thamorri coppers had an outline of Thamorr stamped into their surface. And now all of Thamorr was drowning in ale. There was only one way to save it.

Tristan lifted his cup to his lips, swallowing the disgusting ale with practiced speed. Three gulps were all it took to drain the cup. He slammed it down on the table barely an instant before the bearded man did the same. The small gathered crowd shouted and jeered. Tristan grinned, wiping his mouth before reaching for the small pile of silver in the middle of the table. It was almost impossible to cheat at Save Thamorr, but the quick fingers that made him such an expert cheat at cards had always made him better than the average man at the skilled drinking game. Usually he won by a much larger margin than that, though. He made a mental note to practice more with his left hand, or to make like Cam and gouge Clem's brand out of his skin.

He counted out the silvers carefully, then added them to his pouch. With these, plus the coin he had won playing Flaxman's Cup with a set of loaded dice he had lifted off an unsuspecting drunkard, he was up to about three crescents in silver. Not bad for a few hours' work. He grinned to himself. The rush of winning felt even better knowing he didn't have to give a single copper to Callum Clem.

"Who's up for another—" he started, then broke off as the common room door opened. A very windswept Evelyn Linley stepped in, her curly red hair tangled around her face. “Excuse me a moment, gentlemen. I’ll take more of your coppers later,” he said, slinging the table a knowing wink. The men grumbled or guffawed appreciatively. By the time he was three steps away, they were already involved in some other game, and he was completely forgotten.

“Did you get it?” he whispered.

“Not here” was all Evelyn said, glancing around anxiously. She seemed oddly spooked, the way his younger brother had always looked after hearing a scary story—peering around every corner before turning, as though expecting an attack.

He followed Evelyn out of the common room and up the staircase to their room. When they got inside, she locked the door behind them, then checked the tiny wardrobe, behind the moldering curtains, and under the bed before taking a deep breath and sinking into the stained armchair beside the window. Tristan waited for a few seconds, and when she didn’t speak, he thrust his arms out.

“Well?”

Evelyn shook her head. “It wasn’t there.” She leaned forward, resting her forehead on her left thumb and forefinger. “I dug that room apart. Nothing.”

Tristan opened his mouth, then closed it again.

Then finally said, "If it wasn't there, what's all the secrecy for?" So far everything she had said could have been shouted in that common room for all to hear, and no one would have had any idea what it meant or why they should care. There had to be something more. Had Asher mastered the Quill already? Winter was fast approaching, it was true. Were they finally out of time?

"Asher and Rafferty came into the room while I was still there."

"Asher and—" Tristan's eyes bugged out of his skull. "Did they see you? Do we need to leave? Now?"

"We need to leave, but not because they saw me. They didn't. But I overheard . . ." Evelyn scrubbed both hands over her face, then looked up at him. "Callum Clem is alive, Tristan."

For a few seconds, everything went silent. A ringing filled Tristan's ears, like his head was a gong that had just been struck. "What?"

Evelyn pushed herself to her feet, running a hand over her hair in an attempt to smooth it. It didn't work. She grabbed the satchel they had shared on the way to Carrowwick and began throwing their belongings inside. It didn't take long. "He's alive and has turned up in Golden Port, apparently." She faced him, eyes blazing, thrusting the satchel into his arms. "He has the Quill, Tristan. I know he does. Why else would he abandon his little empire? Leave Carrowwick?" She took a breath, trying to smooth her hair again. "He swapped the Quill for a fake and fled. Maybe before any of us even set foot in the Catacombs that night."

Tristan fingered the strap on the satchel, his teeth grinding together almost painfully as he studied the wicked brand on his right wrist. Callum Clem in charge of the Lottery had been bad enough. Callum Clem gifted with the ability to control every Adept servant in Thamorr? Tristan remembered the way the world had spun when he placed his finger on the Quill. The way he had seen through a thousand eyes at once. How he had stopped the beast attacking Ryia from splitting her throat an instant before its talons came screaming down. His stomach curdled. Clem would have no desire to stop the Adept monsters he touched from attacking someone. Once he mastered the Quill, all of Thamorr would burn.

"So what do we do?" he asked.

Evelyn was already walking toward the door. "What do you think we do? We go to Golden Port. Now, before the slippery git has the chance to escape again. Without horses it'll take us a little longer, but I think we can make it in a week or two if the weather holds."

"You want to go on *foot?*"

"Do you have a better idea?"

Tristan cocked one eyebrow. "You do know this is a dock town, right?"

"I lived here a lot longer than you bloody did," Evelyn said. "Which means I also know booking passage on a ship costs coin—coin we don't have."

"Speak for yourself," Tristan said, smirking as he walked a silver half across the backs of his knuckles.

"How did you—" Evelyn started, then she broke off. "Has anyone ever told you you have a ruddy gambling problem?"

"Is it *really* gambling if I never lose?"

"For Adalina's sake, you're annoying." Evelyn turned the rusted doorknob. "Let's hop on the first ship heading out of this pisshole."

"And into the next pisshole on our tour of the seedy underbelly of Thamorr," Tristan said sourly.

Evelyn turned back in the dark hallway. "Did you just say 'piss'?" She tutted. "Your manners tutors would be so disappointed."

"Say that a little louder, would you?" Tristan said, peering over both shoulders. They were alone in the corridor.

"Oh please," Evelyn said, starting down the creaky stairs. "Your wrist is more likely to get us killed in this bloody place than your real name."

Tristan hastily stowed his branded right hand in his pocket as they walked through the common room and out of the Cellar Mouse. Night was already lifting outside, the sky taking on the deep, purplish crimson of early dawn. Suddenly

Tristan felt exhaustion pulling at his limbs. If he had known they would be setting off again so soon, he would have taken some time away from his gambling to sleep. Then again, they might not have had enough gold to buy their way onto a ship. Walking all the way to Golden Port on a full night's sleep would be a lot more tiring than walking to the docks without one.

They skipped over the seedier docks to the south, heading straight for the trade docks north of the Lottery. They found a ship bound for Golden Port within minutes. A fur-trading vessel out of Boreas. Tristan wasn't sure how many people in a place like Golden Port could afford furs, but he wasn't about to question it—especially not since the captain only charged them three silvers apiece for passage, provided they weren't carrying anything that would cause trouble with the Disciples prowling the docks, and provided they didn't need a cabin. Tristan was ready to cough up some extra gold for the cabin, but Evelyn scoffed and marked them out a corner in the back of the crew's quarters.

He thought about mentioning how dangerous it could be for a woman in a place like this . . . then he remembered all the times he had seen Evelyn draw that sword of hers. In truth, the crewmen surrounding them were in a lot more danger than Evelyn was, should they decide to try anything stupid.

Fortunately, none of them did. After the terror-inducing experience of having a pair of Disciples search them cap to trousers on the Carrowwick docks, the journey was short and uneventful. They set sail just after noon and sailed through the evening and the night. By the time the sun rose, vibrant and pink on the horizon to the east, the men were running around on deck, shouting orders in Borean, pulling ropes, and lowering oars to steer the ship safely into the harbor at Golden Port.

Tristan had only been to Golden Port once before. That time, he'd had both Ryia and Evelyn at his back, and still had been profoundly relieved that they left the city the same day they arrived. People said the Lottery was the disease of Carrowwick. If that was true, then Golden Port was a city whose disease had conquered its host. Sure, Golden Port had merchants and guards, but they lived in small pockets surrounded by slipshod structures and seedy storefronts . . . and most of them were tangled up with whatever syndicates prowled these streets anyway. Tristan didn't know the names of the gangs here, and he didn't want to. The less time they spent in this festering pit of a town the better.

"So," he asked, shouldering their meager pack as they stepped off the gangplank and onto the dock. At least there were no Disciples gliding along the streets here. Yet. "Where do we start looking?"

Evelyn patted her sword, like she was assuring herself it was still there, though he was pretty sure it hadn't left her waist since they left the Shadow Keep. "You know the man better than I do."

Tristan snorted. "I don't even think Clem's own mother really knows Clem." The phrase "Clem's mother" sounded odd to his ears. He supposed the man had to have a mother—he had to have been born, after all—but it was impossible to picture the Snake of the Southern Dock as a small child, sitting on a bended knee.

"Right, then. I guess we should start at that tavern." She set off heading north, long legs taking such quick strides that Tristan had to jog to keep up.

"Why?" he asked, feeling ridiculous as he trotted along beside her. He glanced up at the swinging sign they were walking toward: the fisherman's hold.

"Because it smells like they're frying fish, and I'm bloody starving."

The tavern reminded Tristan instantly of the Miscreants' Temple. Not only was it run-down and dingy, yet oddly homey, but it was also far too busy for this early hour of the morning. Of course, the rules of upper-class society rarely applied to the shadowy corners of Thamorr. In fairness, if you spent your nights working at one of the taverns or loading merchant ships, then going for an ale at seven in the morning was hardly any different from a respectable merchant reaching for a glass of Gildesh red in the evening when his day was done, was it?

The rail of the bar was filled with lone men and women in mud-covered boots and salt-stained coats, and about half a dozen of the tables held folks smoking, playing cards, or breaking their fast with large slabs of the fried fish Evelyn had smelled from the street.

Evelyn moved to settle down at a table beside the door, but Tristan waved her on toward the bar. He plopped down beside a grizzled man with a mane of gray hair and fingers so callused they would have made Nash's palms look like the hands of a noblewoman. The barkeeper was a woman. She was even taller and thinner than Evelyn, but she didn't look delicate. If anything, she reminded Tristan of a spear; hard, steely, and deadly. Her grayish-blue eyes surveyed them for a moment, and then she raised one dark brown eyebrow.

"What are you looking for?"

"Breakfast," said Evelyn.

At the same time Tristan said, "A man."

Her eyebrow climbed another few inches and Tristan flushed. "I mean, breakfast. But we just arrived in the city this morning, and we're wondering if you've seen a . . . friend of ours."

"It's possible." The barkeeper picked her teeth

with her tongue. "I see a lot of people." Tristan counted out five coppers and slid them across the bar top toward her. She eyed the coins a second, then scooped them up. "Give me just a few minutes."

They ordered a breakfast special each, which was a slab of fried cod paired with a flaky biscuit drizzled with Dresdellan honey. It cost them a silver half apiece, but it was the first decent meal Tristan had eaten since leaving his cushy prison in the Shadow Keep, so it was worth every single copper. He was licking the last bits of grease from his fingers, Evelyn scooping the last traces of honey from her empty plate with her last bit of biscuit, when the barkeeper finally returned.

She leaned over the bar toward them. The bones in her chest stuck out like the rungs on a ladder. "So. You're looking for someone. A *friend*."

The way she said the word "friend" made Tristan certain she knew they were actually looking for an enemy. Thankfully, in a place like this, people didn't worry much about secondhand blood on their hands. If she could earn a few coppers helping them find Clem, what did she care what they meant to do with him when they found him?

"His name is Callum Cl—" Evelyn started.

"You think anyone uses their real name in a place like this?" The barkeeper waved her off. "Names aren't gonna help me."

"We're looking for a . . . well-dressed man," Tristan said slowly.

"Well, that already narrows it down," the barkeep said, sucking on her teeth.

Tristan licked his lips, thinking. Clem would have had to flee Carrowwick with only what he could carry. He would probably have had to spend a fair bit of coin buying passage here, just like he and Evelyn had. "Well-dressed, but without gold. He's probably staying somewhere far from the trade docks."

"Hmm, I'm not sure. I'm havin' some trouble remembering. . . ." She tapped her fingernails on the bar top.

Tristan rolled his eyes. He had expected this. He pulled another pair of coppers out of his purse and walked them across his knuckles, dropped them on the bar, and pushed them across to her.

She scooped them up, then leaned in closer. "I remember now. I haven't seen any man like that. Sorry for your luck." She grinned and cocked her head. "You all done with these? Great, I'll just take them, then." She cleared their empty plates and disappeared behind the swinging doors to the kitchen.

"Shite," Evelyn swore.

"Yeah, I was afraid of that," Tristan muttered. He peered into his purse. Six silvers and four coppers winked up at him from the depths. Enough for another meal or two in this part of the city. Maybe enough for a bed in a much shadier part, but not for more than one night. Definitely not enough for horses. Whatever happened here, they would be leaving on foot.

He turned instinctively as he felt a tap on his left arm, then looked up, turning to see it was the grizzled old sailor seated next to him at the bar. "Hey, String Bean, I think I know the git you and Red are after."

"Why is it always Red?" Evelyn grumbled under her breath. But Tristan held up a hand.

"You've seen him? Here in the city?" Tristan asked, turning.

"No, but I heard about him. Heard he was here." The man's right bicep twitched, almost unconsciously.

Tristan swallowed, noting the size of the muscle hidden underneath the man's dirty coat. So far, he seemed friendly. Or as friendly as a stranger in Golden Port was likely to be, at least. Hopefully he'd stay that way.

"Do you know where he is?" Evelyn asked, leaning forward.

The man leaned back, folding his arms across his chest and scratching his beard with one beefy hand. "I don't know for sure, but last I heard, the prat was seen down on Skuller's Lane. Careful, though. He's got his ruddy beasts with him."

"His beasts?" Tristan asked, perplexed.

The sailor leaned forward, looking around

before whispering, "Kinetics. Two of 'em. Nasty-lookin' things. At least four rebrands on each of 'em."

A chill slithered down Tristan's spine. He remembered the night Clem had won those Kinetics. He had seen it, in the alleys of the Lottery. Seen the glint in the Snake of the Southern Dock's eye as he watched his creatures tear an unfortunate merchant to shreds.

"Where is this Skuller's Lane?" Evelyn asked, eyes narrowed in focus. Tristan dragged himself from the horrible memory of thrashing Kinetic claws in time to see the sailor point toward the southeastern corner of the tavern.

" 'Bout four streets that way. Make a left and head back toward the docks. When you see the slags selling *vitalité* out in broad daylight, you'll know you've made it there."

Tristan swallowed. Skuller's Lane sounded charming. Then he frowned. "Why are you telling us all this? For free, I mean."

The man gave a deep chuckle. "Because I can tell Callum Clem isn't your fucking friend." He rolled up his left sleeve a few inches, tilting his arm to show them a greenish tattoo. A tattoo of a woman with eagle's wings. A harpy. One of the men in Harlow Finn's gang, then—the gang Clem had run out of Carrowwick over the summer. He rolled the sleeve back down with a wink. "Happy hunting."

With that, he turned back to his ale and his pipe, not saying another word.

But he had given them exactly the clue that they needed. Callum Clem had been spotted in the city, most recently someplace called Skuller's Lane. Shooting one last glare at the scamming barkeep, they stalked out the door and into the near-blinding sunlight.

As they walked through the mucky streets, Tristan was vaguely aware that autumn must be quite nice this far south. He associated autumn with biting winds and the first morning frosts, but here, so close to the border with Gildemar, autumn seemed to mean crisp air and warm sunshine. No wonder the Gildesh were so jolly all the cursed time. Not only did they have the best wine in all the kingdoms of Thamorr, but it seemed they had the best weather to boot. Maybe that was why his father hated them so much.

Four streets south and east, they turned left and found themselves someplace where even Ryia would have kept one hand on her hatchets at all times. There were men passed out on stoops, their eyes rimmed with the vivid red found only on the faces of dormire's blood huffers. Stalls of foul-smelling fish were set up right next to stalls selling small bags of the little Borean pellets Ivan had bought for their trip to the Guildmaster's island, vials of thick liquid Tristan could only assume were poison, and bundles of dried, spiky

Gildesh leaves that were mashed up to form *vitalité*.

Tristan noticed a few suspicious eyes turning their way. He elbowed Evelyn in the ribs.

"Don't walk like that."

"Like what?" she asked indignantly.

"Like a guard. Slouch your shoulders a little bit or something." Tristan mimed the motion.

"Oh shut up," Evelyn snapped back, but she did slouch just a bit, relaxing her shoulders and resting her hand on the hilt of her sword in a way that looked more cocky and less regimented. She still looked a bit formal, but more like a hired sword and less like a soldier coming to kick off a raid.

Tristan was just about to ask where she thought they should start looking when he caught sight of a small crowd gathered just outside a shop halfway down the lane. Something bubbled low in the pit of his stomach. Intuition. Intuition mixed with a healthy dose of dread. The Harpy in the tavern had told them to go to Skuller's Lane . . . and now there was a crowd on the street far too early for any sort of crowd to be gathering in a place like this. There was no way the two things weren't connected.

He turned to Evelyn. Her lips were pressed together so tightly that they looked almost as pale as the rest of her freckled face. She nodded curtly, and he knew she was thinking the same thing. He returned the nod, and they fell in step side by side, stalking toward the crowd.

They stood gathered at the stoop of a weaver's shop. A battered sign hung over the door, featuring no words, just a ball of yarn and a pair of crossed needles, positioned like the skull and crossbones of a freebooter flag. The shop was completely silent, which was odd in itself. Tristan hadn't spent a lot of time around weaver shops, but he wasn't sure he had ever heard the one in the Lottery go completely silent. There was always at least one loom clattering somewhere in the darkness.

"Why Bornchev?" a woman with stringy gray hair was asking.

"Maybe he owed the Skullrats some crescents he couldn't pay back?" asked a man in a fisherman's coat.

The woman shook her head. "He's been livin' above this here shop since before I was even born, and he never caused a speck of trouble."

"Half the Skullrats grew up on his bloody stories," piped in a rotund man. "More likely they'd run through his killer than they would do anything like this to him."

They grew silent, narrowing suspicious eyes in Tristan and Evelyn's direction as they approached.

"What happened here?" Evelyn asked.

"Who's asking?" asked the fisherman.

Tristan felt Evelyn's hackles rise, and he held a hand out to stop her. "We're hunting someone. Someone dangerous." He nodded at the staircase they were all clustered around. "Something tells me he might have been here."

The round man looked Tristan up and down. "You lot are bounty hunters?"

Tristan understood the suspicion—he didn't exactly look the type. But maybe Evelyn did. Thankfully, she picked up on the game immediately, widening her stance and slipping into her best impression of Ryia Cautella. It was dead-on, from the smirk to the carnivorous glint in her eye.

"We are," she said, running her tongue over her teeth. "And I'll tell you one thing: the son of a bitch we're after is no Skullrat."

The gray-haired woman shuddered. "Well, I'll tell you, there's no way in Felice's deepest hell that one man did what happened up there."

Tristan's stomach bubbled and curdled sickeningly. He and Evelyn shared a look, then Evelyn said, "The man we're after isn't alone." She paused, picking at her fingernails for a second, then nodded up the stairs. "Want to stand aside so we can take a bloody look?"

"A *bloody* look is exactly what you'll get," the round man said.

Tristan didn't like the sound of that at all, but before he had the chance to even think about it, the crowd had parted down the middle and Evelyn was leading him up those creaking, driftwood stairs. The door to the apartment was open. Tristan's first thought upon walking into the room was that he was glad it wasn't summer. The cool air filtering in through the cracks in the walls and the open doorway was the only thing that kept him from vomiting every bite of his too-expensive breakfast onto the floor.

If he hadn't overheard the conversation at the base of the stairs, he wouldn't immediately have known the figure in the apartment was a man at all. Blood pooled all over the floor, and odd pieces of flesh clung to everything: the walls, the furniture, even the cursed ceiling. If Tristan closed his eyes, he could see it happening. See Callum Clem standing there, cold and unfeeling, watching as his trained mutts tore into this poor man's skin, pulling him apart at the seams. If this was the kind of damage Clem could do with just two Kinetics at his beck and call, imagine what he would be capable of when he could pull the strings of the entire Adept population. They had to find him before he destroyed all of Thamorr.

"Clem's work?" Evelyn asked, prodding a disembodied leg with one toe.

"Absolutely," Tristan said, wrinkling his nose.

"Great. So, to find him we just need to figure out why in Felice's bitterest hell he decided to kill this poor man."

"Gold?" Tristan guessed.

Evelyn raised an eyebrow, gesturing around the apartment. "It doesn't exactly look like he was a ruddy lord."

"He was a storyteller."

Tristan nearly jumped out of his skeleton at the sound of a new voice. It came from near the door. He turned to see one of the people from the crowd. An old man with yellowing teeth and a sallow face who hadn't spoken before. It was clear why—his voice was scratchy beyond belief, like every word was being dragged up a throat made of sanding paper and rusted needles.

"A storyteller?" Evelyn asked, perplexed. "Why would anyone want to kill a ruddy storyteller?"

The man in the door shrugged. "No one *did* want to kill him for near fifty years in the bloodiest street in Golden Port."

Tristan's head started to clear as they left the gore-soaked apartment behind them, but still, the pieces didn't fit together. The more they learned from the crowd, the less things made sense. He was an old man who told stories to travelers for coins and to children for free. He had a bit of a drinking problem, but he had lived above the weaver's shop for as long as anyone could remember and had never stolen so much as a leaf of pipeweed.

"What about before he came to Golden Port?" Evelyn asked, chewing on the inside of her cheek. "Any chance he was a no-good son of a bitch then?"

"Unless the man after him was near eighty years old, I doubt that matters," said the stringy-haired woman. "I don't know where the man came from—"

"Boreas," chimed in the gravel-voiced old man who had scared them in the doorway.

"No shit, Gabriel," she said, rolling her eyes. She turned back to Evelyn. "If he had any enemies back then, I'd think Felice's hounds would have come for them by now, eh?"

She had a point. Outside of lords and kings, no one lived much past sixty or seventy in Thamorr—not unless they were very lucky or very rich. Besides, Tristan was already certain that Clem had done this. Whoever this poor old storyteller had been before coming here was irrelevant. But without knowing why Clem had killed this man, how would they know where the Snake had gone? How would they be able to track him down again?

"Well, this day is about to get even worse."

Tristan yanked himself from his thoughts as the round man spoke. He followed the man's gaze, looking toward the ramshackle stretch of docks that held fishing boats and smugglers' ships. His heart dropped into his stomach. A sleek, narrow-masted sloop with vivid blue sails peeked from between the buildings.

"Now, it's been a long-ass time since I seen one of them," said the man in the salt-stained fisherman's coat. "Who do you think they're here for? Miriam and Francis's kid?"

"No, that kid is almost two, you git," said the stringy-haired woman. "Named and everything. Has to be—"

"They're not here for a baby," Tristan said. His voice was shaking slightly, but he had never been more certain. He turned to Evelyn. She was white as a sheet. "Looks like we're not the only ones on Clem's tail."

Evelyn shook her head, growing somehow even whiter. "He won't be after Clem."

"What do you m—"

"He never saw Clem on that island."

Realization crashed over Tristan. The only thieves the Guildmaster had seen the day of the auction were the ones in the bell tower. Clem hadn't been inside the bell tower when their schemes all fell to pieces. But Evelyn had.

Tristan thought he saw the memory of that horrible day reflected in Evelyn's gaze as she whispered, "He's looking for me."

CHAPTER TWELVE
Nash

"Are you ready to sail?"

Nash looked up at the voice. All she could see was Ivan's silhouette. She looked back down to the game of stones she was playing against herself. "Sail with what, exactly, Rezkoye? In case you forgot, we don't have any twice-damned sai—" She broke off mid-word as the Kinetics appeared in the doorway of their room at the Gull's Gullet behind Ivan, each carrying a thick canvas bundle. Sails, folded up tight. "Where did you get the coin to buy those?"

She didn't need him to answer; she already knew. She had seen Clem ransack Bornchev's apartment after the massacre. Seen him take every last copper the poor man had squirreled away over the years. To sum up, these sails had been bought with the blood of an innocent old storyteller, and Ivan Rezkoye didn't seem to give a single shit. And to think, there had been a time, not all that long ago, when Nash thought there might be a kind man behind that icy exterior . . . but no. No use thinking of that now.

There was no point in resisting. Golden Port was filled with sailors who would cut a hundred throats to get their own ship. If Nash wouldn't sail *The Hardship* for Clem, he would just set his Kinetics on her and find someone who would. Now that she had seen those two Adept rip someone apart firsthand, she had to admit she was scared senseless at the thought.

The Hardship was ready to sail before nightfall. She and the Kinetics outfitted the vessel with its new sails . . . though "new" wasn't quite the right word. They were riddled with patches and holes and bird droppings—enough of each that Nash wondered if they had just bought their old sails back for twice the gold they were worth. Not that it mattered. If Clem got his way, they would all be filthy rich and ruling the world before winter came crashing down on Boreas. If he didn't, they'd all be dead.

That sure put things into perspective.

The sun dipped below the horizon just as *The Hardship* pulled away from the docks at Golden Port, leaving the blood-soaked memory of Gavril Bornchev behind them.

Nash cleared her throat. "What's our heading?"

"Have you forgotten your dear storyteller's tale already?" Clem said, his voice thin with amusement. Nash could have throttled him. "We make for Boreas. For the Reclaimed Castle."

"The Reclaimed Castle," Nash repeated. "Now I wonder if *you've* forgotten Bornchev's story."

"And why is that?" Clem's voice took on a

dangerous tone. She didn't even have to look at him to know his ice-blue eyes had narrowed in challenge.

"The Guildmaster and all his Disciples couldn't find the dagger when they raided that twice-damned castle," Nash said. "You honestly don't think King Andrei is going to just let us waltz right in and take it, do you?" She looked to Ivan, imploring him to talk some sense into the Snake. She should have known by now that he was no ally to her. Not anymore.

"We will not *waltz* in," Ivan said. He paused, considering. "Or rather, we *will,* but we will not do this as ourselves."

"Precisely," Clem said. He leaned back against the rail, his now shoulder-length blond hair tossing in the sea breeze. Even in the lowest pits of the Golden Port gutter, the Snake had found the means and the time to have a decent wash. He tapped his pristine fingernails along the rail. "Did you know that, just two days ago, our old friend Tolliver Shadowwood openly declared war on Gildemar?"

Nash blinked. She didn't know what she had expected him to say, but it definitely wasn't that.

Clem shared an irritatingly knowing look with Ivan, then flashed a reptilian smile. "Yes, for the first time in a hundred years or more, two of the kingdoms of Thamorr may be going to war. What will dear King Andrei do in such a situation, Ivan?"

"He will call together a meeting of the Borean lords," Ivan said stiffly.

Clem picked one set of perfectly clean fingernails with the other. "And how many lords are there in the kingdom of Boreas?"

"Dozens."

There was a long silence. Nash ran her hands over her tangled black hair. "So you think you can just, what, throw on some furs, claim to be Lord Fredrik von Volkfier or some other made-up name, and march right past the *medev* into the Reclaimed Castle?"

"Of course not," said Clem. "No doubt the Borean king knows the names of all his lords, even if none of the rest of us do."

"Then what exactly is your plan?"

"Simple," Clem said, scratching his chin. "We enter as one of the existing lords."

Nash's stomach twisted. She studied the horizon for a second, adjusting the mainsail and their heading a hair as the sail began to luff. "I think someone will notice if there are two lords with the same name in the room."

"There will not be," Ivan said. "We will ensure that one of the invited lords does not attend the meeting."

"How do you suggest we do that?" Nash asked, wheeling on Ivan to stare him down. The infuriatingly handsome Borean man stared right back for a few seconds, then blinked and looked away. He never answered, but it didn't matter. Nash already knew what he and Clem intended to do.

Bornchev the storyteller's blood hadn't been enough to satisfy their thirst. Now they had to prey on some innocent lord. Murder him and steal his identity just to go chasing after some stupid knife that would give Callum fucking Clem far too much power for any man, let alone a man like him. There was no way Ivan was truly okay with this. He still had a heart inside that icy, Borean exterior—she had seen the evidence of it herself. Seen him spring into action to save Ryia and Evelyn back on the island . . . and wasn't he the one who'd said they couldn't sell the Quill to an unpredictable, violent man like Tolliver Shadowwood? Who was more violent and unpredictable than Clem, especially in his current state?

There was something else at play here. Something he wasn't telling her, because he didn't trust her to know.

Clem and Ivan plotted on deck through the night. They would sail directly for Volkfier to target a minor lord by the name of Gavik Piervin. Piervin was Clem's favorite type of target—powerful enough to get through the door, unimportant enough that none of the real players in the game really knew his face. Once the real Piervin was out of the way, Clem would take his place. His Kinetics would accompany him, and Nash would shave her head and join their ranks, posing as another of his Adept guards. That was all important, of course, but the real key was Ivan.

With Piervin's name and a bit of luck, they could get through the door, sure, but they'd never get within a line cast of the dagger's hiding place without a distraction. That was where Ivan came in. He would not be entering as a lord or an Adept servant, and there was only one other type of man allowed in the Reclaimed Castle for these negotiations. *Medev*. It would be up to Ivan to infiltrate the *medev*'s ranks and set the distraction that would allow Clem to go for the dagger.

Honestly, it wasn't the worst plan Nash had ever heard . . . except for the parts that made her stomach feel like it was full of half a dozen wriggling eels. She tapped her fingers along the edge of the namestone resting against her chest. *Ma, what would you think of me if you could see me now?*

When the sun finally started to burn away the darkness of the night, Clem rubbed his hands on his trousers, then made his way through the hatch, ready to sleep off his night of heinous plotting. Ivan sat on the crate he had been using as a chair for a few more minutes, staring off into the distance, studying waves tinged with the brightest pinks and most vibrant oranges. When he finally moved to stand, Nash waved to the Kinetic that was still awake. Clem had ordered the other to rest two hours ago, and he was still curled up in a ball a few feet from the prow.

"Hey, watch the wheel for a second, would you?" she asked.

The Adept walked over, blank-faced as ever, seized the ship's wheel, and stared straight north over the waves. Not for the first time, Nash wondered if any old Adept could take the helm like that or if the man Clem had stolen these two from was a sailor of some sort who had taught his Adept rigging and lines and how to plot a course.

She left the Adept to his steering, striding across the deck. Nervous sweat slicked her palms. Felice, she hated that. She wiped them on her trousers.

"Ivan, hold on," she said. Her voice sounded small. She cleared her throat. "Wait for just a second."

The disguise-master stiffened, halting mid-step and turning on the deck to face her. "I know what it is you are going to ask me, Nash."

"And what is that?"

The morning sunlight glinted off his blond hair as it riffled in the wind. "The same thing you asked me the last night we were all trapped on this *verdammte* ship." He turned his eyes on her. They were colder than usual. "You are going to ask me to betray Callum."

"Well, we don't have to put it like that," Nash said, cocking her head to one side. "What if instead, I ask you to . . . save an innocent man's life?"

Ivan snorted, a slight huff of air that barely counted as more than a breath. "I assume you are referring to Piervin?" His face grew hard. "There is no such thing as an innocent lord in Boreas, Nash."

"Maybe not," Nash said slowly. "But whatever this Lord Piervin has done, I'd be willing to bet all the gold in Thamorr he hasn't smiled as he stood by and watched his Kinetics savage an innocent man." Ivan swallowed, and Nash took another step toward him. "And that's the man you want to give *more* power to?"

"It is not that simple, Nash. I have *vortkom* I must keep."

Vortkom. One of the Borean words Nash knew from her years trading with smugglers from the north. It meant "promises."

"Promises you have to keep to whom?" she pressed. She gestured toward the closed hatch across the deck. "To Clem? Because I guarantee you, he wouldn't keep a promise to you if he could make a single twice-damned copper by breaking it."

"That is not—" Ivan started. He broke off, turning to look out over the sun-speckled waves. His left hand drifted up, like he was going to run it through his hair, but it paused just behind his left ear. When he lowered it, turning back to face Nash, she knew she had lost the battle. "I will take Callum into the Reclaimed Castle to free . . . the dagger if it takes my last breath from me."

His hesitation on naming the dagger was the only indication of any uncertainty. His hands were steady and his jaw set. There was no point in arguing anymore. Ivan Rezkoye, her closest ally in the flight from the Guildmaster's island, the only one of the Saints of the Wharf Nash thought she could truly trust, was gone from her now. He was Clem's man, through and through.

"Fine," Nash said, her voice sharp as a razor blade. "Then get used to the slick of blood on your palms, Rezkoye."

With that she shouldered past him, making her way down the hatch and into her own cramped cabin. She lay awake for hours, twisting her ma's namestone around and around on its leather strap in the darkness. She never heard Ivan come down the ladder behind her.

CHAPTER THIRTEEN

Ryia

"Get your ass up or get left behind."

"Whuzzat?" Ryia blinked, then winced as sunlight pierced her corneas.

A large shadow moved in to block the light. Joslyn. The pirate stretched a hand down toward her, and Ryia grasped it, allowing Joslyn to pull her to her feet. She scrubbed both palms over her face, then blinked, looking around. The harsh gray lines of Duskhaven were gone, giving way to a small, grimy-looking town buzzing with chaotic energy.

The captain of the barge called out orders to men and women positioned on the edges of the craft, and they dug long wooden poles into the greenish-brown waters of the Rowan, steering the flat, broad boat toward the river's edge. And there, on the northern banks of the river, sat the Edalish city of Fallowton. Ryia recognized it by the distinct buildings, made completely of dark gray clay.

She turned her eyes west. The greenish waters of the Rowan widened, churning and sloshing as they collided with the deep blue salt water of the open ocean. Vivid white sails dotted the horizon beyond, sailing in and out of Fallowton's harbor. The city was smaller than Carrowwick, but its energy was the same. The same energy Ryia had sensed in every dock town from Boreas to Briel—frantic, crowded, and tinged with the smells of fish and greed.

The barge had made good time down the Rowan, the sky was bright, but the sunlight was still pale with the sleepy orange glow of early morning. There would only be a few minutes until they docked, then the barge would unload its shipment of ale and grain, take on barrels of fish and whatever else the poor saps of Fallowton had to trade, then turn right around and pole its way back up the river to Duskhaven.

She stretched and yawned, then turned back to Joslyn. "Relax, it'll take them a few hours to unload. We can take a second and plan our next move before we—"

But before she finished her sentence, Joslyn had already taken off running. She planted both hands on the rail of the barge, then pushed off, vaulting over the few feet of water and landing with a puff of dust and the clatter of boots on the worn stone path lining the riverbank.

"Or we can just charge into the city without thinking," Ryia griped under her breath. Was this how Evelyn felt every time she took off without warning? Maybe she would have to stop doing that.

She shook the last bit of sleep from her limbs, then sprang after the pirate, easily clearing the rail and the water in one massive bound, landing nimbly on solid ground just beside Joslyn.

"This way," Joslyn said, hurrying into the tangle of clay-and-stone shops and houses behind them as angry voices rang out from the deck of the barge, calling curses and shooting rude hand gestures.

"Mind telling me why we decided to piss everyone off and jump overboard instead of waiting five minutes until the barge was docked?"

"I promised the captain we'd pay him when we docked in Fallowton." Joslyn looked over her shoulder with a shrug. "Technically, we never docked, so I don't owe him a single copper."

Ryia snorted. "Well, they're going to dock eventually. And when they do, I'd imagine they'll tell whatever pissant guards patrol this mud pit to arrest us, so I hope your plan has a stage two."

"It didn't until just now," Joslyn admitted, grinning over her shoulder. "But it looks like that lazy bitch Felice has finally decided to wake up and give us a twice-damned break." Ryia raised an eyebrow, and Joslyn pointed west toward the harbor. "You see that mast?"

"I see a lot of masts, Joslyn. It's a harbor." But as she looked out over the rooftops toward the tangle of sails, she saw the one Joslyn must be talking about.

It stood a little higher than the rest, toward the northern edge of the harbor. A small flag hung at the top, just like many of the other masts crowded there. A telltale, Ryia had heard Nash call it. A little scrap of fabric that flapped around to tell the helmsman what way the wind was blowing . . . Could they not *feel* the wind on their faces? Most of the telltales were solid and bright, but the little flag on top of the mast at the northern end of the harbor was black as pitch, except for the sigil emblazoned in vivid white stitching. A narrow, curved shape, pointed at one end.

An Ophidian fang.

"Your crew?" Ryia asked.

"Or some dumb son of a bitch thought it was a good idea to steal my ship." Joslyn tutted her tongue against her teeth as they veered left down another street, ignoring an aggressive vendor waving a bunch of carrots in their faces. "Either way, we're leaving the city on the *Fang*."

Ryia gestured to her hatchets. "You really think I can take an entire shipload of enemy freebooters by myself?"

"I guess we'll find out," Joslyn said darkly. Then she chuckled and punched Ryia in the arm. "Relax. I was messing around. It's my crew."

"How do you know?"

Joslyn just tapped the side of her nose in response, and Ryia understood. The ship smelled clean. They were still a ways out of range for

Ryia's senses to pick up on it, but she knew if the men on board were enemies, it would smell like a twice-damned mortuary to Joslyn right now.

If the bargemaster had sent the guards in this city to search for them, they were doing a shit job of it. Or maybe Joslyn was just doing a great job of keeping them clear of trouble. Every so often, Ryia thought she caught a whiff of danger, a hint of mulched earth and dried blood wafting on the wind, but the pirate was always three steps ahead of her, steering them down an alley or cutting through the common room of an inn, where the scent was replaced by the smells of piss, fish, and fresh-baked bread.

They left the crumbling clay buildings behind them, boots thudding hollowly on the wooden planks of the Fallowton docks.

"There she is," Joslyn said softly. Her tone was almost reverent—a tone Ryia had heard Nash use a hundred times when talking about her own ships.

Ryia turned toward the docks and saw it. The *Ophidian Fang*. Where most of Nash's smuggling ships had been smaller, unobtrusive vessels, the *Ophidian Fang* made no attempt at subtlety. The galleon towered above the other ships on this stretch of the docks. Its hull was stained so dark it almost looked black, even in the midmorning sunlight. The ship flew no flags, aside from the tiny telltale, flapping in the wind high above them, but it was unmistakably a freebooter vessel. Seemed risky to put in at a proper city like this one.

"Oy, shithead," Joslyn called out as she approached Fallowton's dockmaster.

"Maybe not the best way to start a conversation," Ryia said.

"It's all right; I know the man," Joslyn said.

"You know me," Ryia countered. "Doesn't mean I want you to start calling me shithead."

But the dockmaster's lips spread into a wide smile as he turned to see Joslyn approaching.

"Well, well, well." He clasped her hand in a firm shake, pulling her in to place his other hand on her elbow before releasing her. "I heard you were captured."

Joslyn waved him off. "The infamous Salt Beard is never captured. Where did you hear that rubbish?"

"From your crew," the dockmaster said, gesturing toward the docks behind him.

"You know better than I do that those saps all have bilgewater for brains," Joslyn said, clapping the dockmaster on the shoulder.

"That so?"

Ryia turned as a new voice joined the conversation. If they had been in Carrowwick, Ryia would have immediately assumed the man strolling up the dock toward them was one of Harlow Finn's Harpies. He was shorter than she was, but at least twice as broad, with swirls of fading blue ink peeking out from the torn neckline of his shirt and the sleeves of his cloak. His hair was long and tangled with a beard to match, and he wore both in thick, ropy braids.

"Derrik," Joslyn said, stepping forward to slap the man on his shoulder. "How in the hells are you?"

"Better than you, from the looks of it," he said, scanning her filth-stained clothes and the bruised-looking bags circling her eyes. "Where'd the bastard take you?"

"The Shadow Keep."

Derrik's left eyebrow twitched up toward his hairline. "How'd you wriggle your way out of that one?"

Joslyn grinned, grabbing Ryia's shoulder and ushering her a step forward like an overeager mother introducing her daughter to a new suitor. "I made a new friend. Derrik, meet the Butcher of Carrowwick."

"The Butcher of Carrowwick, eh?" the man said, stretching a hand toward her. "Wonder what you did to earn a title like that."

Ryia shook the man's hand. Then she ran her tongue over her teeth, tapping her fingers along the row of hatchets lining her belt. "Oh, you know, this and that."

The dockmaster feigned examining an invisible pocket watch. "Well, would you look at the time! I'd better be off." He patted Joslyn on the shoulder. "Good to see you're still in business. Until our next visit."

" 'Visit,' " Joslyn chortled as the man walked away. "He's a nice man for a skorp addict."

"Skorp?" Ryia asked. "Really?" The drug was made from the venom of groundmaster scorpions, a rare breed that only lived in the driest corners of the Brillish deserts. She had never seen an addict of the drug who wasn't batshit crazy . . . not to mention one who still had all his teeth.

"Yeah." Joslyn watched the dockmaster disappear into the crowds farther south along the docks. "I introduced him to the smuggler who brings it in for him. Weedy little fucker, but he doesn't dare piss me off, so he's reliable enough. But if I weren't around anymore . . . well, let's just say poor Dockmaster Wynne here wouldn't be the first man to get screwed over by that smuggler."

"Ah, that's why he was so relieved to see you," Ryia said. Joslyn provided him with a substance that was going to ruin his life, so he felt inclined to do her infinite favors. Kind of a cruddy dynamic, no matter how she looked at it.

She shook herself. If the man wanted to spend all his time and coin on skorp, that was his concern, not hers. And if Joslyn could profit off his terrible decisions, well, that was just good business. But still, the idea made her ears ring with a voice that sounded an awful lot like Evelyn Linley's.

But the time for talking about Wynne the doomed dockmaster had passed. She fell into step behind Joslyn and Derrik as they strode down the docks and onto the deck of the *Ophidian Fang*. The warm reception they had gotten from the dockmaster was nothing compared to the twice-damned party that broke out on board the *Fang* as soon as the crew caught sight of their beloved Salt Beard, back from torture, imprisonment, and certain death.

Before Joslyn had been taken, the *Fang* had been cornered in the Yawning Sea—Shadowwood's men closed in from one side, the Guildmaster's blue-sailed sloops from the other. When it was clear there was nowhere else to run, Joslyn had picked the lesser of the evils, taking the ship's rowboat in the middle of the night and rowing over to the Edalish warship to turn herself in. The crew told the rest of the story over a traditional Fallowton breakfast of baked oats and potatoes.

The Disciples had caught up with the *Fang* the morning after Joslyn had disappeared. They had searched the ship, ignoring all sorts of stolen gold and other assorted illegal things. They had all found that lucky but strange, but Ryia didn't. She knew what those bastards were looking for on the *Fang*. A rogue Senser who had escaped from their clutches before they could sell her off like livestock.

It didn't take much convincing to get the *Fang*'s crew to ready the ship and prepare to set sail. They had been languishing in Fallowton for weeks now, arguing whether they should try to rescue their captain or wait it out and hope she made it back to them on her own. But aside from bickering among themselves, they'd had nothing to do but eat and drink and gamble for days. Some men would have been thrilled with that to-do list, but these were sailors. They loved the open ocean as much as Ryia hated it. Before the sun was even halfway up, they had already pushed away from Fallowton Harbor and into the sparkling waves of the Yawning Sea.

If Ryia had thought Joslyn reminded her of Nash back in the prison cells of the Shadow Keep, they were almost indistinguishable from each other at the helm of a ship. Sure, Nash had thick, dark hair where Joslyn's shaved head gleamed golden brown in the sunlight, and Joslyn was missing the sharpened canines from Nash's infamous smile, but they both came alive at sea. They had the same laugh, the same shine to their eyes, the same easy stance and comfortable leadership.

A pang ran through Ryia's stomach at the thought, and she shook herself. Was she actually *missing* Clem's favorite smuggler? Feeling guilty for leaving her for dead back in Carrowwick? Felice, what was happening to her? She'd be writing poetry and learning the damned lute next if she wasn't careful.

It took just a little over a day for the tall, thin spires of the Bobbin Fort to appear on the horizon to the southeast. The crew took turns heading down to the cabins belowdecks to rest, and even Ryia spent a few hours curled up like a faithful hound dog in a corner of the deck, but Joslyn never left the helm for a second. Ryia rubbed the sleep from her eyes, pushed herself to her feet, and padded across the deck to stand beside her.

"Back on the *vitalité*?" She'd heard a person could stay awake for days at a time on the drug.

"Hmm?" Joslyn asked. She turned to face her, showing eyes lined with tiredness. "No, not yet. I just . . ." She trailed off, and Ryia narrowed her eyes.

"Just what?"

"How sure are you that your friends are in Carrowwick?"

"I—" Ryia broke off. How long had it been since she had sent Evelyn and Tristan ahead without her? It had been too easy to lose track of time in that twice-damned cage. "I don't know," she finally admitted. "But if we're going to help them steal and destroy that Quill, we have to start looking for them somewhere, right?"

"Well . . . there is something else we could

try." Joslyn was silent for a long moment, then turned to face her again. "What are the stakes here, Cautella? If we don't find your pals, what happens?"

Ryia ran her tongue along her teeth thoughtfully. Was Joslyn going to bail on her? She could make her think twice about that.

"What happens? Well, the Quill is currently out in the world, probably in the hands of an idiotic slumlord from Carrowwick. It's only a matter of time before he figures out how to use it." She cocked one eyebrow. "You think being chased by the Guildmaster was bad? At least he operates by a set of rules. Wyatt Asher is as ruthless as a starving street dog." She fixed Joslyn with her most carnivorous stare. "We don't find Evelyn and Tristan, we die. Maybe not today, maybe not tomorrow, but someday soon, and at the hands of a twice-damned maniac. Those are the stakes."

"So, the stakes are life and death?" Joslyn asked. She stared at her for a second, then cracked a smile, turning back to the horizon. "I can work with that." She lifted her nose, sniffing the air in a way Ryia recognized all too well.

"What are you doing?"

"Finding your friends." Joslyn sniffed again, wrinkled her nose, then turned her head a bit to the south, sniffing again.

Ryia snorted. "That's not how Senser magic works, Salt Beard." She looked around hurriedly, but there were no crew members close enough to overhear. Still, she lowered her voice. "Have you forgotten? I've got that particular skill set too. You can't trick me."

"Tell me, then, Butcher. How does that . . . *skill set* . . . work?" Joslyn asked, adjusting their course a hair, then sniffing again.

"You can detect *danger,* not people. Not objects. Felice, if Sensers could sniff their way to anything they liked, people would be using them like twice-damned hunting dogs."

"I am detecting danger," Joslyn said. She sniffed again, wrinkled her nose in displeasure, then readjusted course. "You just told me if we don't find your friends, we die, right?"

"Right."

"Okay, so every path that doesn't lead to your friends smells like shit to me now."

Ryia stared at her blankly as she reasoned out what the pirate had just said. Then: "So you just follow the one path that doesn't smell like shit, then?" She shook her head in disbelief. "Does that really work?"

"Not always." Joslyn shrugged. "But it worked when I first escaped the island. I knew if I didn't find a ship that would take me into their crew fast, I was deader than a bleeding man in Shark's Cove. I went to the only ship on the docks at Ruby Isle that didn't smell like a corpse rotting at the bottom of the ocean and . . ." She thrust her arms out, gesturing to herself, her ship, her crew. Obviously she had survived.

"Well, let me guess," Ryia said, sighing. "Carrowwick smells like shit."

"Carrowwick always smells like shit," Joslyn chortled. "But yeah, right now it smells a few degrees ranker than usual."

"And what way smells as sweet as an Edalish meadow, then?"

Joslyn sniffed the air a few more times, then lifted a finger, pointing. South. South and east, to be more precise. Ryia picked between her teeth with one jagged fingernail, thinking. Tristan and Evelyn had no ship, no gold, little to no supplies. They had set out for Carrowwick . . . but what if something had changed? For Felice's sake, Ryia had never anticipated meeting another free Adept in the cells of the Shadow Keep, joining her crew, and sailing south on the fabled *Ophidian Fang* pirate ship. Who was to say Tristan and Evelyn's path hadn't gone similarly batshit crazy? Maybe Wyatt Asher's eyes were set on greener pastures, now that he had the whole world in the palm of his hand.

"Let's follow that nose of yours," Ryia finally said.

Ryia woke to a boot kicking into her ribs.

"Wake up. We have a complication."

She blinked, glaring up at Joslyn, towering

over her, silhouetted against the bright blue sky. "Is that complication the fact that not sleeping for three days makes you a twice-damned nightmare to be around?" she asked, massaging her rib cage sourly.

Joslyn just pursed her lips and shook her head, raising one hand to point over the right-hand side of the ship.

Ryia pushed herself up, and the breath left her lungs as she turned to look. They had arrived at a familiar harbor. The run-down, sludge-filled docks of Golden Port. But that wasn't the complication. The complication was the set of too-blue sails peeking out from the other masts crowding the harbor.

"Let me guess," Ryia said. "Everything just smells like shit now?" There was no more path to follow. Evelyn and Tristan had to be here—the *Quill* had to be here—that was why the Disciples had come to Golden Port. She could feel it in her bones.

"Yep." Joslyn glanced over her shoulder toward the helm, where one of her crewmen stood, hands on the wheel, eyes on her, clearly waiting for instruction.

Ryia licked her lips, thinking fast. "All right, lower one of those little rowboats for me. I'll take it in and—"

"Who are you, Hotar the Heroic?" Joslyn snorted, naming one of history's most famous

Brillish warriors. "You try to row in there on a damned dinghy, and you'll be dead before you get within a net's cast of that Quill."

Ryia grinned. "I think you're forgetting just how . . . skilled I am."

Joslyn cocked one eyebrow. "And I think *you're* forgetting that you're not the only one on this ship who wants to see that Quill turned to splinters."

Ryia's grin dripped off her face. "What are you planning, then?"

"I'm planning to keep you alive long enough to find those friends of yours," Joslyn said. Then she raised her voice and said, "Putting in at Golden Port!"

"Putting in at Golden Port!" echoed a few other voices.

"Putting in at *vitalité* port," said the reedy man at the helm.

"Shut the fuck up, Fagan," Joslyn chortled.

As they drew nearer to the docks, Ryia got a closer and closer view of the ship attached to those aggressively blue sails. It was larger than the sloops she had seen in the past, and it looked newer, finer. Her stomach dropped and tossed, her lip curling with a mix of fear and anger. She had never seen that ship before, but she knew it wasn't just any old Disciple ship. It had to be the ship of the Bastard King himself—her old enemy, the seventh Guildmaster of Thamorr. Joslyn's knuckles grew white as she gripped the helm like she was choking a man, and Ryia knew the pirate had come to the same conclusion.

The men lashed the ship to an open stretch of dock, and Joslyn turned to them. "All right, I can't tell you what's going on just yet, but my new friend and I are on a bit of a suicide mission." She grinned. "If you want to clear out, head out into the city and stay here. If I survive what I'm about to do, you'll be welcome back on the *Fang* whenever you find us in port again. If not . . . well, find yourself another twice-damned captain and get back to work. If your curiosity gets the better of you, though, outfit the ship with fresh supplies as fast as you can and be ready to cast off at any second." She cocked her head at Fagan. "If I make it back to the *Fang*, I promise I'll spill all my secrets as soon as we're clear of the harbor, deal?"

No one spoke.

Joslyn nodded at Ryia. "Ready?" She leapt over the side rail and landed with a thud on the dock. The dockmaster at Golden Port was clearly just as friendly with the pirate as the one back in Fallowton—he pretended he didn't even see her and Ryia as they hurried past, making their way toward the cluttered structures of the city beyond the docks.

"Nice speech," Ryia quipped, struggling to keep pace with Joslyn's long strides without jogging. "Of course, we're done for if they all decide to scarper before we get back, but I'm sure you thought of that already."

"Scarper?" Joslyn laughed. "Felice, you spent too long in Dresdell if you're using words like 'scarper.'"

"A single day in Dresdell is too long," Ryia snorted back. She'd probably picked the word up from Evelyn. And if they didn't find her and Tristan in this tangle of streets before the Guildmaster did, she'd never get the chance to learn more piss-poor Dresdellan slang. Her pulse ticked up a few beats, and she picked up the pace.

"They won't all leave," Joslyn said confidently. "For one, most of 'em are suckers for gossip. They leave, they don't get to know what we're up to." She lifted her nose, sniffing sharply, then dragged Ryia into the nearest tavern. An instant later, Ryia saw the distinctive flick of a deep blue cloak swish past the window. "And secondly, they might look like a bunch of cheats and wretches, but they're the most loyal bastards in all the three seas."

"I knew another captain who thought her crew was loyal," Ryia said darkly. "Until almost the whole lot of them stabbed her in the back for a few free trips to the nearest whorehouse."

"What captain might that be?" Joslyn asked, eyebrow cocked.

Your damned twin, Ryia thought. Before she

had to answer out loud, Joslyn apparently forgot the question, darting back out the door and into the alley. She turned the opposite way the Disciple had gone, heading southwest. Her eyes were tight with concentration, her nostrils flaring constantly as she veered left down one street, then right down the next. She dragged them into an apothecary, then dragged them back out past the protesting shopkeeper into the back alley, heading still farther south.

Ryia was about to ask whether they were running *away* from the Guildmaster or *toward* Evelyn and Tristan when she heard a familiar voice cry out in alarm.

"No, Evelyn, turn back! I just saw Nash!"

"Nash? Oh, I'll take that smuggling git. Where is she?"

A narrow-bladed sword snapped free of its sheath, leveling at Joslyn's throat.

Well, maybe "level" was the wrong word. Evelyn stood a good head shorter than the pirate, so the blade tilted up at a steep angle, its point tickling the hollow in Salt Beard's neck. Ryia slowed her steps to a walk, rounding the corner to see Evelyn and Tristan. Relief blossomed in the pit of her stomach. They looked like hell, but they were alive and unhurt. So far, at least.

"Where is he, you bloody traitor?" Evelyn hissed, pressing the blade against Joslyn's throat. A tiny bead of blood formed on the point of her sword. "Where did you hide that twice-damned Quill?"

Tristan was the first of them to notice Ryia. His eyes about doubled in size, and he tugged on Evelyn's coat. "Evelyn. Evelyn, it's—"

"Can't you see I'm a little busy?" Evelyn snapped back, eyes still fixed on Joslyn.

The pirate raised her hands mockingly, then cocked her head to one side. "Aren't many men who've held a sword at my throat before. Or women. They're all feeding the fish of the three seas now. Care to join them?" She smiled widely.

"You cocky jackass—" Evelyn started. Then she blinked, studying Joslyn's teeth.

Ryia grinned, taking a step forward and putting a hand on the flat of Evelyn's blade. "Simmer down there, Linley. That's not Nash."

"Who in the hells is this Nash person?" Joslyn asked. No one answered.

"It's not . . ." Evelyn trailed off, then finally looked at Ryia. She blinked. Then blinked again. Her free hand twitched, like she was going to reach out to Ryia, to grab on to her. She seemed to think better of it and pressed her palm firmly to her side.

Ryia thought she saw a hint of relief glimmer in her eyes. Evelyn had been worried about her. The thought of Evelyn Linley lying awake, fretting over her being trapped in the Shadow Cells, warmed Ryia's cheeks. And not in an unpleasant way.

"How in Adalina's grace did you get here?" Evelyn finally asked, clearing her throat and breaking the weighted silence that had fallen over them.

"She's got a ship," Ryia said, hurriedly nodding to Joslyn. Then she reached out with her Kinetic magic, feeling the energy pulsing from within Evelyn's sword. The note it sang to her was clear as the skies over Fairvine, and it felt almost as familiar to her as her hatchets did. *Probably because it feels a lot like Evelyn.* She pushed that thought away. Snapping her magic like a whip, she sent a vibration twanging through the needle-thin blade. It shook in Evelyn's grip, almost springing free of her fingers. "And I've got some new tricks."

"You—how did you—" Evelyn started, looking down at her sword like it was a snake that had nearly bitten her. Ryia winked.

"Do you want to get captured by our old friend the Guildmaster, or do you want to get out of here?"

CHAPTER FOURTEEN
Tristan

The knots that had started to form in Tristan's stomach the second he and Evelyn had abandoned Ryia in his father's dungeon finally started to loosen. Ryia was alive. Ryia was safe. She had escaped from his father and traveled half the length of the world to find them. Not only had she managed to break free, but she'd made a new friend along the way, it seemed. A friend who looked way too much like Nash for it to be coincidence.

But Ryia's new ally wasn't Nash. She was none other than the infamous pirate Salt Beard. Tristan supposed he had never given much thought to what Salt Beard would look like, but he had expected them to have . . . well, a beard.

But what the real Salt Beard lacked in facial hair, she definitely seemed to make up for in knowledge of the streets of Golden Port. Tristan could barely keep up as she darted around turns, cutting through shops and taverns and inns, slipping through alleys and shady corners, trying to steer clear of the swirling blue cloaks and snapping footfalls of the Disciples who had come to hunt them down.

"How in Felice's bitterest hell did he find you, anyways?" Ryia whispered as they hurried past a bakery that smelled like absolute paradise. Tristan's stomach rumbled despite his massive breakfast, but they scurried on.

"I'm not sure," Evelyn said, sounding uneasy. "Maybe one of the Disciples in Carrowwick recognized me? Followed us here?"

"Why is he even looking for you, anyway?" Salt Beard asked.

Evelyn hesitated, but Ryia nodded. "She knows about the Quill."

"You told her about the Quill?" Tristan burst out. The more people who knew about that wretched thing, the more likely it was to fall into hands that would use it to destroy them all. Though it was already in Callum Clem's hands, and he supposed it couldn't get much worse than that.

"Yeah, she told me about the Quill," Salt Beard said, lips twisting, amused. "And then I sailed her here on my ship to rescue your asses. You're welcome."

"You haven't rescued us yet," Tristan muttered darkly. If anyone heard him, they ignored the comment.

"Ryia and I were the last people the Guildmaster saw on the island the day it was stolen," Evelyn explained.

Ryia chortled. "That, and Linley here threw a twice-damned hatchet at his head."

Salt Beard reared around, looking impressed. "Did you? Shame you didn't hit him."

So the pirate was an enemy of the Guildmaster's too? Or did she just hate anyone in any position of power, like Clem did? Tristan put the thought aside. None of that mattered now. The only goal was escaping this cesspit of a town before the Guildmaster and his beasts slaughtered them all.

They went another three streets without incident, aside from shrugging past an aggressive dormire's blood dealer and fending off four separate pickpockets. Then Salt Beard and Ryia slammed to a stop, both of them looking like they'd just been smacked in the face.

"What?" Tristan asked, brushing himself off after crashing into Salt Beard's back. The docks were so close he could smell the salt of the ocean over the scents of rot and body odor that clouded the rest of this foul city. "We're almost there."

"It's him," Ryia said quietly. She bared her teeth.

"Him? Who is 'him'?" Tristan asked, but he didn't need an answer. There could only be one "him" that made her face go that pale with rage. The Guildmaster.

"Where is he?" Evelyn asked. Her red curls whipped around her as she tried to look in every direction at once.

"He's standing watch at the docks," Salt Beard said. "He's got to be."

There were still at least two rows of buildings blocking their view of the docks, but Tristan couldn't get a word in edgewise to ask how they knew the Guildmaster was there.

"Is there another way to your ship?" Evelyn asked.

"A way to the ship at the docks . . . other than going to the docks?" Ryia snorted. "My gut says no. Joslyn?"

Tristan was confused for a second, then realized that Salt Beard could hardly be the pirate's given name.

She chewed her lip for a second, then shot Ryia a sidelong grin. "I think I've got a way."

Joslyn's "way" turned out to be banging on the door of a smelly old shack to talk an equally smelly old man into lending them a rowboat so rickety it looked like it must have been built during the Seven Decades' War. Tristan wiped his hands on his trousers as he took his seat on one of the benches. The sides of the boat were slimy with something greenish and unpleasant. Joslyn grabbed one barnacle-encrusted oar, and Evelyn grabbed the other.

"One of these days, you and I are going to board a ship from the bloody docks again, Butcher," Evelyn said sourly.

Ryia leaned back, laying her head on the stern

of the tiny boat and kicking her feet up to rest between Evelyn and Tristan on the front bench. "Where's the fun in that?"

Salt Beard guided them slowly through the harbor, weaving in and around the skeletal masts and rickety docks. Tristan had just been in this harbor a few hours ago, and even then, early in the morning, it had been bustling, filled with the sound of laughter and swearing and clattering footsteps. Now it was eerily quiet. Hardly even a gull cried out, even though the sun blazed high overhead. The sailors and fishermen they saw all wore grim faces, going about their business with light-footed steps like they were afraid they would wake something horrible if they trod too loudly.

Tristan's stomach flipped as he caught sight of a tall, thin man between the hulls of two of the ships towering over them. He was dressed all in swirling blue robes, his head a mass of intricate tattoos. Tristan had seen the Guildmaster enough times to recognize that easy, confident stance, like he owned the docks he stood on, and everyone on them. Recognize the impatient tap of his long-nailed fingers on the edges of his bell sleeves.

"Shit." Joslyn grabbed on to the dock nearest them, pulling them back into its shadows just as the seventh Guildmaster of Thamorr turned his head, combing the ships surrounding them with his piercing blue-gray eyes.

They waited in the shadows for a few seconds, then Ryia and the pirate took a deep breath in unison, sharing a look, and Joslyn and Evelyn started rowing again. Tristan wasn't sure he had ever seen Ryia trust another person as much as it looked like she already trusted Salt Beard. A pang of jealousy shot through him. It had been months before she had even trusted him to deliver a message. Now she was putting all their lives in the hands of this newcomer after what, a few weeks huddled in the darkness of his father's dungeons?

Of course, he couldn't exactly be upset with Ryia for not trusting him. He *had* abandoned her back on the Guildmaster's island. He should just be thankful she hadn't slit his throat. But he wasn't the only one who had noticed the bond between Joslyn and Ryia. Evelyn hadn't said a word, but she was sitting awfully stiff on the bench behind him, her jaw clenched tight.

Joslyn stopped them twice more before they reached the towering ship near the northern edge of the docks. It was a galleon, if Tristan's father's seafaring lessons had been worth a single copper. A handsome ship made of dark wood with clean, white sails and a masthead that looked like a giant serpent. An Ophidian, he realized, remembering Salt Beard's infamous ship was called the *Ophidian Fang*.

They never set foot on the dock, instead rowing

around to the broad side of the ship until a ladder came into view, the rungs built right into the hull, leading from the water's edge all the way up to the ornate rail high above them. Joslyn peered up the ladder, then reached a hand toward Ryia.

"Give me one of those little axes."

Tristan snorted. The only time Ryia Cautella parted with one of her hatchets was when she threw it at whatever idiot was bold enough to challenge her. But his jaw dropped as she reached for her belt, sliding one throwing axe free and spinning it around in her palm to hand it, handle first, to the pirate.

"Thanks," the woman said with a grin. She wiggled the axe. "Can't have anyone sounding an alarm by accident."

"You're going to kill one of your own crewmen?" Evelyn asked, disgusted.

Joslyn shot her a look but didn't explain. She clamped the handle of Ryia's throwing axe between her teeth and started up the ladder, waving for them to follow.

Tristan grabbed on to the ladder next with Evelyn close behind him, and Ryia bringing up the rear.

"It's me, idiot. Shout and we're all dead," said Joslyn above him.

Tristan craned his neck to see her pressing her hand over a reedy man's mouth with one hand, holding the hatchet to his throat with the other.

"Fuck's sake, Captain," the man hissed, wriggling himself free of her grip. "The docks are too boring for you now you've seen the inside of the Shadow Keep's cells, or what?"

Joslyn hopped free of the ladder, stepping aside to make room for Tristan and the others to come up on deck behind her. "Just get the ship readied as quickly and quietly as you can. Anyone not on board the second she's ready to sail stays behind."

She tossed the hatchet backward without looking. Tristan flinched, but Ryia caught it deftly, threading it back into her belt without so much as a blink.

"If you were going to put your hand over his mouth, what in Adalina's fury did you need the bloody hatchet for?" Evelyn asked.

Joslyn looked back and cocked her head. "In case he was fool enough to scream anyways."

As she stalked away across the deck, Evelyn shot Ryia a look. "*This* is the person you've decided to ally us with?" she hissed.

Ryia shrugged. "Unless you have a ship I don't know about, we don't really have a choice here, Captain." Evelyn opened her mouth as if to argue, then shut it again. Ryia patted her awkwardly on the shoulder. "Glad you two are still alive, by the way."

Evelyn cleared her throat. "I'm . . . I'm glad you're still alive too."

Something blossomed between the women. An energy, almost tangible in the salty air. Tristan frowned, his mood souring. He stepped forward, positioning himself in the middle of them, then glanced anxiously at the docks, where the Guildmaster was no doubt still lurking around, hunting for them.

"Let's hope we stay that way a little longer," he said drily.

It only took Salt Beard's crew a few minutes to get the ship ready to sail. They had already been mostly ready, according to Ryia—ordered to be prepared to shoot off from the docks at a moment's notice. They managed to pull away from the harbor, unfurling the sails and heading out into the open waters of the Yawning Sea, without alerting the Guildmaster that they had slipped his net. Relief trickled through Tristan's veins as he watched the vivid blue sails of the Disciples' ship shrink alongside Golden Port on the horizon behind them.

They sailed straight west until the coastline of Thamorr became no more than a dot in the distance . . . then disappeared altogether. When they were surrounded by nothing but tossing waves and screeching gulls, the skinny man Joslyn had threatened when they first came on board cleared his throat.

"So, are you going to tell us what pile of sea sludge you've gotten us all into now, or should we wait till dark to fit the mood?" he asked, voice dripping with sarcasm.

"No, you've all waited long enough," Joslyn said. She exchanged a look with Ryia, who hesitated, then gave the smallest of nods. "You may have noticed those blue-cloaked bastards back there in Golden Port. That won't be the last we see of them on this job."

She laid out the facts about the Quill. That it was an artifact belonging to the Guildmaster, that it was incredibly powerful, and that a man named Wyatt Asher had stolen it.

"Er, actually, Asher doesn't have it," Tristan cut in.

Ryia blinked, raising an eyebrow and turning to face him. "The bastard lost it already? Who's got it now?"

Tristan and Evelyn exchanged a look. Evelyn finally took the burden of breaking the news.

"Our favorite piece of human shite, unfortunately," she said. "Callum Clem's alive. He double-crossed us before we got the chance to double-cross him. He's got the Quill."

Ryia's face paled. She seemed to be struck dumb.

Joslyn frowned. "Who is this Callum Clem? Is he another—" She broke off abruptly, then cleared her throat. "Is he Adept?"

Callum Clem? Adept? Tristan shuddered. "Thank Adalina, no, he isn't."

"Then why do we give a shit who he is?"

"Remember how I described Wyatt Asher as a rabid gutter rat?" Ryia asked Joslyn. Her voice sounded hollow. Joslyn nodded and Ryia grimaced. "Callum Clem is more like . . . well, they call him the Snake of the Southern Dock."

A few of Joslyn's crew made noises of assent. They had heard of the Snake.

"He's calculating," Tristan said.

At the same time, Ryia and Evelyn said in unison, "He's a prick."

Linley and the Butcher shared an amused look, then Ryia said, "If anyone will figure out the same thing my father did . . . it would be him."

Joslyn winced, nodding. Evelyn went ashen. Tristan traded confused looks with Salt Beard's crewmen. Finally, the reedy man, whose name turned out to be Fagan, spoke up.

"Most of us don't know your twice-damned father, Cautella."

"No need to brag," Ryia said. Then she swallowed, turning to Evelyn. "Did you know that, in order to use the Quill—to *really* use it, not just grab the reins for a second—you need to be Adept?"

Tristan shut his mouth. He had been about to argue that he had already used the Quill. But Ryia was right: he *had* only managed to grab the reins for a second. He shuddered as he remembered the flood of images, the wave of power too great for his body to hold . . . and then the way that wave had receded, faster than it had come, leaving him too weak to run. Too weak to *stand*.

"So we're saved, then," Tristan said. "Clem's a vicious son of a snake, but he's no Adept."

"Not yet," Ryia said darkly.

"Not yet? What the hell do you mean not *yet?*" asked one of the crew, a heavyset man with a tangled beard. "You can't just *become* Adept."

"That's what everyone told my father."

There was a long silence, filled only with the sound of flapping sails and cawing gulls. Tristan finally swallowed. "Your . . . father was Adept?" He didn't know anything about Ryia's father. He didn't know anything about her life before coming to Carrowwick at all, honestly. Most of what she had told him was probably lies, he had known that all along, but he had never expected this.

"Not my father . . ."

Ryia paused, then raised a hand in front of her. Tristan felt the blood drain from his face as one of the hatchets in the Butcher's belt wiggled, then flew up to her outstretched hand, seemingly of its own accord. Nausea curled in the pit of his stomach. He hadn't been seeing things back in his father's wine cellar. Ryia really *was* Adept. And apparently, she hadn't been born that way. Her *father* had done this to her? Hatred pulsed through Tristan's veins, though he had never met the man.

Several of the crew jumped backward. Fagan

cursed and tripped over a coil of rope behind him, crashing to the deck. Evelyn's jaw tightened, and Joslyn looked completely unfazed. The pirate and the ex–Needle Guard captain already knew, then. He had known Ryia longer than either of them, and still, she hadn't seen fit to trust him with her secret. She had come to rescue him from Duskhaven, but she would probably never *really* trust him again. That thought made him almost as nauseated as the idea of her being a twice-cursed Adept.

Almost.

"How did you . . . ?" Fagan asked, brushing himself off as he pushed himself back to his feet.

"I'm not here to give anyone a twice-damned tutorial," Ryia snapped, baring her teeth at him. "Look, we need to find Callum Clem before he figures it out. We need to take the Quill from him before he's able to use it."

"And then what?" Tristan asked. His voice sounded somehow both hoarse and squeaky. He cleared his throat. "Say we figure out where Clem is going. Say we catch him and steal Declan Day's Quill out from under his nose. Then what?"

Ryia turned her jet-black eyes on him, cocking one equally jet-black eyebrow skyward as she held her hatchet out in front of her. "I'm going to hack it to a thousand pieces. Then I'm going to scatter those splinters all across the three seas so no power-hungry asshole can ever have even the faintest prayer of tracking them down and fitting them back together."

Tristan swallowed. "So, when the Quill is destroyed, what will happen to the newborn Adept?"

"They'll just grow up on the mainland, you git," Evelyn said. "What did you think would happen to them?"

Tristan's mind flooded with images of a world where any cloaked man or corseted woman could be concealing Adept powers. His queasiness grew so strong he felt his knees start to weaken. And it wasn't just that. Without the auction and the Guildmaster holding the kingdoms in check, what was to stop rulers like his father from marching off to war every few years? What was to stop the *Adept* from rising up and claiming that the crowns of Thamorr should be theirs? By the time the first freeborn Adept hit maturity . . . the world would be a tinderbox, ready to burn.

"Not just the newborns, either," Joslyn said, cutting through his thoughts. The pirate gestured vaguely east, back toward the mainland, hidden by tossing waves and the curve of the world. "Every poor sap wearing a black robe and a brand will be free as soon as that Quill is broken."

"How d'you know that?" Fagan asked, wrinkling his nose.

"Is there anything I *don't* know, Fagan?" Salt Beard asked, grinning.

The pit in Tristan's stomach widened into a chasm. His father had said something similar, back in that dusty wine cellar, he now recalled. They wouldn't need to wait for the world to fall to pieces, then. It would happen immediately. He could see it already—merchants, lords, and kings slaughtered in their beds by their Adept servants the instant Ryia took her hatchet to that precious Quill. His gut lurched again as images flashed before his mind's eye. Images of his father's Kinetics, leaping into action. Images of the fighting pits on the Guildmaster's island. Images of the poor, destroyed corpse in that apartment back in Golden Port. With all the Adept free and independent . . . Thamorr would crumble in a day's time.

"And why would we destroy this Quill when we can sell it?" a weathered-looking woman on Salt Beard's crew asked.

Joslyn snorted. "Who in Felice's darkest hell would you want to sell it to now that you know what it does? Anyone who figured out how to wield it could shut down the free waterways of this land like that." She snapped her fingers in the woman's face.

"We could ransom it back to the Guildmaster," said another man.

Ryia's face grew so red Tristan thought it might explode like a firecracker.

"Fuck the Guildmaster," Joslyn said. "He's

the reason I had to give myself up to Tolliver Shithead back there. No." She ran a hand over her shaven head. "Besides, the Adept are gonna free themselves someday, no matter what we do here. Would you rather be on the side that kept them in chains or the side that helped break them free when that happens?" She cocked one eyebrow.

Tolliver Shithead. He had never heard that one before. But Joslyn's argument was a good one for the crowd on the deck of the *Ophidian Fang*. Most of the crew shifted from incredulous to thoughtful. After all, these men and women were pirates and mercenaries. Aligning themselves with the likeliest victor would appeal to them far more than any sort of call to their possibly nonexistent honor. He didn't like this Joslyn one bit, but he had to admit she was smart.

"All right," Fagan started slowly. "Let's say we agree here. How do we track down this Callum Clem son of a bitch?"

"No idea," Ryia said. She turned to Evelyn and Tristan. "You two tracked him to Golden Port. Did you see him there?"

"See him? No," Tristan said, his mouth twisting sourly. "But we saw his . . . handiwork."

"What does that mean?" asked the round man.

Evelyn tapped her sword hilt absently, addressing Ryia. "He still has . . . company."

Ryia's eyes narrowed. "What do you mean *company?*"

"Ivan. And Nash." Evelyn paused. "And those two Kinetics you said he stole from that one merchant back in Carrowwick."

Understanding crossed over Ryia's face like a shadow. "They killed someone."

Bile surged up Tristan's throat as he remembered the inside of that apartment. The metallic scent of blood, the smears of what had once been a living, breathing man, spread all over the floor. A nod was all he could manage.

"Who?" Salt Beard asked. She leaned forward, her eyes narrowed in focus. It was the first time Tristan had seen her look distinctly separate from Nash, who rarely focused on anything that wasn't an inappropriate joke or a mug of ale.

"That's the part that makes no bloody sense," Evelyn said. She ran a hand over her hair. Rather than calming the vibrant red curls, it just mussed them up further. "He was nobody. A storyteller living in a shite-poor apartment on Skull Street."

"Skuller's Lane," Joslyn corrected. She cocked her head to one side. "An old man? Above a weaver's shop?"

"Yes," Evelyn said. "You know him?"

"I do," the pirate said bitterly. "Anyone who's been to Golden Port more than a handful of times knows him. Boys, this Callum Clem asshole killed Bornchev."

Groans and irritated hisses sounded out from

the crew. Another nail in the coffin—this was personal now. Joslyn had laid out her arguments one after the other, leading her crew to their side of their own accord. This Joslyn was not someone to be underestimated. Tristan made a mental note to keep an eye on himself around her. He didn't want to let something slip. Something that might make her turn on him—or worse, realize what a valuable bargaining chip he was.

"What kind of sick bastard would kill Bornchev?" Fagan asked.

"The kind who heard a story they didn't want anyone else hearing," Joslyn said darkly. She looked at Ryia and said, "Bornchev. That's a Borean name, isn't it?"

Tristan had no idea why that mattered, but Ryia's night-black eyes suddenly sparkled with inward starlight. "You don't think . . ."

"I thought they were all extinct."

"Don't worry—we'll all just wait patiently while you two talk in bloody riddles," Evelyn said bitterly, inspecting her filthy fingernails.

There was a pause; then Joslyn said, "Have you ever heard of the Eis Yavols of Boreas?"

Evelyn raised an eyebrow. "Eis Yavols? You mean the giant bears from ancient times? They've been dead longer than the Ophidians you named your ruddy ship after. Why?"

"Because it's said that a bite from an Eis Yavol can make a regular, non-magic man into an Adept

Kinetic," the pirate said, clearly choosing her words very carefully.

"Said by whom?" Tristan asked, the color draining from his face. He had never heard that story before.

"Borean legends," Joslyn said evasively. She turned her eyes on him. "Probably Bornchev."

"So, what, you think Callum Clem is heading to the Völgnich Mountains to go hunt down an extinct snow bear?" Evelyn asked. "The Snake might be vicious, but he's not a git. Besides, can you imagine those loafers of his cutting through the wilderness?"

Ryia snorted. Even Tristan cracked half a smile, picturing it. Callum Clem was many things, but a mountaineer he was not.

"He wouldn't need the whole bear . . . ," Joslyn mused, stroking her chin with one long finger. "Just one tooth."

"How big is an Eis Yavol tooth?" asked Fagan, picking his own teeth with one jagged fingernail.

Salt Beard held her hands about six inches apart.

"Oh, good. Something even harder to find in the mountains than a long-dead bear," Evelyn said.

"Unless it's not in the mountains . . ." The words were out of Tristan's mouth before he could stop them. His common sense was distracted by a memory. The memory of a trip he had taken with his father as a boy. A trip to the Reclaimed Castle in Boreas.

The eldest prince, Edmon Tovolkov, had bragged to him about an ancient heirloom of the Borean throne. A dagger made of bone.

Not just any bone. A *fang*. The two young princes had snuck into the throne room after dark, and young Prince Edmon had opened a secret compartment in the arm of his father's throne, pulling out an ornate dagger with a six-inch blade made of bone, yellowed with age. The edges were dull as a butter knife, but the tip was still sharp. He could see it glinting in the moonlight in his mind's eye, the Eisfang Dagger. Neither of them had dared touch the tip . . . because Edmon had told him it was cursed.

When he came back out of his thoughts, he saw Ryia staring at him. Her eyes cut through the space between them like the blades of her hatchets. "You know where he's going."

Dread pooled thickly in the pit of Tristan's stomach. "I know where he's going."

By the time the sun began to set, they had a plan. A plan that would take them all the way to the Sea of Boreas in the north. A plan that relied on equal parts luck, bullheadedness, and Ryia's Adept powers.

A plan that made every inch of Tristan's intestines queasy.

That night, he tossed and turned in his bed. He

was sharing a cabin with three of Salt Beard's crew, and all of them snored louder than Roland back in Carrowwick, sounding like they had swallowed a thousand cicadas apiece. Finally unable to ignore the voice in his head a second longer, he pushed himself out of his bed. He padded barefoot across the cabin and rummaged in his pack until he found what he was looking for: a scrap of parchment and a stick of charcoal.

There, in the darkness, he scrawled a note. A note that simultaneously calmed the nausea coursing through him and sent a wave of guilt crashing over him. A note outlining every inch of the plans they had just formed up on that deck.

When he had finished scrawling his note, he shoved it in his pocket, sneaking away from the still-snoring men in his cabin and into the passageway beyond. A ship this size always had a messenger cabin. He followed the sounds of restless flapping and occasional birdsong until he found it. There was just enough light from the moon sneaking in the porthole for him to make out the colors on the dyed feathers of the birds' bellies. Finally, he found the color he was looking for, reached into the cage, and grabbed the bird gently around the back, pinning its wings to its sides.

He bound his note to its leg with shaking hands, then crept back through the passageway and up the series of ladders leading to the main deck of the ship. The night was frigid cold, autumn winds whipping across the deck, sending his overlong hair into his eyes. He pushed it back with his wrist, edging along the side of the deck, keeping out of the eyeline of Fagan, who was at the helm. Tristan was thankful Ryia had managed to talk Salt Beard into taking a few hours' rest. He didn't relish the idea of trying to sneak past the seasoned pirate captain while she was awake.

When he reached the stern, he raised both hands, cupping the bird gently. "Fly quickly, little friend," he whispered into its feathers. "The fate of Thamorr depends on you."

Then he let it go, watching it flap its tiny wings until it disappeared completely into the darkness.

CHAPTER FIFTEEN
Ivan

Two thoughts filled Ivan's mind as he watched the Borean city of Volkfier bloom on the horizon before them. First, that the last time his feet had been on Borean soil, he had been running away from the men who had captured Kasimir. Second, that Kasimir would *klatsch* him silly if he could see how much he was shivering in the northern winds. Ivan shook his head. After only a few years in the south, he had become a squealing *kindt* about the cold and the snow.

In Dresdell and the southern parts of Edale, autumn meant reddening leaves, gray skies, and chill winds. In Boreas, it meant the light snows of summer were behind them, soon to be replaced by the heavy snows and bitter gales of the long, dark winter.

The journey north had been long and quiet. Callum was in better spirits than he had been in since the night they had stolen the Quill from Wyatt Asher, but his quiet, satisfied smirks did not cancel out the anger seething from Nash's very boots. When she was forced to speak, the smuggler's voice was even colder than the winds whipping across the waters to redden their cheeks and freeze their fingers and toes. Ivan was alarmed to realize how much he missed her easy smiles and foul-mouthed joking now that they were gone. Perhaps if he told her about Kasimir, she would understand . . . he considered it only once, then tucked the thought away.

To tell Nash about Kasimir would be to risk Callum discovering his secret. To risk the Snake of the Southern Dock learning that his faithful disguise-master was not faithful after all, simply using him toward his own ends. That was not something Callum would take well. It was likely he would kill Ivan out of anger. Even likelier that he would ensure Kasimir's demise as well out of spite. No. His friendship with the smuggler had been nothing but a distraction. It was for the best that it had ended.

At least, that was what he told himself.

"Pulling in at Volkfier," Nash said from the helm.

Her voice sounded flat. Ivan did not blame her. She did not want to be on this adventure any longer, but she was their only ally with a ship. If she were to try to abandon them now, Callum would certainly send his Adept dogs barking after her. Surely she knew that. And so she had stayed.

"Come on, boys, let's get her to shore so we can get some damned coats," she said. She always spoke to the Kinetics as though they were regular crewmen. Ivan was not sure if this was out of true respect for the mindless Adept or out of self-delusion—an attempt to pretend all was normal on board *The Hardship*.

Perhaps it was a bit of both.

Callum appeared from the lower deck as soon as he heard the call. As far as Ivan knew, the Snake had never been this far north before, but the cold did not seem to bother the man. His cheeks were tinged with pink, and his knuckles were white as they grasped the *saltz-sprict* railing, but he did not shiver or hunch his shoulders. Instead, he stood tall and proud, like the figurehead on a royal ship, his eyes burning with blue fire. That expression of passion that had inspired crowds when it shone in Kasimir's eyes inspired only dread in Ivan when he saw it in Callum.

Not for the first time, doubt clouded Ivan's mind. Helping Callum would lead him to the Reclaimed Castle. It would help him free Kasimir, if he were to cast his stones in the right order. But what kind of world would he be freeing Kasimir into if Callum were truly victorious? Was he being a *dummklav* to think that Callum ruling Thamorr would be any better than King Andrei ruling Boreas? After all, both men were hard, cruel, and ambitious. The only difference was Callum was also ruinously clever. Perhaps Nash had been right. Perhaps they were making a massive mistake.

But it was far too late to turn back now. The

Saints were destroyed. Kasimir rotted in a cell. Ivan had no more allies, and nowhere else to go.

Harsh shouts and the smell of pine smoke filled the air as *The Hardship* bumped against the docks at Volkfier. It was the kind of town every smuggler and pirate up and down the coast knew well, but the kind that was often overlooked by the reputable people of Boreas. Relatively small, the city crowded itself along the coastline, stretching longer miles along the icy western shores than it stretched away from them inland to the east. An ox-drawn cart filled with crates of *stervod* plodded down the snow-covered street. A pair of men walked the opposite direction across the docks just behind them, each holding one end of a net that had snared a massive *snefisk*, a Borean fish as long as Ivan was tall, sporting a pair of daggerlike blades on its face. A stall at the edge of the docks held a woman selling *konigcrabben* to passersby, pulling the massive crabs from baskets and trading them for a few silvers apiece.

Despite all his doubts and dread, a sense of calm washed over Ivan. The peace that comes from arriving home after a long day. He had spent years in Dresdell, long enough that it had come to feel comfortable to him. Now he could not deny that it had never truly felt like home. Boreas was where he belonged.

Callum left Nash behind on *The Hardship*. She

was to guard the ship, he said, but Ivan knew his true reason for leaving her behind. He was less observant than usual, consumed with dreams of power as he was, but Nash's doubts would have been visible to the smallest *kindt* or the blindest elder. She was still involved in their plans to steal the dagger, but it seemed her stomach had grown too soft for Clem's methods. Bringing her with them this day would only put them all at risk.

Unnecessary risk was something Callum Clem avoided at all costs.

Nash did not seem to mind being left behind. Of course, she had always felt more at home on the deck of a ship than she had on land anywhere in all of Thamorr, but this relief was more than that. Perhaps she did not want to witness Callum killing another man in cold blood for his scheme. Or perhaps she was afraid she might be fool enough to try to stop him.

Either way, the smuggler did not even mutter a goodbye to Ivan and Callum as they exited *The Hardship*.

"*Namirt?*" the dockmaster asked, swooping from nowhere almost the instant their boots touched the snow-dusted wooden planks of the dock.

"Bornchev," Ivan said without thinking, sliding a pair of coppers into the man's gloveless hand. He winced internally, instantly glad that Nash had not been near enough to hear that. It was bad enough that Callum had robbed the dead man, but to use both his name *and* his gold? That was perhaps taking things a bit too far.

The dockmaster asked if they had come to sell anything. Ivan held his arms out to indicate they were empty, explaining they had come only to restock their ship with supplies before heading farther north.

The man looked them up and down a moment, then said. "*Peltzmann ta Grulnik*." He nodded his head to the east behind him.

"What did he say?" Callum asked, picking at his fingernails.

"He said there is a fur trader on a street called Grulnik," Ivan said, vaguely amused. "I do not think he believes our wardrobe is suitable if we are traveling farther north."

"We will have a new wardrobe soon enough," Callum said thinly.

That they would.

Lord Gavik Piervin held a small estate just outside the limits of Volkfier, overlooking the cliffs north of the city. It was no simple feat to walk into a lord's manor, no matter how minor, but Ivan Rezkoye was no simple man. He was one of the *Fvene*. A member of his brother's sophisticated resistance force. True, it had been a number of years since he had last served in Boreas, but he had not forgotten his lessons.

Kasimir had researched every lord in all of

Boreas. After all, when they managed to topple King Andrei and the Tovolkov line, it would be the lords who would *bickern* and squabble over the chance to take his place. Many of the lords of Boreas had been on Kasimir's list of men to remove from the conversation before they truly became a threat. Gavik Piervin had been low on the list, but he had been among them.

As the lord outside one of the smaller ports in Boreas, Piervin was not an overly influential man, but he was ambitious and he was foolish; a combination that would have become dangerous, had he ever somehow managed to come into power.

Without his customary stash of fabrics and face paints, Ivan's usual methods of sneaking into places he did not belong were out of the question, but disguise was not his only strength. He had one left that was far greater still—knowledge. In this case, the knowledge that Gavik Piervin was an arrogant *bastrak* who would never take notice of someone as lowly as a servant. Fluent in Borean and dressed in his travel-rumpled clothing, Ivan could easily pass for a kitchen worker, blending in with the housekeepers, cooks, and laundry maids entering through the manor's back door. He purchased a basket of fresh fish on the docks and marched right into the kitchens.

The house and grounds were both bustling with energy. Grooms prepared sturdy northern horses, and servants outfitted a carriage painted to look like an eagle in flight. Inside the manor, food was cooked, and casks of wine and *stervod* poured into bottles for travel. Lord Piervin would be leaving for the Reclaimed Castle within the next few days at the latest, possibly this very afternoon. Ivan would need to move quickly.

Falling into the comfortable but hurried stride of a servant too busy to stop and talk to anyone, Ivan bustled through the ornate corridors of the manor. Furs hung on nearly every wall. Bears and wolves and deer. Furs were a sign of status in Boreas. The poor of the northernmost kingdom lived most of their lives outside in the cold, so if a man insisted on walking around draped head to *tüse* in warm furs, it was a sign that he was used to sitting inside by the warmth of a fire.

Ivan found Piervin's living quarters without difficulty. Borean manors were all the same, more or less. Windows lined only two walls of the home, those facing east and west, for the sunrise and sunset. The northern and southern sides of the home were hidden by the roof, which slanted all the way from the top floor to the ground outside, to prevent the large winter snows from building up on the rooftops and causing them to cave in. That meant northern and southern chambers were reserved for servants' quarters, larders, and other areas the lord would never visit.

The lord's chambers were usually the largest,

on the ground floor, facing west (so he would not be awakened by the light of the rising sun). Ivan did not so much as glance over his shoulder as he bustled past a surly-looking maid carrying a chamber pot. Looking over his shoulder would indicate that he did not belong. That would raise suspicion. Kasimir always said that a man who moves with confidence is a man whom other men do not question. His brother's words held true. No one made any move to slow his progress as he entered the chamber and eased the door shut behind him.

Ivan was unsurprised to find Lord Piervin's wardrobe stuffed full of furs. Cloaks made of fox fur and bearskins and elk lined with mink. The contents of this wardrobe likely cost more gold than the entire *verdammte* manor. Shooting a quick look toward the still-closed door to the empty chamber, Ivan pulled the folded linen sack from inside his shirt and began piling furs into it. A pair of finely stitched trousers, an undershirt made of Brillish silk, and then the finest, most *ghastlich* cloak in the wardrobe, a monstrosity made from the pelts of two bear cubs, one stuffed head adorning each shoulder.

With his bag packed full of Lord Piervin's vile clothing, Ivan turned back toward the door. Now to return to Callum with the loot and take to the woods to set fire to the lord's carriage as it left the manor. The lord would have more Adept than

Callum had, and guards beside them. There was no way to kill Piervin without destroying the carriage as well. This much had been clear in their long discussions on *The Hardship*.

Of course, they would need to arrive at the Reclaimed Castle in *some* kind of carriage . . . but that was something they could sort out later. Nash was skilled at stealing ships; perhaps her talent would translate to land.

As Ivan reached for the doorknob, a series of shouts and thuds sounded outside the door. His jaw clenched as he heard the unmistakable shriek of steel blades against iron scabbards. The top of his mind fluttered fearfully, wondering what could be happening, but deeper in, he pulsed with dread. He already knew the truth. After all, Callum always prided himself on keeping the core of his plans from even his own crew.

By the time Ivan made his way back to the kitchens, he found them sullied with blood and gore. The cooks who had been busy preparing supper when he had last passed through were now slumped over on the floor, motionless but for the blood seeping from their bodies. Ivan swallowed as he saw the basket of fish he had brought in, sitting beside the still-roaring ovens.

Feeling as though he were trapped in a dream, Ivan left the kitchen, winding through the corridors of the manor. Every few turns, he found more bodies. They were spread out, clearly caught by surprise during preparations for Lord Piervin's departure. A laundry maid here. A guard there. Ivan toed the first black-robed figure he came across nervously. The poor creature's head lolled sideways, revealing its mark. A Senser. A few corners later, Ivan came across the first dead Kinetic. He stopped looking at the bodies altogether a short while after that, simply following the *klattern* of footsteps and sound of muted shouts. They led him up a winding staircase to a gilded wooden door at the western end of a long hall.

He eased the door open, and in that same instant, he felt his worn boots leave the floor.

One of Callum's Kinetics held him by his collar, lifting him into the air as though he weighed no more than a *fëder*. Fear coursed under Ivan's skin, though Kasimir had trained him too well to ever let the expression show on his face. An instant before the Kinetic dashed his skull against the door frame, Callum snapped his fingers once. The Kinetic stopped, lowering Ivan to the floor and stepping aside as though it had not just been inches from killing him.

Ivan brushed his collar. It was now smeared with blood from the Kinetic's hand. The blood of a dozen innocent servants and guards. A mark like that would not come clean no matter how much he rubbed at it. He tried all the same, then looked up at the chamber when he had finally given up. It was a study. The walls were filled with shelves lined with dusty books, and a large wooden desk sat in the center of the room. The fine carpets were of Gildesh weave, all splattered with blood.

There was only one corpse in this room. A man of perhaps forty years. He wore a long mink stole and loafers made of burgundy-stained leather. Lord Gavik Piervin. Callum examined the man shrewdly, then stooped to the floor, relieving the dead man of his fine shoes. He held the loafers up, cocking his head to one side.

"To complete the effect."

"Callum," Ivan said slowly. "I thought we had agreed to stop the carriage on the road. You were supposed to be visiting the *fierverker* I told you of, getting the blasting powder we needed to send Lord Piervin's carriage to *Yavol*'s realm."

"Yes, but this way we get to save a good bit of gold we would have spent on that blasting powder, Mr. Rezkoye," Callum said primly, still examining his new loafers. He looked up, shooting Ivan a chilling smile. "And we can now make use of Lord Piervin's carriage, as well." He walked across the bloodstained floor and patted Ivan on the shoulder in a manner that was somehow both jovial and a warning. "Our resources are limited on this job, Ivan. I must ensure I am making good use of all our investments. This way, we also ensure that there are no witnesses to blow the whistle before we arrive at the Reclaimed Castle."

"And you did not see fit to inform me of this change, why?" Ivan asked.

"Because my smuggler has softened that icy Borean heart of yours, Mr. Rezkoye," Callum said. "I couldn't risk you trying to stop me."

Ivan did not pull back as Callum took the bag of clothing from his grasp and began pawing through it. He pulled the bear cub cloak out with a chuckle. "Ah, if there is one thing I have always loved about the nobility, it is their dauntless approach to fashion."

He slung the cloak around his shoulders and left the room. The Kinetics followed closely, and Ivan trailed along in their footsteps, his eyes locked to the floor. There had been no need to murder a dozen or more servants. And . . . Ivan tightened his jaw. Lord Piervin had both a wife and a daughter. *No witnesses.* He doubted Callum had let them escape to sound the alarm. So much unnecessary bloodshed, all to save a handful of crescents on *fierverken* and a carriage. Perhaps Nash was right. Callum was too dangerous to wield the true power of the Quill.

But it was too late for those thoughts. Ivan's teeth ground together behind his thin white lips as he and Callum walked out into the thin white sunlight, swirling with thin white flakes of snow. He was closer to saving Kasimir than he had ever been. In just a few days' time, they would arrive at the Reclaimed Castle. Callum would find his dagger . . . and Ivan would find Kasimir. Just a few more days, and all of this would finally be over.

CHAPTER SIXTEEN
Evelyn

Evelyn Linley was no stranger to long seafaring voyages these days, but she had to admit that none of her previous journeys compared to the trip to Volkfier. For starters, it was bloody cold. An uncomfortable chill sank into her bones about halfway up the Edalish coastline, and it never went away. The wind was cold. The sea spray splashing up on the deck was cold. Even the ruddy stars in the sky looked cold, like tiny chunks of glittering ice floating high above the snowy clouds.

Salt Beard's ship was almost as large as the one she had sailed on with King Duncan Baelbrandt when she was with the Needle Guard. It was quick, too, cutting through the waves like a needle through cloth. When Salt Beard herself was at the helm, the *Ophidian Fang* seemed to zip through the fierce gales of the Sea of Boreas all the faster, though maybe that was just Evelyn's imagination.

All said and done, it took them only eight days to reach Volkfier. Eight mornings of watching Ryia test the limits of her new powers, toying with coppers and forks and discarded socks.

Eight days of playing dice with Salt Beard's crew, talking every tiny detail of their plan to death; eight nights of sinking into sleep in her cabin belowdecks, dwelling on the thousand laughs Ryia had shared with the pirate captain that day.

Evelyn wasn't sure what in Adalina's darkest hell had happened back in the cells under the Shadow Keep, but the Butcher and the pirate were thick as bloody thieves now. More than that, Evelyn had the sense that Ryia was keeping secrets from her again.

Not that any of that should have surprised her. Ryia Cautella kept her secrets closer than most men kept their wives. She breathed lies like they were air and was about as easy to pin down as a cloud of smoke. Maybe that was what was pissing her off. It had taken Evelyn months of listening to the Butcher's lies for Ryia to start trusting her. And it looked like Joslyn the pirate had swaggered in and won that same trust or more in a twice-damned fortnight.

"Volkfier ahead!"

Evelyn whipped her head toward the voice. Salt Beard's first mate, Fagan, stood at the prow, peering out through a pocket telescope. In between snowflakes fluttering from the sparse clouds, Evelyn saw the outline of a town. It sprawled up and down the coast, an organized mass of sturdy, squat structures with angled rooftops stretching all the way down to the snowy earth on either side. The city stretched only a few miles inland, but at least twice that far north and south, only stopping its northern crawl when it reached a sheer cliff that cut straight up into the sky.

"Ready to show that sword of yours some action for once?"

Evelyn barely stopped herself from jumping at the sound of Ryia's voice just behind her. She tapped the hilt of her needle-thin sword, as always, at her hip. "This sword's seen plenty of action," she scoffed. "You'd better hope it doesn't see much on this job, though. I'm not exactly chinless, but I still don't like our odds against a bloody castle full of *medev*."

"*Medev*." Ryia tutted her tongue. She leaned up against the rail. She looked less sickly than she had aboard *The Hardship*, but still, her cheeks were a good two shades greener than usual. "They're just regular men in stupid hats who've been following orders so long they've forgotten how to use their own brains."

"Maybe they've forgotten how to use their brains, but they still know how to use a blade."

"Brainless sword fighting is kind of your specialty, though, isn't it?"

Evelyn cracked a smile at the insult. This was the most Ryia had acted like herself around her since they had met back up in Golden Port. "Fuck off."

The Butcher just grinned. Her hair had grown, the tangled black waves dusting her earlobes as she turned her head, facing into the wind and staring toward the docks. Her hair wasn't the only change, though. Ryia Cautella always sported a collection of bruises and scars, but the ones she had picked up in Shadowwood's dungeons were unlike anything Evelyn had ever seen on her face. Her nose had changed shape completely, clearly broken and poorly healed, maybe more than once. The yellowish remnants of half-healed bruises ringed both eyes and circled her narrow throat. Evelyn hadn't asked what had happened, but whatever it was made her hate Tolliver Shadowwood more than she had hated any other man in her life.

When she had picked up her sword and taken her vow back in Dresdell, she had promised never to harm an unarmed man, but if Tolliver Shadowwood was lacking a sword the next time she saw him . . . well, she might just make a twice-damned exception.

The silence stretched another long moment, then Ryia pushed herself away from the rail. "We're almost there. Someone should go get His Highness from belowdecks so we can kick off this cursed plan."

She began to walk away, and Evelyn reached out, grabbing her upper arm without thinking. Remembering how much the Butcher hated to be touched, she let go immediately, as though Ryia's skin was blazing hot, but the other woman didn't flinch away, just turned to face her.

"What?"

Evelyn raised one eyebrow. "You know what." She pursed her lips. "Is there any way I can talk you out of this?"

The Butcher's plans always fell somewhere between "risky" and "bloody insane," but this one tipped even the scales of the latter. Evelyn had pretended for months that she was only allying with Ryia because she was her best hope at destroying the Quill before someone dangerous used it for something awful . . . but after watching her get dragged off into the darkness by those Kinetics back in the Shadow Keep, she had to admit there was more to it than that.

The thought of Ryia putting her neck on the line for this mission again made her heart feel as icy as the Borean winds whipping her hair.

There weren't many ways to get into the Reclaimed Castle. Only four types of people were allowed in: *medev*, servants, invited guests, and prisoners. As the crown prince of Edale, Tristan could enter the Lords' Negotiations as a guest, bringing Evelyn as a guard, but they needed more than that. In order to ensure they could get to the dagger before Clem did, they would need to make sure everyone was looking the other way. A diversion. They needed someone inside the castle who wasn't in the negotiating chamber.

None of them spoke a ruddy word of Borean, so passing as a servant was out of the question, and trying to don a *medev* helmet was about as good a death sentence as spitting on a man wearing one. That left one option.

Evelyn had tried to volunteer, but Joslyn had pointed out pretty quickly how foolish that would be—without Adept powers, Evelyn would truly just be stuck in the cells above the Reclaimed Castle until she died, or until King Andrei saw fit to release her.

From the stories she had heard, it would be the former.

There was no dungeon in all of Thamorr that was a *pleasant* place, but the dungeons of the Reclaimed Castle were among the worst of them. Walls that were made of ice as often as they were made of stone. Some men and women left to rot away in the freezing darkness, others strung up by their wrists and dangled off the edge of the bloody cliffside until the wind stripped their skin from their bones. Ryia was tough, but though she would never admit it, she was still weak from her stay in the Shadow Keep.

What if she didn't survive the Reclaimed Castle?

"I'll tell you what," Ryia said. "If Callum Clem never turns up here in Volkfier and we were wrong about this whole twice-damned venture, then sure, I'll let you talk me out of it."

"Then I hope the bastard never turns up," Evelyn muttered.

They pulled into the docks, bobbing to a stop in the icy surf. They didn't have any papers for docking, but Evelyn wasn't stupid enough to ask what they planned to do about that. She had spent enough time around the criminals of Thamorr by now to know that someone like Salt Beard would have a plan for coming into port. Whatever that plan was, Evelyn missed it, but before she knew it, they were all ashore. Joslyn appeared almost disappointed at the feel of solid ground beneath her feet, but Ryia looked like she might kneel to the snow-covered cobblestones and kiss them.

"What now?" Evelyn asked.

"I was thinking a cup of *stervod.* Maybe some nice roasted elk—you ever had elk before, Linley?" Joslyn started.

Evelyn shot her a glare. "I meant about . . . you know." She mimed a dagger strike to indicate the Eisfang Dagger.

Ryia snorted. "Subtle."

"We'll have to comb the city, won't we? For any sign of . . . *Clem.*" Evelyn whispered the name, glancing over her shoulder. No one was close enough to overhear. To be fair, she wasn't entirely sure any of the people on this street spoke Thamorri Common, anyhow; all she heard was Borean, from the crab hawkers and the fishermen and the shopkeepers shouting from their doorways.

"Well, if we're combing a city this size, I'd rather do it on a full stomach. How about you?" Joslyn said, pushing to the head of their group.

They followed the curve of the docks, Joslyn scanning the signs hanging from the doorways of the taverns and inns on the next street. Could she read Borean?

"Is that what I think it is?" Tristan suddenly piped up. It wasn't fair that his curls just fell handsomely around his face with the swirling snow while hers puffed up like a ruddy storm cloud if they were touched by even a hint of wind. Evelyn turned to follow his gaze.

Shite.

There was no mistaking the ship cozied up along the northern edge of the harbor. She had lived on the ruddy thing for a month back in the summer. In that time, it had felt like a home, a prison, and, in the case of their escape from the island, a beacon of hope. Now it filled her gut with lead. If *The Hardship* was here, it had to mean Callum Clem was here. If Callum Clem was here, that meant the mission would go ahead as planned. Ryia was going to let herself be slammed into an unforgiving cell from which, despite all her arrogance, she might never escape.

Curse Callum Clem. The man ruined everything.

Evelyn nudged Ryia with her elbow. "How's the ship smell?"

Tristan stiffened uncomfortably, but Ryia raised one eyebrow and grinned. She closed her eyes, turning her nose in the direction of *The Hardship* and sniffing. She shared a look with Joslyn before turning back to her.

"Like a fresh Borean winter's day."

Clean—Clem wasn't on his ship, then. The thought simultaneously sent a thrill of hope through her and made her bloody skin crawl. If he wasn't on board the ship, it meant he was out here somewhere in this crowd. He could be lurking behind any corner. But if he wasn't on board the ship, it meant maybe she had one last chance to save Ryia from a terrible death in the Reclaimed Castle. To save *them all* from a terrible death in the Reclaimed Castle, honestly.

"What do you think the chances are that the git left the thing on board?"

Ryia snorted. "Less than one percent."

But Joslyn was tapping her chin thoughtfully. "I don't know. This city's full of pickpockets and thieves. And he might have a fancy little lockbox on his . . . er . . . *ship*." Her expression made it clear she didn't think *The Hardship* was worthy of that title. "Might be worth a peek."

The four of them strode toward *The Hardship* in a tight little knot. Evelyn drew her cloak around her as another gust of wind blew in from the Sea of Boreas. The cloak had been warm enough in Edale and Dresdell, but this far north the damned thing might as well have been made of lace for all the good it did. Tristan looked similarly miserable. Joslyn was prepared for the climate this far north, wearing a patchwork coat made of the fur of at least half a dozen different types of animals. Ryia wore a thinner cloak even than Evelyn's, but she didn't shiver once. Was that the Kinetic magic in her blood, or just her single-minded focus on getting the Quill from Callum Clem? Evelyn didn't know.

The Butcher kept her nose to the air like a hunting dog on the verge of baying, sniffing every few steps to make sure their path was still clear. Salt Beard looked more like their old friend Nash than ever as she swaggered across docks at the front of their pack, cutting through the crowds just by radiating pure confidence. Just like Clem's smuggler, Joslyn wasn't *intimidating,* except maybe in size. She looked bloody jovial, actually. But Evelyn had been in enough fights to know anyone *that* cocksure knew how to handle themselves in a scrap. The Boreans on the docks could sense it too, scurrying out of their way without protest.

Of course, the pirate sigils stitched proudly into Salt Beard's ramshackle fur coat probably helped there as well.

It was a flash of those sigils and the pirate's snow-white teeth that convinced the nearest *dockmenne* to stand aside, allowing them onto the dock holding *The Hardship* without a word or a hint of papers or even gold. No wonder Ryia was so in awe of Salt Beard. She commanded respect on land just as easily as she did on her ruddy ship. Adding her to their team had already saved their skins at least twice . . . so why in the hells did Evelyn hate her so much?

She ground her teeth as Ryia glanced at Joslyn again. If she was being honest with herself, she already knew why she hated the pirate.

"Still clean," Ryia said finally. "But we'll need to be quick. Who knows when the bastard will come back."

"I'll stand guard," Tristan said hurriedly. Evelyn had the impression that he just wanted to stay off that ship so he could run away at the first sign of Clem.

Joslyn looked amused and nodded. "I'll stay with the runt."

Ryia eyed the ship apprehensively. Evelyn knew she didn't like going belowdecks. Even on Joslyn's ship, which was basically a bloody palace floating on water, being belowdecks always made the Butcher nervous.

"Why don't you search up top? I'll take the hold," Evelyn said.

"Whatever you say, Captain" was all Ryia said.

But Evelyn thought she saw a flash of relief in her pitch-dark eyes.

Stepping aboard *The Hardship* was a bit like stepping back in time. So many of Evelyn's miserable memories were tied up in the lines of this ship. Rainstorms and boiling-hot sunshine, fleeing from freebooters and Disciples and the guards at Carrowwick Harbor. But there were good memories too. Like the spot on the rail where she had watched Ryia fight off two Disciples single-handedly. The rowboat Ivan had rescued them in, dangling off the back end of the ship. The spot at the prow where she had cast her father's ring into the surging waters of the Luminous Sea.

"You going to check the hold or keep staring at the deck all day?" Ryia asked.

Evelyn snapped back to the present. "Oh shut it, Butcher."

Ryia just grinned at her, and the hairs on the back of Evelyn's neck shivered in a way that had nothing to do with the whipping northern winds.

The hatch was already open. Evelyn's senses sharpened. That seemed uncharacteristically careless for a man like Callum Clem, but he was an arrogant git. Maybe he was just getting too cocky for his own good. Pulling her hood tighter around her chin, Evelyn eased herself down the ladder and into the darkness of the hold.

Before her eyes even had time to adjust to the

dimness, she felt a flash of ice-cold steel at her throat.

"If you know what's good for you, you'll march your skinny ass back up that ladder and find another ship to pillage."

Evelyn recognized the voice instantly. Nash. The real Nash.

"If you know what's good for you, you'll get that bloody hunting knife away from my throat," Evelyn said back.

The blade faltered, and Nash took a step back. "Linley?" She looked drawn and tired, and she had sheared all the hair from her head, but aside from that, the smuggler looked the same as ever.

Evelyn spun around, pulling her hood back and cocking her head to one side. "Surprise."

"What—what are you doing here?"

Evelyn stepped past the smuggler, peering around as her eyes adjusted to the dim light of the hold. Crates had been hammered together to form makeshift cabins. She slipped into the closest one. Nothing but a slightly swaying hammock. "You know what I'm doing, Nash. I'm looking for something you helped Clem steal." She ducked into the second cabin. Another hammock, a mirror, and a bag overflowing with fabrics. Ivan's quarters, then. "Maybe you'll remember it? Little thing, about yea big"—Evelyn held her hands six inches apart—"has the power to destroy the bloody world. Ring any bells?"

"The Quill isn't here," Nash said. "But Clem will be soon, with his Kinetics in tow. If you're interested in keeping that curly-haired head of yours, you're going to want to get the hell out of here."

"Of course you're going to tell me the Quill isn't here," Evelyn scoffed. "You're with him."

"I'm not—" Nash started. She swallowed the sentence, though—probably because it was an obvious lie.

Kind of hard for Nash to say she wasn't with the Snake when the final cabin on *The Hardship* was so obviously his. Even when Callum Clem was presumed dead and on the run from, well, everyone, his penchant for finery followed him. A blue rug covered most of the deck. It was small, but finely woven, maybe Gildesh in make. Instead of a hammock, Clem had nailed a real bed to the hull of the ship. Or, more likely, he'd made Nash do it for him. A fine bronze lantern sat on a small table in the corner, unlit, and a chest beside the table was packed full of clothing. Fine doublets and loafers and coats fit for a feast at the Bobbin Fort. Very sensible clothing for a long sea voyage—the prat.

Evelyn rummaged through the clothing, shaking out all the pockets. She pushed aside the papers on the desk next, then riffled through the sheets on the bed. She wasn't really expecting to find the Quill—if it was here, Nash would be trying to stop her instead of standing at the entrance to the cabin, arms folded.

"Would it be too much to ask for you to put everything back where you found it?" Nash asked. Evelyn shot her a glare, and the smuggler sighed. "Okay, fine, I'll do it myself. Unless you'd rather he knew you were here?"

Evelyn turned, eyes narrowing suspiciously as she watched Nash carefully restack the papers on the desk, then move to the trunk, folding and stacking Clem's clothing again. "Why would you help hide that I came here?"

"Because Clem left me behind to guard the ship. I doubt he'd be too pleased if he came back to find the place ransacked and me without a scratch, do you?"

"I could give you a few scratches, if that's what you want."

Nash snorted. "I can't say I wouldn't deserve it if you did. I—"

She cut off abruptly, looking up as heavy footfalls fell on the deck above them, followed by the creak of the ladder leading down into the hold.

"He's on his way" came Joslyn's voice from the makeshift passageway outside the cabin. "Where the fuck did you get to? That bastard, Keln—Clam—whatever his name is, he's coming back. Did you find the—"

The pirate broke off, looking between Evelyn

and Nash as she thundered into Clem's cabin. She nodded at Nash, still looking at Evelyn. "Who the hell is this?"

"Clem's smuggler," Evelyn said. She looked at Nash. The smuggler's face had gone completely slack. She was staring at Joslyn like she had never seen a human face before.

Although Evelyn couldn't blame her. If some sod had come along looking like her twice-cursed reflection, she probably would have gone mute too.

But it was more than that. Nash didn't look surprised, she was bloody *glowing*. Her eyes shone as she looked from Joslyn's face to her height, something burning particularly bright in their depths as she gazed at the pirate's shaven head.

They really did look almost identical. She had wondered if it was just a flaw in her memory that had made her mistake the pirate captain for Nash back in Golden Port, but now, seeing them side by side, she realized it was a mistake anyone could make easily. She froze, an idea forming in her brain. Was it really a mistake *anyone* could make?

She looked back at Joslyn, and the sparkle in the pirate's eye told her they were thinking the same exact thing. Salt Beard gave her a nod. If Clem really was coming, they would need to move quickly.

Nash was so enthralled with the appearance

of her mirror image that she didn't even flinch as Evelyn drew her sword from its sheath. She started to turn as Evelyn raised the weapon and lifted a hand to block as Evelyn brought the hilt crashing down. But the smuggler was too slow. Her eyes rolled back into her skull, and she slumped senseless to the deck.

"That was what you were thinking, right?" Evelyn said, kneeling to the deck to strip Nash's boots from her feet.

"Never hurts to have a man on the inside." Joslyn caught the boots easily as Evelyn tossed them her way, then slipped them onto her own feet in place of the ones she had been wearing. They were a perfect fit.

"Any chance you two are related?" Evelyn asked, grunting as she rolled Nash over to relieve her of her salt-stained coat.

"Maybe," the pirate said evasively. There was something off in her tone. "Never knew my parents. Who knows what they did after they shipped me off to that damned orphanage." She looked back at Nash's face, examining it critically. "Or before."

Evelyn frowned. She had always felt like her parents preferred her younger sister, Nialla, to her, but to keep one child and give the other to a ruddy orphanage? If Nash and Joslyn really were related, then their father was even worse than hers.

Getting Nash into Joslyn's clothes was more difficult than getting the smuggler out of her own. She was almost two hundred pounds of pure muscle, after all. Evelyn was no weakling, but still, by the time they finished rolling Nash's limp form into Salt Beard's fur coat, they were both soaked in sweat.

"Anything I should know about her?" the pirate asked as they finished up.

"She's foul-mouthed," Evelyn said, grunting as she helped Joslyn push Nash to seated. "And cocky. And she talks of nothing but her bloody ship."

Joslyn grinned at Evelyn, hefting the smuggler up over one shoulder. "I think I can wrap my head around that."

"Ah, there is one thing," Evelyn said, looking at the pirate's smile. She pulled back Nash's lip to show the carefully sharpened canines. "Don't smile."

"Got it," Joslyn said. She ran her tongue over her own teeth with a wince, and Evelyn knew she was thinking the same thing she had thought herself when she first saw those canines. Filing them to points had to have bloody hurt.

Evelyn climbed up the ladder first. Ryia was still standing there, looking at her like she was crazy. "What took so long? You better have found the twice-damned Quill."

"Not exactly," Evelyn said, panting as she

reached back down the ladder, helping Joslyn boost Nash from the hold.

Ryia swore softly as she saw the senseless smuggler.

"Change of plans, Cautella," said Salt Beard. She flashed the Butcher a grin. "I'm sticking around. See if I can bring this bastard down from the inside."

"And what are we supposed to do with this?" Ryia asked, gesturing to the unconscious Nash.

Joslyn shrugged. "Keep her out of sight? I don't know—just get her to my ship and lock her in my cabin or something." She stiffened, her nostrils flaring as she glanced toward the docks. "We don't really have time to chat about it, though. Your old friend will be here any second."

Grumbling, Ryia grabbed Nash's shoulders while Evelyn took her feet, and together they carried her down the gangplank and onto the dock.

"What happened to Joslyn?" Tristan asked, jumping back in alarm.

"Not Joslyn." Evelyn peeled back Nash's lip again, revealing the sharpened canines. "Are you going to help us carry her or what?"

"For Adalina's sake," Tristan muttered. But he took one shoulder from Ryia's hands, and the three of them marched down the docks like some bizarre Festival of Felice processional.

Evelyn shot one last look back at *The Hardship*.

Joslyn stood, leaning against the helm, looking like she owned the twice-damned thing already. Evelyn nodded sharply, then hurried away, leaving the ship and its counterfeit captain in her wake.

Getting back to the *Ophidian Fang* supporting what looked like a dead body was disturbingly easy. No one made any move to stop them; in fact, they jumped out of the way like they thought the body was diseased. Of course, this was Boreas—the place where the Borean Death had originated and wiped out half the bloody population less than a century ago—maybe they really *did* think the body might be diseased.

Evelyn wanted to explain to Salt Beard's crew what they had done, but Ryia and Tristan talked her out of it. What if the crew abandoned them once they learned the pirate was no longer with them? What if they tried to chase Clem down themselves in an effort to defend their captain? They didn't know much about these pirates, but the bastards were definitely loyal to Joslyn. It was a good point, and in the end, Evelyn agreed to go with Tristan's lie—weak as it was—that Joslyn had fallen ill while they were in the city and would have to stay in her cabin for a few days.

Apparently the crew was used to Joslyn falling ill. They looked the other way as they carried Nash on board. Maybe Salt Beard had a habit of getting pissed onshore—or maybe she had a penchant for something even stronger than ale or *stervod*. Either way, by the time the sun sank below the waves, the still-senseless Nash was locked tight in Salt Beard's cabin, the crew had filtered off into the taverns and dice halls of Volkfier, and Tristan had slunk off to warm himself belowdecks, leaving Evelyn and Ryia alone on the main deck of the *Fang*.

Evelyn had taken Joslyn's fur coat. She wrapped it tighter around herself, shivering in the cold evening winds. Ryia still wore only her old threadbare cloak, though she had pulled the hood up. It flapped in the breeze, throwing deep, flickering shadows across her still-bruised face.

"Are you sure you want to do this?" Evelyn knew there was no point in asking, but she had to. She had to try, one last time. "Maybe now that we have Joslyn on the inside, we won't need to—"

"Nash's head was shaved," Ryia said, looking out toward the winking lanterns and glowing windows of the city.

". . . What?"

The Butcher turned to face her. "Nash. Her head was shaved. That means Clem plans to sneak her in with his Adept. However he plans to get into the meeting chamber, you can bet that stick up your ass that Joslyn will be in there with him. Which means we still need someone outside that room."

"And you're sure it has to be you?"

"Unless you've gained Adept magic since the last time you asked me this question."

"And what if something goes wrong?" Evelyn asked. "What if you can't get out?"

Ryia whipped around to face her. Evelyn's breath caught as the Butcher's jet-black gaze pinned her in place. "And what if Callum Clem gets Kinetic powers? What if we give the weapon that has held Thamorr hostage since the Seven Decades' War to the twice-damned Snake of the Southern Dock?"

Evelyn's lips twisted into a bitter smile. "I didn't realize you were the noble type."

Ryia cocked her head to one side, amusement sparkling in her eyes. "Chalk it up to a bad influence."

And just like that, with nothing more than a flip of her cloak, she leapt over the rail and off the ship. Evelyn watched her shadow slip through the docks. She swore she saw Ryia pause at the edge of the city, looking back, just for a moment.

Then she was gone. A lump rose in Evelyn's throat. Gone again, maybe for the last time.

CHAPTER SEVENTEEN

Ryia

Fear was nothing new for Ryia. But this kind of fear—a sinking sense of guilt and dread that was less associated with the *medev* base she was about to break into and more associated with the look on Evelyn's face? That was new.

But what did Evelyn expect her to do? Give up on the plan, let Clem get the dagger and take over the whole cursed world just to save herself?

She really *was* sounding like a noble prick these days, wasn't she?

The woman she'd been a few months ago would have chewed this version of her up and spit her out like a lump of tobacco. Then again, the woman she'd been a few months ago had also been a lonely, selfish asshole.

Hood up, boots crunching in the filthy, well-packed snow lining the streets, she cut her way east through the city of Reusig. The trading hub was smaller by far than Volkfier. She'd arrived in the bustling riverside town that morning, hitching a ride with some dour-faced traders down the fast-flowing Shielriev river. She flexed her gloved fingers, reaching instinctively for her hatchet belt, but of course it wasn't there.

It would have been stupid to bring it along just to let the *medev* confiscate it. Still, she felt naked as a Gildesh whore without it. She knew that, with a little luck and a lot of focus, she could control just about anything with her Kinetic powers—even now, she could hear the bricks and barrels lining the streets singing to her—but for over a decade that belt had been both her weapon and her shield. Her only armor against a world that wanted to kill her for what she was. For what her father had made her.

Sure, that belt was also the thing that had been used to *make* her into what she was. And maybe the fact that she still clung to it after all these years was, as Joslyn had said, fucked up, but so what? Everyone was a little fucked up in one way or another. Those hatchets had stolen the lives of half a hundred Adept. Someday soon, she would use them to save the lives of thousands of those unlucky bald bastards.

But first, she had to get captured and dragged into a cell. She didn't need weapons for that. From her time in Boreas, Ryia knew there was only one offense guaranteed to get someone sent to the fabled cells above the Reclaimed Castle—treason. Anything less, and she might find herself locked in some other lord's cellar or just executed outright. But King Andrei had been struggling to put down the revolution started by the man known only as *Haisefven* for the better part of two decades at this point. Rumor had it that the Shark of the North himself had been caught some years ago, but whether or not that was true, the flames of his revolution burned on. Any traitor would be brought in for questioning.

Of course, "questioning" really meant "torture," but it was best not to think about that too much. Dwelling on that piece of the plan was likely to make her crawl back to Evelyn on hands and knees and beg the ex-captain to hide her away until this was all over. The old Ryia would just have snagged one of these shaggy-ass horses and ridden off into the snows to wait out the storms in the Völgnich Mountains.

But no. This new, stupid-but-noble Ryia had sat down with the few Boreans in Salt Beard's crew to pinpoint where the nearest *medev* weapons hold was and how to get there. There was one just a few miles northeast of the city. The weapons shipped from Edale came in through Volkfier before being delivered to the hold, but it was rumored that there was also a stockpile of blasting powder from the mountain mines lurking there.

Breaking into a heavily guarded weapons hold that also possibly held a large quantity of powder that could reduce a stone wall to pebbles . . . unarmed. What could possibly go wrong?

She made it out the snow-covered east gate just before nightfall, then took the road north.

It didn't take long to figure out that not many travelers ventured this far north. Why would they? Aside from this weapons stockpile, the only things north were the mountains and a few small villages specializing in trapping and drinking too much *stervod.*

Ryia knew she didn't look like a *medev*, and she had a feeling with her brown skin and dark hair, she didn't look much like a far-north Borean trapper, either. The thick pine forest on either side of the packed-snow road was full of the kind of shadows she had been taught to lose herself in when working with that group of highwaymen in the south of Edale. Even if there weren't any of those purse-cutting bastards this far north, there were probably wolves and bears and worse lurking in those snow-covered trees.

But Felice was on her side for once. She stalked through the trees, seeing wolf tracks but no wolves, hearing nothing but the occasional hooting of lonely owls and the rustle of branches and smelling only pine and snow—none of the cloying, decayed scent of danger. Just a few hours into the night, she saw it. A large clearing. Climbing the nearest tree to get a better view, Ryia peered out into the moonlight.

It was a *medev* facility, all right. Built entirely from stone, the structure slanted up toward the sky like a man-made mountain. It was surrounded on all sides by thick stone walls, and a quick lap around the tree line showed there was only one gate. At least four *medev* stood guard there, two on top of the wall and two at the base, the reddish plumes on their stupid helmets fluttering in the northern wind as it howled through the trees. But Ryia had never had much use for gates. The outer wall would be easy enough to get past. Even from this distance, she could see half a hundred toeholds on the way up. No, the challenge would come with the tower itself.

Like all the structures in Volkfier, the *medev* weapons hold was built with slanted walls. Unlike those dock-town buildings, however, there were no corners to this base. Instead, the structure was shaped like a cone. Ryia could see ice glinting in the moonlight, slicking the smooth, ground-stone walls as they angled straight from the ground to the point at the top. Sure, there were a few holes that must have been windows or arrow slits, but they were way too far apart to serve as handholds.

She glanced down at her gloved fingers, flexing them. “Up for a challenge?” she asked them.

As usual, they didn’t answer. But their silence felt anxious rather than cocky. She shook her head. Stupid. If ever there was a time it would be okay to fail, it was now. The goal was to get captured, after all.

Just as Ryia had expected, the outer wall was no challenge. Easier than scaling the outer fortifications of the Bobbin Fort, and that was saying something. The top of the wall was hardly wide enough for one man to walk. A pair of *medev* patrolled, one pacing along the southern and western stretches of wall, the other taking the east. No one seemed to bother to patrol the north—there was no gate over there, after all, and who was going to storm them from the mountains? An army of goats? A few dozen angry fur traders?

Ryia was uninterrupted as she scaled the northern wall, slipping down into the field surrounding the weapons hold itself. Normally the snow coating the ground would have presented a problem, but now she just trudged right on through, leaving a neat line of very obvious boot prints in her wake. When she reached the place where the slanted roof met the crunchy snow, she looked up doubtfully. It was steep and smooth and covered with ice.

But if she wanted to be sure she was taken to the Reclaimed Castle and not just shoved in whatever holding cell this backwoods shithole might have, she needed to look like she was a real threat. A real threat wouldn't slide down the side of the building like it was a twice-damned laundry chute, landing in the waiting arms of a *medev* guard. No, a real threat would be found *inside* the building. Preferably deep inside the building, pillaging through the stock of weapons, but at this point, Ryia would settle for just indoors and on her feet.

The first window was about three body lengths up the side of the roof. She could see it—or rather, the lack of it—from here. An indent in the slanted wall of stone. If only there were a single handhold between the ground and there . . . but there was nothing. Not even her Kinetic abilities could help her here.

Or could they?

Ryia shot a glance over her shoulder. Still no sign of any patrolling *medev*. She would have smelled them coming, anyway. She returned her attention to the slanted roof. More specifically, to the carefully sanded stones. If she closed her eyes, she could feel their vibrations tugging at her. Hear the gravelly sound of their song—a hundred or more individual tones, one for each stone that made up the wall. Tugging on them all was out of the question . . . but tugging on just one?

Maybe.

She isolated one stone—the one just a few inches higher than her outstretched hand. A dark gray one with a flattened top. Then, reaching out with her Kinetic power, she pulled. The stone groaned and protested, hesitant to break free of its icy home. "Come on, you son of a bitch," she muttered, gritting her teeth. Ryia's heart jumped into the back of her throat as the ice around the stone cracked. Pouring every last ounce of her concentration into wiggling that one little rock, Ryia narrowed her eyes. Finally, she heard the telltale scrape of stone on stone as the sanded rock inched forward. After she'd pulled it from the wall just enough to latch her fingers around its edge, she released a breath and her focus at once.

"Now, that's handy," Ryia panted, grinning. She pulled herself up using her newly made handhold, then repeated the painstaking process. Every few feet she pulled another stone loose with her Kinetic magic, then another, and another, making a ladder up the side of the ice-coated hold.

She didn't stop until she reached the top window—the one situated right underneath the point of the conelike roof. Then she paused to catch her breath. After a few moments, she pulled herself closer to the window and flattened herself against the curve of the roof, listening carefully. Throughout her climb, there had been movement on the other side of the stones. A few footsteps here, the rattle and scrape of metal there. Now all was quieter than a crowded tavern after Roland told one of his jokes. She sniffed the air delicately, then nearly fell backward off the wall.

If it was so quiet, why did it smell like a cesspool of death and decay?

Staying flat against the roof, Ryia peered sideways through the window. It was still night, but her eyes were well-adjusted to the darkness at this point. Through the thin glass pane, dusted with snow, she saw . . . nothing. Some shadowy boxes, stacked in neat rows. A floor so clean it reflected the silvery light of the moon shining through the window. A door on the far side of the room, with a thin band of light underneath it. There were shadows outside the door; Ryia could see them moving, blocking that band of light, then letting it shine through again. Guards. Two of them, by her count.

Two guards wouldn't smell that dangerous . . . especially not from the far side of a closed door. Would they?

It was against all her experience and instinct to ignore the stench of danger and death, but the goal of this mission was to fail, to get caught. Running toward danger was the only way to do that. Holding her breath, Ryia reared back, then leapt forward, speeding toward the windowpane boots-first.

The cold-brittle glass shattered like crystal, tinkling to the floor. Far quieter than Ryia had anticipated—why did that never happen when she was *trying* to be quiet? Still, the sound of her boots hitting the stained-wood floor was loud enough. The crates shuddered as the dull thud echoed through the space. The stench of danger was almost incapacitating now that she was actually inside the room. Whoever was outside that door had to be at least five times as dangerous as the quickest Disciple she had ever faced.

Then her eyes shifted to the crates around her, and her stomach flipped. Unless it wasn't the guards her senses were warning her about. The door banged open, and light flooded into the room from the hallway. Warm torchlight that flickered over the contents of the open crate beside the door. Tiny granules the color of steel but dull as stone. She had seen it before, a handful or less filled every firework, she knew. A small handful made a firework shoot half a mile up into the sky and blow into a thousand pieces.

What would an entire *room* of the stuff do?

Well, she had wanted the guards to believe she was dangerous enough to be worth the trouble of carting her to the Reclaimed Castle. The bastards would have to believe that now.

Remembering her instructions from Salt Beard's Borean crew members, Ryia stiffened her back, staring down the red-plumed *medev* as they stalked into the room. Then she shouted, "*Salu Haisefven*!"

Hail the Shark of the North.

The *medev* were just as quick as she remembered from the last time she had fought them. She could have dodged them, could have wriggled free, back out the window and into the night. She probably could even have escaped with a few pocketfuls of blasting powder, if she'd wanted to.

But that wasn't the plan. So she let the bastards knock her down and bind her arms. She let them throw a bag over her head. She sensed the blow coming, but made no attempt to dodge as the left-hand *medev* clapped her firmly across the temples.

Then she slumped to the floor.

She awoke to the sound of rattling and the bite of cold wind on her face. When she opened her eyes, she found herself in a carriage. Well, not so much a carriage as a cage with wheels. It shook and clattered as it bounced over the uneven, frozen dirt of whatever Borean road they were on. Two shaggy horses pulled the cage, and half a company of *medev* marched alongside it. Ryia pushed herself up, tapping on the bars next to her to get the attention of the nearest *medev*.

"Hey, you mind telling me where we're headed?"

The only response she got was the point of the *medev*'s broadsword leveled at her throat through the bars. It wavered with his every step, but only barely. He withdrew the blade a few seconds later, threading it back into his sheath without looking, eyes still locked on the snowy, rolling hills before them. These Borean bastards prided themselves on being as obedient and regimented as Adept soldiers, she remembered. She would get no answer from them.

The next seven days passed measured in gusts of cold northern winds, cups of half-frozen water, and chunks of stale bread and dried meats. Ryia ate only the bread, tossing the meat out of her cage with an upturned lip. Most sane people would say it was stupid to turn down food when she was literally starving, but she would wager none of those men had been force-fed human blood for three years chained to the wall of a cellar. So, fuck them. If she ever tried to eat meat again, she knew she would just retch it all back up anyway. Might as well save herself the trouble.

No one had told her where they were headed, but by the end of the fifth day, she already knew. Their road wound and curved, snaking around snowbanks and over narrow bridges crossing ice-slicked streams, but she knew in the end it would lead them to the giant mountain sprouting from the horizon to the east. Faustnich was its proper name, but everyone south of the Borean border just called it the Fist. It was a monstrous pile of rock and snow rising up from the otherwise lightly rolling countryside. A deep lake with a glasslike surface lay in its shadow, and surrounding the lake was the bustling city of Oryol, the Borean capital.

There was no castle at Oryol, or at least not one that was visible to the casual eye. The kings and queens of Boreas were even more dramatic than the royals in the south. The fort in Oryol was known as the Reclaimed Castle, and it had been built into the Fist itself, its corridors carved like tunnels, its stairwells snaking up the sides of the jagged cliffs, its chambers buried deep within the heart of the mountain.

The Boreans believed the dark counterpart of their god lived beneath the ground. They believed it to the point that they burned their dead instead of burying them, as to them, burying a body was as good as handing it to *Yavol* with a bow around its neck. So, by digging *up* the ground and building their castle inside the mountain, the first king of Boreas said he had reclaimed it from the darkness—hence its ridiculous name.

Nonetheless, Ryia had to admit that the Reclaimed Castle was a sight to behold. She wrapped her fingers around the bars of her cage, craning her neck to try to get a better look as the cart rattled and rumbled through the streets of Oryol and toward the castle gates. The rock face rising to greet the setting sun was dotted with windows and ornately carved balconies. Stairwells wound up and down the sides, carved from pure white stone that made it look like the servants were bustling up and down stairs made of nothing but snow.

But snowy stairs and fancy balconies weren't what she had come to the Reclaimed Castle to see. The castle gates creaked open to let them in. Ryia lounged back against the corner of the cell as the jail cart bounced over the ice-slick cobbles. The yard inside the gate was crawling with *medev*. They patrolled in neat rows, their stupid little plumes jutting up from their helmets, making them look like Brillish songbirds trying to find a mate.

The *medev* were supposed to be the most elite fighting force outside the Disciples, but Ryia counted the chances she had to escape. Even without using her newfound Kinetic powers, she could have bolted three times—once when they first opened the cage to drag her out, again when the door guard fumbled his keys and took two tries to unlock the door to the prison, and a third when they removed her shackles to shove her into her cell at last. But she wasn't trying to escape—not yet, at least.

Instead, she put on a big show of falling to the floor face-first, eyes squeezed shut, hands up over her face when the *medev* locked her away. She lay huddled there, the picture of defeat and submission, until the elite guards' clanking footsteps faded into silence. When they were finally out of earshot, she pushed herself to her feet and examined the bars in the small window on the massive iron door to her cell. She ran her palms over them. They were solid, but rusted. She could feel the brittleness in their song already. That window would be a tight squeeze, but still, breaking out of here would be a twice-damned picnic. Ryia hugged her cloak around her as a chill wormed into her bones.

She frowned. No, that was more than a chill. It was *wind*.

She turned around slowly, eyes widening as they took in the back wall of her cell. Or rather, the lack of one.

A set of rusted bars ran from floor to ceiling, but other than that, the wall was wide open to the whistling winds and the piercing snows. The prison was located far off the ground, near the top of the Reclaimed Castle, looking out over the barren, snowy wasteland outside Oryol. The cliff face outside the bars dropped straight down to the ground, flatter than Ivan Rezkoye's emotional range. Like the slanted walls of the armory Ryia had broken into to get here, it was slick with ice and snow.

Even if there were no bars to stop someone from leaving the cell, without Adept abilities, the only thing a prisoner would accomplish by trying to climb down that wall would be plummeting to his death, dashed against the spiky rocks far below.

"You wouldn't happen to have a flint and some wood?" Ryia asked jokingly, rubbing her hands together as she turned to the cell across from hers.

A man sat huddled in the corner. He was buried

underneath a filthy pile of fabric that might once have been a cloak. His long blond hair was matted with dirt and frozen in places. He lifted his head, revealing a gaunt face half-concealed by a tangled beard. His cough sounded frail, but when his eyes locked on hers, they were sharp as daggers. Sea green and glinting with curiosity and energy. He looked her up and down appraisingly.

"Southern Edale" was all he said. His accent was thick, his voice hoarse.

"What?"

"You are from southern Edale. How did you get here?"

Ryia shifted her weight uncomfortably. She *was* from southern Edale, but no one had ever called her on that before. She nodded toward the corridor outside. "The *medev*—how did you think I got here?"

"You know what I am asking."

His voice was measured and calm.

Ryia plopped down on the floor and stretched out her legs. "I raided a *medev* weapons cache." She leaned closer to him, lowering her voice. "I'm with the resistance, you know. *Haisefven*. All that shit."

Out of the corner of her eye she saw his lips twitch. "You are one of the *Fvene*?"

"Yep," Ryia said. "And who the hell are you?"

The man studied her for a long moment. "My name is Kasimir."

CHAPTER EIGHTEEN
Ivan

Ivan did not say a word the entire walk back to the harbor at Volkfier. He could not have spoken even if he wanted to. With every blink he saw the bodies of the innocent, lying slain in the halls of Lord Piervin's manor. Lord Piervin himself had been something of a monster, but the maids? The cooks and servants? They had been regular, poor, hardworking Boreans. The very same people he and Kasimir had spent their lives trying to protect. And Callum Clem had murdered them without a second thought.

Callum would be a worse tyrant than the *Keunich* had ever been. This had all been a mistake. Ivan felt sick. But he had to believe it was not too late to set things right. Perhaps Nash still had a plan. If she did, he would not be fool enough to stop her this time. She had been right all along. How had he been so blind?

The smuggler stood at the helm of their little ship, hood covering her head as she looked out over the tossing waters of the Sea of Boreas. Clem did not even give her a passing glance as he hurried up the gangway.

"Pack anything you need, Nash. We leave

for Oryol at sunup," he said over his shoulder, slipping belowdecks for whatever last-minute preparations he had on his twisted mind.

The blood-soaked Kinetics took their positions on deck, standing on either side of the hatch Clem had just disappeared through. Ivan stood on the dock a long time, staring up at Nash's silhouette, regal and statuesque against the darkening horizon. She had tried to warn him about Clem after leaving Carrowwick. And in Golden Port. And again on their voyage up the coastline to Volkfier. Ivan had not listened. How shameful it would be to admit his mistake only after so much blood had been spilled.

Swallowing his pride, Ivan strode up the gangway. He stopped just behind Nash, then cleared his throat.

"Nash, I—" he started. But he broke off when the hooded figure turned to face him.

The woman standing on the deck of this ship was not Nash. She was the same height, her face the same shape, and she was dressed in Nash's clothes, but the look in her eyes was different. Harder and more unforgiving than the Nash he had come to know so well.

"Who in *Yavol*'s name are you?"

"Don't you recognize your own ship captain?" The fake Nash smiled. And there was the proof. Her canines were unsharpened.

"Do not play coy with me," Ivan said, taking

a step closer. "What have you done with Nash?"

"Are you feeling all right?" asked the fake Nash. She lifted a hand as though to feel his forehead for fever. He ducked out of reach.

"Do not make me call for Callum," Ivan said. He shot a meaningful look toward the Kinetics guarding the hatch behind them. "You will not like what happens next if I do."

The fake Nash took a deep breath in through her nose and smiled again. "You're not going to call for Callum Clem." She studied him intently with the eyes that were at once nearly identical to and wildly different from Nash's. "You're afraid of him, aren't you? Fuck, the others were wondering why you joined up with his psychotic ass, but none of them guessed it was something as simple as cowardice." She gave him a disapproving nod. "I think you should take that as a compliment."

Ivan clenched his fists. "It is *not* cowardice." Then he paused, the rest of the impostor's words sinking in. "What do you mean, 'the others'?"

Fake Nash just smiled her non-Nash smile. "I think you already know."

The Butcher and Captain Linley. It had to be. They had survived the Catacombs and had come looking for Clem. Were they on the ship as well? Ivan looked around, and the impostor chuckled.

"They're not on board, Rezkoye."

"Where are they? Where is Nash?" Ivan asked again. He was surprised at how relieved he felt to know Ryia and Evelyn were alive. Alive and close by. Nash would be happier with them than she had been with Clem . . . if they allowed her to join them, that was. Would they have taken her alive? In their eyes she was a traitor, just like him, was she not? A shock of dread coursed through him at the thought of Nash's eyes, wide and unseeing, drained of their light and life. He forced the image away.

Fake Nash shrugged. "Somewhere close by, probably. There's no use looking, though. You'll see them in a few days anyways. The fourth of Seteber is the exact date, I believe?"

The day of the council meeting in Oryol. Ice-cold wind whipped through Ivan's hair as he faced the impostor. "You know about it, yes?"

He did not dare elaborate, in case this impostor did not know about the dagger Clem sought. But why else would Ryia and the others have come to Boreas? Why else would they be planning to go to the Reclaimed Castle on the exact date of the *verdammte* council meeting?

"With my help, your old team knows a lot of things."

"Is that so?" Ivan narrowed his eyes. "Who are you?"

The woman leaned casually on the helm, cocking her head to one side. "Let's just say every sailor off the coast of Gildemar pisses their pants when they see my sails coming."

Ivan examined the fake Nash critically. Impossible . . . this woman could not be Salt Beard. But now that he thought of it, he was unsure there had ever been actual accounts confirming Salt Beard was a man. This woman was certainly bold and cocksure enough to fit the description. But how in Gott's name had the Butcher managed to get the most infamous pirate in the Luminous Sea to join her vendetta against Callum Clem?

The same way she got the rest of us to join her vendetta against the Guildmaster just a few months before, he thought wryly.

"Look, Rezkoye," Salt Beard said, coming a step closer. She nodded toward the hatch. "You're afraid of that jackass now. Imagine how scary he'll be with the power of Declan Day's Quill."

Ivan stiffened. "I did not join with Callum out of fear," he argued again.

"Ambition, then?" Salt Beard gave him a look that could only be described as pitying. "I don't know the man, but from what I've heard, he's not exactly the type to farm out power to a second-in-command."

Ivan was growing angry now. This filthy pirate wearing Nash's clothes knew nothing about him. She had no idea what she was talking about. What was at stake. He poked a finger into her sternum. "Do not accuse me of such petty aims."

The pirate just shrugged. "Sorry, Rezkoye, so

far you strike me as the petty type. A coward who teams up with a tyrant to save his own ass—"

"It is not my own *arsch* I am trying to save!" Ivan finally burst out. He had trained for years to keep his emotions in check, but between what he had just seen in Lord Piervin's manor and Nash's unexpected absence, he was feeling raw and out of control.

"Aha," the impostor said, raising an eyebrow. "Now we're getting somewhere. Whose ass is important enough to burn the damned world for?"

Ivan was silent for a long moment, lips buttoned tight. But as he stared down the impostor, his resolve began to waver. He had carried this secret for so many years, and all it had done was drive him into the service of the most sinister *arschlache* in Carrowwick—perhaps all of Thamorr. He should have told Nash his true motivations weeks ago. Perhaps she would have been able to talk some sense into him.

He had lost his opportunity—he could not tell Nash now. But somehow he could not control his tongue as it slipped, spilling his darkest secret to this woman who shared Nash's features. "My brother." He sank to the deck, hugging his knees tight to his chest.

The impostor sucked her teeth. Then: "Noble. But you realize if Clem destroys Thamorr, your dear brother's not going to have anywhere to live, right?"

He did realize that. Ivan stared at his boots, studying the blood spatters. He had been feeling these doubts for weeks now, if he was being honest with himself. But after what he had just seen at the manor, he was certain of it. He had bet on the wrong horse, as the real Nash would say. But the race had already begun. If Nash was elsewhere, if she did not have a plan . . . Ivan could not see a way to stop it now.

There was a rustling of fabric. Ivan looked up as Salt Beard lowered herself to the deck beside him. "So, where is this brother of yours?"

"The cells above the Reclaimed Castle in Oryol." Ivan could picture it now, Kasimir, stuck in one of those open-walled cells, shivering in the biting winds and freezing snows for years on end. He pulled himself out of his thoughts as he heard Salt Beard laughing beside him.

Turning, he saw the pirate nearly doubled over, rasping with mirth. Anger clawed up his throat, but before he could retort, Salt Beard wiped her eyes and said, "I think it's time for you to switch sides, Rezkoye."

"And why is that?"

Salt Beard grinned her harsh, un-Nashlike grin at him again. "Because as it so happens, we've already scheduled a prison break as part of our plan."

Ivan felt as though he had been hit in the head with something very heavy. "You are planning to break into the cells within the Reclaimed Castle?" It was *seicherende*. Certain death. "There are easier ways to commit suicide, if that is your intent."

"Into? No. But we're planning on breaking *out* of them. Or at least, one of us is."

Even more impossible. If there was a way to break out of the cells in Oryol, Kasimir or his *Fvene* would have found a way, would they not? "If that is your plan, then *one of you* will be trapped in Boreas for a very long time," he said sourly.

The pirate just tutted her tongue in apparent disappointment. "I thought you knew the Butcher better than that, Rezkoye."

Ivan sat in silence for a long moment, staring up at the star-strewn sky. Ryia had a talent for getting into places she did not belong, yes . . . and she also had a talent for getting out of them. She had gotten out of the bell tower on the Guildmaster's island, slipped out of the Bobbin Fort more times than he cared to try to count, and apparently wormed her way out of the Catacombs the night Callum Clem had lifted the Quill from under Wyatt Asher's nose. Was it likely she could escape the *Keunich*'s prison? No. But there was a chance. And right now, perhaps a mere chance was enough.

Finally, Ivan cast a sidelong glance at the pirate. "All right," he said. "Let us hear this plan of yours."

• • •

For five long days Ivan sat in the deceased Lord Gavik Piervin's carriage with Callum Clem and his two Kinetics, stitching in silence. His disguise had been complete since before they left the harbor at Volkfier, but the tiny tweaks and last-minute adjustments he made as they bumped along the northern road helped him to calm himself.

Salt Beard, whose true name was Joslyn, had volunteered to steer the carriage, sitting out in the blistering autumn winds and tending the horses. Thankfully, Clem did not question this. So far, it seemed the Snake was still not aware that his smuggler had been replaced by a convincing double . . . but then again, it was always difficult to know what Callum Clem was truly aware of.

Clem ordered "Nash" to stop the carriage just outside the city of Novkal. Ivan had been to the city only once before—when Kasimir had sent him and five other members of the *Fvene* here to set fire to the very building he was now planning to infiltrate. Ivan could see the tip of it over the pines already, stretching into the gray autumn sky. The most elite *medev* base in all of Boreas.

In his mind, Ivan could still see the flames licking up the steep-angled roof. See the smoke pouring from it, sending tendrils of their temporary victory snaking between the stars. Of course, the *medev* had put a stop to the fire and rebuilt more quickly than a snowrabbit ran across an open field. But for Kasimir, the goal had never been complete destruction. It was about sending a message, he always said.

It was about showing the people of Novkal that their *medev* captors were not gods. That they could be touched. Harmed.

That they could bleed.

"I know I don't need to explain to you how important it is for you to get inside the castle," Clem said, barely looking up from the paper he was reading as Ivan opened the carriage door and stepped out into the fading light. "Without your support on the inside, this entire operation will fall apart, Mr. Rezkoye."

"Do not worry, Callum. I will be inside when you arrive." He shot a glance toward Joslyn, sitting on the hard bench at the front of the carriage. "I will see you in two days, Nash." *If Clem has not discovered your betrayal before that,* he thought. With that, he turned toward the city of Novkal.

Clem needed him inside to start the distraction that would give him and "Nash" the window required to find and lift the dagger, but there was a much more pressing reason that Ivan needed to ensure he made it into the base. To ensure he embedded himself into the company of *medev* that would travel to Oryol to provide security—and a show of force—for their *Keunich* during the upcoming discussions. He smoothed his counterfeit *medev* uniform as he slipped into the woods, away from the carriage. Like a true *medev* uniform, this one was deep red, lined with black fur and finished with black trousers.

Soft pine needles covered Ivan's tracks as he snaked through the trees, making his way toward the Novkal city gates. They were well-defended: half a dozen *medev* were visible on top of the spiky wooden wall, and no doubt countless others milled around just inside. Even the Butcher would have trouble breaking into a place like this. But it was not Ivan's style to break into any place. He preferred to walk in through the front door.

He waited on the edge of the trees for a long while. Long enough for the shadows to stretch and the cold of night to begin its creep up his spine. *Schiss.* Three years in the warmth of the south and he was as weak in the cold as a Brillish cactus. But Kasimir would cure him of his weakness again. Just as he had done the first time, submerging him in the *Höllefluss* during the dead of winter until he could feel the pain no more.

If it meant Kasimir returning to him? Ivan would gladly go through that torturous training once more. He would dive into those frigid waters a hundred times if it meant he could see his brother's face again.

As the pale gray skies deepened to the color of charcoal, Ivan saw what he had been waiting for. A *medev* patrol, marching in formation, heading for the gates. It was then a simple matter to loop around behind them, creeping from the trees when the line turned the corner, just out of view of the guards keeping watch high above, and bury himself within the line. The rest of the men held helmets at their sides. Ivan had no helmet just yet, but he had come prepared. He pulled a red plume from the pocket of his disguise. It was made from delicately cut silk from Lord Piervin's wardrobe rather than from feathers of the Borean firebird, but the *medev* surrounding him had been trained to keep their eyes ahead, and Ivan trusted that the ones above would see only what they expected to see—a tuft of red beside each soldier's left hand.

The gates creaked open, and the line marched inside. Ivan glanced up at the wooden arch above him as he marched alongside them. He had made it into the base. Tomorrow, he would join these near-silent guardians on their long, cold march to Oryol. And then, finally, after three long years, Kasimir would be free.

CHAPTER NINETEEN
Evelyn

"Nash is awake."

"Hunh?" Evelyn grunted, rubbing her eyes as she pushed herself to seated. She had fallen asleep slumped on the deck of Salt Beard's ship, watching the last of Ryia's shadow disappear into the night.

She squinted up at the brightening sky, blinking as Tristan's face appeared above her.

"Nash is awake," he repeated.

Evelyn scrubbed her hands over her face. "Right. Let's go see if we can get the ruddy traitor to turn her cloak again, shall we?"

If Evelyn had been expecting a fight from Nash, she was sorely mistaken. She had barely set foot inside Salt Beard's cabin when the smuggler willingly and angrily started blurting out Clem's plans. Within the span of five minutes, Evelyn had the full picture. Clem would be dressed as a Borean lord, Ivan as a *medev* guard. Both would be inside the negotiations at the Reclaimed Castle by the time she and Tristan arrived. If Clem hadn't discovered Joslyn was a double by then, she would be in disguise as one of Clem's Adept.

"Who in Felice's name *was* that, by the way?"

Nash asked. She looked shaken, like she was remembering seeing a ghost. Evelyn could understand why—she had once met a Gildesh merchant who was her brown-haired, blue-eyed double, and even *that* had been unnerving. Joslyn and Nash looked almost identical in every way. Enough that Evelyn was certain Nash must be questioning whether or not her father had taken some liberties with his marriage vows.

"That was Salt Beard," Tristan piped up as he finally strode into the cabin from the passageway outside.

"You!" Nash burst out, her lip curling as she studied the boy. *That's right,* Evelyn realized. The last Nash knew, Tristan Beckett had betrayed them all on the Guildmaster's island and left them for dead. "I risked my ass to try to save you, you fucking—"

"Nash," Evelyn said, reaching a hand out to calm the smuggler. "Relax, he's on our side."

Nash eyed the boy suspiciously. "That's what we thought last time."

As much as Evelyn appreciated Nash's intel (if it was indeed the truth), the fact remained that the smuggler had been with the enemy until they had knocked her out and dragged her off his ship. With how she had reacted to Tristan's reappearance, Evelyn would have thought she might have understood the fact that they weren't about to trust her outright, but she had fought like a starved cat when they said they were going to leave her behind. In the end, Evelyn had been forced to alert a few members of Joslyn's crew that the person locked in the captain's cabin was not actually Salt Beard and insist that they post guards to keep her put.

Evelyn looked back at the *Ophidian Fang* as she and Tristan left the harbor behind them. "What do you think the chances are that ship is still there when we get back from Oryol?" With Salt Beard nowhere to be found and no wealth to be seized in a port this small, she doubted the crew would stick around in this half-frozen wasteland.

Tristan snorted. "I'd say somewhere between zero and zero." He glanced back nervously. "But at least if they sail off, Nash will be trapped at sea and won't be able to rat us out to Clem."

"You really think she would do that?"

"She betrayed you once."

"So did you."

It was a cheap shot, and they both knew it. Tristan had been coerced by the Kestrel Crowns. Nash had picked the wrong team all on her own. There was a long silence; then Evelyn asked, "How much do we have?"

Tristan was picking through a jingling bag of silvers. They had put together every last copper they had, combined with the coins they had managed to shake from Nash's pockets before she came back around. "Two crescents, thirty-four halves, and nine coppers."

"Enough to buy a carriage?"

"There's one way to find out."

It was enough. *Barely* enough. Tristan returned from the stables outside Volkfier leading the weakest-looking pair of shaggy northern horses Evelyn had ever seen, pulling what had to be the rattiest carriage in all of Boreas. She surveyed the creaking cart as it rumbled to a stop in front of her. "You seriously think anyone will believe the prince of Edale is showing up in this bloody thing?"

"The prince of Edale *is* showing up in this bloody thing, though," Tristan pointed out.

Evelyn rolled her eyes. "You think anyone will believe your father *sent* you here in this bloody thing?" she amended.

Tristan shrugged, wrenched the carriage door open, and tossed their bags inside. The whole thing groaned like it might simply fall apart. He then jumped in himself, reaching a hand down to her. "Maybe I'm in disguise to protect me from people angry at my father for trying to rip the world to pieces."

Evelyn considered it. He had a point. "We'll just have to hope these are enough to get us in the door when we get there," she said, patting the bag on her own shoulder.

Tristan's packs were filled with food and water for the seven-day journey to Oryol, but Evelyn's held something even more valuable. Given that Ivan Rezkoye had chosen to stick with the Snake, they didn't have anyone to sew them perfect disguises for the job, but they *did* have Joslyn's wardrobe to pick through. The pirate captain had several nice cloaks, all of which were too broad in the shoulders for the lanky prince of Edale, but they had found a vivid green one with a mink-fur hood that fit Tristan reasonably well. Evelyn had had even more luck with her own disguise, as Salt Beard appeared to have stolen an actual Shadow Warden uniform at some point during her sea voyages.

Evelyn didn't want to think about what had happened to the uniform's previous owner, but it fit her almost like it had been made for her. Women were frequently made into Shadow Wardens in Edale, Tristan had said. They were usually employed as assassins instead of guards, but hopefully no one would question Prince Dennison's choice to bring a female warden with him to Boreas. Evelyn's thin Dresdellan sword would rattle around a bit in the wide scabbard, but all in all, the costumes made them look pretty bloody grand as a pair.

Evelyn and Tristan bumped along the rolling road to Oryol. Either the *medev* were as good at peacekeeping in Boreas as King Andrei always claimed, or the shoddy state of their carriage didn't invite attention, because they had no trouble with highwaymen, thieves, or bandits anywhere along the way. With ample rest and a good supply of food from one of Tristan's packs, the old horses held up pretty well. Back on their voyage to the Guildmaster's island, Ivan had always insisted that everything was a bit tougher in Boreas. Hopefully that same rule would not apply to the job. If it was somehow tougher than the job that had almost gotten them all killed on the Guildmaster's island, there truly was no hope for them here.

During the days, she and Tristan sat huddled together on the driver's bench of the carriage, talking over every last detail of their plan for the thousandth time. During the evenings, they warmed tea on a campfire and munched down their modest suppers, and then Tristan would nod off inside the carriage while Evelyn sat staring into the distance, thinking about the Butcher of Carrowwick.

Salt Beard had unlocked something in Ryia. That something had clearly helped her survive the dungeons beneath the Shadow Keep and had brought her back to them in Golden Port, so Evelyn was grateful to the pirate, of course . . . but she was also jealous of the stupid git. She knew that was ridiculous, though. Evelyn watched the smoke from their dying fire spiral up toward the stars night after night. Whatever strength Joslyn had helped Ryia find was the only thing that would save her from despair and possibly death in those blasted cells in Oryol. And the new power she had helped the Butcher unlock would save all their arses when the time came.

Evelyn had never been one for prayer, but she sent a little one up to Felice each of the seven nights they were on the road. Hoping that the goddess of luck would keep Ryia out of harm's way, that everything would go to plan when they arrived in the Reclaimed Castle. Even if it didn't, she prayed that she would at least get the chance to see Ryia again. The idea that their goodbyes back at the harbor at Volkfier might have been their last scared Evelyn almost as much as the idea of waltzing into the Reclaimed Castle with the goal of stealing from the twice-damned king of Boreas.

The night before the Lords' Negotiations, Evelyn didn't sleep a single ruddy second. Even after Tristan came to relieve her from her watch, she just sat in the darkness of the carriage, staring up at the moldering slats of the roof and dwelling on all the things that could go wrong. Tristan took first shift steering the next morning, and somehow the rattling bump of the carriage's creaking wheels on the uneven, frozen ground lulled her to sleep at last. She awoke to Tristan flinging the carriage door open, blinding her with thin, white sunlight.

"Time to get dressed?" she asked blearily, rubbing her eyes.

"I think so," Tristan said, clambering into the carriage and shutting the door behind him. He riffled through the bags, throwing Evelyn her gray uniform and matching gray cloak before pulling his own extravagant costume out. "I saw several other carriages on the road this morning. A few coming from the west like us, but the roads from the north and south are starting to converge, which means we can't be far from the *Keunichsweg*."

The *Keunichsweg*. King's Road, in Borean. The place where all the major roads of the kingdom joined together to lead travelers in one path through Oryol's single gate. From there, they would need to travel through the capital's streets to the inner wall of the city, and through a second gate to the Reclaimed Castle itself. Hopefully Tristan's face would be enough to get them in. As it always seemed to go with these plans, however, getting back *out* was going to be the kicker.

Evelyn shrugged out of her borrowed furs, boots, and trousers, and pulled on the boring, slate-gray pieces of the Shadow Warden uniform while Tristan wriggled out of his own traveling clothes and donned the regal (if slightly over-large) garments from Salt Beard's wardrobe.

When he finished, he perched himself on the moldering bench of their ratty carriage, thrusting his arms out.

"What do you think? Princely enough?"

Evelyn cocked her head to one side, studying him as she fastened the last few buttons on her Shadow Warden uniform and clipped the cloak around her shoulders. "Make sure you keep the shoes hidden, and I think you're good."

Tristan looked down at his travel-worn boots. "Good point." He pulled the hem of the bright green overcoat over his toes, hiding the distinctly non-regal shoes. "Thank Adalina Joslyn is so tall."

He was right. The young prince wasn't exactly short himself, but Joslyn was tall enough that her coat would easily cover his feet even when he stood. Evelyn straightened her uniform. "What about me?"

Tristan gave an exaggerated shiver. "You look exactly like my recent nightmares."

Evelyn chuckled at that. "Perfect." She swung the carriage door open and leapt out onto the frosty grass beyond. She missed her heavy fur cloak within seconds. "Next stop Oryol, Prince Dennison," she said, giving a curt bow.

Thank Adalina for the sunshine, because without its meager warmth, Evelyn was pretty sure she would have frozen to death before they even reached the gates. Much sleeker carriages pulled by much healthier-looking horses approached from every direction, thumping down the hard-packed roads of Boreas.

They were still several miles away when Evelyn first caught sight of the Borean capital. Sunlight glinted off the waters of the mirror lake surrounded by the sprawling mass of buildings with chimneys belching woodsmoke into the northern skies. The land outside the city walls was dotted with farms, just like Carrowwick, but where the Dresdellan farms were filled with flax and barley and wheat, these farms seemed to grow only things that were harvested from beneath the ground. It was too late in the season for potatoes with the frost. Maybe beets? Either way, farmers tilled the fields dressed in threadbare dresses and trousers, barely a scrap of fur among them.

Evelyn shivered. Ivan had always said the Boreans were a hard people, but for Felice's sake, she couldn't imagine removing even a single thread of her outfit in this cold.

She caught sight of her first *medev* just outside the city gates. Red-plumed helmets stood on either side of the open gate, searching every carriage that rumbled through. More red plumes winked from the towers dotting the wall. Were *medev* trained archers as well? Hopefully she wouldn't have to find out today.

The *medev* who approached their carriage barked several orders in Borean. Evelyn had learned a bit of the language during her Needle Guard training but was nowhere near fluent. She was able to scrape together enough words to tell them they were the royal party from Edale, here for the Lords' Negotiations.

The *medev* looked skeptical. "King Tolliver is inside this *pizhlache* of a carriage?" he asked.

"No, Prince Dennison is inside this *pizhlache* of a carriage," said Tristan from inside. He slid the splintered shutter up, treating the *medev* to a haughty glare Evelyn couldn't help thinking Ryia would have smacked off his face in half a second.

"*Heuheit*," the *medev* nearest the window said, bowing. There was a Borean word Evelyn definitely knew—the term for "Highness" or "Majesty," used for royals from the other four kingdoms of Thamorr. "Apologies," he said, reverting to Thamorri Common. "I did not know the *Keunich* was expecting you."

"He isn't," Tristan drawled, inspecting his fingernails as though bored. He really played the role of a spoiled arse well. "Why do you think we have arrived in this horrible carriage instead of one of my father's? My father has instructed me to represent Edale in these discussions, but he knows the situation is . . . ah . . . delicate. He didn't want to risk me being stopped on the road."

As they had expected, the *medev* didn't have a response for that. After all the crap Tolliver

Shadowwood had pulled in recent months, the Edalish flag would hardly have been a welcome sight in any of the other kingdoms. They might just make it through the gates with their ramshackle carriage after all.

The two *medev* conversed for a few moments in such rapid Borean that Evelyn couldn't even begin to follow it. She tried her best to look stoic and bored. It was difficult when the freezing winds wouldn't stop trying to rip her bloody cloak off. After what felt like an eternity, the *medev* on the right sounded a whistle. Four other plumed guards appeared as though out of thin air, snapping to attention in front of the carriage. Evelyn held her breath. Would they really arrest the crown prince of Edale?

"A royal escort," the *medev* said. Evelyn gave a silent sigh of relief. "To ensure the inner gate does not give you trouble."

"Finally, some competence," Tristan said in apparent exasperation. He really was a bloody nightmare as a prince. "Lead on."

With that, Tristan snapped his moldering shutter shut, and Evelyn prodded the exhausted horses, following the small company of *medev* through the streets of Oryol toward the inner gate of the city.

For all the talk about how foreign the kingdom of Boreas was, Evelyn thought the streets of its capital looked awfully familiar. Sure, the roofs were more slanted, stretching all the way to the ground, and yes, the streets were made of earth and snow instead of cobblestones, but there were still rowdy taverns and merchants hawking their wares. Where Carrowwick and Golden Port always smelled largely of fish, the streets of Oryol were filled with the richer smell of spiced, roasting meat. Caribou or elk, most likely. After seven days of eating steadily staling bread and cheese on the road, the smell was enough to send Evelyn's mouth watering. Children wrestled, and servants took out the washing; *medev* patrolled the streets like the Needle Guard back in Carrowwick. All in all, it felt good to be in a proper, bustling city again.

With the help of their *medev* escort, they sailed through the streets. The inner gate creaked open to let them pass, and Evelyn almost jumped as the shutter directly behind the driver's seat of the carriage slid open.

"Which of those do you think belongs to Clem?" Tristan asked in a very low voice, head poking through the newly opened window over her shoulder.

"I'm not sure," Evelyn responded, eyes combing over the dozens of carriages lined up at the base of the mountain that formed the Reclaimed Castle. "I would say the one that looks most like it belongs to a prat, but that could be any of them."

Tristan snorted.

They saw no sign of Clem as they pulled their carriage into position. Or at least, Evelyn didn't think she saw him. She narrowed her eyes, staring down the heavily fur-clad men dismounting the carriages all around them as she tethered their horses and moved to open the door to let Prince Dennison out. Nash may have abandoned Clem, but the Snake still had Ivan on his team. Any one of these sods could be Clem in disguise, for all she knew. . . .

She eyed a man about the size of an ice bear, thick blond beard stretching down to the center of his rotund belly. Well, okay, maybe not *any* one of these sods.

"Prince Dennison Shadowwood."

Evelyn's eyes snapped up at the voice. It was female. Deep and husky, laced with the thickest Borean accent she had ever heard.

"Queen Isabeth," Tristan said, inclining his head slightly as Evelyn helped him down the carriage steps. "I am surprised that you would see fit to greet me yourself."

His tone was one Evelyn had heard in the Bobbin Fort many times—that special, noble tone used to simultaneously show respect and disdain.

The Borean queen's response was just as two-faced. "I am surprised the absent king of Edale would see fit to send an envoy to this discussion."

Absent king. That didn't sound good. If Tristan caught on to this troubling slight, he gave no sign of it.

"If you continue to refer to his crown prince as an 'envoy,' I have no doubt that I will be the last one he will bother sending," he said coolly.

"And what a *schaemde* that would be," said Queen Isabeth. Evelyn had always thought the Borean queen was terrifying from afar, but that was nothing compared to how she seemed up close. Her eyes were sharper than steel, her two-inch fingernails just as sharp. Her face would have been gorgeous if it hadn't been so haughty. Her cheekbones looked as though they could cut glass, and her smile was at least as cold as Callum Clem's.

But Tristan—Dennison—was fully locked into his identity as prince of Edale, and he didn't back down.

"It would indeed be a shame," he said, smiling his own empty, cold smile, "if my father were to leave Boreas out of his considerations." He looked around, as though surveying all of Boreas in one glance. "After all, any trade in or out of Boreas must pass through Edalish seas or country. If that were stopped . . ." He tutted. "Well, let's just say, sooner or later, I think the people of the north might get sick of their sugar beets."

The queen didn't respond, but the way she pursed her lips together told Evelyn that Tristan had won their little pissing contest. She turned in a flurry of fine furs, stirring up a small snowstorm behind her as she stalked back up the wide stone steps rising like smoke into the sky above them. The doors at the top of the stairs were at least four times as tall as Nash was, made of white stone carved to look like icicles. It was stunning—and a pretty on-the-nose metaphor for the Borean queen, Evelyn thought. Beautiful and delicate-looking, but hard as iron and cold as the waters of the Sea of Boreas.

"Are you sure that was wise?" Evelyn asked out of the corner of her mouth as she and Tristan made to follow. "Riling up the bloody queen like that?"

"You've met my father, have you not?" Tristan asked, mounting the steps and looking up at the massive doors apprehensively. "He doesn't tend to negotiate politely. If we want anyone to believe he sent me, I'll have to follow that lead."

"And hope he doesn't find out you're here until we're long shot of this place," Evelyn added, glancing over her shoulder like she was expecting to see Tolliver Shadowwood pull up in his own grand carriage any second.

"I don't think we'll have to worry about that," Tristan said grimly. "Based on the queen's commentary."

The absent king of Edale. The phrase buzzed around them as they paraded up the stairs and into the entry hall of the Reclaimed Castle. From the few snatches of Borean Evelyn managed to translate, it sounded like none of the lords of Boreas had heard from King Tolliver Shadowwood in months. It was rumored that he hadn't been seen even by Edalish eyes since the end of Augusta. Since around the time Evelyn herself had seen him. Some speculated that the Edalish king was dead. Evelyn thought it was more likely the man was plotting something terrible.

Oh, how much more peaceful the world would be if shite men would stop plotting shite things.

Evelyn lurked a few steps away from Tristan as he traded niceties in broken Borean with the other lords present for the negotiations. She held herself at attention, keeping her face a guard's mask of calm and focus, trying not to think about the fact that somewhere near, Ryia Cautella was trapped in a Borean cell. She swallowed the thought, scanning the growing crowds milling around the hall, dripping in furs and finery. Twice she thought she saw Callum Clem, but each time it just turned out to be another blond-haired, blue-eyed man. Adept Kinetics loped solemnly after their masters. Evelyn studied each of their faces in turn as well, looking for Joslyn, but again she came up empty.

She didn't see a face she recognized until they were being herded into the Negotiation Chamber.

And that face was Ivan Rezkoye's. The disguise-master was up to his old tricks again, nearly unrecognizable in head-to-toe *medev* gear, half his face hidden by his plumed helmet, the other half by a close-cropped blond beard. His sea-green eyes showed no sign of surprise or dismay as they met her gaze. Instead he gave her the barest nod.

What in Adalina's deepest hell did *that* mean?

The Negotiation Chamber was larger than the entry hall by far. The ceiling stretched so high above them that Evelyn could see sunlight snaking in through windows carved in the summit of the lower peak of the Fist above them. Furs and banners hung from the walls, and a pair of roaring fires bookended the space, flames almost as large as the common room of the Miscreants' Temple back in Carrowwick contained in mammoth braziers.

A table had been set in the center of the room, longer than half the roads in the Lottery and made of what appeared to be cherrywood. It must have cost a ruddy fortune to ship that much of the southern wood this far north. But as fine as the table was, it paled in comparison to the defining feature of the room—the place where the Eisfang Dagger was hidden, if Tristan's account was to be trusted.

King Andrei's throne.

The throne was positioned at the head of the table, or more accurately, the head of the table was positioned before the throne. The royal seat was made of solid, jet-black obsidian. It seemed to grow from the floor of the room, its ornately carved back stretching up and snaking almost all the way to the ceiling a hundred feet above them. The back branched off like limbs of a massive tree, the tendrils of stone stretching down toward the fur-drenched man lounging on the cushion placed on the throne's seat.

King Andrei was just as foul as she remembered. His broad face was curved into an obnoxious sneer as he surveyed the lords filing in through the arched doorway. A few lords were already positioned around the table, crowding the seats closest to him, and the entire throne was ringed by *medev* and Adept servants. Gout had taken King Andrei's mobility some time ago, but what did he bloody care? All he had to do was snap his fingers, and half a hundred swords would be yanked from their sheaths in unison to do his bidding. She had heard rumors of past Lords' Negotiations in Boreas—that it was rarely a negotiation at all, and more of a flattery contest to see who could gain the favor of the *Keunich* enough to ensure protection or supplies for their own manors and fiefs.

Hopefully Ryia would enact her prison riot sooner rather than later. If Evelyn had to sit through a full day of these northern fools licking the boots of their git of a king, she might vomit.

“Warden.”

Evelyn’s head whipped toward Tristan. “Your Highness?”

Felice, she was glad she didn’t have to call him that all the time.

Tristan just pointed toward the table with his chin in response. Evelyn followed his gaze. And there he was. Callum Clem.

He was sitting in the chair just beside the *Keunich*—within a sword strike of the dagger’s hiding place. *Shite*. The Snake nodded deeply as King Andrei drawled something Evelyn couldn’t hear. Did Clem even speak Borean? No doubt Ivan had taught him the basics, at least. He was dressed in a rich red tunic lined with black fox fur. A hideous cloak lay draped over his back, the stuffed head of a bear cub gracing each shoulder. Evelyn fought the urge to curl her lip in disgust.

Three Kinetics stood lined up behind him. Well, two Kinetics and Joslyn. Her false tattoo was less convincing than Ryia’s had been back on the Guildmaster’s island, and the pirate seemed unable to wipe the ghost of a smirk from her face, even for this, but thankfully for her, no one at the table paid the servants surrounding them any mind.

Partially because the crown prince of Edale had just entered the chamber.

If Clem was surprised to see Tristan, he gave no sign of it.

"Prince Dennison," the Borean king boomed. His voice was so deep, it seemed to shake the entire chamber.

"*Keunich* Andrei," Tristan said, claiming the head of the table opposite the Borean king. A bold move—and one Evelyn wasn't sure was wise, as they were now trapped on the far side of the chamber from the dagger. But there was nothing she could do, so she just fell in behind the prince, setting her face in stone and locking her eyes on the throne.

"I trust we can conduct these negotiations in Thamorri Common?" Tristan continued, smiling in that special, priggish way all nobles knew how to smile. "My Borean is a bit rusty, and I would hate to bring my father the wrong message. . . ."

"So that is why you are here? To gather information to bring to your father?" King Andrei said. "A disappointment. I had hoped you were here to share with us all what in *Yavol*'s name your *verdammte* father intends with his bold threats of war in this time of enduring peace."

Evelyn had been afraid of this. As it was, Tristan probably knew less about his father's threats of war than any of the lords in this room. They had no doubt received magpies from Duskhaven with King Tolliver's demands. All she and Tristan knew was what they had managed to overhear in taverns and markets over the past few weeks. She glanced anxiously at the ceiling. *Come on, Ryia. Start the riot . . . do it now.*

But there was only silence. Tristan gave a shrug, settling into his chair more firmly. "I am a bit young to be speaking on the king's behalf, unfortunately, *Keunich*. But I assure you I will carry your questions faithfully to my . . . *verdammte* father."

Beside the king, Evelyn saw Clem turn to the door. She shifted her weight, pretending to scratch her nose so she could peer toward the open doorway herself. Ivan Rezkoye was sidling toward the exit, dressed in his stolen *medev* uniform. He was inches from the door when Clem cleared his throat in the silence.

"My dear *Keunich*, I believe I have some news that may satisfy your disappointment at Prince Dennison's . . . ineptitude."

"Do you, Lord Piervin?" the king asked. "*Geh beinte*."

The Borean phrase for "go on" hung in the air for a long moment. Then Clem smiled his most reptilian smile.

"There is a wanted fugitive in this room."

Evelyn's stomach clenched, her hand drifting toward her sword. Had King Tolliver put out a reward for the return of his son again? But her jaw went slack as Clem stretched a lazy hand out, pointing toward the doorway instead.

"That is no *medev* there. That is Ivan Rezkoye.

Brother to Kasimir Rezkoye, Shark of the North."

A wave of shock rippled through the room, and the look of surprise and betrayal on Ivan's face told Evelyn this was not a part of the plan. At least, not part of any plan Clem had shared with the disguise-master.

The Borean king yelled something Evelyn could only assume translated to *Seize him!* and within seconds, the room devolved into chaos.

CHAPTER TWENTY

Tristan

Callum Clem had always been a no-good bastard, but Tristan still couldn't believe he would rat out his last ally the way he had just ratted out Ivan Rezkoye. In the end, it seemed Clem had strung Ivan along for the same reason he had dragged Tristan into his plot on the Guildmaster's island—to use him as a pawn. Tristan had always thought Ivan was one of the most brilliant people he had ever met, but clearly even brains like that were no protection against the Snake of the Southern Dock.

The true *medev* in the room surrounded Ivan, marching toward him, their poleaxes extended as they backed him up against the raging brazier beside the door. Soon there would be nowhere for Ivan to go but into the fire or into a cell. Tristan wondered dimly for a moment if Ivan was foolish enough to choose the fire. But at that moment, a great rumbling shook the mountain above them. Everyone in the room—apart from the Kinetic servants—glanced upward in unison. Up toward the place where the cells of the Reclaimed Castle lay, several floors above. There was another rumble. Then came the sounds of harsh shouting. Victory rushed through Tristan's bloodstream.

Ryia was here. She had made it into the cells . . . and from the sound of it, she had made it back out of them as well.

All the gathered lords remained frozen as a single *medev* captain, distinguishable by a bright red cape and a plume that stood some six inches above the plumes of his fellows, lurched into the doorway, bowing deeply. The Borean king's thick fingers were clamped over the arm of his throne, subconsciously guarding the secret compartment that held the dagger. Clem's eyes flicked to the same location. Tristan's stomach clenched. He knew where it was hidden. *No, no, no.* They couldn't let him get it.

King Andrei shouted something in the harsh northern tongue, and the *medev* captain shouted back. In their exchange Tristan caught the Borean words for "cells" and "prisoners," and the word *friyleben*, which he could only assume meant "escaped," based on the shade of purple the king's face took on once this word was spoken.

The next thing he yelled must have been an order, because every cursed *medev* in the room snapped to attention. The guards surrounding Ivan faltered ever so slightly, and Tristan saw the disguise-master share a glance with Joslyn across the room. The pirate stood, pretending to be Nash, just behind Callum Clem. For a moment, she did nothing. Then she leapt forward, reaching for Clem's throat.

Horror rocked the faces of the men surrounding the table—Tristan could see why, of course. To their eye, it would seem as though Lord Whoever-Clem-Was-Impersonating's Kinetic had just turned against him. Tristan knew Ivan well enough to know to glance back over his shoulder at him while everyone else gaped at Joslyn and Clem. Sure enough, the disguise-master was already in motion.

He surged toward the door, doing his best to blend in with the rest of the *medev* in identical uniforms now crowding the massive entryway.

Tristan looked back over to Clem's seat. Joslyn had been snared by the Snake's two true Kinetics. They held the pirate back as she kicked and struggled, trying to reach Clem . . . but Clem was nowhere to be seen. Tristan blinked, his heart dropping like a stone. Where had he gone? Tristan's eyes jumped to the throne, fearing the worst . . . but there was no sign of Clem there, either. Yet. The feeling in the pit of his stomach told him it wouldn't stay that way for long.

The rest of the lords at the table stirred. A few began to gather their Kinetics, streaming into the hall behind the *medev* heading to quiet the prison break upstairs. Others cowered underneath the table, muttering prayers to their cruel god in the stuffy darkness. The company of *medev* near the door seemed to have finally realized that Ivan had slipped their net somehow.

The soldier who had been closest to Ivan looked around, utterly bewildered as a taller *medev*—the company leader, no doubt—shouted at him.

Tristan didn't know where Ivan had gotten to either, but he didn't much care about that at the moment. Getting distracted by Ivan was what had let him lose track of Clem in the first place. No, all that mattered now was the fact that the Eisfang Dagger and Callum Clem were both still somewhere in this room. Fear surged through him at the idea of Callum Clem laying hands on the Borean relic. The Snake of the Southern Dock was terrifying enough as he was—but if he became Adept? Tristan shivered. The man would be unstoppable.

"Evelyn, cover me!" he shouted. He didn't know where Evelyn was, to be honest—she might not even have been in earshot—but on the off chance that she was, he definitely wanted cover. Because he was about to do something colossally foolish. His fancy coat billowed and swirled inconveniently as he ducked and dodged through the panicking lords and their guards. The king of Boreas was still sitting in his high throne, surrounded by a dozen *medev*. Would they be enough to stop Clem?

Tristan had been twelve years old the first time his father had brought him and his brother, Ronson, to Boreas. The crown prince of Boreas, Edmon, had been no older than seven at the time.

Tristan could still feel the haunting cold of the chamber at midnight, still hear the dull thump of his stockinged feet on the stone floor as Prince Edmon led the way into the high-ceilinged chamber.

That's it? Tristan had said at the time, peering down at the small dagger with the curved blade that Edmon had pulled from a secret compartment in the right armrest of the throne. He had at least expected the hilt to be crusted over with diamonds or threaded through with beads of gold.

Careful! Edmon had shrieked, yanking the blade from Tristan's hand as he had gone to test it with a finger. *It is poisoned. Made from the fang of an Eis Yavol. Father says it is* seicherende *to touch.*

Seicherende. Certain death. Of course, now Tristan knew that had been a lie. The blade might be poisoned, but the only way that poison meant *seicherende* was if Callum Clem managed to get ahold of it and imbibe that poison. Then it would be *seicherende* for them all.

He glanced back and forth, looking for a clear path to the throne, but there was none. A ring of *medev* surrounded it on all sides. King Andrei still sat, perched on the seat, his swollen fingers white-knuckled as he gripped the right armrest with both hands. As long as the king kept his grip on that armrest, the dagger might be safe . . .

But the last time Tristan had assumed Callum Clem was out of the game, the Snake had managed to sneak Declan Day's Quill out of the Catacombs right under the nose of Wyatt Asher, half a hundred Kestrel Crowns, and Tolliver Shadowwood's strongest Adept servants and Shadow Wardens. Clem always had a plan . . . and then four more plans lined up behind it in case the first ones failed. As long as Clem was still out of sight, the fate of Thamorr was still in danger.

That meant Tristan only had one choice.

Curses.

Shoving his fears down into the pit of his stomach, Tristan kicked his chair aside, using its seat to help him clamber up onto the top of the massive, cherrywood table. From this vantage point, he could see over all the chaos in the room. Joslyn had finally stopped struggling, giving in to the Kinetics who had pinned her against the wall of the room. Clem was still nowhere to be found. A few *medev* took notice of Tristan's position on the table and made to follow, but Evelyn leapt from the crowd, slicing the backs of their knees with her sword.

"Go, Tristan!" she shouted, brandishing her sword as half a dozen more *medev* turned her way. The meaning was clear—she'd do her best to keep them back . . . but she clearly couldn't promise to keep them at bay for long.

And so, Tristan started running.

He vaulted over candlesticks and centerpieces of bloodred flowers, sprinting toward the knot of *medev* surrounding the throne and the king. He might not be able to get out of here with the dagger, but that was hardly even the point. The goal was simple: keep the dagger away from Callum Clem. They could regroup and make another run at the thing later on if Ryia and the others were really determined to destroy it.

The table shook behind him as the first *medev* boots climbed up. He was almost at the head of the table when all the air whooshed from his lungs, sucked from him as the collar of his borrowed coat slammed into his windpipe. A guard had seized the back of the garment, tethering him in place, his outstretched hands only inches from the helmets of the *medev* surrounding the Borean king. Two poleaxes extended toward him next, one from either side of the table, the blades tickling his throat.

"*Heltz*!" shouted three voices in unison. Even if he hadn't known a single word of Borean, the meaning there would have been clear enough. *Cut it out, or we cut you up.*

Tristan froze obediently, raising his arms up over his head. His eyes darted around the room again, looking for Clem. There was still no sign of the slippery snake anywhere. Maybe he had decided to cut his losses and flee?

It was unlikely to the point of being ridiculous.

The sounds of struggle still echoed from the halls outside, but the chamber itself fell eerily silent. The lords huddling under the table slowly moved their chair barricades, sliding back out into the room, still clinging to their Kinetics like children clung to their mothers. The *medev* circling the throne had all turned to face Tristan, lifting their poleaxes toward him, as though two of the deadly weapons pointed at his tender throat weren't enough to stop him.

King Andrei looked up at him with shrewd, pulsing eyes. "Is this what your father has sent you here for, Prince Dennison?" he asked. His voice was calm, but there was rage behind it. "To commit these crimes against the great and superior kingdom of Boreas?"

Thankfully, Tristan was spared the trouble of answering by the renewed sound of kicking, fighting, and shouting in the entry hall. He recognized the shouting voice instantly but was still somehow surprised when he saw the figure dragged through the door by no fewer than four guards.

Nash.

Tristan had no idea how the smuggler had escaped from Salt Beard's crew back in Volkfier, let alone how she had managed to traverse the wilds of Boreas on her own, but there was no doubt that it was her. She strained and thrashed against the grip of the plume-helmeted guards, apparently indifferent to the weapons dripping from their belts.

"Let me go, you pricks!" she said, her sharpened canines flashing in the light of the chamber as she bared her teeth. "I'm trying to save all your skins."

The Borean king watched with mild amusement for a moment, then raised a hand. The *medev* holding Nash let her go. The smuggler gave one last thrash, then smoothed her travel-rumpled shirt and pants hurriedly. "Thank you." Tristan could almost taste the sarcasm dripping from the words.

"What is it you are trying to save us from, *unfründe*?" the king asked, using the Borean word for "stranger."

Nash opened her mouth again, but before she had the chance to reply, another bang rocked the chamber. It was far louder than the one Ryia had produced, and far more violent. It was followed by a second. And a third. Louder and more frightening than blasting powder—no, this was the feeling of the mountain itself straining against them.

"That," Nash said grimly.

The smuggler leapt out of the doorway just as two dozen tall, shaven-headed figures streamed in, dressed all in rich blue robes and dripping with swirling tattoos. Fear and relief charged through Tristan's veins in equal measure as he caught sight of the man at their head. A familiar, drooping face with icy eyes and a feral snarl on his lips.

The seventh Guildmaster of Thamorr had arrived.

CHAPTER TWENTY-ONE

Ivan

It was not often Ivan could say he considered himself foolish, but he had been nothing short of a *dummklav* in planning this deception. He had allowed himself to become complacent—to believe Callum Clem had mentally unraveled enough that he was no longer a proper threat. He had just been abruptly reminded that Callum Clem was always a threat. That *bastaerte*. How long had he known about Kasimir? Had this been his plan from the beginning?

Nash had been right all along. He should not have sided with the Snake of the Southern Dock to begin with. Clem's plans never seemed to benefit anyone but himself. So, forget his plans, then.

But before Ivan had even managed to escape the Reclaimed Castle's throne room, it was already clear that Joslyn's original plan would not work either.

The pirate had not subdued Clem. Instead, she stood, waylaid by the Snake's two true Kinetics, and Callum Clem was nowhere to be found. Perhaps he had already found the mysterious Eisfang Dagger; perhaps he had not. Perhaps he would be trampled to death by heavy *medev* boots. Ivan did not much care any longer. He had gotten this far, he had made it inside the Reclaimed Castle, and, for now, he was free within her walls.

It was time to forget the schemes and plots and return to what truly mattered. It was time to rescue Kasimir.

He knitted himself into the churning mass of *medev* guards, pushing and jostling with the rest of them, following the stream of Borean lords and their Kinetics out the door of the chamber and into the entry hall.

"*Verr es schuchthaus*?"

Ivan turned to the lord who had asked the question *Where is the prison?* He kept his tone flat as he nodded toward the entry hall. "*D'retter.*"

Slang for "over there." Unhelpful and unclear—just like everything the cursed *medev* said and did. The lord accepted the information with a curt nod, then joined the small crowd of overeager defenders snaking through the entry hall and toward an outdoor staircase leading up the side of the Fist. Ivan fell in step with the nearest pair of genuine *medev* and did the same.

Doubt clouded Ivan's heart as he looked over his shoulder. There were at least a dozen Kinetics trailing after their lords behind him, and perhaps twice that many in front of him. In the years since Kasimir had been captured, the *Fvene* had combed through every last record of the Reclaimed Castle in all of Boreas, had bribed servants for information. Every source had said the same. There was only one path to the prisons at Oryol—the narrow, exposed stairwell Ivan was already climbing.

His *medev* disguise would get him up to the cells without trouble. But what were the chances that he could get Kasimir back down this stairway without raising suspicion? He would have to trust the chaos to conceal them until he could devise a better escape plan.

The lowest block of the prisons was an absolute *schissdin*. The top of the outdoor stairwell was so clogged with bodies, even Ivan had trouble slipping through. *Medev*, Kinetics, lords, and prisoners, all battling for the same three feet of doorway. Some calculated steps and a few feet of crawling were all it took to penetrate that wall of furs and flesh. Once Ivan made it past that front line, he gave his eyes a moment to adjust to the relative dimness of the prison.

His eyes widened as he saw the cell doors swinging in the northern winds. Every cell had been breached, their doorways wide and gaping like missing teeth in a grin. When Salt Beard had told him of Ryia's plans, he had assumed she might spring half a dozen prisoners from their frigid pens. But somehow she had overpowered the guards enough to free them all. Kasimir was loose somewhere in these corridors, then. Ivan only needed to find him.

Instinct would tell a prisoner released from his lofty cell to go down as low as possible, to try to reach the ground, but Kasimir would be smarter than that. He would know that the greatest chance of escaping the Fist altogether would be avoiding the guards for as long as possible. And the guards were down, so Ivan went up.

He stepped aside half a dozen times on the prison's narrow, internal stairwell, making no attempt to stop the stray prisoners from joining the riot below. There was no sign of Kasimir. No sign of Ryia yet either, but knowing the Butcher, she was already long gone, perhaps rappelling out the open-air side of her own cell like a *verdammte* spider down to the ground below.

By the time he reached the third floor of the prison, the sounds of chaos were muted, a heavy silence filling the air between him and the *medev* and prisoners downstairs, like a blanket of snow pressed over his eardrums.

"Kasimir?" he called out tentatively, his voice little more than a whisper as he paced past the mangled, empty cells. "Kas—" He stopped mid-step and mid-word as he felt something cold and sharp press against his neck.

"What's this, a Saint caught away from his Temple?" asked a familiar voice.

Ryia Cautella.

The Butcher of Carrowwick pulled the weapon away from his neck. As she paced in front of him, he could see it was a length of iron bar sharpened into a rough, makeshift blade.

"I have to say, I'm surprised to see you here," she drawled. "I mean, not surprised you're in Oryol—I know you're a double-crossing son of a bitch and all that. But here specifically." She gestured to the cells surrounding them. "What game is Clem running that puts you all the way up here?"

"This is no game of Callum's," Ivan said, his voice surprisingly hoarse.

"Let me guess," Ryia said, spinning the makeshift knife around her fingers before casting it carelessly to the floor. "He betrayed you. You're running away, and you're just terrible with directions."

"I am not *verloren*," Ivan said, indignant. The Borean word for "lost" was used as an insult as often as it was a genuine description. The Borean people were historically very strong navigators—had they not been, they would have starved to death in the vast snowy wastelands centuries ago. "I am exactly where I want to be."

Ryia leaned against the nearest cell, knocking on one of the bars. "I can see why. This is a nice place. Cozy. Like a Brillish holiday bungalow."

"Ivan?"

Ivan's head snapped around so quickly he was half-certain he would crack his own neck at the sound of another voice coming from the cell on the other side of the corridor. The breath was sucked from his lungs the moment his eyes found the speaker.

The man in the cell looked like a *leichni*, a beggar. His posture was stooped, his hair tangled and unkempt, his flesh coated with filth, but his eyes still shone a keen turquoise.

"Kasimir," Ivan said. Forgetting Ryia, forgetting Callum Clem, forgetting the *medev* and the Kinetics and the lords downstairs, he walked to his brother, clasping the shoulders of his disgusting cloak and pressing that filthy forehead to his own.

For a few seconds the two brothers stood there, locked in their embrace. Then Kasimir's hands grew to talons on Ivan's shoulders and *Haisefven* pushed him back. "What are you doing here?" he hissed in Borean, his voice low, contorted with anger.

Ivan drew back a step. "Did you expect me to leave you to rot?" he asked in the same tongue.

"I expected you to understand the cause is larger than one man," Kasimir said.

"If either of you is hoping for me to take your side in this argument, I'm going to need you to speak a language I can understand," Ryia piped up from the corridor outside the broken cell.

"Apologies, Ryia," Kasimir said, this time in Thamorri Common. He straightened Ivan's cloak, which had gone askew as he shook him. "This man is my brother."

"Your brother?" Ryia asked, eyebrow raised. She shook her head with a bitter laugh. "For such a big world, it feels awfully fucking small lately."

Muted shouts rose from the floor below them, and Ivan glanced anxiously toward the stairwell. It was still empty, but he did not presume that would last.

"What do you intend to do here, brother?" Kasimir asked, looking at him as though he had lost his mind.

"I am getting you out of here," Ivan said tersely. He looked Kasimir up and down. "We will need to find you something else to wear."

"Good thing we're in the middle of a bustling shopping district, then," Ryia said, looking around as though examining a number of different clothiers.

"There are several downed *medev* on the floor below," Ivan said. "We will relieve one of his uniform."

He began to lead his brother toward the stairwell but stopped when he heard Ryia's soft-footed steps following.

"You cannot come with us, Butcher," he said.

Ryia stopped and cocked her head to one side. Her nostrils flared, then she reached for the nearest cell bar. She took a deep breath, and then Ivan saw the bar begin to vibrate beneath her touch. In an instant it creaked, then broke free three feet below her fingers. Next it broke three feet above her fingers, giving her a long, jagged staff.

"Do you mind ducking for a second, Ivan?" she asked calmly.

"What?"

"Duck, moron!"

Ivan did indeed duck as the Butcher of Carrowwick flipped the staff around in her fingers, then swung it toward his head like she was swinging an axe at a tree trunk.

The pole gave out a ringing gong as it struck something just behind him. Ivan spun to look as the *medev* slumped back into the shadows of the stairwell, his helmet knocked askew by Ryia's crushing blow. The guard's eyes grew unfocused, then slid shut as he drifted into *schlafflandt*, the land of dreams.

A razor-sharp dagger fell from his outstretched hand, landing just a few inches from where Kasimir stood. If Ryia had not reacted, that blade would have slipped itself across Kasimir's throat before Ivan had the chance to react—he was certain of it.

"What was that about me not coming with you?" Ryia asked, cocking her head and hefting her new weapon up on one shoulder.

Kasimir gave a rasping sound that Ivan realized, in surprise, was a chuckle. “Perhaps we should have recruited Edalish merchant *kindte* to the *Fvene* all along,” he said.

Was Ryia from Edale? And a merchant's child? Ivan had known Ryia a year now and had learned only that she was sarcastic and dangerous with a set of hatchets. But his brother had always had a way with people. It was how he had managed to lead a massive revolution from the tender age of seventeen. If anyone could get the Butcher of Carrowwick to sing her stories like a Gildesh bard, it was Kasimir.

Ryia took the lead on the stairwell, Kasimir close behind, Ivan bringing up the rear. Just before they reached the landing for the second floor of cells, Ryia threw her staff out, nearly catching Kasimir in the shoulder as she halted them abruptly. Ivan was about to tell her off when he heard the mechanical clank of armored boots on stone. *Medev*. A full company, at least. They surged through the doorway to the second floor, and Ryia waved them forward again.

“How did you know they were coming?” Ivan asked.

Ryia shot a wink over her shoulder. “Just a bit of luck.”

She was lying. Clearly, the Butcher was hiding more than just telekinetic magic beneath that smirking exterior. She was a Senser, as well. But how was that even possible? He studied the back of Kasimir's head as they descended another flight of narrow steps, heading toward the sounds of a scuffle still echoing from the entrance to the prison block. Perhaps his brother knew the Butcher's full story. He would have to ask him once they were clear of this cursed place.

The bottom floor of cells was a bloodbath. Ivan's stomach turned a bit as he surveyed the fallen prisoners, their corpses little more than skin and bone on the earthen floor. There were fallen guards as well. One Kinetic lay limp amid a dozen dead prisoners. A pair of *medev* were askew on the floor a few paces away. Ivan glanced around, then quickly moved to take one's uniform, handing the pieces to Kasimir as he went. Within moments, the majority of Kasimir's wasted, filthy body was covered in black furs, red fabric, and thin mail.

"Where are the guards?" Kasimir asked as he slid a plumed helmet identical to Ivan's onto his head. "The living ones, I mean." *Gott*, his voice sounded so frail.

"Up ahead," Ryia answered, nodding toward the bend in the corridor leading toward the outdoor stairwell.

"How do you know?" Ivan asked, at the same time Kasimir asked, "How many?"

"At least a dozen," Ryia answered, ignoring Ivan's question altogether.

Ivan chewed the inside of his cheek, examining Kasimir. His own disguise might be enough to allow him to emerge from the prison block and blend in with the remaining guards . . . but it would be obvious to anyone giving more than a passing glance that Kasimir did not belong in the uniform he wore. Then there was the matter of the iron-bar-wielding ruffian accompanying them both. There was no chance of the three of them strolling from this prison without a fight.

Ivan had never been much of a fighter, but he grabbed a poleaxe from one of the fallen *medev* as well.

"You know how to use that thing?" Ryia asked, sounding skeptical.

Ivan spun the weapon experimentally. It felt heavy and clumsy in his fingers, which were used to handling quills and needles and coins. "I know the handle is for gripping and the blade is for stabbing. What more is there to know?"

"That's what I thought," the Butcher sighed. She looked to Kasimir. "Are you up for a run, *Haisefven*?"

Kasimir's gaunt face cracked into a smile. "It is all I have dreamed of for three long years."

"Then get those knobbly knees ready," Ryia said. "I'll see you back on the ground."

"Where are you going?" Ivan asked. There was only one possible answer . . . but he could not imagine the Butcher of Carrowwick making such a selfless choice.

"To clear the way for your hobbled-ass brother," she shot back with a grin. "The window's going to be pretty tight. If you miss it, then the *medev* and Kinetics down there will be the least of your worries, got it?" She waved her makeshift weapon in his face, as though her meaning had not already been clear.

An instant later she was gone, sprinting down the hall and around the corner toward the open-air stairwell. The sound of metal clashing on metal quickly followed, and Ivan grabbed Kasimir by the elbow.

"*Reitig*?" he asked. *Ready?*

Kasimir clasped his elbow in return. "*Enfeurich*."

I'll follow.

Ivan swallowed the emotion that surged into his chest at the sound of Kasimir saying those words to him, then turned and began to move down the corridor at a sharp clip. The slap of Kasimir's still-bare feet on the cold stone followed him around the bend and into the light of the setting sun streaming in through the open doorway. The stairs came next. They were a blur of *medev* armor, fine lord's clothing, Adept robes, and whatever rags Ryia was wearing as she spun and twisted among them all. Using the light steps and unassuming air of the *Fvene* infiltrators, Ivan and Kasimir kept their heads low, weaving this way and that through the wholly distracted guards, slowly making their way down the stairwell.

Ryia reached the bottom of the knot of *medev* within a few moments. As soon as she was past them, the window was closed. A company of guards was sent to pursue, the rest ordered to continue guarding the door to the prison . . . but it was a simple matter at that point for Ivan and Kasimir to slip down the steps under the guise of joining the guards pursuing the runaway prisoner. Everyone was still so distracted in their pursuit of the rod-wielding Butcher that they easily made it down the stairs and back into the main castle undetected.

The rest of the guards rushed straight forward, following Ryia into the entrance hall, but Ivan pulled Kasimir into an alcove. His brother was still upright, but barely. He was breathing hard, and two of his brittle toenails had fallen off, leaving a trail of blood droplets in his wake.

Ivan tore a strip of fabric from the hem of his uniform and stooped to tie it around Kasimir's bleeding foot. "*Sindt keuftig*?" he asked. *Are you okay?*

Kasimir gestured down at his foot "*Gott weich nim*." Then he patted Ivan on the shoulder. "*Gott gevt nach*."

Gott takes away. Gott gives again.

Let us hope Gott still has a little more to give,

Ivan thought. If they could make it out of the castle, he was sure they could stow away under a carriage and escape the city. One more stroke of luck. That was all he needed, and Kasimir would finally be free.

But before Ivan could take even one more step, he heard a voice that made every hair on the nape of his neck snap to attention like so many soldiers on an ancient battlefield.

“Let me go! Get your damned hands off me!”

Nash.

What in Gott’s name was she doing here? She was in trouble.

“Wait here,” Ivan said, spitting the words out in Thamorri Common in his haste. Then, throwing all caution to the pits of *Yavol*, he sprinted toward the voice.

“Let me go, you pricks!” Nash shouted. Ivan wheeled around a corner, skidding into the entry hall of the Reclaimed Castle. There were guards and lords everywhere now, but no one seemed to notice him; they were distracted by the thrashing figure being dragged into the meeting chamber by no fewer than four *medev*. “I’m trying to save all your skins!”

The next voice sent a rush of anger up Ivan’s cheeks. King Andrei Tovolkov.

“What is it you are trying to save us from, *unfründe*?” he asked.

Just then, the walls of the entry hall shuddered

and whined, straining under the pressure of something that had struck the mountain outside. Dust spiraled down from the ceiling like snowflakes in a gentle spring storm in the silence that followed. Then another bang shook the chamber. This time, taking the massive front doors with it. They landed with an equally loud crash on the floor, cracking the stone as they careened through the space.

The waning daylight beyond was striped with the shadows of bald-headed, blue-robed figures. Disciples, led by the Guildmaster himself. Ivan felt the blood drain from his face, felt his jaw go slack. Why was the Guildmaster here? It made no sense.

The first words out of the Guildmaster's mouth made even less sense.

"I am looking for a Dresdellan thief by the name of Callum Clem."

"There is no one by that name here, Master Guildmaster," said King Andrei.

"Yes there is! He's in disguise," said another familiar voice. Clem himself. Before Ivan's eyes even found the man, he knew what he would see. The man was still dressed as Lord Piervin, raising one hand and pointing toward the entry chamber.

Directly at Ivan himself.

"We finally meet, Master Clem," the Guildmaster said, turning to face Ivan. He pulled a dagger from his robes, spinning it around his fingers in midair. “You are charged with stealing from the Guilds of Thamorr. And you have been found guilty.”

He snapped his fingers, and the dagger began to fly.

For the next few seconds Ivan felt as though he were underwater, his movements slowed and dreamlike. There was no time to stop it. No time to dodge. Ivan lifted his eyes to the Guildmaster’s, raising his chin defiantly, ready to accept his fate as the dagger spun toward his heart.

Just before the blade struck home, a blur of red and black and matted hair dove in front of him. His brother lifted his head, throwing himself between the Guildmaster and Ivan at the very last second.

Ivan did not even have time to scream before the Guildmaster’s dagger took his brother in the throat.

CHAPTER TWENTY-TWO

Ryia

Ryia had expected to encounter *medev* and Kinetic servants on this job, maybe even King Andrei himself. What she had not expected was the twice-damned Guildmaster. Just the sight of that piece of pond scum masquerading as a man was enough to get her blood boiling. Watching him cut the throat of her newest friend? Well, that was just about enough to make her want to return the favor.

Of course, there was someone else in this castle who felt the exact same way.

"I am not Callum Clem, you *bastaerte*!" shouted Ivan.

This was the first time Ryia had ever seen anything resembling genuine emotion on Ivan Rezkoye's face, and it was terrifying. His eyes almost seemed to glow, and his entire body shook as he catapulted himself toward the Guildmaster.

A suicidal move at best—Ivan wasn't even armed anymore. Thankfully, a six-foot-tall shape dressed in travel-soiled linens tackled him mid-stride. Was that *Nash?* The woman grabbed Ivan by the shoulders and called him a *fucking moron*. Definitely Nash. This was turning into a twice-damned family reunion.

Ryia tapped her fingers along the length of her makeshift weapon as she paced a stride closer to the massive chamber just off the entrance hall of the castle. A knot of *medev* stood at the door, looking dazed. Evelyn was just behind them, face tight, her hand skimming the blade at her belt. Tristan was standing on the table for some reason, five poleaxes pointed directly at his throat. Callum Clem had surfaced just long enough to point the finger at Ivan. He'd then slunk back into the tangle of the crowd, now nowhere to be found.

Apparently, this job was going even better than their last one had.

The Guildmaster's face was devoid of any emotion as he studied Ivan, thrashing in Nash's grip. Felice, she hated that man. "If you are not Callum Clem, the Snake of Carrowwick's Southern Dock, then where is he?" He surveyed the room, frozen in chaos. "He has something of mine. Something I do not plan on leaving this castle without."

From her hiding place in the shadows, Ryia could see that the king had risen to his feet, his *medev* parting to allow him to address the Guildmaster directly. "May I ask why you have come to the snowy wilds of Boreas to find a common thief from the Forgotten Kingdom?"

The rude, potato-faced man had a point. How did the Guildmaster even know Clem was here?

Ryia had gotten so used to the bastard using his Quill to haunt her every step all these years that it hadn't even seemed strange that he had shown up where she happened to be. But he didn't have the Quill anymore, and even if he did, Callum Clem wasn't Adept, so the Quill wouldn't be able to track him down.

"I have more eyes in Thamorr than the seas have fish, Andrei," he said.

The king's face reddened a shade in anger at the casual use of his name in place of his title. "I believe in this case that your eyes may be mistaken, then, Guildmaster," he said tersely. "There are no Dresdellan thieves here. Only esteemed lords of Boreas." He paused, looking back at Tristan with a sneer. "And disgraced princes of Edale."

The Guildmaster took another step toward King Andrei. The Borean royal had at least seventy pounds on the Guildmaster, but he flinched backward anyway. Evelyn would call him a coward for that—but Ryia knew it was smart. A twice-damned field mouse would be a threat if it had even half the Kinetic magic the Guildmaster had coursing through his veins.

"Even if that does turn out to be true, my birds have sung another song to me. A song that sheds new light on the mysteries of generations past."

"If you continue to speak in riddles, I will not be able to assist you, Master Guildmaster,"

King Andrei said coldly. He was pretending not to understand, but even from her hidden vantage point, Ryia could tell that was horseshit.

The Guildmaster knew it too. His face slipped into his most hideous smile. "Then I will speak more plainly. I have been informed of the existence of a relic and have learned something most interesting about that relic's nature. It was once favored by a man named Leonid Avendroth, as chance would have it."

Avendroth. The name took Ryia a few seconds to place. Then she remembered her tutor's history lessons, back from her near-forgotten childhood. From the days before her father had chained her in the manor basement, that was. Leonid Avendroth had once been king of Boreas himself. Before the Guildmaster had marched to the Reclaimed Castle, slaughtered his entire family, and given the throne to a young lord by the name of Andrei Tovolkov.

The king's ruddy face paled three shades, but he said nothing. The Guildmaster took another step forward. "Give me the dagger, Andrei."

"I'm afraid the Eisfang Dagger is no longer Andrei Tovolkov's to give," said a third voice. Quiet, yet somehow also ringing and clear. Ryia's stomach dropped. Callum Clem.

He stepped back out of hiding, emerging from behind the massive throne, spinning something in his fingers. The dagger. Its blade was about six inches long, curved, and as shining white as the robes of Adalina herself. Even from this distance, Ryia could feel the power emanating from the thing. It seemed to radiate with it. More accurately, it seemed like a vortex that sucked all the light in the room into it, leaving nothing but the bright, pulsing white of the dagger.

"You know, the stories really don't do this relic justice," Clem said, staring at the dagger like it was his firstborn child. "Much nicer than that crusty old pen of Declan Day's." His eyes sparkled mischievously as he looked up at the Guildmaster, the picture of smug impudence.

"You must be the actual Dresdellan scum lord I have heard so much about," the Guildmaster said. There was a breath of silence. Then: "Seize him!"

The Disciples flanking the Guildmaster split in half, surging across the room on either side of the table toward Callum Clem . . . but Clem didn't look even remotely alarmed.

"I'm afraid I have no interest in surrendering to you, Guildmaster," Clem said, his voice somehow carrying clearly over the rustle of robes and the pounding of feet. He lifted the dagger, pressing the point of the blade into his palm. "They say that out of every one hundred men to feel the sting of this venom firsthand, ninety of them died. The other ten became gods." His eyes sparkled with madness. "Let's see which kind I am, shall we?"

"No!" Ryia shouted. She leapt from her hiding spot, lifting her makeshift weapon and flinging it toward Callum Clem . . . but it was too late. The dagger parted the skin of Clem's palm. The Snake gasped as his blood welled around the bone blade.

His vivid blue eyes snapped up as the iron bar cartwheeled toward his head. He raised one hand, stopping the bar in midair, a full ten feet from his outstretched palm. He then flicked his wrist to cast it aside. A laugh built in his throat, low and terrible. Still cackling, he lifted the Eisfang Dagger again, holding it out for everyone in the room to see.

"The time of Guilds and kings is over," he said. "No longer will bloodlines define who has power and who has nothing in this world." He lifted his left hand again, then made a fist. The Eisfang Dagger crumbled to dust, the motes of ancient bone wafting down to the floor.

"What will define it, then?" asked a bold lord in a bearskin cloak fastened with a dozen massive teeth. A stupid question—the answer was already obvious to everyone in this room with half a brain.

Clem turned toward him, cocking his head to one side. The lord tried to take a step back, but it was too late. Clem flexed his fingers, and the teeth on the man's cloak jumped to life, embedding themselves in the man's neck. He gurgled, falling to the floor. Clem smiled, answering the man's question, even though he would never hear it.

"Me."

CHAPTER TWENTY-THREE

Evelyn

As the Snake of the Southern Dock, Callum Clem had been mildly terrifying. As a powerful Kinetic hell-bent on usurping every throne in Thamorr, he was a bloody force of nature. She didn't know what she had expected to happen if the worst came to pass—if Clem *did* manage to lay hands on the dagger—but she definitely hadn't expected Callum Clem to take to Adept magic like a ruined merchant took to Gildesh wine.

Within the first thirty seconds, he had disarmed every *medev* guard surrounding the throne. He took their poleaxes and thrust them into the nearest brazier. Their wooden handles crackled and spat as they caught, their blades glowing red-hot as they fell into the cinders lining the braziers' base. Clem then clapped his blood-soaked hands together. He reached his blood-smeared fingers under his coat. Evelyn's stomach turned. She couldn't see the Quill, but as Clem withdrew his hands and spread his arms wide, eyes glittering in triumph, she knew it was there.

Clem then set his jaw, his face locked in a grimace. Evelyn saw what was coming next an instant before it happened. One by one, the

Adept servants in the room stiffened, turning mechanically to face Callum Clem. A muscle under his eye twitched, and for a moment, Clem was immobile. He looked catatonic, or almost as if he was sleeping. Then both his eyes flicked open. Evelyn's face heated, panic creeping through her veins as Clem snapped his fingers, and the Adept servants turned in unison to face down the Guildmaster and his Disciples. They had lost the day. Maybe there was still a way to defeat Clem, but they sure as hell weren't going to do it here and now. They needed to escape this castle while they still had half a chance.

"Tristan," Evelyn hissed, reaching a hand toward the Edalish prince, still standing, horror-struck, on the table. "Tristan, we need to leave."

"The Disciples will stop him," Tristan said. His voice sounded distant, like it was in a dream.

But the Disciples were already scattering, falling back to regroup as Clem and his small Kinetic army battered them with everything they bloody had: weapons, bare fists, waves of power sent pulsing from outstretched hands.

"I don't think they will, Tristan," Evelyn said grimly. "Come on, we need to go. *Now*."

"Don't worry, I've got him," said a voice behind her. Evelyn spun to see Joslyn limping toward her. Her lip was swollen, her left eye heavily bruised, but she was still stronger than Evelyn on her best day, and Evelyn wasn't too proud to admit it.

The pirate grabbed Tristan by the waist, hauling him off the table and throwing him over one shoulder. “Now what?”

“Now we find the others and get the ruddy hell out of here,” Evelyn said. She ducked as the better part of a chair flew across the room from the place where Clem’s Kinetics were still clashing with the Disciples.

They found Nash and Ivan with little difficulty—they were still on the floor by the entrance to the chamber, Ivan struggling feebly against Nash’s grip, Nash still grimacing as she held him back.

“He killed my *brother,*” the disguise-master yelled, screaming the last word like it had been torn from his throat. Guilt crept up Evelyn’s own throat as she stole a glance toward the lifeless figure still dripping blood onto the ruined floor of the Reclaimed Castle hall.

His brother? *Shite*. She could see the resemblance now, in the set of the dead man’s jaw and the blond of his tangled hair. They needed to get Ivan out of the castle, but Evelyn was sure dragging the man away from his brother’s body would be a challenge.

“Can you get them?” she asked Joslyn, nodding toward Nash and Ivan. “I still need to find Ryia.”

“Good luck,” Joslyn said, peering back toward the meeting chamber as Clem’s cold laughter echoed from it again.

The pirate's tone said that going back into that room was a death wish. Evelyn had to admit she agreed, but she wasn't leaving here without Ryia. Her mind jumped back to the moment in the castle at Duskhaven when she had watched, trapped beneath a sewer grate, as Ryia had been cornered by Shadowwood's Kinetics. She wouldn't let that happen again. This time she was leaving with the Butcher of Carrowwick at her side, or she wasn't leaving at all.

The scene back in the negotiation chamber was grim. Bodies littered the floor. *Medev*, lords, even some Disciples lay limp, dripping gore. Evelyn ducked beside one of the braziers framing the doorway, peering out into the room between the fluttering flames.

Come on, Ryia . . . where are you?

"Your Majesty, what are you doing all the way over there?" Clem asked across the room. His tone was playful, like he was having the time of his bloody life. He probably was. They had to find a way to stop him . . . but not here. Not now. All they could do at present was escape or die.

These options were made painfully clear by what she saw next. A fur-clad shape sailed across the room, soaring through the air, dragged forward by invisible hooks. Clem and four of his new Kinetics all beckoned in unison, and Clem's serpentine smile spread wide across his face as King Andrei shuddered to a stop just before him.

"The Guildmaster gifted you the great kingdom of Boreas for no other reason than the fact that you were the lord of the highest-ranking house in the land. You know what I think? I think that is a load of horseshit."

Evelyn had no love for the Borean arsehole, but she still flinched as Clem slashed the life from him with a fallen Disciple's scimitar. One. Two. Three times he slashed him, hacking, seemingly at random. The king finally toppled over, falling to the floor at the foot of the throne with a distinctly final-sounding thud.

That was when Evelyn saw her. Ryia Cautella, creeping down the back of the throne, climbing down it like a squirrel, head down, fingers gripping the tiny crevices in the carven stone, slinking toward Callum Clem armed with nothing but what looked like a small knife, clenched between her teeth.

What in Adalina's name was she *doing?*

With the Borean king dead in the dust, Clem turned his attention to the Guildmaster. The Snake flexed his fingers, no doubt evaluating the Adept magic flowing through his veins.

"I knew I would have to deal with you eventually on my quest to topple the old regimes of this broken world," he said calmly. "But I never dreamed I would have the opportunity to settle this matter so early in my reign. I suppose I should be thanking you for that."

The Guildmaster gave a thin-lipped smile. "There have been countless foolish upstarts like you throughout the histories," he said. "And not a single one of them has lived long enough for the historians to bother penning their name. I see no reason why you should be any different."

Even at this distance, Evelyn could see Ryia roll her eyes at the display of bravado playing out beneath her. The Butcher edged another few feet down toward Clem . . . but before she could do anything too daft, the two overpowered men sprang into action.

The Guildmaster made the first move. He flicked both wrists straight upward. One of the massive braziers upended itself, sending a wave of burning hot embers and ash streaming toward Clem. But the Snake was ready. He clenched his fists, punching them upward in a poor mimicry of an uppercut. One of the gigantic slate floor tiles ripped itself free, popping up to shield Clem from the burning projectiles. The Snake then pushed outward, sending the wall of slate screaming toward the Guildmaster. The man leapt sideways, springing inhumanly high into the air and landing some fifteen feet to his left. Two of his Disciples weren't quite so lucky. Evelyn winced when she heard their bones crunch, their bodies mangled by the gigantic slab of rock as it slammed into them.

Clem and the Guildmaster prowled around

each other like a pair of jungle cats, sizing one another up for a moment. Then, in a blink, they were at it again. The Guildmaster waved a hand, summoning a poleaxe from a fallen *medev* and sending it screaming toward Callum Clem. Clem summoned a discarded shield to counter. The poleaxe ricocheted off the shield with a resounding gong. Clem then whipped the shield sideways like a discus, his magic-fueled limbs giving the projectile far more speed than any normal man could produce. The Guildmaster caught the shield in his bare hands. He gnashed his teeth, then wrenched the cold steel in two, ripping it like it was made of paper. The metal gave a grating shriek as it parted. Both jagged halves became weapons in their own right as the Guildmaster flung them back toward Clem.

The two men fought with fervor and fury. Evelyn's eyes flicked back up to Ryia, still clinging, upside down like a spider, to the shadowed edge of the throne, waiting for the right moment to strike. But she had to know it was hopeless, didn't she? Clem was holding his own against the bloody Guildmaster. The man who had trussed Ryia up in invisible bonds within the first thirty seconds of their own fight back on the island just a few months ago. Even if she could get close enough to the Snake to stick him with that tiny blade, she would undoubtedly die in the attempt. Evelyn had to stop her.

But she hesitated as Clem drifted back toward the throne, his latest dodge putting him into Ryia's range. The Butcher had the element of surprise on her side. What if this was it? Their only chance to stop Clem and save Thamorr? Could Evelyn really throw that away to save the life of one woman? For a moment she hovered, torn between instinct and duty. In that instant her decision was made for her.

The Guildmaster seized the collar of Clem's coat with his magic, yanking him back, strangling him with the suffocating layers of fur and silk. Clem broke free seconds later, but Ryia was already in motion. She pushed off from the throne, going into a free fall from twenty feet up in the air, her knife pointed straight down, aimed at the Snake's neck. For a second, Evelyn thought there was a chance the Butcher would win.

Then she saw the smile on Clem's wormlike lips.

She was running before her brain could even register how foolish that was. She yanked her sword from its overlarge, Shadow Warden scabbard, sprinting around the brazier and using the legs of one of the toppled chairs to catapult herself onto the table. She was still ten steps from Clem when he whirled around on the spot, reaching out and catching Ryia midair by her throat with one perfectly manicured hand.

It was a bloody miracle her neck didn't snap

with the force of it. Maybe it was Ryia's own Kinetic powers that saved her, or maybe it was just Evelyn's fierce prayers to Felice. Either way, Ryia struggled in his grasp for a moment, then finally managed to spin her knife around in her fingers, slicing up and scoring a deep gash in Clem's wrist. His fingers spasmed as she severed the tendons there, and Ryia crashed to the table. Seeing the opening, the Guildmaster and his remaining Disciples pressed forward again, swarming Clem and his band of Kinetics. Their fight resumed just as furiously as before, but Evelyn didn't care.

"Ryia," she gasped, skidding to a stop beside the Butcher's crumpled form. She sank to her knees, rolling Ryia over and pulling her half into her lap. Bruises were already forming around her long throat.

"Linley?" Ryia asked, her voice twice as raspy as usual. "What are you still doing here?"

"Looking for you, idiot," Evelyn said.

"I think running back in here makes *you* the idiot." Ryia struggled to sit up. "Where's Tristan? And the others?"

"Already out," Evelyn said. "And unless we'd like to become a snack for whatever carrion feeders live this far north, we should follow them. Quick, while the bastard's distracted . . ."

But when she looked up, Evelyn knew it was already too late for that. Clem might only have one functional hand now, but he still had almost twice as many Adept on his side as the Guildmaster—a ratio that was growing by the minute, from the looks of the dead Disciples dotting the floor of the chamber.

"Come on, let's go," Evelyn urged, helping Ryia to her feet. Then they both crashed down again as the table rocked and shook beneath them.

"You always were a slippery one, Butcher," Clem's voice said. "I should have listened to the voice in my head that told me to slit your throat and cast you into the Arden the night you first came to me looking for work."

"I would have ripped your spine through your throat before you had the chance to lift whatever letter opener you call a knife," Ryia grunted back.

"Perhaps," Clem said calmly. "But I'd like to see you try that now." At that moment he thrust both his good hand and his bleeding one skyward. The six Kinetic servants nearest to him did the same. Evelyn's stomach dropped out from under her as the massive table groaned, then began to rise through the air.

They were twenty feet up in the air before Evelyn had a chance to think. Then thirty. For Adalina's sake, how high were the ceilings in this cursed room? But that was a stupid question—the castle was a literal mountain. This room spanned nearly its full height. Even with all the armor and Kinetic ability in the world, the chances of the two of them surviving the fall when Clem inevitably let the table come crashing down were less than zero.

"Ryia, I—" Evelyn started, but the Butcher held up a hand.

"Shut up."

"What?"

"Shut up," Ryia repeated. "I'm trying to think." Her voice was flat and calm, but fear lined her face as her eyes screwed up in concentration, searching for a solution Evelyn was certain did not exist.

"There's no way out this time, Ryia," Evelyn said softly.

"There's always a way out, Captain," Ryia said. She looked around them one more time. They were very near the ceiling now. The light streaming in from the windows was almost blinding, the deep orange of sunset. Evelyn's heart skipped as Ryia's face split into a smile. "And I've just found it."

"You've just found . . . what, exactly?" Her voice sounded so bloody high-pitched, but that was the panic setting in. The panic stemming from their imminent deaths at the hands of a power-mad syndicate lord turned conqueror.

There was a short pause as Ryia stared past her, studying something intently. She appeared to be counting, or perhaps timing. When she finally looked back to Evelyn, her gaze was so intense it sucked every last wisp of air from Evelyn's lungs. "Do you trust me?" she asked.

Evelyn hesitated. Swallowed. "Yes."

Emotion flickered behind Ryia's eyes, but she seemed to stifle it as quickly as it blossomed. "Good. Then jump."

"Jump?"

"Yes, jump. Now!"

Evelyn took a deep breath, closed her eyes, and jumped. For an impossibly long second there was only the darkness of the insides of her eyelids, the rush of air all around her, and the feeling of doom rising up to meet her. Then the air whooshed from her lungs all at once as she landed on something solid. Something much closer than the floor would have been. She opened one eye, daring to peek. The first thing she saw was Ryia's outstretched hand, ready to help her to her feet. Then she saw where they were, and the world spun for a second.

They were perched on a stone outcropping jutting from the side of the wall of the chamber. The ledge had certainly not been there a second ago. *Ryia.* She must have pulled the stone loose from the wall, forming a platform with her newfound Kinetic magic.

"You okay?" Ryia asked, and Evelyn realized she still hadn't taken her hand.

"I'm fine," Evelyn wheezed, clasping the

Butcher's hand and letting her pull her to her feet. She winced, favoring her ribs on the side where she had landed.

"It would have been a softer landing if you'd jumped the first fucking time I told you to," Ryia said. The words were harsh, but Evelyn had traveled with her long enough to know it was the mercenary's own strange way of showing compassion.

"I'll remember that next time."

"Go ahead and remember it now," Ryia said. They both peered down toward the floor of the chamber. The Guildmaster was throwing everything he had at the Snake, but Clem was fending him off again and again, pressing the powerful Kinetic backward toward the chamber door.

Ryia's eyes snapped back up to Evelyn's. "Climb out that window."

True to her word, Evelyn didn't hesitate this time. Despite the bruises blooming all over her body, she grabbed the frigid windowsill, hauling herself through and out onto the snow-slick mountainside beyond. She heard a vicious crack that she knew was the ledge Ryia had made splintering away from the wall. Whirling around, she thrust both arms out, barely catching Ryia's wrists as the Butcher started to plummet back down into the hall below.

"I've got you," Evelyn grunted, hooking her

right foot around a stone for support and planting the left one on the earth beneath her. Panting, she pulled back, dragging Ryia up until she was able to grab hold of the windowsill herself, using her inhuman strength to pull herself up and out onto the mountainside.

For a few seconds, they lay in the snow, drenched in the glow of the setting sun, catching their breath. Evelyn spoke first. "Well, that went as planned."

"When do our jobs ever go as planned?" Ryia asked. She sprang to her feet, pulling Evelyn up beside her. "Come on, we need to get moving. If that bastard hasn't already sent Kinetics after us, he will soon."

Without Ryia's Kinetic abilities, Evelyn would have plummeted down the mountain to her death about a dozen times. But with a few rocks carefully teased from their normal resting spots to make handholds, inhumanly sharp eyes to guide their way, and Ryia's hands grabbing on to her before she could fall, they made it safely to the ground, slipping through the last few feet of snow and scree just beside the northernmost portion of the city's inner wall.

"Now what?" Evelyn asked, dusting herself off and helping Ryia to her feet again.

Ryia peered around, looking for an escape route. "Now we find a way out of this death trap," she said.

Just then, something burst around the corner—an extravagant carriage drawn by two sleek, hardy-looking horses. Ryia's eyes were closed, her hand pressed to the wall. A few stones started to pull their way free of the pattern, jutting out just enough to form hand- and footholds. But her breathing was calm and steady. If her senses hadn't picked up the approaching carriage, that had to mean it wasn't a threat . . . right?

"For Felice's sake, did you guys roll down the side of a mountain, or what?" asked a familiar, jovial voice.

Nash.

She was sitting in the driver's seat of the carriage as it thundered toward them. Her unnaturally sharp canines flashed in the fading light of dusk as she reined the horses to a stop just beside them. The door opened, revealing Tristan, Ivan, and Joslyn all inside.

"Nice carriage," Ryia said, taking Tristan's hand as he reached out, pulling her in. "Where'd you get it?"

"Same place she got all those ships of hers, I'm sure," Evelyn said darkly, climbing in after her. It was a tight fit, to say the least, but they managed it.

"Well, what did you expect me to do after you assholes left me behind?" Nash asked. There was the sound of reins slapping and the carriage bumped forward.

The inner gates lay on their sides some ten feet from the wall, clearly bashed in by the Guildmaster and his Disciples as they approached. There were no guards left to stop them as they cantered out from behind the inner wall and through the streets of Oryol, leaving Callum Clem and his reign of terror behind them.

For now.

CHAPTER TWENTY-FOUR
Nash

The only thing more foolish than fleeing across Boreas on foot was fleeing across Boreas in a carriage they had clearly stolen. And so Nash insisted they sell the cart to a man with a grand total of three teeth in the first village they passed through after leaving Oryol. Not long after that, everyone decided they hated her for making that decision. The carriage was too risky—it stood out too much. Made them a target. But, Nash herself had to admit, what looked like a Kinetic, a prisoner, a *medev*, a Shadow Warden, a prince, and a smuggler all traveling together, trading turns on a pair of horses, probably stood out just as much.

The days and nights all blurred together as they moved from town to town, bleeding their coin purses dry on less conspicuous clothing, lumpy beds with moth-eaten sheets, and cups of *stervod* that had all too clearly been cut with water. The morning tea was always lukewarm and flavorless, as were the evening meals. Joslyn lamented the lack of *vitalité* in their supplies in a joking manner that Nash surmised was not actually a joke at all. But their ramshackle crew moved east at a steady clip all the same, driven forward by a simple fact.

Clem had gotten the dagger.

And after using it for his own gain, he'd destroyed it, per his custom.

During their first night on the road, sitting in a deserted inn common room in some shithole town just east of Oryol, Joslyn vouched for Ivan. In turn, Ivan pulled himself from the depths of his grief long enough to share that Nash had wanted to leave Clem for months now. All in all, Nash would have to be an idiot to think Ryia and the others trusted her any further than they could carry her on their backs, but they were able to hold a shaky peace, at least. An alliance if nothing else—bonded by their mutual desire to stop Callum Clem from setting the whole damned world on fire.

After at least two weeks on the road, they finally caught sight of their destination—Roulsk. It was a sleepy town about twice the size of Volkfier, positioned on the northeastern coast of Boreas. Nash had heard of the city before but had never traveled far enough around the northern curve of the Borean peninsula to see it herself. Smoke rose into the sky, thick and black, forming unnatural clouds that hung like heavy curtains over the harbor and the Sea of Boreas beyond.

Just north of the city lay the mines—coal mines, to be precise. The coal that powered the forges in all five kingdoms came from these mines, Nash had heard, which explained why the ruling family of Roulsk, the Vulpuns, were wealthier than the other fifty-some lords of Boreas combined. Nash wondered dimly if Lord Vulpun had survived the attack in the Reclaimed Castle. But as they drew closer to the city gates, Nash caught sight of something that drove that question from her mind: dozens and dozens of red-plumed soldiers.

"What in Felice's name are this many *medev* doing in Roulsk?" Nash asked, wrinkling her nose. "Even in the days before the first Guildmaster, I have a hard time believing any army would march their asses this far north."

"The *medev* have a great interest in Roulsk," said Ivan. His voice was hoarse from disuse. This was the first time Nash had heard him speak in days. She didn't blame him—Joslyn had told them all the story one night after Ivan had slunk off to bed. He had spent the past three years trying to find a way to save his brother . . . had sacrificed everything he believed in to side with Clem in hopes of rescuing him, only to watch him die minutes after doing so.

Nash's stomach clawed with guilt whenever she thought about the way she had talked to him these past few weeks. If only she had known about Kasimir, then maybe things could have gone differently. But there was a coldness between them now. A block of ice not even the sunniest of days could melt.

“What interest could they possibly have in this place?” Ryia asked, shivering violently in the icy winds. Autumn had come on hard, bringing snow and frigid temperatures that only got more frigid the farther north and east they moved. “Or are all *medev* just complete masochists?”

“Do you see that building there?” Ivan asked, pointing toward a structure just beside the feather-strewn tower of the Messengers’ Fellowship. Black smoke belched into the sky from its chimney, the thickest Nash had ever seen. “That is where they make the *Tron vun Yavol*.”

In Thamorri Common, the name translated to “Tears of the Underworld.” A badass name for a badass piece of equipment. Nash had seen them in action before—had used them herself back on the Guildmaster’s island. Tiny, spun-glass spheres filled with hard-packed coal dust primed to spread and expand when the capsule was broken. The soldiers of Boreas had used them for cover since the years of the Seven Decades’ War back in the days before the first Guildmaster. The mysterious capsules were at least half the reason those plume-helmeted pricks were considered the most dangerous fighting force in Thamorr, outside of the Disciples.

Of course, they would be in third place now, Nash thought grimly, since Callum Clem was building his own Adept army. She had expressed a hope that the Guildmaster may have crushed Clem's little resistance back in the Reclaimed Castle that first night on the road . . . but Evelyn and Ryia had squashed that optimism in three seconds flat.

"From what we saw in there, I think the Guildmaster would've been lucky to escape with his head on his ruddy shoulders," Evelyn had said.

"And that was the Snake still getting used to his new powers," Ryia had reminded them.

It was a grim thought. The Clem they'd seen in the Reclaimed Castle was terrifying, and that was only a fraction of the power the Snake of the Southern Dock would wield once he truly learned to master his Kinetic magic and the power of the Quill.

"I still don't understand how he was so strong," Evelyn had mused, staring into the flames like she was hoping to find the answer in the sparks dancing up from the logs. "The Guildmaster has wielded magic his whole life; he should have been able to kick Clem right in his arse."

"The Eis Yavol poison in the Guildmaster's blood has been diluted over the generations," Salt Beard—Joslyn—had answered flatly. "Your pal Clem just got a fresh dose. He's probably the strongest Kinetic alive."

A strange thing for a pirate from Gildemar to know so much about, but Nash already knew

Joslyn was no mere pirate. She was an Adept. And not a manufactured one, like it seemed Ryia was, either. No, Joslyn had been born with this power, but under a different name.

Joslyn was Jolie, her long-lost sister—she had to be. Nash had known it the second she had laid eyes on her back in the hold of *The Hardship*. She had Dad's strong jaw, just like Nash, and his height, of course. It was easy to see why, at a glance, they seemed almost identical, but someone looking closer would see that Jolie—Joslyn—had Ma's thinner nose, where Nash had gotten their grandfather's broader one. See that the pirate's shoulders weren't quite as wide as Nash's, taking more after their mother's tall, willowy frame than their father's broad and powerful one.

And if Joslyn was really Jolie, then of course she would know intimate details about the Adept and their history. She had been taken to the Guildmaster's island. Nash had seen her dragged from Ma's arms with her own two eyes. She must have somehow escaped from the Disciples after growing old enough to walk, but before having her blood taken for the Quill. What a tale that had to be. Nash glanced sidelong at Joslyn, walking straight-backed a few paces away, pretending not to notice Nash was staring at her. She always pretended not to notice.

When they reached the gates of the city, they found their way barred by the poleaxes of the *medev* standing guard on either side of the entrance.

"*Sagt sichen zielen*," said the guard on the right.

Their entire crew looked to Ivan in unison. Felice, he looked ill. His face had a gray pallor to it, the bags under his eyes so deep you could almost tuck a pair of silver crescents into them. Back in Carrowwick, he had been handsome in an almost boyish, youthful way. Now he looked like a grizzled—though still unfairly attractive—soldier returning from war.

He spoke to the guard in such rapid Borean Nash couldn't imagine how even a native speaker of the language could follow it, but whatever he said appeared to do the trick, because in the end the guard stood aside, allowing them to pass into the soot-stained streets of Roulsk.

"What was that all about?" Tristan asked, glancing over his shoulder to see if the guards were out of earshot.

"Didn't you study Borean with your prissy little tutors growing up?" Ryia asked, eyebrow raised.

"Didn't you use to *live* in Boreas?" Tristan shot back.

Ryia shrugged. "Turns out when your job is sticking up merchants on the road, you don't need to know much of the language."

"Anyway," Evelyn cut in, putting a hand on Ryia's shoulder to stop her from saying anything more. "What did they say?"

"They were asking to see if we were with Callum Clem. Only they did not call him Clem."

"What did they call him?" Joslyn asked.

Ivan turned his eternally haunted stare on her. "Eis Lischka."

Eis Lischka was the Borean term for the polar foxes that hunted on the large open plains of the northern kingdom. They were small, but fierce and clever, moving in large packs to claim lands from everything including ice bears and smaller villages of people.

"I can see Clem's head growing from that nickname already," Nash snorted.

"I do not doubt it," Ivan agreed. His eyes flicked to hers, just for a moment. So strange that they had been traveling together in this very small group for weeks now, sharing rooms at the inns and sharing benches when they managed to find carriages willing to take them a few miles in the right direction . . . and that might be only the second or third time the man had actually met her gaze.

"So the Boreans are planning to fight back?" Joslyn shook her head. "I don't think that's going to end well for them."

"Probably not," Ryia agreed, "but they might buy us a little time to get our act together."

"Forgive me if I am not eager to trade hundreds of Borean lives for a few more days of planning," Ivan snapped.

"No one would expect you to be eager," Evelyn said gently.

They had all been walking around Ivan like he was sitting on a mound of blasting powder these past few weeks. Nash knew him well enough to know that he blamed himself for his brother's death. Blamed himself for the fact that Kasimir had taken the dagger intended for his own throat. It wasn't his fault. She had tried to tell him half a dozen times, but he always seemed to walk away just an instant before she managed to get the words out. He wasn't ready to forgive himself yet. Nothing she said could change that.

"All right, we're in a hurry, and this town smells like smoke and bear shit anyway. What do you say we get the fuck out of here as soon as possible?" Ryia asked.

Nash nodded, then turned to share a look with Joslyn. A shiver spanned her shoulder blades as the pirate's eyes met her own. As her *sister's* eyes met her own. Joslyn cleared her throat and looked away, holding herself a bit stiffer than was natural. Nash stared a heartbeat longer, then averted her eyes as well. *If only Ma was alive to see this.* She touched the namestone beneath her thick woolen coat. If her spirit really was trapped in this stone, she would be beside herself to see her two daughters alive and free, working together.

Hopefully, she would be so happy that she

wouldn't even mind what they were working together to do.

"Ready to do some . . . peaceful ship watching?" Nash asked, acting like the last moment's shared, silent recognition had never happened. It had been weeks now, and no one on the team had so much as mentioned their near-identical appearance. It was like everyone could sense that Joslyn wasn't ready to talk about it yet. But if the time didn't come soon, Nash was pretty sure she was going to explode.

"I'm readier for the step that comes after," Joslyn chortled. She shook her legs out. "I'm not used to my feet being on solid ground for this long."

"Weren't you rotting under the Shadow Keep for two months before I broke your ass out?" Ryia asked.

Joslyn rolled her eyes. "Thank you for reminding me, Cautella." She glanced around the streets as a light snow began to fall, then pointed at a sign hanging over the door of a squat building sandwiched between a butcher and what looked to be a dye shop. "Sell these horses somewhere, then wait at that tavern. And be ready to move when we come back for you."

"Shouldn't we be buying supplies?" Tristan asked.

"Don't you worry about that, little pup." Joslyn grinned. It was even more cutting at the edges than Nash's own smile, despite the unsharpened canines. "Nash and I will take care of all of that."

With that, Joslyn set off east. Nash hurried to keep up as they snaked through the streets, dodging piles of horse droppings and bowing at everyone they passed in the Borean custom, trying to stand out as little as possible—a challenge, to say the least, given their tall statures, near-identical faces, and Gildesh-dark skin.

As Ivan had requested, they avoided the northern part of the docks, where the common fishermen and poorer merchants docked, aiming instead for the ships flying flags featuring a stag with pickaxes for antlers. That was the sigil of the Vulpun family. Ivan appeared to have no issue whatsoever with stealing from them.

"All right, so what can you sail?" Joslyn asked as they posted up in the shadow of a foul-smelling tannery, peering out over the maze of naked masts crowding the snow-dusted docks. She was still holding herself in that not-quite-natural way, like she wasn't sure what to do with her arms. This was the first time they had been alone together in their travels. The weight of the silence about their shared blood felt even heavier without the rest of the crew around.

"It's not a question of what I can or can't sail," Nash said, chewing the inside of her cheek. "It's a question of what we can sail with two expert helmsmen and a mostly useless crew." On the trip to the Guildmaster's island, she'd had a few members of her usual crew along for the ride, and ever since, she'd had Clem's Kinetics to help out. Now it truly was just her and Jolie—Joslyn—plus four people who didn't know a mainsail from a bedsheet.

Joslyn snorted. "Fair." She narrowed her eyes, posture relaxing a bit as she continued to study the ships. "So, what, something with a lateen rig?"

"A lateen rig?" Nash asked. "Are you crazy? You want to sail half the coast of Boreas on a boat so small we won't even be able to stretch our legs out without dangling them overboard to tease the sharks?"

"Fair, fair," Joslyn said. "What are you thinking, then?"

Nash chewed her lip a moment longer; then her face split into a wide grin as she spotted it. "There."

It sat tethered on the very southern tip of the docks. Nash had always known it as a catboat, though she didn't know what they called it up in Boreas. A small, low-profile sailing ship with a gaff rig—the type her father had called a "child's rig" growing up. Was it ideal for a long journey? Absolutely not. The Vulpuns' catboat was bigger than most Nash had seen, but still, probably only used by Lord Vulpun and his kin for pleasure cruises or jaunts down the coastline to one of the neighboring eastern dock towns of Boreas.

It wasn't perfect, but it would do.

"Good eye, there, Nash," Joslyn said, now staring at the same ship. "Shouldn't take much to outfit her, and she's small enough that she'll slip by unnoticed in most ports if we need to stop for supplies before we get to Edale." She paused for a long second, then said, "Where did you learn so much about ships and sailing, anyway?"

"My dad." Nash swallowed, carefully avoiding the pirate's gaze. "But I think it's just in our blood."

Joslyn's eyes snapped to hers. "*Our* blood?" Though she was being pointedly skeptical, it was obvious that she knew the truth.

"I know who you are." The words Nash had kept locked inside for weeks suddenly spilled out, all at once. "You're an Adept. Who escaped from the Guildmaster's island."

"What makes you think that?"

"Because I remember the day you were taken from us by the Disciples."

Joslyn said nothing for a long moment. After a few seconds of silence, Nash plowed on before she lost her nerve and the moment passed.

"Your name was Jolie. Before. Ma only cried for about a week after it happened, but she was never the same. None of us were."

"I . . ." Joslyn paused to clear her throat as her

voice cracked. She still wasn't looking at Nash. "I had a name?"

"Yeah," Nash said, chuckling despite herself. "Everyone on the street said Ma was mental for bothering. But we couldn't help ourselves."

Joslyn blinked, then cleared her throat and scoffed. "What makes you so sure that baby was me?"

Nash raised an eyebrow, then gestured between them. "I'm sorry—do you meet many people with faces as gorgeous as ours?"

Joslyn snorted. "You're the first."

"As I thought," Nash said, grinning. "You know, I spent years avoiding the routes I knew Salt Beard took. If I'd let you capture me once, we could have met a long time ago."

"Only if I hadn't killed you first."

"I would've liked to see you try." Nash laughed, then paused for a second. "How did you do it? Escape from the Guildmaster, I mean. Or were you sold and . . . released somehow?"

"I was never going to be put up for sale," Joslyn said bitterly. "I was the ol' Guildmaster's pet from the second I caught my first hint of danger."

A Senser, then, Nash thought. Then the rest of Joslyn's words sank in. "You would have become a *Disciple?* Felice, Joli—Joslyn. Why did you run away from that?"

The wind blew Joslyn's matted-fur collar up around her face. "Because I knew not all of us would be so lucky." She trailed off, her eyes losing focus.

Nash watched her a moment. "It was to help someone else escape too, wasn't it? Someone you knew would be sold."

"I tried." Joslyn was quiet for a second, then said, "Her name was Marie. Only friend I had on the island. Great person, but a shit Senser." She cleared her throat. "I didn't think I could live with myself if I stayed on as a Disciple and she got her brain scrubbed cleaner than a nobleman's asshole. I figured if we tried to escape, either we'd both make it or we'd both get caught and executed."

"Marie got caught; you got away?" Nash guessed.

"No, we both got away," Joslyn said. She gritted her teeth, eyes growing distant as she stared blankly toward the catboat. "But the merchant who agreed to break me out had never signed on to have a second, weaker Adept tag along."

"He didn't . . . kill her?" Nash said, aghast. But of course he had. The merchants of Thamorr were just as ruthless as the thieves—and twice as crafty. If the deal had been for one Adept, that was all that would get through. Additional risk wouldn't be tolerated.

"Threw her overboard to drown." Joslyn turned to face Nash, lips slipping into a dark, bitter smile. "Don't worry—I returned the favor the second I got the chance." She stretched out her arms, shaking the emotion from her face and voice. "And that's the story of how I stole my first ever ship."

"You started off with a fancy merchant's vessel?" Nash asked, grinning to lighten the mood. "No wonder the *Ophidian Fang* is a twice-damned floating palace."

"I'd take a floating palace over that oversized barrel you drifted north in," Joslyn shot back, returning the grin.

"I'll have you know that oversized barrel has taken us along almost the entire perimeter of Thamorr at this point."

"Honestly, I'm not surprised—none of the pirates I know would bother trying to steal a dinghy like that."

They traded insults the entire walk back from the docks toward the tavern where Ryia and the others were waiting. By the time they returned to the group, Nash was filled with a warm, cozy feeling she hadn't had since before Ma had died ten long years ago.

When this was all over—when Clem was sinking to the bottom of the ocean, and the Quill along with him—she was going to be a part of a family again.

CHAPTER TWENTY-FIVE

Ryia

After sailing for weeks on the *Ophidian Fang*, even *The Hardship* would have felt cramped. The little boat Nash and Joslyn had lifted from the harbor at Roulsk felt like a floating coffin. There were benches on the top level with barely enough room to swing a hatchet in the space between them, but belowdecks was worse. It was too short to fully stand. Ryia, Evelyn, and Ivan had to hunch over to avoid smacking their skulls on the beams above them, while Tristan, Joslyn, and Nash nearly had to crawl. There was enough room for some sleeping mats and supplies, but not much else.

The rich asshole who owned this ship clearly only used it for day trips, because Ryia couldn't imagine a fur-clad Borean lord crawling on hands and knees into the belly of this cramped beast.

At least the theft had gone smoothly. Between Ivan's knowledge of the Vulpun family's inner workings and Joslyn's and Nash's combined experience in sailing—and stealing—ships, they were out of the harbor in the time it took a single cloud to roll across the moon. The following day, they stopped in a small trapping village just off the coast to stock up on supplies and give Ivan a chance to hide the Vulpun sigils on the sails with some clever stitch work.

The goal now was to trek this little skiff south as fast as possible. They knew exactly where they needed to go. Clem had shown his hand back in Boreas—the moron.

No longer will bloodlines define who has power and who has nothing in this world.

What will define it, then?

Me.

His goal was clearly to wipe out all the royals and replace them with hand-selected puppets—or maybe no one at all, choosing to rule all of Thamorr under a single banner: that of the Snake of the Southern Dock.

A terrifying thought, for sure. But it meant they knew where he was heading. From Boreas, logic would take him to the Shadow Keep to exterminate Tristan's whole line, then to the familiar streets of Carrowwick to take out the Baelbrandts. If they could sail fast enough, they could beat Clem to Dresdell, warn King Duncan, and mount defenses. They had underestimated the bastard back in Oryol. It wasn't a mistake Ryia planned on making again. This time, Clem was going to die, and the Quill would be destroyed. They would save Thamorr and the Adept in one fell swoop.

Tristan always seemed a bit squeamish when

discussing this plan, but Ryia had a feeling it had something to do with them all knowing that Clem planned to hit Edale next . . . and the fact that they weren't going to make any effort to stop him. She was sure the little prince turned con man had nothing resembling love for his father anymore, but she knew the boy had a mother, too. And a brother and sister. If Clem had made good on his promise back in the Reclaimed Castle, then not a single member of the Tovolkov line had been left alive to challenge him. She had to imagine he'd take a similar tack in Edale. By not trying to beat Clem to Duskhaven, they were sentencing Tristan's entire family to death.

Their second day at sea, Joslyn taught them all how to steer the catboat. That must have been why she and Nash had chosen to steal this stupid bucket—a child could sail it. Just one hand on the mainsheet, another on the tiller, and *don't lay us up on any twice-damned rocks,* in Nash's words. Ryia volunteered to steer as often as possible after that—she felt less nauseated when she had some control over the bobbing and weaving of the ship. Besides, what else was she going to do? Relax in the gravelike sleeping quarters below?

Her time trapped beneath the Shadow Keep may have broken her of her claustrophobia to some extent, but she wasn't exactly skipping at the idea of going somewhere she couldn't feel the wind on her face.

Their sixth night at sea was the quietest yet. The water spread out in front of her, looking like glass as it reflected the moon and the stars glinting in the sky above. The frigid northern air was finally starting to mellow out, and the coastline to the right changed slowly from the snowy white of Boreas to the grayish slate cliffs of Edale. The ship was just as silent, the rest of the crew sleeping soundly beneath her feet.

Ryia glanced over her shoulder toward the hatch leading belowdecks at the sound of someone climbing the rungs of the incredibly short ladder. Maybe they weren't all sleeping. It had to be no later than one in the morning—Nash wasn't supposed to take over the helm from her for another three hours at least.

But it wasn't Nash. Ryia couldn't stop herself from smiling as the curly red hair of Evelyn Linley appeared from the shadows instead.

She turned away to hide her grin. "You should be sleeping, Captain."

"I would be, but Tristan is sleeping heavily enough for all of us," Evelyn said, hoisting herself up onto the deck. In the few seconds before she eased the hatch back down, Ryia could hear the droning snore of the sleeping prince echo up through the narrow chamber. "Like a ruddy army of carpenter bees," Evelyn griped.

Ryia snorted.

Evelyn crossed the tiny deck in two steps,

settling onto the bench across from Ryia. For a long moment, they just sat there, Ryia keeping one hand on the tiller to hold their course, Evelyn leaning into the wind.

"It's so peaceful out here, you'd never know the whole bloody world is falling apart," Evelyn finally said, breaking the silence.

Ryia looked over at her. Her face seemed to almost glow in the moonlight, her long curls fluttering in the gentle breeze that swept over the water. She cleared her throat, looking forward again. "Yeah, after a few nights out here, I'm starting to think maybe Nash has a point about the open ocean after all."

"Is that why you always volunteer to take the night shift alone?" Evelyn asked. Her eyes sparkled. "And here I was, thinking it was just so you could empty your guts in peace."

"No, that's just an added bonus."

She had been able to hide her seasickness well enough back on *The Hardship*, but here, there was nowhere to go. Everyone in their party knew her weakness now. Though thankfully, she was finding she was less and less nauseated by the tossing waves each day. She really was coming to appreciate the sea. Maybe in time she could learn to love it. Or, at least, learn not to hate it.

Another long silence stretched between them, comfortable and peaceful. Ryia stared off into the distance, adjusting their heading any time she noted that they were drifting too far from or too close to the shore to the west. The back of her neck prickled as she felt Evelyn's gaze on her—not with her Adept senses, just the regular, run-of-the-mill intuition she had been born with.

"What are you staring at?" Ryia finally said.

"Nothing," Evelyn said. A flush crept up her pale, freckled cheeks, and she looked away. "I just . . . I'm glad we made it out of there, is all."

"We're not out of the swamp yet, Captain."

Evelyn cleared her throat. "As long as we don't have to split up again."

Ryia grinned, glancing over. "What, did you miss me?"

The captain met her eye, solemn and unflinching. "Yes."

There was another long silence. Ryia's heartbeats suddenly came in triplets. She wasn't sure what she'd expected Evelyn to say, but that wasn't it. Finally, she forced a chuckle and said, "I've seen the trouble you all get yourselves into when I'm not around—I'd miss me too."

"Right, like you never get yourself into trouble."

Ryia grinned, adjusting the line in her hand, pulling the sail taut against the wind again. "Yeah, it's a good thing you keep showing up to drag my ass out of the fire at the last second." She paused, frowning, then turned toward Evelyn again. "Why in Felice's darkest hell do you keep doing that, anyway?"

Ryia had made dozens of alliances in the years since she'd fled from her father's home. Of those, few had stuck around when things got tough. Only the people on this ship had stuck around after finding out what she really was. And only the woman sitting on the bench across from her had actually risked her own life to try to save Ryia's—she'd even done it twice now. Once back on the Guildmaster's island, and again in the Reclaimed Castle.

"I'm pretty sure you know why," Evelyn answered.

"Let me guess," Ryia sighed, straightening her back in her best imitation of Evelyn's perfect posture. "Honor and the integrity of teamwork?"

"Not exactly."

"Ah, I know," Ryia said, pulling the tiller toward her to steer them a hair farther to the right. "You just feel guilty about all the times I've saved *your* skin."

Evelyn seemed like the type of person to always make sure things were square. *You scratch my back; I'll scratch yours.*

But the captain shook her head. She smiled, but there was something nervous in the expression. "Wrong again."

"What, are you keeping me alive because you found someone else who's put a bounty out on me, or—"

"I have feelings for you, you git," Evelyn interrupted.

Ryia froze. Blood thundered past her eardrums, and her stomach somehow both fluttered like a soap bubble and sank like a stone. For all these years, she had known friendship to be out of reach—she had never even dared to think about anything more. Love was nothing but a set of dormant coals sputtering to death in the pit of her belly. It was why she'd spent so many crescents at whorehouses over the years. For her, loneliness was something that could only be solved with one too many cups of ale and a paid companion for the night. She had known that for years now.

"You wouldn't if you knew—" Ryia started.

"If I knew what?" Evelyn challenged. "If I knew you worked as a mercenary? Do I need to remind you how we met?" She slid closer on the bench, leaning forward. "If I knew you were being hunted by some of the most powerful arseholes in this world? Bad news—so am I." She cocked her head to one side, her deep brown eyes boring into Ryia's jet-black ones. "If I knew you'd been tortured and tormented into believing you were a monster? Face it, Butcher. I know all about you, and look." She gestured down at herself. "I'm still bloody here."

It was true. Evelyn Linley had seen damned near every side of her in the past few months. Had known her as the fearsome, coldhearted

Butcher of Carrowwick. Had witnessed her at her weakest and her strongest. Had seen every one of her scars, physical and mental. And she was still here. Solidly, stubbornly here.

That had to count for something . . . right?

Before she could let her doubts stop her, Ryia leaned in. The moment Evelyn's lips met hers, the dying coals in her chest sparked and caught fire once again, warming her from the inside out despite the chill autumn winds buffeting the ship. She felt Evelyn's lips smile against her own as the captain pulled her closer. Ryia knit her fingers into the curls at the nape of Evelyn's neck, and for an instant and an eternity, they were connected.

This was it—the feeling she had both craved and run from her entire life. Not just desire, but understanding and acceptance and attachment. A sense of belonging. The feeling that maybe there was a spot of sunshine for her in this dark, horrible world after all.

Then Evelyn stiffened against her, and the feeling evaporated in her chest.

"I'm sorry," Ryia said, face burning as she pulled away. What was she doing? "I shouldn't have—"

"Oh, don't even try it with that—you definitely *should* have. I would have preferred if you'd been less of a milksop and done that a long time ago, actually," Evelyn said. She shifted her gaze from Ryia's eyes to just over her shoulder. She lifted a hand to point. "It's just . . . what is that?"

Ryia's stomach dropped as she followed Evelyn's point. Smoke billowed into the sky far in the distance, blotting out the stars to the west as it poured up from the earth like blood from a corpse sinking into deep water.

"Whatever it is, it can't be good."

Evelyn went below to wake the others. The second Joslyn appeared on the deck, she covered her nose and met Ryia's eye. Ryia couldn't smell anything from here, but Joslyn's senses were a hell of a lot stronger than her own. But still, big surprise—who could've guessed that a fire half the size of Oryol was dangerous?

"It's Clem," Tristan said, mouth twisting sourly. "It has to be."

"Now, come on—we don't know that. Clem might still be up in Boreas," Nash said.

"Who else would want to burn down half of Edale?" Tristan countered.

"Maybe no one," Nash said. "It was a dry summer; Edale's got forests. I've seen it before—one lightning strike in the wrong place, and *poof,* miles of trees and villages, just gone."

They bickered back and forth for a minute before Ivan cut in. Felice, he looked like shit these days. He had let his long hair grow unkempt and tangled, and there were bags under his eyes no matter the time of day. They looked particularly hollow in the silvery light of the moon.

"There is one way to discover for certain what has happened here," he said.

"He's right. We should stop in the next coastal town we see for news," Joslyn agreed. She shook the canteen in her hand. "It'll be good to stock up on fresh water, anyway."

"Stock up on *vitalité*, you mean," Ryia muttered under her breath.

"No," Joslyn said firmly. She clenched her fists, then loosened them. Then she cracked a grin. "Whatever *vitalité* I'd find in a town like this would be shit anyways."

"Probably," Ryia agreed. She gave the pirate a grin. Maybe she'd manage to kick the habit altogether after all.

Nash took over the tiller, and Ryia let herself nod off on Evelyn's shoulder as the smuggler steered them toward the shore. Despite the danger and the foreboding smoke rising from the horizon, she swore she saw a small smile on Evelyn's lips as she settled in. The thought sent a hint of the warmth she'd felt when they were alone stealing through her gut again.

Did that make her soft? Ryia realized she didn't really care.

The closest town was an Edalish village by the name of Brookgrove. It was so small, Ryia thought she could have thrown a hatchet from one end to the other even without her Kinetic magic. Little wooden houses, inns, and shops stood almost on top of one another, like they were all crowding together to get a look at the ships coming into the harbor. Rows of wheat stretched out to the west of the city, the fields stripped clean and bare from the summer harvest. Cliffs jutted up to the north, and south lay countless apple trees full of hard, green fruit that wasn't quite ripe.

"You think a place this ruddy small will have any idea what's going on?" Evelyn asked, looking around doubtfully as Nash steered the catboat into the harbor.

"They definitely know what's going on," Tristan said.

"What makes you so sure?" Ryia asked, yawning and stretching.

The prince pointed toward the tallest building in Brookgrove. "I doubt all those birds are bringing love letters."

The building flew the banner of the Messengers' Fellowship. Flocks of magpies swooped around the upper windows, the scrolls tied to their legs rustling together as they jockeyed for position, all trying to enter the tower at once.

Joslyn led them through the narrow streets and into a tavern called the Apple Grove. Within five minutes of sitting down, they had already heard the news.

The Shadow Keep had fallen. Tolliver Shadowwood had not been heard from since then; it was presumed that their king was dead.

A mysterious stranger leading an army of Adept Kinetics had swept through the Edalish countryside and taken the entire city of Duskhaven in a single night.

"Craziest thing was, the army never breached the gate," the barkeep said, glancing around like he was scared Clem and his army might burst through the door of the Apple Grove at any minute.

"Never breached the gate?" Evelyn asked. "How the bloody hell did he take the city, then?"

"The Adept," Ryia guessed.

"I know he has an army of Kinetics, but they'd still have to batter down the gate to do any good, wouldn't they?" Nash asked.

"I meant the Adept *inside* Duskhaven," Ryia said darkly.

The barkeep pointed at her with the empty glass in his hand. "Exactly right. The Adept inside the city turned on their masters all at once, killed them all. Then opened the gates for that bastard to walk right in."

Tristan looked ready to vomit. He shared a glance with Ryia, and she knew he was thinking the exact same thing she was. Clem had taken the Adept inside the Edalish capital without even laying eyes on them, then taken the city itself without ever lifting a twice-damned finger. A cold chill crept down the length of Ryia's spine as she turned to Evelyn next. At this point, they might be lucky enough to beat Clem to Carrowwick, but if they did . . . what then?

Even with the Needle Guard on their side, they would have maybe a thousand bodies inside the walls fighting against at least twice that on the outside. A thousand regular men and women fighting against two thousand Adept? Those odds weren't just bad; they were impossible.

The rest of the conversations they had in the tavern only made those odds sound worse. There were birds coming in from all over Edale, saying that the invader was traveling from city to city, turning all their Adept and then razing everything to the ground. If Clem managed to hit every major city in Edale before moving on to Dresdell, that would at least slow the bastard down . . . but it also meant he would probably be arriving with a force of closer to three thousand Adept servants.

Some of those would be weak, sure. Some would barely be able to sniff out an arrow streaming toward their throat, or would be just a hair stronger than the average Gildesh wrestler, but still. Three thousand Adept, all fighting under one banner? That hadn't been seen since the days before Declan Day.

After hearing the same news from half a dozen more travelers and villagers, Ryia led the group out the door and back into the streets. They were quiet now, the skies filled with the vivid pink light of early sunset. In a nice, wholesome place like this, most people were probably holed up in their little houses, cooking up what might be their last ever family dinner, if Callum Clem decided to swing this far east.

Tristan broke the silence first. "You all know what we have to do, don't you?"

"Hop on that catboat and sail east until we find a new speck of land that hasn't gone completely to shit?" Joslyn said.

"I'll second that," Nash said.

"No." Tristan looked at Ryia, his eyes threatening to slice her in half. "We need to find our own army. One stronger than Clem's."

"Where exactly do you expect to find such a thing?" Ivan asked. "The *medev* are the strongest army in all of Thamorr, and he *slichte* through them like they were made of snow."

Silence fell over them as they walked through the quiet streets, heading back toward the harbor. Then Tristan said, "I can think of one stronger."

Ryia's stomach clenched as she finally caught his meaning. She skidded to a stop in the mud. No. *Hell* no. "You can't be serious."

"He has the numbers. And they're powerful," Tristan argued, stopping alongside her.

"And just as evil as Callum fucking Clem," Ryia shot back.

"That's debatable."

“Does anyone else want to clue us in here, or . . . ?” Nash said, looking between them.

“Prince Moron here wants to ally us with the Guildmaster,” Ryia said, jerking a thumb toward Tristan.

Joslyn and Evelyn both shouted something to the effect of *Are you crazy?* Ivan made a sound somewhere between a bear’s growl and a cat’s hiss deep in his throat. But Nash just looked on thoughtfully.

“We’re going to have to, aren’t we?” she said after a pause.

More spluttering from Joslyn and Evelyn. A silent yet deafening glare from Ivan. But Ryia didn’t say anything, just watched.

“No, listen,” Nash said, raising two hands to quiet them. “Clem’s got the Quill, which means he can take over any branded Adept in Thamorr, right?” She winced, pointing between Joslyn and Ryia. “That means that the only Adept who *could* fight with us, other than you two, are with the Guildmaster.”

“Too bad the Guildmaster wants us dead,” Joslyn said. “Next suggestion.”

“You don’t think he’d be willing to make peace? After what you saw back there?” Tristan gestured vaguely north, clearly indicating the nonsense back in the Reclaimed Castle.

It was true; the Guildmaster and his posse had gotten their asses kicked by Clem and his newfound Adept magic. And Clem was a far greater threat to his power over Thamorr than Ryia or Joslyn had ever been. He had the numbers, the fighters . . . and they had knowledge of Clem. Would the Guildmaster be willing to stop hunting Ryia long enough to send Callum Clem screaming into hell?

More importantly, would she be able to resist cutting the smirk from his smug face if she had to look at it every twice-damned day?

Maybe, maybe not. This alliance would be short-lived, if they could breathe life into it at all.

"Do we even know he is still alive?" Ivan asked coldly.

"He's alive," Ryia said, stomach churning as she mulled over their options. That bastard wouldn't have gone down that easily.

"A pity," Ivan said.

"Don't tell me you're considering this," Joslyn said, reading Ryia's expression. "You can't possibly trust him to—"

"I don't trust anyone," Ryia interrupted, out of reflex more than anything else. The statement wasn't exactly true these days, but it was true enough in the sense that she had no intention of willingly backing herself blindly into one of the Guildmaster's traps.

"Why are we even considering an alliance if we're expecting to be stabbed in the back?" Evelyn asked.

“Because we’ll be ready to stab him first,” Ryia said. The seeds of a plan had taken root in her mind.

She shared a look with Joslyn, and they had a wordless conversation. Finally, the pirate shook her head in submission, shrugging as if to say *fine.* Then Ryia turned back to the group.

“Anyone have four coppers?” She looked back at the birds swirling around the tower of the Messengers’ Fellowship. “We have a letter to send.”

CHAPTER TWENTY-SIX

Tristan

It took just two days for the Guildmaster to reply to Ryia's message. Tristan was relieved, of course. Clem was cutting through the countryside of his homeland at that very moment. But a small, illogical part of him wouldn't have minded if he had taken a day or two more. Brookgrove was a peaceful town, the kind of place Tristan had dreamed of settling down in once he escaped from his father and Clem—once he could live the life he wanted to live.

Also, he wasn't about to complain about sleeping on a straw bed in an inn instead of curled up on the lower deck of that tiny catboat.

"What does the weasel have to say?" Joslyn asked when Ryia returned to the inn common room the second morning, clutching a scroll bearing the Guildmaster's vivid blue seal.

Evelyn and Nash both perked up. Ivan remained sitting in his chair, staring into the fire like he was hoping the flames would swallow him whole. He had been like that ever since they left the Reclaimed Castle, but it had gotten worse since they'd agreed to try to ally themselves with the Guildmaster. Privately, Tristan thought it was quite childish for him to let a personal grudge outweigh what was clearly going to be best for all of Thamorr. Not that he would ever have the guts to say something like that to the man out loud.

"The weasel has agreed to meet with us," Ryia said, lips twisting sourly like she wasn't sure if that was good news or not. "Tomorrow, in the middle of Haven Bay."

Haven Bay was a small inlet on the southeastern coast of Edale. It sat at the mouth of the Aspen River, a waterway that could lead them straight to the Arden and back to Carrowwick if they snaked through the right lakes and streams.

"Tomorrow?" Nash asked through a mouthful of the apple tart she was eating. The inn's kitchens always smelled like cinnamon and baked apples here, and Nash had probably eaten thirty of those tarts since they arrived. "We need to pull out right now if we want to make it to Haven Bay by then."

The crew packed what few things they had and left the friendly innkeeper and his wife with a wave as they made their way back to the tiny catboat waiting for them at the dock. Tristan watched the small town wistfully as they pulled away, staring at the lanterns winking to life in every window as the sun sank lower and lower in the sky. What would happen to these people if they failed? If Callum Clem succeeded in wiping out all the kings and queens of Thamorr, taking rule of the entire continent under his cruel thumb?

Or worse yet, said another voice in the back of his skull, *what will happen to them if* Ryia *succeeds?*

Because Ivan Rezkoye was not the only member of their crew who was letting personal feelings get in the way of what was best for Thamorr. Ryia planned to destroy the Quill of Declan Day. To let the Adept of the world run free and unchecked. Once they were free, what was to stop them from forming an army all on their own? How did she plan to stop them from becoming brigands or thieves, using their magic to rob and steal and maim innocent people like the ones living in the town of Brookgrove? What did any of their crew intend to do to stop it, for that matter? None of them had so much as spoken up against Ryia's plan to destroy the Quill and set Thamorr aflame alongside it.

Tristan clenched his fists, watching the winking lights of Brookgrove disappear behind the rolling coast as they sailed south. If no one else would look after what was best for Thamorr, then it was up to him.

They reached Haven Bay just after sunrise. Tristan stretched the sleep from his limbs as he emerged from the dark, cramped underbelly of the catboat and settled onto the bench beside Ryia, who had once again offered to steer them through the darkest part of the night. At least she had gotten some sleep in the inn at Brookgrove. Tristan was relieved to see the dark circles under her eyes had lessened.

"You want me to take the tiller for a bit?" he asked, yawning.

"What, are you afraid I'm going to ram the bastard?" Ryia asked.

"I mean, I am now, a little." Tristan grinned. His stomach fluttered as she shot him an exasperated smile in return. For a second, it felt almost like things between them were back to normal—back to how they had been in Carrowwick, in the days before they'd ever heard of the cursed Quill of Declan Day. His grin faded as he glanced at the bay beyond, at the single, tall-masted sloop anchored there, waiting. "You don't think he'll pull anything . . . funny, do you?"

"I never knew the Guildmaster to be much of a fucking comedian."

"You know what I mean."

Ryia pulled a small glass vial from her pocket and asked, "What do you think these are for?" The vial was full of deep purple liquid and stoppered with a tiny scrap of cork. Dormire's blood.

Tristan fingered the identical vial in his own pocket. They had to meet with the Guildmaster—

they didn't have a choice. But that didn't mean any of them planned to blindly trust the man. At the first sign of foul play, the plan was for all of them to dash their vials on the deck, hold their breath, and run. It was the same trick Ivan had used on the Harpies back in Carrowwick. Would such a simple ruse work on beings as powerful as the Disciples? Tristan's grip tightened around his vial, feeling doubtful. Hopefully they would have no need to find out.

Ryia stomped hard on the deck beneath her with both leather-booted feet. "Wake up, you sons of bitches," she called to the rest of the team. "We're here."

The Disciples' sloops had always looked small from a distance. Up close the ship was a lot more intimidating—though of course that could be because they were approaching it in little more than a rowboat. The deck stood tall enough over that of their stolen Borean catboat that a pair of Disciples had to throw down a rope ladder for them to climb. Tristan noticed Ryia's moment of hesitation before grabbing hold of the rungs. She was nervous, maybe even afraid. Evelyn followed close behind—no surprises there. He fought to keep the bitterness from his mind as he watched the redheaded swordswoman disappear onto the deck.

When Ivan reached for the ladder next, Nash frowned in surprise.

"You're coming?"

"Why would I not join?" Ivan retorted.

But Tristan didn't blame the smuggler for her question. Ivan had done nothing the past three weeks but brood and make waspish remarks against the Guildmaster—none of it suggested he was dying to chat with the man face-to-face.

"Er . . . ," Nash said, sharing a look with Tristan.

Ivan just turned, grabbing the next rung. "If I cannot stop this alliance from being made, I can at least be there to make sure you do not promise away everything."

"Oh, don't you worry about that," Joslyn said, clapping Nash on the shoulder and grabbing the ladder after Ivan as she called up to him. "That asshole isn't getting a lick more than the least we can get him to take—he might not even get that, by the time I'm done."

"You might want to lower your voice," Tristan said, wincing and looking up at the deck of the sloop like he was expecting the Guildmaster to be there, leering down at them. Thankfully, he wasn't.

Nash followed the pirate up the ladder, leaving Tristan to bring up the rear alone. The energy on the deck of the Guildmaster's ship was so tense, Tristan thought it might snap like a ginger biscuit at any moment. A dozen Disciples stood surrounding the Guildmaster, four Sensers and eight Kinetics, judging from the tattoos. *Are these all who survived the fight in the Reclaimed Castle?* There had been more than twenty of them when the Guildmaster arrived in Boreas. He saw Ryia's eyes combing over the numbers as well and knew what she was thinking.

Their bargaining position was better than they had even hoped.

After a series of tense greetings, the group found themselves down in the Guildmaster's cabin. It was massive, taking up at least half the lower deck of the sloop. Portholes lit the space with the natural light of the rising sun. A neat bed stood in one corner, a long table taking up the center of the space, laden with fancy Gildesh fruits and loaves of thick bread studded with nuts and raisins.

"Wine?" the Guildmaster asked, pouring himself a small glass of rich red wine from the decanter beside a plate of thinly sliced cheese.

Nash instantly grabbed the nearest cup. Ivan gave her a look that could freeze the southern sea, and Nash set the cup down glumly, slumping into the closest open chair empty-handed instead.

"No one?" the Guildmaster asked after a moment. He shrugged, then set the decanter down and settled himself primly in the chair at the head of the table. "Suit yourselves."

"Can we cut the shit and get to business?" Ryia asked. She did not take a seat, though there was one right in front of her, choosing to stand awkward and tall in the cabin, arms folded like a toddler who had been told they could not have any more sweets.

"I see you are as charming as ever, Miss Grayson," the Guildmaster said.

Tristan saw Ryia priming for one of her trademark cutting responses and thrust one arm out toward the Guildmaster, the other toward the Butcher.

"Ryia, uh . . . Guildmaster," he said. He realized he had never addressed the Guildmaster directly before.

"You may call me Master," the Guildmaster said.

"Master?" Ryia snorted, incredulous.

"Yeah, I'm done calling you that," Joslyn added, lowering herself into the chair opposite him and propping her boots up on his table.

"Master," Tristan interjected, trying his best to keep the peace. "We appreciate your willingness to meet with us. We have a common enemy, which makes us allies."

Ivan, who was leaning against the hatch leading to the passageway outside the cabin, muttered something in Borean. Tristan didn't catch the words, but he could guess what they meant all the same.

"At least one of you has a sense of decorum," the Guildmaster said. He grabbed a loose grape from the plate in front of him and popped it into his mouth.

"Sorry, Martin," Ryia said.

"It's *Master,*" the Guildmaster corrected.

"That's what I said, Martin."

Joslyn snickered loudly a few seats away. Tristan had to stop himself from rolling his eyes. Ryia's irreverence was one of the things that had drawn him to her back in Carrowwick, but did she really not see that they didn't have the upper footing here? He had hoped they could all set their grudges aside long enough to make an agreement—even if it was an agreement Ryia and the others planned to break.

"So, Martin," Ryia continued. She leaned forward, placing her palms on the table. "We have a plan that will stop Callum Clem from slithering his army over the rest of Thamorr."

"And?" the Guildmaster asked, raising one eyebrow. "Did you simply come here to brag?"

Evelyn stepped out from Ryia's shadow and lowered herself into the seat at the Guildmaster's left. "Clem is using the Quill of Declan Day to gather an army."

"Yes, I have heard," the Guildmaster said, feigning disinterest. "Marching across the map, attracting Adept servants like flies to refuse as he goes."

"Yes," Evelyn agreed. She swallowed. "Your

Disciples will soon be the only Adept in Thamorr outside of his control."

"Thanks to your greed," Ryia interjected.

The Guildmaster shot her a side-eyed look but otherwise gave no sign that he had heard her. "That is unlikely," he said. "Have you not noticed the man's pattern? His mastery over the Quill is still quite amateur." His face remained flat, but his icy eyes betrayed a hint of unease. "It will be years before your Clem can control more than a handful of Adept at a time without losing control of his own body."

"I would not bet on that if I were you," Ivan said stiffly.

The Guildmaster glanced over at him, brow raised. "So, you require my army, is that it?" He sat back, swirling the wine in his cup, considering. "I wonder, then, what I need your help for?" Tristan saw Ryia's hand twitch toward the pocket holding her capsule of dormire's blood. If the Guildmaster noticed anything strange about the motion, he didn't mention it. His expression was smug when he looked back up from his wine. "Tell me: What is to stop me from taking you all prisoner for aiding Clem in the first place—"

Joslyn opened her mouth to argue.

"—or for hiring a traitorous merchant to help you run away from your destiny to serve as a Disciple?" he finished, giving the pirate a level stare. "If it is my army you need, what is to stop me from simply making my own plan to stop Callum Clem without you?"

Tristan's stomach dropped. He began to toy with the capsule in his own pocket, rolling it between his fingers. But Nash jumped in without skipping a beat. Slapping Joslyn's hand back before she could stop her, Nash reached out and grabbed a slice of the thick bread, topping it with some of the pale yellow cheese and taking a bite.

"You don't know the man like we do," she said around the mouthful. "He's as crazy as a damned fruit fly these days, don't get me wrong, but he's brilliant." She swallowed, wagging the bread in her hand at him. "You're free to try this without our help, but trust me, you will fail. And that bastard is moving fast. I don't think you'll have time for a second attempt here."

The Guildmaster was quiet for a long moment. His gaze raked over each of them in turn, and Tristan was overcome by the distinct feeling that he could see *into* them. See through their false offer of partnership right to their intent to betray him. Then his gaze flickered to the deck above. Ryia caught the look; so did Ivan. They all knew the Guildmaster was thinking of the Disciples on deck . . . and by extension the Disciples he'd lost back in the Reclaimed Castle. He had already seen the consequences of underestimating Callum Clem. He was too smart to make the same mistake twice . . . wasn't he?

Finally, he leaned back in his chair and said, "I will agree to an alliance. But I will first set some terms."

"And what might those terms be, Martin?" Joslyn asked.

The Guildmaster gritted his teeth, clearly displeased that Ryia's nickname for him was spreading. "When this is all over—when Clem is stopped and put to rest—I want the Quill."

"Like hell," Joslyn growled.

At the same time, Ryia contributed a simple "Fuck off."

Evelyn laid a hand on Ryia's forearm, then turned to the Guildmaster. "If those are your terms we can't accept them."

"Yeah, what's to stop some other son of a bitch from stealing it again someday and starting this whole mess all over again?" Nash asked. She reached for the fruit plate next, helping herself to a bright red strawberry. "No dice, Martin. Either the Quill is destroyed, or we don't help."

The Guildmaster's jaw twitched. "You do realize that without the aid of the Quill, the Guilds will fall?"

"You say that like it isn't the whole bloody point," Evelyn shot back. Ryia beamed at her.

They had known he would ask for this, of course. In Tristan's mind, if they were already planning to go back on their word, they should just accept this offer and be done with it. But

Ryia and Joslyn had both insisted that would tip the Guildmaster off to their betrayal. Here and now, Tristan had to admit it was a compelling point . . . because the moment the Guildmaster nodded slowly, indicating he would give up the Quill, Tristan knew the man intended to betray them in kind.

"I see your point," the Guildmaster drawled. "I am a reasonable man, despite anything you might believe to the contrary." He shot a pointed look at Ryia and Joslyn. "There is one other set of terms to which I will agree."

"We are listening, *schwiensucher*," Ivan said.

Tristan wasn't familiar with that particular Borean term, but he couldn't imagine it was an honorific.

"We will enact your plan, with my army, to defeat this Callum Clem. You may destroy the Quill of Declan Day. The Guilds will remain, but will take in only Adept who wish to serve." He paused, looking back at Joslyn and Ryia. "But in return, the two of you will join my ranks. You will agree to be bound to service for the rest of your lives, following orders as unquestioningly as the rest of my loyal Disciples."

"And how exactly do you plan to make us do that?" Ryia asked. Her tone was light and flippant, but there was a tenor of fear behind it.

The Guildmaster smiled. "Without the Quill, compliance will be a bit more difficult—it's true.

But there are other . . . more *traditional* methods of breaking a person."

Evelyn's fingers tightened into a fist on the table. Tristan didn't blame her; his own stomach had twisted itself into a knot the second the words left the Guildmaster's mouth. Even if they planned to try to weasel out of this agreement, there was no guarantee they would actually be able to at the end of this. The idea of the spirited Butcher of Carrowwick spending the rest of her days wearing the Guildmaster's invisible chains made him want to vomit.

Ryia was silent for a long moment. "So, let me be clear. You'll give us your army to help stop Clem, allow the Quill to be destroyed, and stop kidnapping infants from their sobbing mothers' arms if we just agree to come to your little island of nightmares?" She shared a look with Joslyn. "Kind of makes us sound like assholes if we say no, doesn't it?"

Joslyn sighed. "Well, I'd hate to be an asshole."

The Quill destroyed. The Guildmaster still in power. Ryia stuck as a slave. If, by some chance, this deal actually went to plan, it would be on the worst terms Tristan could have imagined. The conversation continued to buzz around the cabin as the odd group of allies hashed out the details of their plot, but Tristan wasn't listening anymore. He was busy formulating a plan of his own.

Beneath the table, he tore a scrap of his linen undershirt free. When he was certain no one was looking, his hand darted across the table, snagging one of the charcoal writing sticks littered on its surface and returning it to his lap. While the rest of the party continued to argue, he scribbled fiercely on his makeshift parchment.

He looked back up just in time to see Ryia stand and extend a hand toward the Guildmaster.

"You have yourself a deal, Martin."

The Guildmaster smiled his frigid smile and accepted the handshake.

Ryia and Joslyn worked out the details of their plan with the Guildmaster as Nash and Evelyn chewed worried holes in their cheeks. Ivan was still glaring daggers from the corner. The Guildmaster agreed to return to his island, load his Disciples onto their ships, and sail for Carrowwick Harbor while their party traveled by the riverways to approach Carrowwick from the west in hopes of beating Clem there and convincing the Baelbrandts to cooperate. Then they would all lie in wait for Clem's forces to arrive and hopefully end this uprising once and for all.

Finally, they all stood, and the Guildmaster said, "This has been a pleasure."

"No it hasn't," Ryia said brightly. "Here's to hoping one of us dies in Carrowwick so we never have to do this again."

And with that, their crew filed out of the cabin, heading back onto the deck and down the ladder to the catboat. Tristan lingered for a moment, making sure he fell to the back of the crew, then extended his own hand toward the Guildmaster.

"Thank you for agreeing to meet, Master," he said.

The Guildmaster grasped his hand, and there was the whisper of fabric sliding against fabric as his makeshift parchment slipped from his sleeve into the Guildmaster's. Then Tristan clambered down the rope ladder back onto the catboat, where Evelyn was already talking.

"You know he only agreed to make that bloody deal because he's planning on using your nose as a replacement for his precious Quill, right?" she said, pointing at Joslyn. "If he doesn't manage to double-cross us and take the Quill back altogether, that is."

From what Ryia had said, Joslyn was the most powerful Senser the world had ever seen. The powers didn't usually work that way—allowing a Senser to locate something with their magic—but she had used that power to find him and Evelyn back in Golden Port. Could the Guildmaster use it the same way?

"He's free to try," Joslyn snorted. "I'll drown myself in the damned ocean before I use my senses to drag some poor sod into a life like that."

"You might not have a choice," Nash said

somberly. "He said he knows how to break people the old-fashioned way."

"All he'll find out if he tries is that I'm not so easy to break," Joslyn said.

"Perhaps someone should take the time to find out if *he* is easy to break," Ivan interjected.

Evelyn pointed to him in agreement. "Yes. After Clem is dealt with, we topple the Guildmaster himself. Sink his bloody island to the bottom of the Luminous Sea."

"I'm pretty sure that's not how islands work," Ryia said. "Besides, I'm not giving that asshole a twice-damned thing if I can help it."

"And if you can't?" Evelyn asked. "If he manages to force us to make good on our promises?"

"I've escaped the man before," Ryia quipped. "I can do it again."

The pair of them continued to argue as Nash pulled in the anchor, hoisted the sail back up against the wind, and steered them toward the mouth of the Aspen River. Tristan stared out across Haven Bay at the Guildmaster's ship. They, too, were hoisting their sails, preparing to sail south around the curve of Thamorr toward the Guildmaster's island. As he watched them, he could see, superimposed against the sky, the words he had penned on that scrap of linen.

I will get you the Quill so you can restore the balance of Thamorr. Meet me on the southern docks of Carrowwick Harbor the day Clem invades.

In return, you will help us defeat Clem, and you will allow Ryia to live out her days on the mainland as a free woman.

If you agree to these terms, send up a signal before we leave Haven Bay.

It was not the first letter he had sent the Guildmaster. The first had been soon after leaving Golden Port, from a magpie in the rookery on Salt Beard's ship.

The team had wondered how the Guildmaster had found them in Oryol, but all had seemed to agree he must have been tracking Clem for some time, trying to reclaim the Quill. The truth was that Tristan had told him exactly where to find them. He had hoped the Guildmaster would have arrived sooner—that he would have been able to stop Clem before he'd found the dagger. Take the Quill back to the island, stop the threat before it had even begun. But his message had traveled too slowly. The Guildmaster had been moments too late, and they had lost the day.

This time, however, they could not lose without all of Thamorr falling to chaos and darkness.

Tristan watched the Guildmaster's ship anxiously as it tacked south against the wind, growing smaller and smaller in the distance. Would he truly not agree to this bargain?

Then he saw it. The signal. A wine bottle flew

high into the sky from the deck of the Guild-master's ship, soaring up above the mainsail, silhouetted against the midmorning sun. It burst in midair, showering vivid red wine down over the waves, shards of glass sparkling as they tumbled from the sky.

That settled it, then. He was going to betray Ryia once again, this time in order to save her. He studied her for a moment, watching her scarred face as she stared toward the coastline of Edale, growing on the horizon. Would she understand? Or this time, would she hate him forever?

But he knew it didn't matter. Not to him. Ryia's life and the fate of Thamorr were at stake, and Tristan would do whatever it took to protect them both.

CHAPTER TWENTY-SEVEN
Ivan

In the days following the troubling meeting with the Guildmaster, the tossing waves of the Sea of Boreas were replaced by the steady flow of the Aspen River. Then the rushing rapids of the Rowan dumped Ivan and the others into Lake Primrose on the northeastern border of Dresdell. Lake Primrose stretched into a series of creeks that finally widened into the Arden River. In all this time, they saw no sign of Callum Clem and his army, other than the occasional billows of smoke rising high into the sky, marking another city that had been stripped of its Adept and left in ashes, but they heard the tales in every town in which they stopped to get supplies.

Tales of a vicious man on horseback, leading a pack of rabid Adept beasts. Attacking cities, destroying lords and noblemen, and stealing their Adept before moving on. Ivan wanted to believe the stories were exaggerations, but after what he had seen back in Oryol, he could not be certain.

Was this all his fault?

He had always known Callum Clem was a dangerous man. A *lischka*, a fox, who saw the rest of the people in this world as chickens in an unguarded coop. Nash had been right from the start. They should never have allied themselves with the Snake of the Southern Dock. He had known what Clem would do—that the man would never stand to see rivals rise up to meet him. That he would strike down every king and queen in this land. But, blinded by his hopes of freeing Kasimir, he had not cared. He had traded the freedom of Thamorr for the freedom of his brother. And in his haste, he had doomed both.

Kasimir's eyes bulged as the blade entered his throat. His frail knees shook, unable to carry his meager weight any longer. He crashed to the floor of the Reclaimed Castle, dust settling around his still body.

Ivan blinked the wetness from his eyes, staring intently at the horizon, watching the too-familiar silhouette of Carrowwick grow closer and closer. He had relived that moment a hundred times since leaving Oryol. Perhaps a thousand. The moment of his brother's death. The death he had caused.

No. He gritted his teeth, shoving the emotion down. It was the *verdammte* Guildmaster who had doomed Kasimir—and Thamorr alongside him. Without his intrusion, Ryia and Evelyn's plan could still have succeeded. They could have prevented Clem from laying hands on that accursed dagger, and Ivan and Kasimir could have fled through the streets of Oryol, returning to the life they had lived before the *medev* took him away.

He struggled to shove his anger and grief away, folding the emotions up and tucking them into the furthest recesses of his mind. Andrei Tovolkov was dead, but the reign that had replaced him—the reign of Callum Clem—would be far worse for the Borean people than the *Keunich* had ever been.

And the fault for Clem's reign lay largely upon the Guildmaster's head. Thanks to the Guildmaster's meddling, Clem had managed to rise to power. And now, for reasons only Gott would ever understand, it fell upon their crew to set things right.

The longer Ivan brooded on the subject, the more certain he was: the Guildmaster was the root of all that was evil in this world. And instead of scheming to cleave his head from his shoulders, they had *joined* him. Even setting his anger at Kasimir's murder aside, Ivan knew their decision to ally with the Guildmaster was unforgivably foolish.

The man had agreed far too quickly to allow the Quill to be destroyed. That could mean only one thing—he meant to betray them. He would use them for their plot to stop Clem—the only threat to his power in this world—and then he would line them up and *slichte* their throats. Ryia and the others might think they were smart enough to outfox that betrayal, but Ivan wasn't too proud to admit when he was outmatched. The Guildmaster would destroy them all.

Nash steered the catboat down the last mile of the Arden River, gracefully looping the *tinzig* ship around to tether it to the docks. The same stretch of the docks where *The Hardship* had been tethered when they had first stolen her, Ivan was almost certain. A pang shot through the hollowness in his stomach at the thought. Had that truly only been a few months before? He felt ages older now. An ancient, wasted man trapped in the body of his younger self.

Joslyn jumped off the ship as they pulled into an open slot on one of the moldering docks, trailing a long stretch of rope she used to lash them to one of the slime-covered posts. One by one, they stepped off the catboat and back onto the streets of Carrowwick. Nash offered Ivan her hand to help him down, and after a moment's hesitation he took it. It was the most they had interacted in a month or more. Since Ivan had caught Nash trying to steal the Quill before they ever put in at Golden Port with Clem. For an instant, he imagined a world where he had not stopped her. Where he and Nash had stolen the Quill and fled to shore, leaving Clem to flounder on his own.

Of course, such dreams were foolish. Callum Clem was too sharp to allow his pockets to be picked like that. He would have sounded the alarm, and Ivan would have watched Nash get pulled to pieces by Clem's first Kinetics.

"All right, are you lot ready for this?" Evelyn asked, brushing herself off. She stood prouder in Carrowwick than Ivan had seen her stand in any of the villages and cities along the way. As though her old guard training activated within her the moment her boots touched Baelbrandt-ruled soil.

Tristan straightened his tunic. They had spent their last few silvers on it back in the village of Lockhorn, some twenty miles up the river. A waste of good coin, Ryia had said, but Ivan knew the truth. He had made his entire career in Carrowwick off appearances. For their plan to work, Tristan needed to look not like Tristan Beckett, pickpocket, but like Dennison Shadowwood, Crown Prince of Edale. Rightful king of Edale, perhaps, if the rumors were true and Tolliver Shadowwood was dead.

Of course, it was unlikely their plan would work anyhow. Tristan and Evelyn hoped to gain an audience with King Duncan II at the Bobbin Fort. A disgraced guard and a runaway prince, coming to beg him to send all of his Adept guards away. It was what Kasimir would have called a *draumwerkern missonen.* A dreamer's mission—doomed to fail. It was far more likely that King Duncan would imprison the both of them.

But of course, they could not fail. If they did not get the existing Adept out of Carrowwick before Callum arrived, then they would all be destroyed before the Snake ever set foot inside the gates. They needed to somehow get all the Adept on a ship far enough out in the harbor, trapping them in a floating prison where Callum could not use them to destroy the city from the inside out, even once he used the Quill to master their minds. For the rest of their brilliant plan to even *begin,* they needed Callum Clem to enter the city.

"Wish us luck," Tristan said. He gave Ryia his usual sheepish grin, but there was something new there—guilt? Perhaps he already knew they would fail as well.

"Best of luck to you," Ivan said stiffly. "And to us."

While Evelyn and Tristan attempted to use their fallen statuses to gain access to the king of Dresdell, the rest of them would be combing the harbor, looking for a ship large enough to fit every branded Adept servant in all of Carrowwick.

"All right, we should probably start north by the—where the hell are you two going?" Nash stopped mid-sentence as Ryia and Joslyn broke away from the docks, moving to follow Tristan and Evelyn to the Bobbin Fort.

"We're going with them," Ryia said, as though it was the most obvious thing in this world. "You didn't seriously think it would take four of us to find a ship, did you?"

"Will it actually take four of you to get into the Bobbin Fort?" Nash asked, incredulous.

Ivan had to agree—if anything, bringing a known pirate and the Butcher of Carrowwick along would make it more difficult for them to gain entry to the fort.

"It might take all four of us to get *out* of the Bobbin Fort if Clem decides to aim that magic Quill of his toward Carrowwick while we're in there," Joslyn pointed out. "That place is *crawling* with Adept." She wrinkled her nose. "I can smell the danger from here."

"And what about us?" Ivan asked coolly. "There are Adept in the city as well, and we have not a single weapon between us."

"Hey now, I have my trusty blade," Nash said, flipping her tiny dagger between her fingers. It was no larger than a letter opener and would be hard-pressed to stop a pickpocket, let alone an Adept Kinetic bent on sending them to *Yavol*.

"We have not a single weapon between us," Ivan repeated. "What do we do if we suddenly find the docks crawling with Adept controlled by Callum?"

"Run fast." Ryia considered a moment, then fished into her belt. She pulled out a single throwing axe and handed it to him, handle first. "And don't miss."

A moment later, the four of them were gone, lost to the tangle of familiar streets steeped in memories that seemed almost to belong to someone else. An Ivan Rezkoye he had been, rather than the one he was now.

"Anyway," Nash said, cutting through the silence the others had left in their wake. "I was saying, we should cut north. There won't be anything bigger than a caravel on the slum docks down here. What we're going to want is probably an Edalish trade ship—the ones that bring the iron and steel are usually pretty damned big."

They walked in silence for a long moment. Finally, Ivan cleared his throat. "I am sorry. For trusting Callum."

Nash looked at him so sharply Ivan almost lost his footing. Her eyes were so bright and piercing, swirling pits of copper, sucking him in. "Why didn't you just tell me about him? Your brother." She inclined her head.

Ivan swallowed. "I did not tell you because I did not think you would understand," he finally said. Then he amended that. "I was *worried* you would not understand."

"And you thought I'd better understand you deciding to partner with the biggest scam artist we knew for no reason?" Nash shook her head. The docks were quiet this time of the morning, just a few drunks stirring in the shadows of buildings, a handful of ships pulling out for the day, and the calling of gulls high above. "After Bornchev . . ." Nash trailed off.

Ivan's stomach curled. The old Borean storyteller in Golden Port. The man had told Callum exactly what he had asked for. Had invited them into his home. Had offered them his *stervod.* And Callum had murdered him all the same. And still, that had not swayed Ivan from the Snake's side.

Perhaps everything that had happened since, everything he had learned and endured, was Gott's way of punishing him for his mistakes. And if that was true . . . He thought of the Piervin manor in Volkfier. The dead bodies littering the corridors and the garden. His punishment was surely not over yet.

"I should have trusted you," Ivan said. His voice was hoarse. He cleared his throat, collecting himself before continuing on. "But now I am asking you to trust me."

"Trust you about what?"

"We cannot work with the Guildmaster."

Nash stopped short. Ivan had been ready for this and stopped alongside her. "It's a little late for that, Ivan," she said weakly.

"I do not mean we should try to stop him from coming here," Ivan said. He looked out over the glistening waters, examining the sunrise with distaste. "I do not think we could stop him if we wanted to. I am just saying we should be careful.

He is not as honorable as he would have us believe."

Nash sighed, scrubbing a hand over her forehead. "Look, Ivan, there's not a single one of us who actually trusts the man. We know he's a twice-damned rat. He kidnapped my baby sister, remember? He'll try to steal the Quill back before we can chop it to pieces, we know that. But Ryia has a plan. Besides . . ." She met him with that piercing stare once again. The one that stopped his breath right in his throat. "The Guildmaster has had the Quill for what, fifty years? And he has never gone on a murdering rampage across the continent. If it's between trusting him and handing the keys to this world over to Callum Clem, I know my decision."

"So, you would side with the man who murdered my brother?" Ivan said. Emotion cracked his voice.

"This is bigger than your brother, Ivan," Nash snapped. "How many people have died because of your little rescue mission? Maybe if he was still alive, I could understand your motivation here, but he's gone, Ivan. Fucking over this whole operation to get even with the Guildmaster is not going to bring him back."

"You do not think I understand that?" Ivan said. He was shouting now. A pair of gulls took off in alarm at the volume of his voice, but he did not care. "I understand that Kasimir is gone. That there is nothing that will bring him back. But the Guildmaster will not stop. He is cleverer than Ryia—than any of us. He is ruthless, and he will be expecting our betrayal; I know this."

Nash looked around, holding a hand up to settle him as a few nosy heads poked out of nearby windows, a few shouting for them to "Shut the hell up, would you?"

"Ryia isn't alone in this. You forget: we have Jol—Joslyn now too." Pride swelled in Nash's voice. "My sister has outsmarted the Guildmaster a hundred times before. I think she can manage it one more time."

Ivan shook his head, frustrated. How could Nash not understand? Was this how she had felt when he had insisted on supporting Clem? It was infuriating. "Nash, I have a plan—"

"No!" Now Nash was the one yelling. "Ivan, I am *done* with plans. I am done with schemes and plots and whatever else you want to call them. If we hadn't betrayed Ryia and the rest of them in the first place, Bornchev would still be alive. Clem would never have gotten control of the Quill. We wouldn't be in this fucking mess." She flung her arms out. "Maybe Kasimir would still be alive."

Ivan's blood ran cold. "So, you think it is my fault that my brother is dead?" he asked, his voice barely more than a whisper.

Nash blanched, but it was too late.

“Forget it,” Ivan said bitterly. “We will trust the Guildmaster. And if it leads us to *Yavol*’s realm, just know that the blame for that will lie in your hands.”

They did not speak again until they found the ship. A massive carrack on the trade docks. She flew the flags of the Edalish iron merchant guild, just as Nash had suspected. They would not have to worry about stealing it—if the king agreed to send off the Adept, then he would ask the merchant for use of his ship. The merchant would comply. It was something that was agreed upon when docking in any large port.

“How do you think the others are faring?” Nash asked. Her voice was too casual, too light. Trying to cover up the strife from the fight they were still engaged in, behind their icy tongues and fiery glares.

Ivan did not respond. He had caught sight of something on the horizon that had made his cheeks pale and his stomach knot like a sailor’s rope. Blue sails. Dozens of them, crowding the horizon, approaching around the cliffs to the south. Nash was right about at least one thing, then. It was too late for doubts or schemes now.

The Guildmaster had arrived.

CHAPTER TWENTY-EIGHT
Evelyn

Evelyn Linley had paced the floor of King Duncan's audience chamber in the Bobbin Fort more times than she could count, but the castle felt foreign to her now. Unfamiliar and unfriendly.

Given how she had last left the Bobbin Fort—disgraced and stripped of each and every one of her honors—she had not been expecting a particularly warm welcome, but the one she got was even more hostile than she had imagined. If Tristan had not been there—Dennison Shadowwood, possible king of Edale—she was certain she would have already been lashed to the walls of the Hackle Cells some five stories beneath their boots.

As it was, the four of them were stripped of their weapons at the door and pushed to their knees on the hard stone floor just before the throne. Ryia had given her a wink as the guard took her sword. The Butcher had wiggled a finger slightly, causing the blade to vibrate for a moment in the guard's hand. The man had hardly noticed, but Evelyn knew what it meant. If things went south, Ryia could get their weapons back.

Of course, she wasn't sure how much good a few bits of steel would do them here, surrounded by guards and Adept and walls of stone. At least she would be able to die with a blade in her hand.

"Evelyn Linley," the king boomed. His voice was just as strong as she remembered it, affected with the proper Dresdellan accent that was so different from the low-Dresdellan tones one heard in places like the Lottery. "After you were expelled from your post for allowing the Butcher of Carrowwick to maim my nephew with impunity, you were seen by several fellow guards on the run with members of a local criminal syndicate." He glared down at Ryia, on her knees at Evelyn's right. "And now you come to me with one of those same criminals in tow, the most wanted pirate on the western coast, and a man claiming to be the lost prince of Edale."

"Yes, Your Majesty," Evelyn replied. There was no point in denying any of it—it was true.

"You must know that I have more than half a mind to cast you into the cells," he said coolly, as though he were commenting on the weather.

"That is why you should believe me when I say we have come to Dresdell with a dire warning," Evelyn said, struggling to keep her calm. The stone floor dug into her bony knees. She shifted, and the guard behind her gave her a shove. Her face hit the floor, and she felt her lip split. "Why else would I return?" she asked, pushing herself back up onto her knees and wiping blood from her mouth.

"To attempt to overthrow my command, perhaps?" the king mused. He stood, pacing back and forth on the platform holding his throne. "To steal something precious from my vaults? Why does any criminal do what they do?"

"I have no intent to steal your throne, Your Majesty," Tristan said, voice muffled as the guard behind him forced his face down toward his chest. "In fact, we come here to help you defend your throne. I am sure you have heard the stories of what has happened in Boreas and Edale?"

"Weak, oversized kingdoms that fell to a common brigand," the king said, disdain dripping from his tone.

Had he always been this much of a prat? And she had served him for years. Adalina, how had she not seen this before?

Evelyn opened her mouth to counter, but Joslyn beat her to the punch.

"And you think Dresdell is so much stronger? Are you kidding me?"

"Joslyn, shh—" Evelyn hissed. She turned back to the king. "Have you heard how those kingdoms fell? How the brigand who attacked them managed to gain entry to the city?"

"Spies and traitors, from what I have heard," the king said, his ruddy nose still up in the air. "But we have no such traitors here. Every member of the Needle Guard has been screened and tested for loyalty."

"It's not the Needle Guard you need to worry about," Ryia said. "It's the tattooed sons of bitches surrounding them."

"My Adept?" The king laughed. "I do not imagine a common street rat like yourself has spent much time in the presence of Adept servants. They do not have minds or souls. They cannot betray me any more than a sword can betray the guard who wields it."

Evelyn glanced nervously toward Ryia, afraid she'd lose her temper and show him just how easily a sword could betray its holder when a telekinetic Adept was in the room. But she held herself in check, thank the goddesses.

"The Adept will be turned against you," Tristan piped up. "If you keep them here in the city, they will betray you, possibly to your death. We have a ship waiting in the harbor. We ask that you send your Adept to—"

"A ship?" The king gave a mirthless laugh. "You would come to my castle, a group of marauders, thieves, and impostors, and ask that I send away my most powerful guards? Place them on a ship in your care? Do you truly think me so simpleminded?"

"Consider for a moment, my king, that there are powers in this world you don't quite understand," Evelyn said.

"Consider for a moment, *Miss* Linley, that Carrowwick is the most secure city in all of Thamorr. That the walls of the Bobbin Fort have never before been breached, even in the days before the first Guildmaster—"

"Because no one ever found them worth breaching," Ryia muttered.

Could she not hold that tongue of hers for a few seconds longer? The king's face took on a purplish hue. Evelyn sighed, knowing what was coming next.

"I believe you have been sent by the brigand who has attacked Boreas and Edale to weaken my defenses, and I will not stand for it," the king said. "Guards!" he snapped. "Take them to the Hackle Cells."

"No!" Evelyn shouted at the same time Ryia said, "Fuck off!"

The guards behind them snared their arms while the ones ringing them from the outside leveled their narrow-bladed swords at their throats. Evelyn looked to Ryia out of the corner of her eye. The Butcher cocked her head slightly, asking the silent question: *Is it time?*

Evelyn sighed. She had hoped for a better outcome. But if the king wouldn't listen, then that was that. They would be in trouble if there were still Adept inside the city when Clem attacked, but if they were in the cells when he came, they would be, as Ryia liked to say, completely fucked.

She gave a slight nod.

Ryia flashed her wolfish grin, turning her attention to the swords at their throats. But an instant before the Butcher could use her magic to begin yanking them free of the men's hands, there was a shift in the room.

They were too late.

The Adept Kinetics flanking the king began to blink, too fast for a normal man. Too fast for an Adept, even.

"Your Highness! Run!" Evelyn shouted. But there was no time to run.

The Adept turned on their king in unison, one grabbing him by his legs, the other by his throat. The nearest Needle Guard soldiers shouted and turned their swords on the Adept, but they fell to the other Kinetics in the room almost immediately. Evelyn cringed at the shock of pure fear in King Duncan's eyes as the two Adept gripping him yanked, tearing him in half at the waist.

"I'd say that's our cue to leave," Ryia said, watching with distaste as the king's disembodied legs twitched on the floor. Still on her knees, she formed a fist, then yanked her arm backward.

The guard holding Evelyn's sword barely seemed to notice as the slender blade left his slackened grip. It soared into Evelyn's outstretched hands as she leapt to her feet. Ryia's hatchet belt flew across the room next, followed by Joslyn's jewel-encrusted Gildesh cutlass. Tristan, who was about as handy with a blade as a toddler was with a fork, had no weapon. He clambered back to his feet, empty-handed, trying to gather as many of the Needle Guard as he could.

"Tristan! On your left!" Evelyn shouted. A small Adept Kinetic was darting toward him. An instant before the freshly brainwashed woman made contact with the prince, she was met with a wall of black fabric and blacker hair. Ryia.

The Butcher grappled with the Adept. "Get to the door, moron," she grunted at Tristan.

The boy didn't need to be told twice, and neither did Evelyn.

"This way," Joslyn shouted. Her nostrils were flaring, her face contorted in disgust. Evelyn could only imagine how rank this room smelled with senses as strong as hers. But if anyone could find them a safe path out of this, it would be her.

The room became a blur of Needle Guard armor, Adept robes, and blood. Fear spiked through Evelyn's veins like a drug, dulling her senses and sending her heart hammering. She had dealt with danger before, but never like this. It wasn't even just the immediate fear of being torn to shreds by brainwashed Kinetics that took over her—it was the larger fear that this battle was already lost. That they were too late. Was the Guildmaster even here yet? If not, he would arrive to find nothing more than a burned husk of a city drenched in blood.

"Keep it together, Linley." Ryia's voice came from behind. The Butcher lay a hand on her shoulder. "We're getting out of here, okay? I promise."

Evelyn glanced down at Ryia's hatchets. The bits were covered in blood and gore. She wondered for a moment if the blood belonged to Needle Guard or Adept, but the hollow expression on the Butcher's face told her the answer. She had been forced to kill Adept today—and she was splitting the blame between Clem and herself, from the looks of it.

"You had to—" Evelyn started, but Ryia cut her off.

"Joslyn, that beak of yours find us a safe path out of this shithole yet?"

"Working on it," the pirate shot back.

Ryia's nostrils flared, and she spun around again, lifting her hatchet just in time to catch a charging Adept in the wrist. His hand flopped to the floor with a wet smack, leaving him with a bleeding stump. Evelyn reared back, planting a front kick to his chest with every ounce of her strength. He must not have been a very strong Kinetic, because he fell back a pace.

"Work on it *faster,*" Ryia huffed.

And then they were on the move again. Joslyn led them on a winding path through the throne room, ducking behind pillars and columns. Evelyn tried to get as many of the Needle Guard as possible to follow, but most of them were still desperate to avenge their king, the gits.

"The king is dead—save your bloody kingdom!" she shouted more than once. But her logic fell largely on deaf ears.

They had nearly made it to the massive stone doors when Joslyn suddenly froze. A Kinetic who had just made short work of three Needle Guard charged directly for them. The pirate's cutlass hung limp in her grip as she stared at the charging man.

"Kill it! Kill it! Kill it!" Tristan screamed on a constant loop.

But Joslyn just stood there.

Ryia grimaced, twirling her hatchets around her wrists, then catapulted herself up into the air, pushing off Tristan's shoulders. The prince stumbled and nearly fell as the Butcher somersaulted over Joslyn's head, landing a two-booted kick directly in the Kinetic's face.

Joslyn shook her head, the spell evidently broken, then waved them on, sprinting toward the door without looking back. Ryia caught up as they streamed out the door, a new blood splatter painted across the front of her throat. She glanced at the dozen Needle Guard Evelyn had managed to round up. "This it?"

"So far," Evelyn said weakly. There were still

at least twice as many in the throne room, and four of the king's Valiers . . . though who knew if they were alive at this point.

"Nope. If the others aren't with us now, they've made their choices," Ryia said. "Joslyn, get the other door."

Joslyn and Ryia each grabbed one of the heavy stone doors, slamming them shut.

"A Kinetic can break through that in half a second," Tristan said. His voice was still high-pitched with panic. Evelyn wasn't surprised—they had just been swarmed by two dozen of Clem's new bloodthirsty, brainwashed Adept.

"You don't think I know that?" Ryia griped back. She had both hands raised up in front of her, her eyes closed. Evelyn knew she was feeling the energy of something—listening to its song. There was a sharp crack, and the stone floor beneath the door shuddered. Then half a dozen shards of stone spiked up from the floor, splintering off from the ground to form a barricade. It wouldn't stop a strong Kinetic forever, but hopefully it would buy them enough time for the Guildmaster to arrive.

"Is she . . . what is she?" asked one of the few Needle Guard who had been smart enough to follow them.

Ryia shot him a wink. "One of a kind."

A pang shot through Evelyn as Ryia grinned at her. She *was* one of a bloody kind. And she had agreed to sell her soul to the Guildmaster to save them all.

The grin fell from Ryia's face as she turned to Joslyn. "Are you okay?" she asked in a low voice.

"Yeah, I just—"

"You knew him," Ryia guessed. The Kinetic who had made Joslyn freeze. Of course. It must have been someone she'd grown up with on the island. "Well, he's out a kneecap and a nose, but he should still survive the day."

"What does it matter?"

"If we win?" Ryia cocked her head. "It matters a whole fucking lot, I'd say."

And Evelyn knew what she meant. If they won—if they got the Quill from Clem and destroyed it—then every branded Adept could go free. If they destroyed the Quill, then that dead-eyed man who had attacked them would regain his mind. He would have the chance to become truly, fully human again.

The ramparts were already filled with shouting Needle Guard by the time they made their way up the steps. It was clear why. From here, they could see over the city walls to the open flax fields beyond. The manors on the hills to the north were already burning. Evelyn wondered dimly if her parents' manor would survive the day. But the thought didn't last long—she was distracted by the host gathered at the gates of the city.

Ryia had estimated two or three thousand Adept. Evelyn could see now that she had been off by at least five thousand.

"What in Felice's darkest hell?" Joslyn said.

"Oh for fuck's sake." Ryia glanced back at her, something that looked an awful lot like fear pulsing behind her jet-black gaze.

"For fuck's sake is right," Evelyn said. She watched as the Needle Guard positioned themselves on the outer city walls and peppered the forces with arrows. Clem, seated on a handsome Edalish warhorse at the head of the army, batted the projectiles aside like they were blades of grass, wafting on the wind.

Even against a non-magic army, the Needle Guard weren't trained for sieges, for war. No soldier had fought in a real war since Declan Day had proclaimed himself the first Guildmaster of Thamorr some three hundred years ago. But against Adept . . . their attempts to fight back were nothing short of pathetic. In all the time they watched, not a single of Clem's Adept fell to their attack. Instead, the black-robed masses marched steadily closer to the city gates.

"We need to get up there," Evelyn said, gesturing toward the walls.

"To do what?" Joslyn pointed out. And she was right. Aside from Ryia's throwing axes, they didn't have a ranged weapon among them.

"There's still hope," Tristan said. Evelyn turned

to face him. He absolutely glowed as he raised a hand to the west.

There, Evelyn saw a cluster of blue-sailed ships. The Guildmaster and his Disciples. He had honored their agreement—he had made it in time. Relief and dread battled for control of her emotions at the thought. If the Guildmaster was here, there was a chance they were all saved . . . and that same chance meant he would force them to hold to their bargain. She studied Ryia's face as the Butcher stared at the approaching sloops. If they survived this day, Ryia could be a prisoner until the day she died.

The sound of screeching iron and splintering wood brought Evelyn back to the present. Clem's army had breached the gate, and his Adept, clad in travel-worn, tattered robes, flooded into the city.

"All right, *now* we have to get down there," Evelyn said.

But before they could even move, a sea of flapping blue silk poured into the city from the docks. The Disciples.

"I can't believe he actually showed up," Ryia said.

"Of course he did," Joslyn said waspishly. "His ass is on the line here too."

Clem's Adept fought with the ferocity of starving beasts, but they were disorganized. The Guildmaster's force operated like a single, massive creature. Sensers guided the Kinetics, warning them of incoming attacks while the Kinetics used their scimitars, swords, and spears to cut through the approaching army.

Evelyn winced as she saw the attacking Adept falling in droves, bleeding out in the streets and gutters of the city. Suddenly she was glad to be up here, her sword clean and her conscience clear. After all, Clem's Adept weren't her enemies, not really. They were enslaved. It wasn't their fault their master was insane.

But even in the few minutes they watched, the tide of the battle turned again. Clem's forces were just too many for even the Disciples to handle. It wasn't long before the corpses of Disciples started to join those of the branded Adept. And Clem himself hadn't even joined the fray yet. Cowardly Callum Clem, full to the brim with raw, untainted Adept Kinetic magic. They were going to lose unless they did something drastic.

Evelyn avoided Ryia's gaze for as long as she could, then finally turned to face her.

"We're not going to win this one the old-fashioned way, Linley," Ryia said. Her voice was hoarser than usual, and she fidgeted with the hatchets on her belt. She was nervous. As she should be.

Evelyn had hoped that with the Guildmaster's help, they wouldn't need to attempt their plan at all. But that didn't seem realistic anymore.

"You don't have to—" she started, but Ryia cut her off with a kiss.

Evelyn knew it could only last a few seconds, but she let herself sink into it. Breathing in the Butcher's scent, trying to memorize the feel of the curve of her back beneath her fingertips. Then, much too soon, Ryia pulled away.

"Keep it together, Linley. I'm a hard one to kill," she said. "And a hard one to catch." Then she turned to Tristan, who was still watching the battle with horror etched on his face. "Ready, Prince Dennison?"

"Don't you mean Prince Bait?" Tristan griped.

Because that had been their plan all along. Callum Clem wanted to wipe out all the royal lines in Thamorr. Well, one member of that elite group was standing right on these ramparts with them. Tristan would lure Clem to the Lottery, where Ryia would be lying in wait. Then came Evelyn's least favorite part of the plan: Ryia would attack Clem.

The Guildmaster believed Ryia intended to kill Clem and take the Quill. Evelyn had no doubt the Guildmaster would have Disciples standing by to pluck the precious device from Ryia's exhausted fingers the second Clem's heart stopped. That they had a scheme to return the Quill to the Guildmaster, and maybe take Ryia captive, too. Or just slit her throat. But in truth, Ryia had no delusions that she could win a fight against

Clem. After what they had seen back in Oryol, even Evelyn had to admit that it would take more than a healthy dose of luck for Ryia to scrape a victory. Maybe the Guildmaster knew this too—maybe he was counting on it.

What the Guildmaster wasn't counting on was Tristan. Ryia would distract Clem long enough for Tristan to pluck the Quill from his pocket and crush it to dust. Then the Guildmaster would have no way to double-cross them, and the Snake of the Southern Dock's conquest would be over at last.

A haze of tears clouded Evelyn's vision as she watched Tristan and Ryia disappear into the city, leaping across the close-knit rooftops as they searched for Clem. No matter what happened here today—no matter if the Quill was destroyed or not, if Clem struck Ryia down, or if she actually managed to win—no matter what happened, Evelyn would lose Ryia today. Either to the afterlife or to the Guildmaster's service. There was no winning. Not for her.

But there was no time to dwell on that now. There was still a battle raging below.

"You ready?" she asked Joslyn.

Joslyn raised her scimitar, the sunlight glinting off its blade. "Ready as I'll ever be."

And with that, the pair of them charged down the stairs, through the gates, and into the war-torn city.

CHAPTER TWENTY-NINE
Ryia

It had been a long time since Ryia had killed an Adept servant. Back in that throne room, she had been forced to kill three. Three perfectly innocent souls being swung around like puppets on strings, and she'd had to snuff them out to keep herself and her friends alive.

She would never forgive Callum Clem for that.

Maybe her rage would be enough to overcome the obvious difference in their Kinetic power, but she highly doubted it. She wound around Flaxen Row, heading deeper into the Lottery. No, she was charging toward her own death right now; that much was pretty damned certain. If Clem had been as strong as he was back in Oryol approximately four seconds after gaining Kinetic magic, she wasn't eager to see what he had learned in the past few weeks.

The Miscreants' Temple loomed at the end of the road in front of her. She still remembered the first time she'd seen the Saints' tavern, almost two years ago now. She had taken a river barge all the way to Carrowwick, not too different from how they'd arrived today, though she had been coming from the Gildesh city of Vitrennés that time. She had worked on a vineyard there for six months before the Disciples tracked her down. Six months of backbreaking labor in the hot sun, keeping her head down, and still the Guildmaster had found her. After that she'd said, *Screw this,* found the most despicable crime lord she could find, and gone back to what she knew best.

The tavern was as silent as the Borean wastes they had trekked across just a few weeks before. Clearly, no one had been inside in a long time. The windows were boarded up, and a plank was nailed across the door. Just one tug, amplified by her Kinetic strength, was enough to pop it free. She had wondered what had happened to the rest of the Saints after Clem skipped town. Rolf, Cameron, Roland, and the others. Evelyn and Tristan had come back to Carrowwick a few months ago, surely they knew . . . but she had never asked. She hadn't wanted to know. And based on the bloodstains covering the dusty wooden floors of the Temple, she still didn't want to.

A few streets away, she could hear screams, the clash of steel, and the chime of breaking glass. Clem's Adept were still sweeping through the streets. She wondered if the Adept they'd locked inside the Bobbin Fort had managed to break free yet. She used the busted leg of one of the Temple's tables to prop the door open, then stepped back into the shadows to wait. She didn't have to wait long.

Tristan skidded around the corner, long legs wheeling comically in unison with his equally long arms as he sprinted through the propped-open door. She barely got a look at his bright red, sweat-slicked face before he vaulted over the bar in a single bound, landing with the crunch of broken glassware. She had never seen a non-Adept run like that in her life. She shook her head, grinning despite the seriousness of the situation. Fear was a hell of a drug.

The grin dropped from her cheeks as a dozen more figures rounded the corner. Where Tristan had been sprinting like his life depended on it (which, to be fair, it had), Clem moved with the slow, deliberate pace of a cocky bastard with nothing to fear. Somewhere along his path of destruction through Boreas and Edale, he'd found time to do some shopping—or more likely, some pillaging. He wore a fine silk shirt under a leather surcoat trimmed with white fur and fastened with buttons of gold. Only Callum Clem would dress like he was attending a fox hunt for a twice-damned city siege.

Ryia wrinkled her nose as he drew a pace closer. He might be dressed like a prissy lord, but he absolutely reeked of danger. To be clear, Callum Clem had always smelled a bit dangerous. It was why she had signed on to work for him instead of either of the other syndicate lords in the city those many months ago. Where Wyatt

Asher and Harlow Finn had smelled of nothing but body odor, smoke, and ale, Callum Clem had carried a whiff of death with him wherever he stepped.

That whiff was now a torrent, streaming over the alley and up her nostrils like rapids streamed over rocks in a river. It was an effort not to gag, honestly.

Clem sauntered another step closer to the door to the Temple. "Come out, my dear prince," he called to Tristan.

He didn't know Ryia was there, then. But why would he? None of the Adept behind him were Sensers, and he didn't have Senser magic himself. It was unlike Clem to underestimate the power of one entire strain of Adept magic just because it didn't give him the ability to rip someone's arms from their sockets.

He hadn't brought any Kinetics with him either, but then again, why would he? As far as he knew, he was stalking a gawky, non-magical teenage prince who got blisters using a twice-damned steak knife. Tristan—Dennison—was no match for Clem, and Clem knew it.

"Blood has no place in choosing the rulers of my new Thamorr. And, sadly, that Thamorr cannot rise until the old one falls. In order for us to have equal footing among all men, the old order must die. You understand."

Equal footing among all men. What absolute

horseshit, coming from a man using his power to enslave thousands.

Fear prickled the back of Ryia's eyes as she spun her hatchets around her wrists, taking a deep breath. She was probably going to die today. But between an early grave and a lifetime of either wearing the Guildmaster's chains or resuming her life on the run from him, she'd take the grave any day.

Still, she couldn't stop the image of Evelyn's face from darting across her vision as she leapt from the shadows, hatchets raised, striking toward Callum Clem's unarmored head.

She was a good three feet away when Clem turned to face her. He was clearly unarmed, but there was no fear on his face. He lifted one hand slowly, almost carelessly. *Shit.* She froze, midair, floating, hatchets poised, still ready to strike.

"Well, well, well, if it isn't the Butcher of Carrowwick," Clem said calmly. "I had a feeling Oryol wouldn't be the last I'd see of you." He flicked his wrist like he was swatting a gnat, and Ryia went flying ten feet across the room. She lost her grip on her hatchets as she smashed through three upturned tables before finally crumpling against the far wall.

From her position, on the floor, she could see Tristan's wide-eyed stare peeking out from behind the bar. In order for him to pickpocket the Quill, she would need to find out where Clem was hiding it. Which meant she had to stay alive at least a few more minutes. Easier said than done.

She rolled out of the way as Clem sent a chunk of splintered wood catapulting toward her. It embedded itself in the moldering floorboard she had been lying on a moment before. On her knees, Ryia pulled two throwing axes from her belt, whipping them at Clem and using her Kinetic magic to guide them toward his exposed throat.

"You always were a quick one," he said, casually batting the axes aside with a blast of his own Kinetic energy.

Ryia formed her hands into fists, pulling back. The axes swooped around like a pair of circling gulls, spinning toward Clem again. And again Clem easily pushed them aside.

"So, that is what you are, then," he mused. It was the first time he had truly seen her Adept powers on display, apart from whatever glimpse he might have caught of her and Evelyn's escape back in Oryol. "I suppose it does explain quite a lot."

His face was serene, and he stood, leaning comfortably against the nearest table, but Ryia saw one of his fingers twitch, and then the smell of danger surged to her right. She lifted her right-hand hatchet just in time to deflect her own throwing axe as Clem sent it spinning toward her.

Her left-hand hatchet came up next. The other axe she had thrown ricocheted off its blade with a sharp ping. She shot him a cocky grin—a grin that contorted into a grimace as the hatchets in her fingers suddenly took on minds of their own. Her elbows splayed outward as the hatchets turned in, leveled at her own neck. Her muscles strained as she fought to keep the bits from severing her windpipe.

Clem stalked toward her, hands outstretched like a puppeteer as they fought for control over her weapons. This jerk was about to kill her without breaking a twice-damned sweat.

The Snake's next step landed lightly on a lopsided rug, and Ryia saw her chance. She let go of her hatchets, ducking beneath them as the bits sliced through where her throat had been an instant before, then reached out with both hands, tugging on the intangible string of Kinetic magic connecting her to the threadbare carpeting. The rug slid beneath Clem's loafered foot, sending him sprawling to the floor.

Ryia's heart skipped in her chest as something glinted at Clem's neck, swaying out from underneath his silken shirt as he scrambled back to his feet. Something long and ornately carved, dangling from a chain of pure gold.

The Quill.

She gestured toward it. "I'd think you could afford nicer jewelry nowadays," she said. "Then again, a charm filled with blood and gore does seem fitting."

Hopefully that was enough of a hint for Tristan. Before she could even steal a look at the bar to see if he'd gotten the message, Clem charged at her with more speed than a galloping warhorse. His hands were at her throat faster than she could react, lifting her into the air. She flailed for the two throwing axes still tucked into her belt, but the next instant she found her arms pinned to her sides by her former boss's Kinetic power. The Quill bobbed against his chest, its chain reflecting the sunlight filtering in through the slats in the boarded-up windows of the Temple, seeming to mock her.

Tristan hadn't been able to steal the Quill. She was about to die for nothing. Evelyn's face swam behind her eyes again as the blackness started to creep in.

CHAPTER THIRTY
Tristan

The moment Tristan had spotted Callum Clem, fighting his way through the streets of Carrowwick, he knew their plan was going to end in disaster. Clem had been frightening enough back in Boreas. With a proper army at his back, a dozen or more new royal murders under his belt, and a better handle on the unnatural powers he'd gotten from the Eisfang Dagger, he was utterly horrifying—less like a man and more like a specter from a tale used to scare children. *Eat your supper, or Callum Clem will come for you in the night*.

Still, this plan was the only one they had. If Callum Clem got to keep the Quill, then all of Thamorr would be in ashes before the first winter snows hit Edale. If anyone else got ahold of it, things could be the same or worse. The only way to ensure that the world was saved was for Tristan to get his hands on the Quill, then get it to the Guildmaster.

When the Guildmaster put his bleeding thumbprint on the side of the device and regained control of all the Adept, he could send Callum Clem screaming into Adalina's deepest hell.

And so Tristan had gathered every last ounce of his courage, shouting to get Clem's attention. Then, without looking to see if the Snake was following, he ran like hell.

Puddles of filth and blood and sick splattered up as his boots pounded the streets, but he didn't care. He didn't even spare a glance for Ryia as he streaked into the Miscreants' Temple, leapt over the bar top, and landed with a crunch on the broken glassware and scattered cutlery lying on the floor. It took him a few minutes of gasping with his head between his knees to catch his breath. Clem was talking, something about blood and the fate of Thamorr, but Tristan could barely hear him over the sound of blood rushing past his eardrums.

A loud slam forced his heart into the pit of his stomach. He peered around the edge of the bar to see Ryia sprawled on the floor against the wall, her limbs tangled with the shattered legs of several tables. Had Clem just *thrown* her? He had known this plan was risky, but he had never actually dreamed that Ryia might *die.* Tristan watched, helpless as Clem batted aside every one of Ryia's attacks like he was lazily fanning the air on a hot summer day.

Then she pulled the rug out from under him, quite literally, and Tristan saw it. *The Quill.* There it was, dangling from the Snake's filthy neck.

If he could just get his hands on it, this would all finally be over.

But before he even had the chance to move, Clem's hands went to Ryia's throat. Her arms twisted up behind her back, forced into place by Clem's magic. Her eyes began to bulge. There was no time. Even if he stole the Quill and got it to the Guildmaster, no one would be able to get back here in time to save Ryia. He had to do something. Now.

He looked around, patting the dusty floor hopelessly. His fingers finally closed around a heavy wooden cup. That might do the trick.

Without giving himself time to consider just how stupid this truly was, he sprang upright, lobbing the cup directly at Callum Clem's head. The projectile hit home with a hollow-sounding thunk that might have come from either the cup or Clem's skull. Possibly both. It was as large as a tankard, heavy enough that a normal man would have been knocked back a pace by the impact at least, but Clem was no normal man. Not anymore. The Snake rounded on him slowly. When Tristan saw the rage burning in his vivid blue eyes, he knew he was about to die.

Ryia slumped back on the floor, gasping, as Clem raised his hands toward Tristan instead. Tristan squeezed his eyes shut, preparing to be torn to shreds . . . but at that very moment, something burst into the Temple behind Clem, taking nearly half the door frame with it. Tristan dared a peek, and his heart stopped. Not something. Some*one*.

A man stood silhouetted against the destroyed doorway.

He was barely recognizable without his crown or his fine clothes. His hair was in shaggy disarray, and he had the scruffy beginnings of a beard, but there was no doubt in Tristan's mind. It was his father, King Tolliver Shadowwood.

His father's eyes were still bright as they hungrily surveyed the room, but there was something . . . *off* about them. Something different. A brimming, buzzing energy that hadn't been there before, even in his maddest moments. The pieces clunked together in Tristan's skull as he stood, frozen behind the bar, staring.

His father had somehow survived Clem's attack on Duskhaven. He had just burst through the door like a bull on *vitalité*, vibrating with power and energy.

Somehow, Tolliver Shadowwood had gained Adept powers.

"King Tolliver," Ryia said drily across the room, still rubbing her bruised throat. "You look well."

Obvious sarcasm, seeing as the king was wearing little more than rags covered in burn marks and great swaths of mud.

"Looks aren't everything, my little test subject,"

Tristan's father said. His voice was scratchier than Tristan remembered. Smoke damage? How much of Duskhaven had burned, he wondered? "Thanks to you, I am more powerful than I could have ever imagined."

Ryia balled her fists. "I didn't tell you *shit*."

"No, but in the end, I did not need you to." His left eye twitched as he bared his teeth in a smile. "Once I knew it was possible, it was quite simple to figure out how." He pulled a flask from his belt, shaking it. The contents sloshed around loudly inside. "You know, now that I'm used to it, I even find the flavor enjoyable."

"You sick son of a bitch," Ryia said as her face contorted in disgust.

Tristan didn't understand. Then his father opened the mouthpiece on the flask and took a long swig of its contents. A drop spilled down his chin. Deep red, but thicker than wine. Much thicker. His stomach turned. It must have been blood. Adept blood.

His father shivered as he swallowed, shaking his arms out. He bared his teeth again; the smile was ringed in red this time. "Don't worry, I won't share your little secret. We can't have others out there challenging my power, can we?"

"So that's what you're here for?" Ryia asked, hands slipping to the two throwing axes still lining her belt. "To kill me, so no one else can learn what you've become?"

"Not exactly. It isn't you I've tracked halfway across the continent, after all." His power-drunk eyes swung sideways, landing on Callum Clem.

"You've come for revenge, is that it?" Clem asked. He began to twirl his fingers behind his back, and Tristan saw Ryia's discarded hatchets rise in the shadows.

"No," Tolliver said. "I've come for what's mine." He lifted a finger to point at Callum Clem. Or, more specifically, at the Quill dangling from his neck.

Then King Tolliver Shadowwood lunged for Clem.

CHAPTER THIRTY-ONE

Ryia

As if one asshole with newly acquired Adept magic wasn't enough, the entry of a power-drunk Tolliver Shadowwood to the mix meant Ryia had two on her hands. Fantastic.

Where Callum Clem had taken to his new magic like a bird to flight, Shadowwood seemed to be adjusting to his new Adept powers more like a cat to water. Thrashing about an awful lot, obviously uncomfortable, but somehow managing to keep himself afloat. The Edalish king might not have mastered telekinetic powers just yet, but what he lacked in finesse, he made up for in brute strength.

Clem smiled coldly as he yanked one arm forward, flinging Ryia's hatchets at Shadowwood from across the room. Instead of using his own magic to knock them aside, Shadowwood just lifted his arms, apparently indifferent to the pain as the blades lodged themselves in his forearms. With blood dripping off the ends of his elbows, hatchets still lodged in his flesh, the king swung at Clem like one of the Gildesh battering rams of old. The scene was pure chaos. But that meant Clem was distracted.

Ryia pulled her two remaining throwing axes from her belt, kissing each one on the handle before letting them fly. Then she reached out, feeling the invisible threads connecting her to the weapons. The magic sang in her bloodstream as she spurred the axes on, sending them spinning so fast they were little more than shining blurs in the air, heading for Callum Clem's throat.

The Snake lifted his hand at the last second, stopping one axe, then the other in their airborne tracks. As they clattered to the floor, he formed a fist. The front of Ryia's cloak crumpled. *Here we go again,* she thought. Her boots skidded across the floor, scoring lines in the dust as Clem dragged her toward him. She was inches from his outstretched hand when Tolliver the ram struck again. His hit landed this time, clocking Clem firmly in the jaw with one magically propelled fist.

Individually, Clem was more than a match for both her and Shadowwood . . . but together, could they beat him?

Just as the thought began to buzz around inside her skull, she caught a whiff of fresh danger. She ducked right as Tolliver Shadowwood's other fist came careening toward her.

"What the hell?" she shouted as he squared up again, ready to aim another punch at her.

"Did you believe we were in this together?" Shadowwood mocked. He stepped forward again, and Ryia gritted her teeth, bounding backward and thrusting her magic out like a pair of lassos, wrapping it around the handles of the hatchets still stuck in Shadowwood's forearms.

The king howled with pain as she yanked the weapons free, snatching them out of the air and spinning them around her wrists as she sized up her two opponents again. Clem was definitely the stronger of the two. If the fight were one-on-one, she could kick the king's royal ass in a matter of minutes, but unfortunately that was not the case.

She grimaced as the scent of danger tugged at her nostrils from behind. She ducked, thrusting both hatchets up behind her to form an X over her back. One of her throwing axes pinged off the steel, ricocheting back to the floor. It was just like Callum Clem to use her own weapons against her.

"Didn't your father ever teach you it wasn't nice to use other people's things without asking?" Ryia thrust her own magic out, whipping the throwing axe around and flinging it toward Clem. It went wide.

"My dear father never taught me a thing," Clem drawled. He ducked lazily as Shadowwood swung for him, then sent a chair flying at the king, knocking him back half a pace. "Outside of a royal decree, I mean."

Royal decree? Ryia raised an eyebrow. "You mean to tell me *you* come from royalty?

Bullshit." She leapt out of the way as Clem brought a ceiling beam crashing down where she had been standing a moment ago. "Royal brats don't end up in the gutters."

Aside from Tristan, she supposed.

"They do when they're mothered by whores," Clem shot back.

"That would make you a bastard, not a royal," Shadowwood replied, grunting as he lifted a table, spinning and chucking it toward Clem like a Brillish sportsman playing discus.

"Perhaps according to you and your ilk," Clem said. "According to me, it makes me the eldest son of King Duncan Baelbrandt the First."

"The rightful ruler of Dresdell," Ryia whispered. Had that seriously been what this was all about? Thousands dead because young Callum Clem hadn't been given the crown he thought he deserved?

"Yes," Clem snarled. Ryia and Tolliver both grunted as the Snake thrust out a wall of Kinetic power. He shattered glassware, toppled tables, and sent them both careening to the floor. "But that was when I realized blood and titles were worthless. The strongest and cleverest should rule the kingdoms of Thamorr, not a bunch of sniveling morons who think they shit gold."

Ryia rolled sideways as Clem sent a whirlwind of power spiraling around the tavern again. It brought her to the space just beside the door to the back room of the Temple. She grabbed the handle, wrenching the door open just in time to block an errant chair. The chair thudded off the peeling paint and landed on the floor. Its leg jammed underneath the door, trapping Ryia behind it for just a moment; by the time she burst free, Clem was on the move again. Thank Felice she wasn't his immediate target this time.

Tolliver Shadowwood flew past, caught in Clem's web as the Snake of the Southern Dock swirled his hands like a fortune-teller. He thrust both palms out, and Shadowwood crashed into the back room of the Temple, landing with the unmistakable crunch of breaking bones. Next, Clem's arms came up like a conductor directing an orchestra, and all five of Ryia's throwing axes extracted themselves from the rubble coating the floor of the Temple, streaking toward the Edalish king. She didn't see the axes find their marks, but she heard them. Several hard squelches at once, followed by the wet splutter of a man exhaling a blood-soaked breath.

Ryia tightened her grip on her long-handled hatchets, keeping light on her feet as she stalked into the room. Clem stood over Tolliver Shadowwood's broken body. The king of Edale had been almost unrecognizable before . . . Now his legs were splayed out at awkward angles behind him, clearly broken. His back was contorted in pain, and four throwing axes impaled him from waist to chest. The fifth hovered teasingly right at his throat.

This was her chance.

The very moment Clem embedded the final axe in Tolliver Shadowwood's throat, Ryia leapt. Her Kinetic power carried her ten feet forward across the room. She flung her arms out, catching Clem in a bear hug and tackling him facedown on the blood-spattered floor.

"What—" was all he managed to articulate. He thrashed in her grip, but she pressed down on the back of his head, grinding his face into the floor.

Ryia ducked, her senses lighting her nostrils on fire as a shard of a broken mug whipped through the air toward her, propelled by Clem's power. It crashed into the wall and shattered. Her face was now inches from the glinting golden chain around Clem's neck. She seized it in her iron grip. Then, with far more force than was necessary, she yanked.

The chain split into three pieces, sending the Quill spinning through the air across the room. It landed on the floor with a thud that was much too loud for such an object. She fought the urge to run and grab it—there wasn't time. Not yet, at least. She had caught Clem by surprise, but he wouldn't be down long. Keeping one hand on the back of his head, she thrust the other toward the ceiling, then wrenched downward with a tug of magic and a prayer to Felice.

Clem's chandelier came crashing to the floor, sending half-stubby candles skittering across the room beside them. But it wasn't the candles she needed. The song of the chandelier's chain was thin and tinny. She latched on to it, pulling it free and watching it slither like a snake toward her. Then she wrapped it around Clem. Once. Twice. Three times. A fourth, just for good measure—there was no such thing as being too cautious when it came to the Snake of the Southern Dock.

The man thrashed like a rabbit in a snare, his face still pressed to the dirt, his arms tied behind his back. His fists clenched, muscles tensing as he tried to break free of his bonds. Next came the wave of Kinetic-powered projectiles. Ryia deflected a handful of them, but most came nowhere near hitting her.

Clem was beginning to panic. He couldn't move. He couldn't see. Somewhere, deep down, the Snake of the Southern Dock knew he was beaten.

Finally, he sagged down against the floor. When he spoke, his voice was muffled by the press of the filthy floorboards.

"From the moment I met you, I knew if I let you live too long, you'd kill me in the end," he said.

"You should've tried to off me sooner, then," Ryia responded. She lowered one hatchet, leveling it at the side of his throat. She reared back, preparing to strike. But just before the bit sliced into his flesh, she hesitated.

Clem chuckled mirthlessly. "What's this? Has the famed Butcher of Carrowwick become bound by mercy at last?"

But Ryia wasn't listening to him. She was calculating. Clem was a powerful Kinetic, it was true, but his army was what had allowed him to ransack all those cities. Once the Quill was destroyed, he'd be no more dangerous than half the other Kinetics they would be freeing of their chains . . . right? What right did she have to take his life, to decide that was the punishment for his crimes?

That Evelyn Linley and her twice-damned honor.

Ryia stepped back a pace.

"Are you really going to let me go?" Clem mocked.

"Yes," Ryia said, still calculating. "Yes, I am." She leveled the hatchet at his throat again. "But you have to get the hell out of here. Go make a quiet life out in the deserts of Briel or the wilds of Boreas. Maybe you'll get lucky and none of the others who want to cleave your head from your shoulders will find you there. Or maybe I'll get lucky, and they will."

She wasn't going to execute the man here and now, but that didn't mean she didn't want him dead.

Clem was still, staring down at the floor for a long moment. Then: "Very well."

Even bound with a blade at his throat, he spoke like he had the upper hand.

She unwound the chains binding him, then gestured toward the door, turning to the place where the Quill rested in the shadows of the room. "Get out of here. And don't give me a reason to slit your throat."

Clem rubbed the places where the chains had dug into his arms, turning to leave. Before she stooped to grab the Quill, the scent of danger nearly ripped Ryia's nostrils apart. *Really?*

She always had said mercy was a curse.

Ryia stood, turning and raising her right-hand hatchet just as Clem pounced. For the first time today, her senses gave her the upper hand. Surprise flickered in Clem's eyes as he leapt straight into her newly raised hatchet blade. It lodged itself neatly in the center of his neck, severing his windpipe and artery in one go.

He opened his mouth to try to speak, but there was only blood. It bubbled from his mouth with a sickening gurgle. Then he collapsed to the floor.

Ryia stood over him, watching as the last spark of cunning light left those sapphire-blue eyes. And just like that, Callum Clem, Snake of the Southern Dock, Terror of Thamorr, Eis Lischka, was no more. After all his power and posturing, he'd died just like any other man: alone and without ceremony.

Shaking herself from her stupor, Ryia whirled around, looking back down to where the Quill had been a moment before. It was gone.

"Tristan?" she called tentatively. "Tristan, you can come out. It's over!"

If he had grabbed the Quill, he would have seen Clem go down. He would know the fight was won. But there was no response except the blowing of the autumn winds through the wide-open doorways. Tristan and the Quill were gone.

CHAPTER THIRTY-TWO
Evelyn

"This way, yes, come on! Leave your bloody things—just save yourselves!" Evelyn's voice was beyond hoarse. Sweat poured down her brow as she furiously waved the merchants and their children on. Nowhere in the city was really *safe,* but there was a small block the Disciples had carved out, just south of the Bobbin Fort. A dozen Disciples patrolled its edges, aided by at least three times as many Needle Guard.

Evelyn hadn't managed to save everyone, not by a long stretch, but she had led at least two hundred innocents hunkered down inside that ring of relative safety, and that was nothing to scoff at. After she and Joslyn had left the ramparts, the pirate had run back to the docks—Nash had planned to sail just off the coast of Dresdell to keep an eye out, just in case Clem had a navy. Joslyn needed to be there to receive her signal and warn the rest of them if he did. An important job, but still, Evelyn wished the pirate could have stayed to help her wrangle these civilians.

She held up a hand, stopping her entourage of a dozen scared citizens of Carrowwick as she peered around the corner of the bakery she had found them huddled inside. The next street was clear.

"Go, go, go," she urged, waving them on. Sword at the ready, she took up a post behind them, eyes sharp. She had managed to avoid direct combat with Clem's Adept so far, but she had a sick feeling in her belly that it was only a matter of time.

They made it to the Disciple-guarded block a few minutes later. Sweat dripped from Evelyn's brow despite the chill winds sweeping through the city as she herded the innocent civilians inside the block. She turned back toward the tangle of streets, wiping her brow as she took a moment to catch her breath. Then she caught sight of a familiar figure picking his way through the streets.

Tristan Beckett.

He was slipping north, away from the Lottery, cutting west toward the trade docks. There was a glint of something in his left hand. The Quill? Evelyn's heart hammered, beating a steady rhythm up her throat until she thought she might vomit the ruddy organ out altogether. He had the Quill, but he was alone. Did that mean Ryia was . . . ?

She couldn't even finish the thought.

"Tristan!" she shouted, waving furiously. Her voice cracked as anxious tears welled in her eyes. She cleared her throat, blinking the tears away. *Pull it together.* "Tristan, here!"

The boy turned, eyes wide as he caught sight of her. She expected relief to flood his features at the sight of a familiar face. Instead, a shadow of fear washed over him. He turned away, sprinting toward the docks at full speed.

What the bloody hell is that about?

A scream sounded out from a few streets away. It sounded like a child. Smoke poured into the sky, black and billowing. A fire. Evelyn took a deep breath, glancing back and forth between the direction of the scream and the corner Tristan had disappeared around for a second. Then she sprinted toward the sound of the scream, dodging through alleys and cutting through buildings. The Church of Adalina stood before her, its tall, stained glass windows shattered and belching smoke.

Time simultaneously slowed to a crawl and raced past with the speed of a herd of wild horses galloping through the countryside as Evelyn charged into the building. She dodged hot spots and falling beams, pulling the neckline of her shirt up over her nose and mouth to avoid the worst of the smoke as she herded every living body she found out of the building and into the street. Twenty-six followed her in the end. Probably less than half the people inside that burning shell, but it was better than nothing.

"Follow me," she croaked to them.

"Follow you *where?*" asked a balding man, a

priest of Adalina, based on his soot-smudged robes.

"Somewhere safe," she said.

But as she led the people to the haven the Disciples had carved out, she found that she had told the priest a ruddy lie. Clem's Adept were everywhere, swarming the streets that had been quiet and calm a few minutes ago. The Needle Guard were doing their best to keep them back, but they were learning just how useless a sword and training could be against Adept magic. They were crumbling like straw men in a fireplace. It didn't take her long to figure out why.

The Disciples were gone. Every last one of them.

The Guildmaster had betrayed them? Now? But why?

Her stomach clenched as she remembered the fear in Tristan's eyes as he caught sight of her. How he had whirled away from her, sprinting toward the docks. Toward the very place where the Guildmaster's ships had been tethered.

That ruddy scheming son of a bitch. He wouldn't seriously have betrayed them again . . . would he?

"Shite," Evelyn muttered beneath her breath. She stowed the survivors of the burning church inside the nearest building—one of her father's lending houses, she noted with distaste. The Linley Manor was outside the city walls of

Carrowwick. Even if she'd cared enough about her estranged family to worry about them, she was confident they were not in Clem's warpath. Pushing the thought aside, Evelyn drew her sword and made for the docks.

Her years in the Needle Guard had taught her all the quickest routes through the city's streets. Cutting through smoldering alleys and shattered businesses, she managed to catch up to Tristan. This time, she didn't give the bastard the chance to run away. Instead of calling out his name, she simply sprinted at full speed, then tackled him to the cobblestones.

"What the ruddy hell have you done?" she growled. "Where is the Quill?" She grabbed his wrists, yanking to turn his palms toward her, but, of course, they were empty.

"I've saved us all," Tristan grunted, his voice muffled. "It's not my fault you're all too thick to see it."

"Too thick to see it?" Evelyn asked. She shoved back, pushing him into the ground one last time before yanking him up by his collar. She then grabbed the sides of his face, forcing him to look at the Carrowwick skyline. At the clouds of black smoke swirling toward the autumn sky. Forcing him to listen to the screams and the crash of breaking glass. "What exactly have you saved, other than your own bloody skin?"

"Ryia," he said.

"What?" Evelyn asked. She was so surprised she almost let him go.

"I saved Ryia."

"Horseshit, I saved myself," said a new voice.

Evelyn almost choked on her relief at the sound. She turned to see Ryia Cautella stalking toward them down the docks, emerging from the smoking shell of the city like a twice-damned phoenix from the ashes. She was bleeding, bruised, and limping, but she was alive.

She held out one blood-encrusted palm. "The Quill, Tristan. Hand it over."

Tristan started to shake but stood tall against her glare. "I don't have it."

"Mm-hmm," Ryia said. Her eyes glinted in her skull like chips of charcoal sparking to life. "And who does?"

She already knew the answer.

"I gave it to the Guildmaster."

Ryia stood there a second, still as stone. Then she reared back, landing a firm punch directly to Tristan's face. Evelyn winced as she heard his nose break.

"I did it to save you," he spluttered thickly, the words nearly drowned out by the rush of blood now spilling from his nose. "I made a deal with him. The Quill for your freedom."

"And did it ever occur to you that there are things I find more important than my own fucking freedom?" Ryia said. She was shouting now. Evelyn didn't blame her—they had both risked their skins to save Tristan from his father, only for the bastard to betray them once more.

"What if you're wrong?" Tristan howled. He yanked himself free of Evelyn's grip, wiping the worst of the blood from his face and staring Ryia down. "You want to destroy the Quill, to free the Adept, but what if once they're free, they decide *this* is exactly what they want?" He flung an arm toward the streets behind them.

Ryia said nothing, and Tristan obviously read this as a moment of weakness. He took a step toward her.

"Can you guarantee me that's not what would happen?" he asked, voice cracking. "Can you guarantee that freedom for the Adept won't just mean slavery for everyone born without magic?"

"No," Ryia said. "No, I can't."

"Then the only way to return some twice-damned sanity to this world is by giving control back to the Guildmaster," Tristan said. "So that's what I did." He wiped his still-bleeding nose again. "The Guildmaster will take control back. He will stop this madness. No one else has to die."

Already Evelyn could hear the screams in the city beginning to quiet. The Guildmaster must be using the Quill to subdue the Adept in Carrowwick.

Ryia was quiet for a long moment. Would she

accept the bargain Tristan had made? It would return peace to Thamorr and free her of the Guildmaster's clutches. It was everything Ryia had ever wanted . . . wasn't it?

But when the Butcher's upper lip stiffened, her eyes snapping back to Tristan, Evelyn knew that wasn't true. Not anymore. Ryia had come a long way from the scared, selfish mercenary she had first met in the back room of the Miscreants' Temple.

"That wasn't your decision to make," Ryia said coldly. "I don't know the mind of every damned Adept in this world, so of course I can't guarantee no one will die if they're all freed. But I can guarantee that if they're *not* freed, there will be thousands of innocent children born who never even get to live."

Tristan swallowed. "It's too late. The Guildmaster has already boarded his ship. He has probably left the city by now."

"We'll see about that," Ryia said. She laid a hand on Evelyn's shoulder. "Good to see you're still alive. Keep a tight hold on that twice-damned traitor for me, would you?"

"Where are you going?" Evelyn asked as Ryia turned, setting off north along the docks.

"To find Joslyn. This isn't over."

CHAPTER THIRTY-THREE

Nash

Nash hated waiting. More than that, she *really* hated waiting with a ship full of Dresdellan sailors who barely knew a topsail from a surrender flag. But it was possible Callum Clem had gathered himself a navy, and someone had to keep a lookout for any warships he might be bringing over to join him.

She stood on the deck of a handsome galleon from King Duncan's own fleet. Though by Joslyn's account, the king had been dead when she had taken it, so as far as she was concerned, it was now hers. Her sister had brought the news and enough sailors to outfit the ship with her when she reappeared after the failed attempt at negotiations in the Bobbin Fort. She and another set of sailors had control of a second galleon still tethered to the docks while Nash bobbed out near the edge of the harbor, being careful to keep Joslyn's ship within sight of her pocket telescope.

Before Nash had left the docks, they had worked out a series of hand signals. If Nash put two hands straight up, it meant enemy ships were inbound. Arms out in a T shape from Joslyn meant the message was received. But so far, there was nothing to report from Nash's side. The horizon beyond the harbor was clear of ships. Judging from the sounds of mayhem coming from behind her, Clem didn't need a navy to take the city. A terrible thought, but a true one.

"Er, um, Captain," said a voice behind her.

Nash turned to see one of the Dresdellan sailors. Obviously he wasn't used to using honorifics to talk to smuggling dock scum like her. She enjoyed his discomfort for a few seconds, then said, "What is it, sailor?"

"We're receiving a signal from the other galleon."

Nash frowned. "What signal?"

"Enemy ships inbound."

"What?" She pulled the telescope from her coat pocket and turned to face the docks, squinting toward Joslyn's ship. Sure enough, she saw her sister's silhouette, tall on the deck of the ship, arms straight up in the air. Enemy ships inbound. But inbound from *where?* She whipped her head back toward the horizon to the west, scanning the entire coastline as far as she could see from north to south. There was nothing. What in Felice's name was Joslyn talking about?

She looked back to Joslyn's ship, wishing they had created a signal to ask *What the fuck do you mean?* when she saw the second shadow next to her sister. Smaller, slighter. Her arms were raised above her head just like Joslyn's . . . a hatchet extended up from each fist.

Ryia? Could they somehow sense ships she couldn't see yet?

Then Nash caught sight of a flock of blue sails pulling away from the docks. Unless they didn't mean Clem's navy.

Enemy ships inbound. What if they meant enemy ships were approaching her, but leaving the city?

Had the Guildmaster betrayed them? Fuck.

Ivan would never let her hear the end of this.

She threw her arms out in a T, then turned to the sailor who had called her attention before. "Weigh anchor, and get the boys down below to their oars. Twice as many on the starboard side. We need to turn around in a hurry."

The sailor hesitated for a second, then saluted and marched away, relaying her orders to the others as he went. Damn, these legal types were obedient. Maybe when this was all over, she'd go straight after all, sign on to serve on some legitimate ship for once. Ivan might let her sail for whatever Borean navy emerged from the wreckage of Clem's coup. Though she didn't much like the idea of living in that cold wasteland year-round. She could work out the details later.

"Coming about!" Nash shouted as the anchor left the harbor floor, hauled back to its resting position by three of the beefiest sailors on board.

"Make sure those chutes are primed with blasting powder."

"What's our target . . . Captain?"

The title came a beat after the question, but Nash ignored that fact. She raised one hand, keeping the other cranking the wheel, pointing at the largest sloop in the blue-sailed fleet pulling out from the harbor.

"The Guildmaster's ship?" one sailor asked incredulously, his voice so high-pitched the words sounded like a gull's squawk.

"Yep," Nash grunted. She pulled the ship around the rest of the way. "Ease up on the starboard rowers, straight ahead now!" Then she turned back to the squawking sailor. "Anyone too chickenshit to go through with this, I recommend you jump overboard and swim to shore immediately."

She heard a few splashes as she turned her attention back to the Guildmaster's ship, but that was fine. Let the cowards swim for the docks.

"Ready the chutes," she said, eyeing the distance between them and the lead sloop. "And light that powder!"

A Dresdellan galleon was outfitted with ten blasting chutes, five on each side. Any good lawbreaker knew that—it was why she had always stayed well clear of galleons when she saw them sailing by. Blasting powder was expensive, and there was a good chance many of them were running empty, but it wasn't worth the risk.

Five of the chutes had a clear shot on the Guildmaster's ship. Not one of them fired.

Nash looked around her. The upper deck was empty. She took a glance over her shoulder and swore beneath her breath. The water behind her ship was churning with splashing limbs. Her entire crew, swimming for the docks.

Ah, she remembered. *That* was why she didn't bother with law-abiding types. Cowards.

The Guildmaster must have gotten the Quill back somehow and decided to flee to his island. She was their only chance at stopping him—their last line of defense. With one move, she could win the day and ensure Joslyn's freedom. All she had to do was sink that ship.

"Fine," she muttered under her breath. "I'll do this my damned self."

She glanced up at the telltale. It streamed straight toward the docks. The wind was blowing southeast. The Guildmaster's ship was southeast.

At least Felice was on her side. If she could only have one ally with her, well, the goddess of luck wasn't a bad option.

She cranked the wheel around, aiming the nose of the galleon straight instead of coming at the sloop sidelong. If there was no one to man the chutes, there was only one way to stop that ship. She was going to ram the son of a bitch.

Her heart hammered in her throat as the wind filled the sails. The galleon picked up speed as she soared over the harbor, aimed right for where the sloop should be. Grabbing her namestone for an extra bit of luck, Nash squeezed her eyes shut.

With a sound like a Borean ice shelf cracking, the galleon smashed into the Guildmaster's sloop. The sound of splintering wood was punctuated by the telltale tinkle of breaking glass. Glass windows? On a ship? No . . . glass *lanterns*. The ones that had lined the passageways belowdecks . . . the same passageways where the chutes were positioned. And their ammunition.

"Oh shit."

The words were barely out of Nash's mouth when the first barrel of blasting powder blew.

CHAPTER THIRTY-FOUR
Ryia

"Do you think she got the message?" Joslyn asked, squinting toward Nash's ship, arms still high in the air.

Ryia's face split into a grin as she saw the galleon haul the anchor up and turn to the left to face the Guildmaster's departing ships. "Give your sister a little more credit than that, Salt Beard. She's figured it out. Now, let's get out there. Which of these do you need me to start yanking on to get this thing out in the open water?" Ryia looked at the complicated web of ropes and rigging suspended over her head.

"Oh no," Joslyn said, still staring out toward the harbor.

"What—oh." Ryia turned and saw the problem.

Nash's ship had a leak, it seemed. Not a leak for water to get in, a leak for cowards to get out. Sailors were jumping over the rails left and right, swimming for shore, leaving Nash alone on the deck. She steered the ship up alongside the Guildmaster's sloop, aiming the right-side chutes toward the ship . . . and nothing happened.

"Now we *really* need to get out there," Ryia said.

"We'll never catch him in time."

"Not if we keep standing here, we won't!"

Joslyn and the few crewmen who had decided to stick around sprinted across the deck like maniacs, hauling lines and loosing sails. As they started to pull away from the dock, Ryia peered out toward Nash's galleon.

"What in the hells is she doing?"

"Wha—" Joslyn spared a glance over her shoulder, then turned back with a grin. "She's going to ram him. Won't be able to get enough speed to sink him in the harbor, but she should be able to slow him down enough for us to catch up."

Ryia grinned. "Nash, you brilliant idiot."

She watched from the deck of Joslyn's galleon as Nash's ship collided with the Guildmaster's. There were five blue-robed figures on the deck, their arms outstretched. Kinetics, no doubt, trying to stop the ships from crashing. But there was only so much Kinetic magic could do against a hundred-ton ship captained by a woman hell-bent on their destruction. The wood splintered, the prow of Nash's ship cracking in unison with the sloop's port side.

"See the way that wood splintered?" Joslyn said. "The beams will stick together now; it'll be almost impossible for the Guildmaster's ship to pull free. It's exactly what I would have done." She shook her head in approving wonder. "Now I *know* we're related."

"Really? The fact that you're fucking identical wasn't enough proof for you, or—" Ryia was cut off as a massive boom shook the air in the harbor.

She whirled around, mouth gaping open as she saw giant pieces of Nash's ship shooting out in every direction. They splashed down in the water of the harbor, leaving the skeletal remains of Nash's galleon behind.

"Shit," Joslyn said. "Shit! Any hand not on the wheel, get to the twice-damned oars!"

Still numb, Ryia followed the stream of crewmen heading belowdecks. She grabbed one of the oars, helping the small crew row the massive ship faster and faster. It wasn't a large harbor. They reached the wreckage of Nash's ship in minutes.

By the time Ryia made it back to the upper deck, Joslyn was already gone. A rope dangled from one of the beams up ahead, swaying in the wind. Ryia grabbed it and took a running leap, swinging herself onto what was left of the other galleon.

"Nash!" Joslyn was yelling, digging through shattered timbers surrounding the place where the helm had been. "Nash!" She ripped a toppled sail aside, searching underneath.

Ryia's ears pricked at the sound of labored breathing coming from behind her. She turned, falling to her knees to chuck aside the remains of what might once have been the port-side rail. Underneath, pinned beneath the splintered mainmast, was Nash.

She didn't look good. She was facedown on the deck; a puddle of blood surrounded her head like a crimson pillow, and her legs were splayed out behind her, bent in directions legs weren't supposed to bend.

"Joslyn! I found her!" Ryia shouted. Her voice broke, but she didn't have time to be embarrassed. She grunted, worming her hands underneath the beam trapping the smuggler. "Help me with this."

Joslyn grabbed the other end, and between the pirate's muscles and Ryia's Kinetic strength, they managed to lift the beam free.

Nash coughed as they gently rolled her over. Blood dripped from between her lips, and her legs just flopped limply, like the legs of a corpse. Bile and something that felt suspiciously like grief crept up Ryia's throat. They weren't going to be getting Nash off this ship.

"Nash, it's all right, we're here, we've got you," Joslyn said. She cradled her sister's head in her lap. Nash blinked, dazed for a moment, then coughed again, spitting out a mouthful of blood.

"The Guildmaster!" she burst. "You need to get him." She paused to catch her breath, then threw her left arm out to point. Her right arm was clearly shattered. Ryia could see the bone sticking out from the skin. "He's going to get onto another ship and escape. You have to go now."

"I'm not going anywhere," Joslyn said.

Nash swallowed, clearly summoning the energy to shout again, but Ryia pushed herself to her feet.

"No, she's right. You stay here and . . . look after her," Ryia said. "I'll go after that son of a bitch." She looked down at Nash. "And when I get back, we'll get you off this hunk of driftwood, all right?"

Nash's eyes met hers. She nodded once, forcing a smile. They both knew this was the last time they'd see each other. Nash was hovering on Felice's doorstep. She wouldn't be in this world by the time Ryia got back. But the smuggler was right—there was no time. The Guildmaster still had the Quill. His men still had ships. If he was still alive, he could still escape. Then Nash would die for nothing.

Fuck that.

Ryia sprinted across what was left of the deck of Nash's ship, Kinetic magic aiding her as she leapt over some of the more gaping holes. She held her hatchets at the ready as she darted across a splintered beam that spanned the two ships. There was no telling how many Disciple scimitars were about to greet her, but the Quill was here. She wasn't leaving this ship without it.

The Guildmaster's sloop was eerily quiet as she stepped on board, but she wasn't fooled. It was obviously a trap.

Or perhaps not.

Blue-robed corpses littered the deck. They must have been a hell of a lot closer to the blasting powder than Nash was when it blew. Nash's injuries had been mostly from the shock wave—the result of being thrown halfway across the galleon and crushed by the mainmast of the ship. These Disciples had been struck by the explosion itself. Burns covered flesh impaled with bits of shrapnel. Ryia swallowed heavily.

It wasn't easy to make her feel pity for a filthy Disciple, but this was as close as she'd ever been.

She didn't want to look at the bodies, but she had to. One of them was bound to be the Guildmaster.

Ryia was starting to wonder if the Guildmaster had somehow already escaped when she saw him. He was flat on his back, surrounded by the bodies of five other Kinetics. He too was covered in burns and seemed to be impaled, a chunk of shattered wood sticking out from his lower belly. But somehow—impossibly—he wasn't dead. His eyes were slitted open, watching her approach as ragged breaths rattled through what sounded like severely damaged lungs.

"Miss Grayson," he said. His voice was hardly audible, muffled by the bubble of blood that burst from his lips with the effort of speaking.

Ryia knelt beside him. "I don't know how many times I need to tell you that's not my twice-damned name anymore." She patted at his robes, searching for the Quill. Her hands were soaked in his blood in an instant.

"Is vengeance against me . . . really worth . . . destroying the world?" he asked, struggling to catch his breath every few words.

Ryia stopped her search, pausing to lean back and look him dead in the eye. "If you really think this is about you, you are even more arrogant than I thought," she said. "This is about every Adept not lucky enough to be handed a blue robe."

He gave a choking sound. It took Ryia a few seconds to realize he was laughing at her. "You are not doing . . . the Adept . . . any . . . favors by . . . destroying the Quill," he said. His voice was growing weaker by the second. "Those with power . . . and those without . . . cannot . . . coexist in peace," he said. "Declan Day knew . . . his people . . . could either live in chains . . . or die without them."

Ryia resumed her search, finally drawing the narrow, slender Quill from the right breast pocket of the Guildmaster's robes. She held it up to the sun, examining the curves and whorls in the polished wood. It would be a beautiful thing if it weren't such a sick invention. "You know," she said, looking back down to the Guildmaster, "everyone seems to have their own ideas about all the terrible things that will go wrong if the Adept are freed. But the fate of hundreds of thousands isn't something one man should be deciding."

The Guildmaster narrowed his eyes in focus, lifting one hand a quarter of an inch and focusing on the Quill in Ryia's fingers. It twitched . . . but stayed in her grasp. He let his hand fall back down, too weak to summon another drop of telekinetic magic. Without it, without his guards and his Quill and his island of terror, he really was just a man, wasn't he? A weak, shriveled old man who genuinely believed that imprisoning the Adept was the same thing as saving them.

"Think of this moment . . . in the years to come . . . when . . . you realize . . . what you have done," he finally said, slumping back to the deck.

"Will do," Ryia said. She hopped to her feet, pocketing the Quill.

The ship groaned beneath her. It was taking on water, fast. It would sink any minute. Time to go. She was three steps away when she paused, looking back at the Guildmaster. He was still alive. Either he would drown when the ship went down, or he would bleed out on the deck before he got the chance. Both were slow ways to go.

He deserved it. No question about it. Still, if she didn't see the man die, there was no way to guarantee he wouldn't come back to haunt her someday.

That was it. She hefted her right-hand hatchet, stalking back toward him. This was prudence. Not a mercy. If she told herself that enough times, maybe one day she would believe it.

"I'd ask you to put in a good word for me with Felice," she said, leveling the bit at his bobbing throat. "But we both know you're going straight to the deepest of the hells."

With that, she struck. Quick and clean. He was dead before she even finished the stroke.

Ryia stared down at his limp corpse for a moment, blood pumping fiercely through her veins, pounding against her eardrums so loudly she felt they might burst. The Guildmaster was dead. The man who had stalked her waking hours and her nightmares for all these years. Her life on the run was over. No longer did she have to be on the constant lookout for blue sails on the horizon.

Destroying the Quill was what would set the rest of the world's Adept free, but destroying this man set Ryia herself free. Already she could feel the heavy weights of fear and rage lifting from her chest.

She wiped her hatchet blade on his robes and tucked it back into her belt, patting the pocket where she had placed the Quill. In an instant, she was across the deck and back on the beam joining the Guildmaster's ship to Nash's.

Ryia found Joslyn in the same place she had left her. On her knees, cradling Nash's head in her lap. A lump formed in Ryia's throat. The smuggler's eyes were closed, her body still. She was gone.

"Come on, Joslyn," Ryia said, her voice hoarse

with emotion. "This ship is about to go down. We need to go. Now."

"One second," the pirate said.

"Joslyn, she's gone."

"You think I don't know that?" Joslyn lay two fingers in the middle of Nash's forehead—a common sailor's parting. Then she slid her fingers into the smuggler's collar, pulling out a thin stone disc on a leather strap. The namestone Nash had always worn around her neck. Joslyn pocketed it.

With that, they fled the sinking ship. Ryia stood on the deck of Joslyn's galleon as they made their way back to the docks. She kept her fist clenched tightly around the Quill in her pocket the entire time.

CHAPTER THIRTY-FIVE

Ivan

Ivan had never been much of a fighter. He was a master when it came to disguises and distractions, but he had never learned the sword or the bow. He had been halfway decent with a poleaxe, but that was a weapon he was unlikely to find outside of a *medev* base. He could not fight in the traditional sense, no. But that did not mean he could not do anything to help.

It was his job to keep Callum's Adept away from the docks where Joslyn's ship was tethered for as long as possible. Armed with firecrackers and the few *Trän vun Yavol* he had managed to lift when undercover as a *medev*, he steered Clem's brainwashed servants from one alley to the next, drawing them with noise and light and driving them back with walls of smoke.

The Adept came slower and slower, and then they stopped coming altogether, but still he did not look up from his work until he heard a massive bang sound out from the harbor. Climbing up to the nearest rooftop for a better vantage point, Ivan peered out over the sparkling water. His stomach dropped to his toes when he found the source.

Nash's ship.

Task forgotten, Ivan dropped the firecrackers in his hands, slipping down from the roof and sprinting through the tangle of streets toward the docks. A few turns away, Tristan was running toward him. He grabbed the young prince's arm.

"What has happened?" he asked.

Tristan shook his head, eyes shifting from side to side in fear. "I'm not sure," he said. "I'm going to find Evelyn to bring her to the docks. We'll meet you there."

Ivan nodded, releasing him. The boy ran off, red-faced with effort.

He thought nothing more of the encounter until he wheeled around the corner leading to the harbor, finding himself face-to-face with none other than Evelyn Linley herself.

"Evelyn," he said. "Tristan just went to find you."

"You saw him?" she asked. Her eyes were rimmed with fury. "Which way did that bloody traitor go?"

"Traitor?" Ivan asked. His eyes slipped back to the harbor, where he had seen the explosion. He could see the scene more clearly now. Nash's ship and the Guildmaster's sloop were bound together by a mass of splintered wood. A string of Borean curses slipped through his lips.

Tristan Beckett must have betrayed them once again. Sold them out to the Guildmaster. Nash had been sharp enough to pick up on what had happened, and she had stopped the Guildmaster from escaping the only way she knew how.

Anger and fear warred for control of Ivan's thoughts. He had *told* her they could not trust that *viesel* of a man. When she arrived back on this shore, she would owe him an apology at the very least. Perhaps a stiff drink as well. And Nash would make it back to shore. She had to.

"Yes, which way did he go, Ivan?"

"I do not know," Ivan said, distracted. "I was not watching him; I did not think . . ."

"Shite!" Evelyn's head sagged into her hands. "Sorry, Ivan. I know. None of us did."

"This is not over yet, Evelyn," Ivan said, looking out toward the smoking hunk of wood in the harbor. Joslyn's ship was returning from the scene already. "Perhaps they have gotten the Quill back. Then it will not matter what that *vretch* Tristan has done."

But as the crew began to exit Joslyn's ship, Ivan's breath lodged in his throat.

"Where is Nash?" he asked, fighting to keep his voice steady as Joslyn and Ryia came to a stop before them.

Then he saw the blood-smeared object dangling from Joslyn's fingers, and he did not need them to answer. Nash's mother's namestone. There was only one possible reason why Nash would not be wearing it.

He went deaf for a moment, his chest growing hollow. Nash was supposed to be the *safest* member of their crew during this fight. While they were all running about the streets of Carrowwick, taking on Clem's Adept, Nash had been stationed out in the middle of the *verdammte* water. She had been a lookout, nothing more. She could not be dead.

"The Guildmaster double-crossed us, with the help of a certain bastard prince I see has managed to wriggle his way free again," Ryia said, craning her neck as though she might catch sight of Tristan lurking in the shadows somewhere. She placed a hand in her pocket, pulling something out with shaking fingers. Something small, oblong, and made of wood and stone. The Quill of Declan Day. "Nash stopped him, but . . . she . . ."

Ivan had never seen the Butcher of Carrowwick at a loss for words before. But it did nothing to salve the gaping wound inside him. What had he last said to the smuggler? He did not recall, precisely, but he knew it had not been kind. Bile and sorrow surged up his throat in tandem. He was not sure which would escape his lips first.

In the end, sorrow won out. He leapt forward, grabbing Ryia's collar and shaking her.

"How in *Yavol*'s name could you have let this happen? She was supposed to be *safe*. If you had not allowed the Quill to leave your sight—"

"Ivan, stop," Evelyn said. He could feel the

ex-captain's grip on his shoulders, but he did not care. He shook Ryia again.

"Your *verdammte* grudge with the Guildmaster cost us the job back in Carrowwick. It cost us our place in the Lottery. And now it has cost me the woman I—"

His voice broke, silencing the last word, and he sagged back, allowing Evelyn to pull him off the Butcher at last.

Love. It was not an emotion he had expressed aloud since he was a very small child. But he knew deep in his bones that it was true. Nash was one of the few people in his life who had ever attempted to understand him. And now she was gone.

But it was not Ryia's fault that she was gone, not truly. It was his own.

Ivan had thrown away the only person in Carrowwick who had ever cared about him for the shadow of a chance at saving his brother. Now he had lost them both.

If Ivan had not sided with Callum Clem, Nash would be alive. Tristan might have fired the arrow, but Ivan had as good as handed the boy the bow. His stomach turned again. Finally, the bile escaped his lips. He vomited on the dock between his boots, resting his head between his knees. He remained there, still and silent, staring at his feet.

"Well," Evelyn said slowly, clearly unsure how

to handle Ivan's outburst. "What are you waiting for? Chop that bloody thing into bits. End this."

Ryia set the Quill down on the docks, raised her hatchets, and looked over at Joslyn. "Are you ready?"

Joslyn opened her mouth, then closed it again, like she did not trust herself to speak without breaking into tears. Ivan could understand the feeling. His own eyes were swimming. He stared pointedly at the Quill, avoiding meeting anyone's eye. Taking their silence for assent, Ryia nodded once in agreement, her gaze hard and determined.

The Butcher of Carrowwick took a deep breath, then brought both hatchets screaming down toward the Quill. She swung so hard that she not only severed the ancient relic, but embedded both hatchet blades deep in the soft wood dock beneath it. But she was not done yet. She pulled back again and again, hammering the hatchets down relentlessly. Blood sprayed from the Quill with every cut—far more blood than should have fit inside such a small object.

When the Quill was nothing more than a pile of toothpicks and a deep crimson puddle, Ryia sat back on her heels. It was over. It was finally over. They had won. The Quill was no more, the Adept free, the battle in Carrowwick over. But all Ivan could feel was the shadow of Nash's death, stealing over his flesh like a chill wind. When he looked to Joslyn, he knew she felt it too.

CHAPTER THIRTY-SIX

Tristan

Tristan's heart pounded itself out of his chest and up his throat as he sprinted through the streets, flinching into the shadows any time he heard footsteps approaching. He had managed to shake Ivan with some quick thinking, but no doubt the disguise-master had made it to the docks by now. Once Evelyn told him of Tristan's betrayal . . . well, there was his last possible ally in these city walls, gone.

Maybe he should regret what he had done, but he knew in his gut he could not have made any other choice. Finding balance in this world was a difficult thing. The Guildmasters had managed to walk that line for centuries now. What good could possibly come from throwing that all away forever? And so he had stolen the Quill himself. Now, if the Guildmaster made it back to the island, everything could go back to normal. Adept would just be simpleminded servants again. Kingdoms would be ruled by kings, and wars would be outlawed once again.

No one else had to die.

Tristan froze as he rounded the next corner, finding himself face-to-face with a branded, black-robed Adept. One of Clem's . . . but perhaps not anymore. Had the Guildmaster already retaken control of the Quill? The Adept paused, blinking. Then it lifted one scarred hand to its face. Tristan's pulse jumped another few ticks faster. *No*.

"Where am I?" the Adept muttered, its voice raspy and scratchy from years of disuse.

Tristan's mouth went as dry as the Rena desert. The Guildmaster hadn't taken control of the Quill. No one had. Ryia had gotten her way after all. She had won.

And all of Thamorr was doomed because of it.

He didn't answer the Adept's question. He didn't think he could have spoken even if he had wanted to. His head was spinning, his mind filled with the crushing fog of pure panic. He turned on his heel, sprinting away from the Adept and toward the merchant's quarter. *There*. A carriage stood, abandoned, in the middle of the street. The horses were still tethered, their eyes wide and rolling with fear. Tristan approached the nearest one, hands outstretched.

"Whoa there, boy. It's all right, settle down," he said. He continued to talk to the beast in a soothing tone as he untethered the horse from the cart and gingerly slipped onto its bare back.

The Adept were free. Ryia had won. That meant the Guildmaster was dead. That meant Tristan truly had no allies left. Now he had nothing but powerful enemies. There was only one place in the world he might be safe now.

"Hyah!" He kicked the horse in the ribs, spurring the creature over the cobblestone streets and out through the hole in the gate Callum Clem's army had made when they marched into the city.

His father was dead. He had watched Callum Clem kill him back in the Miscreants' Temple. But King Tolliver had never really been a father to him. No, he had just been another foolish man, so obsessed with power that he let that obsession become his downfall. As king of Edale, Tristan would not allow himself to make the same mistakes.

He left the name Tristan Beckett in the dust behind him as he rode north toward the Edalish border. He had run from his identity—from his destiny—for long enough.

It was time for Dennison Shadowwood to return home.

CHAPTER THIRTY-SEVEN

Ryia

"You're not packing more of that disgusting Edalish ale, are you?"

"Fuck you, the Edalish make a great ale."

"I've met alley cats that make a better brew."

Ryia grinned, adjusting the barrel on her shoulder as she walked up the gangplank. "Sounds to me like you've just admitted to drinking cat piss."

Joslyn shrugged. "If I did, it tasted better than the swill you're bringing onto my ship."

The battle for Carrowwick had ended two days ago. The last of the buildings had finally stopped belching smoke into the sky the day before, but the city was still in shambles. Buildings were shattered husks of what they used to be. King Duncan Baelbrandt II was dead, and he had no heir, so there was another mess.

Many of Carrowwick's Adept had left the city as soon as they blinked their eyes clear, but others had remained, unsure of where else to go. The last memory any of them had was the auction on the Guildmaster's island.

She could only imagine how disorienting it must be to enter a trance as a scared seventeen-year-old and wake up as a forty-year-old man covered in scars you have no memory of getting. It must feel like the worst post-drunken-blackout hangover known to man.

"Where do you want this, Joslyn?"

The voice belonged to a Senser who had decided to name himself Breeze, after the last thing he remembered feeling before losing his mind for thirty years. Even Ryia hadn't had the heart to tell him that wasn't a real name.

He was carrying a crate of neatly wrapped cheeses. One of the advantages of living in the shattered shell of a city—if you had shaky enough morals and you knew where to look, everything was free. This ship was going to be outfitted like a twice-damned nobleman's pleasure cruise.

"Just chuck it over there, and then help me with this rigging, would you?" Joslyn said.

Breeze wasn't the only newly freed Adept milling around the deck of Joslyn's newest ship—the *Seasnake's Revenge*. There was also a Kinetic who had named herself Ana and another Senser who'd decided to go by Argus. Imagine it—having the whole wide world of names to choose from and deciding to call yourself *Argus*.

Ivan was the one who had found Nash's old ship bobbing unattended near the Kestrel Crowns' stretch of docks. Judging from the burned-out shells of the Upper Roost and the Catacombs, Ryia guessed Clem had hit Wyatt Asher's part of town first when he had come screaming into the city with thousands of enslaved Adept at his back. The Crowns must have stolen the ship from the Harpies sometime in the past few months, and Ryia decided that, in Nash's honor, it was time to steal it back.

Ryia jumped a bit as she felt a pair of arms wrap around her waist from behind, then relaxed when she realized who they belonged to.

"Are you sure you want to do this?" Evelyn asked. "It's going to be a long time at sea. You've never been much of a sailor."

"Says who?" Ryia turned to face her, faking an indignant expression. "But yeah. I'm sure. Seasickness or no, this is . . . important." She pulled something from the pocket of her new coat. A heavy stone disc suspended on a leather strap. She watched it spin for a few seconds, then lowered it. "Is he sure he doesn't want to come?"

Evelyn turned to face the city, gazing toward the place where Ivan stood, stuffing his satchel with supplies. "He's sure. Said he's heading north."

"To do what?" Ryia scoffed.

"You know what."

And she did know. His brother was dead, but the movement lived on. Boreas was no doubt a complete disaster at the moment, leaderless and chaotic. It was the perfect time for Kasimir's *Fvene* to swoop in and try to set things right. An opportunity Ivan wouldn't be able to miss. Still, she frowned, looking back to the namestone. The stone Nash had always meant to hang. A stone that now symbolized Nash herself just as much as it symbolized her mother before her.

"He should be there, though. He should be there when we hang this. He knew her better than any of us. If anyone can pick the perfect spot . . ."

It wouldn't feel right to put Nash's memory to rest without Ivan Rezkoye. But maybe Ivan needed to grieve the loss of their smuggler on his own terms. Ryia's collarbones still bore the bruises where he'd shaken her after learning that Nash was gone. Even if he no longer blamed her for the death, she knew their alliance had splintered in that very moment. Nash had been the glue that held their dysfunctional little family together.

"We'll find the perfect spot," Evelyn said. "Even if it takes the rest of our bloody lives."

"The rest of our bloody lives?" Ryia asked, rising from her thoughts. She cocked her head.

"We won't be at sea the whole time—don't worry. We'll give your poor stomach a break or two along the way," Evelyn teased.

"I told you: I'm getting friendlier with the sea every day," Ryia said. "But do you really think I'm going to put up with *you* for that long?"

Evelyn wrapped her arms around Ryia's waist again. "Oh fuck off," she said. She leaned in, her copper curls tickling Ryia's cheeks as she punctuated the retort with a lingering kiss.

"Ready to shove off, lovebirds?" Joslyn called from the far side of the deck.

Ryia turned in Evelyn's arms. "Oh, don't be jealous," she teased.

She and Evelyn helped the pirate raise the sails. They shared one last, nearly wordless goodbye with Ivan. Then Joslyn took the helm, and the ship nosed away from the docks and out into the harbor.

Carrowwick shrank into the distance. From here it didn't even look broken anymore. If Ryia squinted she could pretend it was just the way it had been the first time she arrived, almost two years ago. But of course it wasn't. Nothing was the same. Thank the damned goddesses.

Over the coming years—decades, really—Thamorr would have to reckon with the newly freed Adept. But Ryia was done playing the hero. The world would have to sort itself out without her help this time. New powers would rise to claim the thrones of the kings Clem had slaughtered. And then, probably, even newer ones would slaughter them to make way for the next. The near future of Thamorr was going to be bloody, but at least it would be free.

With Joslyn at the helm, Evelyn at her side, and the wind in her hair, for the first time in her life, Ryia was free too.

ACKNOWLEDGMENTS

They say a sequel is even more challenging than the debut, and I'm inclined to believe they're right. *Thick as Thieves* was a battle from the very beginning, and I'm so thankful to all the people who took up arms beside me or offered me shelter from the storm.

Firstly, I need to thank the team at RF Literary. Abby Schulman, aka the first person in the publishing industry to see potential in me. Without you, this book wouldn't have been written, let alone published. I also want to thank Rebecca Friedman for carrying the torch after Abby decided to leave the industry to pursue their true calling in life. Rebecca, you are a wonderful person, and any author would be lucky to have you in their corner. I also thank Laura Crockett, my wonderful new agent, for believing in my writing and stepping in to support this project and the next!

To Amara Hoshijo, I thank you for your passionate support of *Thick as Thieves*. Without your efforts, this book would not be in print right now, and I cannot adequately thank you for everything you have done. I also thank you for your insightful notes and for understanding and supporting my vision for the *Thieves* duology from the very beginning of our working relationship.

I would also like to thank Joe Monti for your staunch support of the *Thieves* duology and for having lovely conversations about Tolkien lore with me. I also thank Brian Luster, Alexandre Su, and the rest of the production team for calling me on all the times I misspelled something in a language I made up and for finding all the other inaccuracies in the manuscript. You are either wizards or superheroes. Maybe both.

I'd also like to thank the entire editing, design, subrights, and production team that worked on the project at Saga Press. Jennifer Long, Eliza Hanson, Sirui Huang, Erika Genova, Jéla Lewter, Emily Arzeno, Caroline Pallotta, Chloe Gray, Jennifer Bergstrom, Paul O'Halloran, Rachel Podmajersky, and Fiona Sharp. Without all your efforts, this book would not exist in its current form, and I am forever grateful to you all!

I thank Julia McGarry and Tyrinne Lewis for your hard work on publicity and marketing for *Thick as Thieves*. It's thanks to your efforts that the conclusion to this duology will make it onto many readers' radar, and I am so appreciative!

To Kayleigh Webb, thank you so much for your support and amazing efforts on this duology and all the efforts that led to *Thick as Thieves* existing in the flesh (paper?). I also thank Navah Wolfe for seeing the potential in the *Thieves* duology and for kicking off the publishing journey for Ryia & Co. I hope we get to work together again in the future.

I'd also like to thank Christian McGrath for absolutely nailing the cover art for this story. Your visual representation brought tons of readers to this duology. I am forever grateful for your ability to take my words and represent them perfectly in artwork I could never have even dreamed up.

To my parents, Diane and Richard, I want to thank you for your support from day one. Literally. Thanks for understanding your weird, artistic child and for always supporting her weird, artistic endeavors. (psst. "Her" is me. It's me.)

I also need to thank Haley and Mike. You guys were my first-ever beta readers and have always offered me incredible and invaluable feedback on early drafts of my work. It is incredible to be related to fellow nerds who can geek out with me over books, shows, or movies I'm using as inspiration for my latest project.

To Ryan, also, for your unconditional support during all the highs and lows of my publishing journey. Thank you for reading so many truly terrible early drafts and offering pointed feedback that helped shape them into what they are today.

To my nieces, Kaylin and Abby. Love you both more than words can express. Don't read these books yet, they have bad words in them.

This book is also for my writer friends. Hannah,

Genevieve, Greta, Jenny, Mica, and all my other friends in the writing and publishing space. Special shout-out to Kamilah, Chelsea, and Dave, aka the DC Crew! Thank you for keeping me sane, being incredible, and for traveling the weird and wonderful road of publishing with me.

To Adrian M. Gibson, my incredible friend and collaborator on SFF Addicts. Thank you for including me in this wonderful podcasting journey and for encouraging/forcing me to actually read all the books on my TBR.

For Chris and Kevin, my bosses on the other side of my life. Thank you for understanding that writing is the thing that lights my soul up like a Christmas tree and for being flexible with me, enabling me to pursue my dream without tearing all my hair out (or starving).

I also want to thank every single reader who picked up a copy of *Among Thieves*. I am so unbelievably grateful for anyone who took a chance on my story, and I'm so incredibly humbled by the love I've seen from amazing readers around the world.

Lastly, I need to thank my faithful friends, Thorin Oakenshield and Wrex. Thorin for snuggling on my lap and offering feedback by walking across my keyboard, and Wrex for barking ceaselessly and scaring away all the Amazon delivery drivers and kindly neighbors who might actually be murderers in disguise.

Center Point Large Print
600 Brooks Road / PO Box 1
Thorndike, ME 04986-0001 USA

(207) 568-3717

US & Canada:
1 800 929-9108
www.centerpointlargeprint.com